MATLOCK THE HARE

SilverWood

THE RIDDLE OF
TREFFLEPUGGA PATH

GRIFFLES & ILLUMINAE BY PHIL & JACQUI LOVESEY

Published in 2014 by the authors

SilverWood Books
30 Queen Charlotte Street, Bristol, BS1 4HJ
www.silverwoodbooks.co.uk

To discover more about Matlock the Hare and Winchett Dale, visit
www.matlockthehare.com this very sun-turn…

ISBN 978-1-78132-183-6 (paperback)
ISBN 978-1-78132-184-3 (hardback)
ISBN 978-1-78132-185-0 (ebook)

British Library Cataloguing in Publication Data
A CIP catalogue record for this book is available from the British Library

Set in Baskerville MT by SilverWood Books
Printed on responsibly sourced paper

For all those saztaculous Matlock-folk who dare to believe.
May all your pid-pads be crumlush ones…

Contents

Winchett Dale

A 'griffle' or two to the unwary traveller...

It's unlikely, but not entirely impossible that one sun-turn, you might find yourself pid-padding along Trefflepugga Path and down into Winchett Dale. To do this, you would have probably inadvertently stumbled upon one of the many entrances to the path that lie high and hidden in the Derbyshire Peaks.

Once in Winchett Dale, what would await you there? Your first impressions might well be that it looks more or less the same as any of the crumlush valleys and dales in the area, with mountains, woods, limestone-cliffs, caverns and the occasional lake.

However, then you might just notice the creatures…

Some travellers could get alarmed (or 'twizzly', as they griffle in Winchett Dale) at this point. However, the wary-traveller might well stay a while, soon realising that most of the strange creatures don't really represent the 'oidiest' threat whatsoever.

And then, you'd most likely hear them 'griffling' (or talking, as you would say) in Dalespeak, their very own dialect developed over countless generations in all the majickal-dales. If you chose to stay a while, you could well find that the longer you listened, the more you would begin to understand, and might even begin using some of their 'griffles' yourself. Which the creatures would think was 'saztaculous' and 'fuzzcheck', as, by and large, they're a welcoming bunch, although rather 'clottabussed' at times…

Amongst their number, you might spot a green-robed hare, cheerfully going about his majickal duties in the village, dispensing spells and potions, keeping everyone as 'fuzzcheck' as possible. You could be tempted to stop and 'griffle' to him yourself, discovering his name was Matlock, and passing a most peffa-pleasant afternoon'up in his crumlush cottage as he griffled to you about some of his many majickal-adventures. Then as the sun set, and you headed back home, Matlock would also be leaving to greet the even'up, and see just what other 'shindinculous' and 'peffa-twizzly' adventures lie in wait for Winchett Dale's very own majickal-hare…

Some useful 'Griffles' for your Journey…

Briftest – (adj) What you know as 'the best'.

Chickle – (v) To laugh.

Clottabus – (n, colloquial) A bit of a fool. *Clottabussed* – foolish, but mostly harmless.

Creaker – (n) Door.

Crumlush – (adj) The feeling you get inside when all's *saztaculoulsy* well. Cosy, warm, lovely.

Driftolubb – (n) A book. Part of a set of *driftolubbs* used by majickal-hares to find spells, potions and *vrooshers*.

Excrimbly – (adj) Excited.

Fuzzcheck – (sl) When everything's *saztaculoulsy* fine.

Gobflop – (n) To fail at something.

Glopped-up – (n phrase) When something has gone wrong.

Glubbstool – (n) When something has gone *peffa*-wrong!

Griffle(s) – (n) Word(s).

Juzzpapped – (n) Tired, exhausted.

Lid – (n) Sky. *Twinkling-lid* (n) being a night sky full of stars.

Majelicus – (adj) *Peffa*-majickal, the most majickal majick, that can't be *vroosh*ed from books, tinctures or potions. The very heartbeat of our majickal world.

Nifferduggle(s) – (n) Sleeping. To go to *nifferduggles* is sometimes the most *crumlush* part of our *sun-turn*…

Oidy – (adj) Tiny, *peffa*-small.

Peffa – (adj) Very.

Pid-pad – (v) To walk. Humans tend to '*bud-thud*'; wehereas we, more delicate creatures of the dale simply *pid-pad*. Except Proftulous, who *lump-thumps*, and oidy creatures who sometimes *scrittle*.

Russisculoffed – (n) Irritated. From the gutteral noises made by *Russicers* if you go too near to them while they are hoarding *shlomps*. Be warned, they much prefer their *schlomps* to you!

Saztaculous – (adj) Incredible, fantastic.

Shindinculous – (adj) Something that it so *peffa-saztaculous* that it shines out.

Sisteraculous – (n) The absolute being of you. The complimentary part of your *softulous* (body) that if you really take the time to listen to, has some truly *shindinculous* answers to questions you never thought to even ask. Something so many have forgotten how to trust, but we at Winchett Dale rely on most *glopped-up sun-turns*!

Snutch – (n) A few.

Stroff – (v) To be taken to pass into Oramus' eternal care.

Sun-turn – (n) A day. The period of *time* it takes for the sun to rise and fall, before leaving just the *saztaculous twinkling-lid*. Twenty-eight of them make a *moon-turn* (or 'month', as you would *griffle*.)

Twizzly – (n) To feel scared; something rather scary.

Vilish – (adv) Quickly. From the noise made by a woodland creature rushing through the undergrowth, searching for berries, or trying to escape a hungry predator!

Vroosher – (n) A wand-assisted majick spell. From the *saztaculous vrooshing* noise they make!

Yechus – (n) Horrible, awful, hideous; something that might be *peffa-glopped-up*.

Armed with these few griffles, the wary traveller should have little difficulty in easily pid-padding around Winchett Dale. However, in the unlikely event of you ever getting lost, a more comprehensive glossary can be found waiting for you at the end of your journey along Trefflepugga Path…

Map of Winchett Dale

The Journey Begins

1.

Extrapluffs, Proftulous and Dripples

Long before he had his first ever extrapluff as a majickal-hare, Matlock the hare always loved to think about things. Indeed, it was one of his most peffa-perfect ways of passing any sun-turn.

Matlock was, as the other creatures in Winchett Dale always called him, 'a peffa-extrapluffy hare'. And then they would most likely griffle something about what Matlock might be doing in his cottage potionary, or why it was that Serraptomus the krate always had to be so officious, or how Winchett Dale just wasn't the same as it used to be. Which, of course, it wasn't. But then again, it *was*. Everything, including Winchett Dale, always changes, but then, just as majickally, *doesn't* change, either – which was one of the first things Matlock had extrapluffed so many moon-turns previously…

Not that extrapluffing was the only role of a majickal-hare. Far from it. Matlock only really had time to extrapluff when he had finished his many duties tending to all manner of creatures in and around the dale; and were you ever lucky enough to follow him from house to house, chore to cure, vroosher to vroosher – you'd soon realise that there generally aren't enough hours in the sun-turn to sit and have a really good extrapluff anymore.

Matlock's oldest and briftest friend Proftulus had once asked him about extrapluffing when they had both pid-padded to Thinking Lake. Not that Proftulous could really pid-pad anywhere.

As a Dworp, he stood two-hares tall, with possibly the most yechus face and ears in the whole of Winchett Dale. He just sort of lump-thumped along, instead.

"Matlock," he'd griffled, as the two of them sat by the shindinculously still waters of the lake. "What is it that makes 'extrapluffing' so different from 'thinking'?"

Matlock turned to his friend, trying to ignore the murp-worm making its way into the glopped-up recesses of Proftulous' ganticus ear. Instead, he brushed an oidy mirrit from his own long green majician's gown and adjusted his soft cap. The answer, he knew, would most probably sound rather glopped-up to Proftulous. "Well," he griffled, "I suppose it's rather like listening, really. But with your insides."

Proftulous narrowed his large eyes. "Like when my crimple goes all grumbling when I is hungry? And then I eats myself a snutch of tweazle-pies, and I is all fuzzcheck again?"

"In a manner of griffling, then, yes, I suppose so," Matlock griffled, watching a short-winged fluff-thropp circle the lake, greeping excitedly in the late afternoon breeze. "It's like...it's like when I first decided to become a majickal-hare, I suppose."

"You ates tweazle-pies?" Proftulous griffled. "And you didn't give any to me?"

Matlock shook his head, his long hare's ears flapping slightly. His nose twitched with the crumlush smells of autumn, whiskers sensing a fresh chill in the air, the slight dampness all around. "Proftulous, you know peffa-well that I have never eaten a tweazle-pie in my life. I was simply griffling about..."

"Then you should try 'em, Matlock," Proftulous interrupted. "They be peffa-crumlush and slurpilicious."

"Something for another sun-turn, I'm sure," Matlock griffled.

"They be brifter than that yechus niff-soup you's always having," Proftulous insisted, his mind now more or less totally pre-occupied with the most peffa-saztaculous thing for any dworp – food. "Tweazles are right crunchy, Matlock, and their softulous goes all spludge-glopped in your mouth."

"I was trying to griffle to you about 'extrapluffing'," Matlock sighed. "But now I'm extrapluffing that trying to explain 'extrapluffing' is going to be an extrapluff too far."

"Matlock," he'd griffled, as the two of them sat by the shindinculously still waters of the lake. "What is it that makes 'extrapluffing' so different from 'thinking'?"

"Who wanted to know what extrapluffing is?" Proftulous griffled, picking out the murp-worm from his ear and swallowing it in one gulp.

"Well, you did."

"Me?"

"Yes, you!"

Proftulous frowned. "You peffa-sure, Matlock? I simply be griffling about tweazle-pies."

"I know. But before that you were… Oh what's the use?"

"Of tweazle-pies? Well, you eats them, don't you?"

"Indeed…you do," Matlock griffled, extrapluffing that with the light beginning to fade, now might be the peffa-perfect time to slowly pid-pad back to his small cottage on the edge of Wand Wood. Even though he was a good friend, there were really only so many griffles to be had with Proftulous before tweazle-pie reared its crusty-rodent's head. Which was probably the main reason why Matlock had stayed friends with the ganticus dworp for so long – it was Proftulous' peffa-predictability that made him simply, well, Proftulous. He was probably the briftest example of something which had both changed (his ears had seemed to get more and more ganticus over the years, whilst his saggsquack had almost disappeared) and yet *hadn't really* changed at all. Proftulous and his tweazle-pie fascination were as inseparable as Oramus and the moon itself.

"Has there ever been one single sun-turn," Matlock griffled to his lumpen-friend, "when you haven't thought about tweazle-pies?"

Proftulous' large eyebrows narrowed towards the bulbous bridge of his nose. This, Matlock knew, was his 'thinking-face', and as such hadn't really been used too often. He watched, listening as Proftulous made the inevitable series of yechus sounding noises – mostly glopped-up grunts and herreuchs – as he struggled to answer Matlock's question.

"There be that sun-turn," he finally griffled, "when you bliffed the twizzly Berriftomus in Wand Wood…" He scratched at one ear with a ganticus paw. "Oh, no. I had meself a tweazle-pie after that, didn't I?"

Matlock nodded. "You did."

A snutch of moments passed.

"That sun-turn when you be doing your first majick vroosher when you was just an apprentice majickal-hare? You remember, you tried to make the lid all splashy, but you peffa-glopped up?"

"And if I remember rightly," Matlock griffled, in reality preferring to forget how his first attempt to use a hawthorn wand had resulted in four confused disidulas wandering around Chiming Meadows, smelling rather like tuffle-cheese, "you chickled so much, you had to celebrate with a ganticus tweazle-pie."

"S'right, Matlock. I did, didn't I? Peffa-ganticus it was. Stuffed with them!"

Matlock yawned, stood and stretched. "It was, good-friend, it was."

"Finished the lot, though, didn't I?"

Matlock nodded, and the two of them began slowly pid-padding and lump-thumping back to Matlock's small and crumlush cottage, Proftulous trying all the while to remember the one, saztaculoulsy elusive sun-turn when he hadn't, in fact, eaten a slurpilicious tweazle-pie.

It was, Matlock decided, after he had waved his friend goodbye and finally settled into his favourite chair by the piff-tosh, most probably the perfect time for a bowl of his niff-soup, a crumlush truppleberry brew, and afterwards a peffa-hot bath before settling in bed for some well-earned nifferduggles. Which was, of course, the worst thing to decide, for as Matlock watched the small flames dancing and splutting in the piff-tosh, he found himself extrapluffing that something very different from a crumlush even'up was about to occur. How did he know? What caused these extrapluffs? Hare's intuition or majickal sense? Or something else entirely, known to all majickal creatures simply as 'the calling of the Sisteraculous' – a Most Majelicus extrapluffing, that when heard, has to be acted upon peffa-vilishly…

"Scruffling-cafferdoggles!" Matlock griffled, knowing that any plans he might have made for a quiet night were about to change.

A small, squirreled creature with a long, buttoned nose suddenly scrittled into the room and jumped onto Matlock's lap.

"Been nifferduggling in your cupboard have you?" Matlock griffled to his dripple.

The dripple nodded, yawned.

"So what's woken you, my oidy majickal friend?" Matlock griffled, stroking the creature's soft, furry head. "You feel the extrapluffiness too, eh?"

Again, the dripple nodded, incapable of griffling a reply. Not because it still felt sleepy, but because of the peffa-simple fact that no dripple had ever been known to griffle – ever. As familiars to majickal-hares throughout all the Most Majelicus ages, most dripples simply offer complete loyalty, brew the best ever leaf-teas for their masters, spend their waking hours peffa-happy, and their nifferduggling ones dreaming of what they might want to griffle, if only they could griffle. As such, dripples generally make the briftest of all majickal-familiars, each born on the same sun-turn as the majickal-hare they will serve, and when the time comes, leaving to meet Oramus on the exact same sun-turn as their masters, too; bonded through life in the dales, and in the majickal-hereafter, for all eternity.

Not that there aren't differences in dripples. There are many, and not just in size, tail-length, eye-colour or nose-length. Some, it has to be griffled, have quite short tempers, and are prone to being too bossy, with majickal-hares in faraway dales griffling tales of their dripples insisting on peffa-tidy cottages at all times, and sometimes even refusing some more glopped-up creatures through the front-creaker. But bossiness isn't the only potential problem. Matlock had heard of dripples that were so lazy they simply nifferduggled all sun-turn and most of the night, only waking to eat niff-soup. Others only bathed once every harvest moon, and frankly, tended to make the whole hare's cottage smell worse than an abbrolatt's toenail (which, if you're ever unfortunate enough to be near to, or downwind of, is an aromatic experience you're unlikely to forget in a peffa-long time…). Indeed, on the all too rare occasions Matlock did meet another majickal-hare, he always noticed one thing, that the differences in the size and characteristics of their dripple-familiar closely resembled those of its master. And sometimes, when his own dripple might be nifferduggling contentedly on his lap, or busy-silently harvesting niffs in the garden, Matlock would wonder just how much the little, long-eared creature resembled him. Certainly, it was a crumlush dripple, quite smart at times, intuitively extrapluffy in

its own silent way, reasonably tidy, an excellent brew-maker…but…
but…just not that peffa-*excrimbly*, really. It was, Matlock concluded,
the sort of dripple that was simply always there, just drippling.
And Matlock would occasionally wonder about this, alone in his
cottage on the end of Wand Wood. Is that what the other creatures
in the Winchett Dale also thought about him? That he was simply
a majickal-hare, always there, doing majickal things for them, but
generally not being all that excrimbly, and perhaps worse, just an
oidy bit dull?

But on these rare occasions, his dripple would usually interrupt
Matlock's brooding by putting the kettle on the piff-tosh for a
saztaculous brew, removing Matlock's long majician's shoes,
bringing him his peffa-crumlushy comfy slippers, so that all would
seem peffa-fuzzcheck once more. Because to the dripple, Matlock
was simply the most shindinculous and saztaculous majickal-hare
master it could ever have drippily wished for, ever.

Matlock tickled the dripple under its chin. "Well," he griffled,
"although I'm not peffa-certain of much at the moment, one thing
that I am sure of is that these extrapluffs won't go away while I'm sat
here doing nothing in front of the piff-tosh."

The dripple looked into Matlock's large hare's eyes, nodding
intently.

"Something's either already going on, or about to go on, and as
the majickal-hare of Winchett Dale, I have no choice but to find out
what it is."

The dripple nodded again, dutifully scrittling away, returning
a snutch of moments later with Matlock's hawthorn wand as he
slowly got to his pid-pads. It had been a long sun-turn, and he was
feeling rather juzzpapped, but the extrapluffs that all wasn't right in
Winchett Dale just wouldn't go away…

In a blinksnap, his mind was made up. He would go out into
the night and find out just what was happening. "You pid-padding
along?" he asked the dripple, as he stood at the front creaker. "Or is
an even'up in front of the piff-tosh more crumlush than a night out
with me?"

The dripple hesitated for a moment, caught it seemed, between
what it should do, and what it really wanted to do. Most times, it

would scrittle up Matlock's robes to ride in his hood as he set out across the dale. But that night was different. Instead, it did the most peculiar and peffa-unexpected thing. It let out a small sigh as it made its way towards the creaker. A tiny sigh, the oidiest sigh Matlock had ever heard, but nonetheless a *noise*. Not a griffle, but a noise from his dripple, the first noise it had ever made.

Matlock stood stunned by the open doorway scarcely believing his long-hare's ears. No dripple had made any kind of noise whatsoever. And yet his dripple had almost definitely sighed.

"You don't want to come, do you?" Matlock slowly griffled, the whole even'up becoming stranger with each passing blinksnap.

The dripple shook its head, lowering it, almost in shame.

Matlock reached down and stroked it. "Well, you be sure to guard the piff-tosh and keep the place warm until I come back." Then he left the cottage and set off into the night, wondering just what it was that had so affected the little creature, and why it was that his extrapluffs that things weren't right were getting stronger with every pid-pad he took into the enshrouding darkness of Wand Wood.

2.

Wand Wood, Krates and Mirrits

All hares, not just majickal-ones, can sometimes get an oidy bit twizzly in a gloomy-wood. As creatures of the open-fields, pastures, hedgerows and borders, they like nothing better than foraging and looking for scented trails, the concealed promise of food therein, especially at night, preferably under the light of a shindinculous full-moon, coming out in the early evenings after sheltering in their forms during the day. Indeed, it might well seem that they hold no real fear of the night, but here you would be wrong, for all the while as they scriffle around, their senses are totally alert, waiting for sudden unexpected opportunities, or unwelcome predators.

Matlock, as he pid-padded through Wand Wood that night, was no different. It wasn't simply his majickal-extrapluffs that told him something was wrong, it was his natural hare sense, too. Some creatures thought that this was the main reason why hares were the only Earthly creatures to be chosen to journey to the majickal dales from The Great Beyond; that a hare's natural senses were somehow already attuned to the more majickal-plane from the very first sun-turn they opened their eyes as leverets. Crucially, some young hares show signs of being better extrapluffers than others, as it had been in Matlock's case, and these are the ones all too often chosen to make the long journey along Trefflepugga Path to begin life afresh as an apprentice majickal-hare in any one of the many waiting dales.

And although Matlock had hardly any memories of his time in The Great Beyond, his most enduring was the first sight he'd had of Chatsworth, his Most Majelicus hare teacher and master, pid-padding towards him across a large open field, upright on just his back legs, dressed in what Matlock would soon come to know as majician's robes and cap, a red crystal glowing on top of a twisted, wooden staff. The young hare had been completely mesmerised by the older stranger, anxious to greet and playfully box with Chatsworth, as other hares slowly and reverentially backed away, sensing perhaps, the red-robed stranger's majickal importance.

And then, in what had seemed to be the most natural thing in the world, Matlock had simply turned, taken one last look at his family of fellow hares, then followed Chatsworth as they began their journey to Winchett Dale to start his majickal apprenticeship under the vigilant and peffa-watchful eye of his new master.

Of the apprenticeship, however, the memories were many; his arrival in the dale, learning how to 'griffle' and pid-pad on just his two back legs, being taught to dress in his robe, prepare food, learning how to read from the many majickal driftolubbs, before finally being presented by Chatsworth with his very own hawthorn wand then practising his first ever vroosher on the High Plateau. Which, inevitably, and as Proftulous still remembered, went predictably glopped-up. However, as the moon-turns passed, and Matlock studied and learnt more about the ways of all dalelore, discovering the plants and creatures of his new special home, his vrooshers grew ever brifter and ever more saztaculous. Some even'ups, he Chatsworth and Proftulous would all pid-pad out together to the High Plateau, Proftulous watching and chickling contentedly as both apprentice and master painted the twinkling-lid above with shindiculous vrooshing light.

And whilst it was all so new, excrimbly and different to the life Matlock had known before, it also somehow felt right, or 'destined' as Chatsworth had once explained to him as the two of them pid-padded along the exact same trail through Wand Woods that Matlock now found himself pid-padding along that night…

The woods were eerily, unnaturally quiet. No creatures scrittled across the leafy floor, no wind made the leaves dance above his head.

It felt to Matlock as if he were the only creature alive in the darkness. When he'd got to where Zhava, The Last Great Elm normally stood, all he saw was a huge earthy bowl, a sign that even she'd uprooted herself and wandered somewhere else. But where? Matlock looked to the bright and shindinculous moon above, making out the familiar face of Oramus on its surface, forever looking down on the dales and all of The Great Beyond.

"If you can hear me, Oramus," he griffled out loud, voice echoing in the gloom. "then I'd love to know just what the driffeljubs is going on."

Matlock waited, listening to his Sisteraculous for any Most Majelicus extrapluffs from above. But no answer came. Even Oramus, it seemed, had gone.

Taking a deep hare's-breath, and with no other option, he decided to go on, pid-padding right through Wand Woods, following the strangely stilled waters of Duckleplip Brook to the banks of the River Winchett, it too just as still, as if it somehow refused to flow into the village of Winchett Dale itself. He took a long look into the darkened waters, lightly brushing the surface with a paw.

"Anybody home?" he griffled, splashing lightly, looking for signs of life; slipdgers, frollfish, jellops or blurfs. Nothing. Not a single water creature appeared or answered.

But then, just a short distance away, came the first signs of life Matlock had heard since leaving his cottage, the unmistakeable sounds of a public-griffling, being held in The Great Hall at the very centre of the village of Winchett Dale itself. Matlock vilishly headed towards the raised voices and occasional rounds of unenthusiastic clapping from juzzpapped paws and talons, wondering exactly why, if a meeting had been called, didn't he know about it? Krates considered themselves to be the arbiters of all order in the dale, and on the sun-turn of any public-griffling would be sure to inform all of Winchett Dale's creatures, insisting on attendance. Normally, of course, as was the way of officious-krates, most public-grifflings were mostly concerned with peffa-oidy matters, but always dressed with much stoic importance by the krates, in order to make them appear peffa-peffa serious indeed. It might be that a giant-harebell needed to be moved from Chiming

Meadows, or that a wandering-fropp had lost a shoe, or that the Majickal Stores wanted to open slightly later on a Scruffsday; but one thing everyone could be sure of was that each trivial, itemised matter would be treated by the krates as if the very beating heart of Winchett Dale depended upon it.

"All these extrapluffs, just for a public-griffling?" Matlock griffled to himself as he pid-padded into the village. "'Tis most glopped-up. And why wasn't I told about it?" An extrapluff coursed through him, bringing possibilities he didn't want to be aware of, as a second weary ripple of pawplause broke from inside The Great Hall.

When he got to the large oak-creakers, another surprise awaited. They were quite shut, the large iron knocker too heavy to turn, and most likely locked from the inside. Matlock considered using a vroosher from his wand to open them, but something in his Sisteraculous told him not to. The last thing he wanted to do was announce his late-arrival with a creaker-vroosher, as they were hardly the most silent of spells. He'd once heard tell of another majickal-hare who'd managed to conjure a silent creaker-vroosher, but frankly this had made him so untrustworthy in his particular dale, that he'd been forced by officious krates to surrender his wand immediately.

A slight skriishing noise from the side of hall made Matlock's long hare's ears twitch. He pid-padded around the old wooden building to see the ganticus shape of The Last Great Elm, the tops of her branches pressed against the high walls.

"Zhava," he whispgriffled, "What are you doing here?"

The ganticus tree looked down at Matlock, her heavy roots constantly shifting as if she was trying to avoid stepping on something. "Matlock!" she whispgriffled back. "Peffa-glad you've come. The other trees in the woods sent me here. They're all twizzly about what's going on. But oh, now I'm here, I rather wish I wasn't. There's mirrits everywhere, all over the ground, trying to climb up my roots and trunk. If they get into my branches, I peffa-swear I shall scream. Please vroosh them away, Matlock, please."

"Zhava, you're scared of mirrits?" Matlock griffled. "You, the Last Great Elm? But they're so peffa-oidy compared to you. Not even murp-worms get twizzly about mirrits."

"I know *that*, Matlock! I just don't like them. They're all wriggly and yechus, and with far too many legs."

Matlock sighed, got out his hawthorn wand and vrooshed the oidy scritting mirrits back into the shadows with a vilish, bright green vroosh. "What's going on in there?" he asked, after Zhava rearranged her roots once more, almost toppling against the side of the hall all with an ominous creak as she did so.

"It's a public-griffling," she griffled, leaning closer to a half-opened window higher up.

"Yes, I know that! But what are they griffling about?"

Zhava listened for some time. "Something. They're griffling about something."

"But what?" Matlock was beginning to feel an oidy bit russisculoffed. It was bad enough not to have been invited to the public-griffling, let alone having to try and listen to a commentary given high above his head by a ganticus tree that seemed more concerned about peffa-oidy mirrits than what was actually going on. "Hang on," he griffled. "I'll climb up."

It seemed like a good idea at the time, but the reality was actually far harder than he thought. Hares, even majickal-ones, aren't really able to climb trees without the aid of vrooshers, and the whole clumsy operation was made all the harder by Zhava constantly shifting and moving her roots as the mirrits inevitably made their way slowly back to her trunk. Twice, Matlock nearly lost his grip, before dropping his wand and helplessly watching it fall to the ground below.

"Zhava, please, stand still!" Matlock griffled, over yet another round of pawplause. He was nearly at the window now and could catch the occasional griffles coming from a peffa-officious, but completely unfamiliar voice. It almost certainly had to belong to a krate, but who? Normally it was Serraptomus, as the most senior of Winchett Dale's three resident krates who would lead public-grifflings, yet this voice definitely didn't belong to him.

"I can't stand still!" Zhava griffled, becoming quite twizzly with it all. "Yechus mirrits are everywhere, Matlock! Vroosh them away again!"

"How can I?" Matlock griffled. "I dropped my wand with all your fretting!"

"I can feel them fluggling right into my bark spaces, Matlock! It's completely glubbstool!"

But Matlock wasn't listening to Zhava anymore, his hare's nose almost at the open window as he tried to make out what was being griffled inside The Great Hall. With one more push on Zhava's branch, he was finally able to see inside. A lone and highly-robed krate stood on the podium, with all three of Winchett Dale's own krates facing the hall, arms folded, their officious uniforms gleaming as Matlock had never seen them gleam before. The rest of the hall was crammed with all the creatures from the village and surrounding dale, with not a single place to sit in sight. It was, Matlock immediately knew, a peffa, peffa-important public-griffling. Even the dale's abbrolat had turned up, and Proftulus' ganticus ears were also clearly visible, obliterating the view of a group of silent-brimmers behind him.

Matlock leaned through the window, listening to the highly-robed krate on the podium, its short krate's arms held wide in a gesture of open friendship.

"…and so I griffle to you all, good creatures of Winchett Dale, that when the dreaded time comes, when the 'something' comes for us all, then we will all have to be ready. But with my help, and if we all pull together, we as a dale can face this, beat the yechus 'something' and be safe once more. For who amongst us hasn't felt twizzly over the last few sun-turns? Who amongst us hasn't felt the 'something' making its yechus and peffa-glopped way here? And who amongst us isn't ready to turn the 'something' into a peffa-oidy 'nothing'? It will take courage. It will take heart. But most of all, it will take a great change in Winchett Dale to beat it. Now, I know that some of you might be thinking 'What great changes do we have to make?' And it would be only natural to think that…"

A voice that Matlock immediately recognised at Proftulous' suddenly griffled, "I mostly be thinking about eating more tweazle-pies, meself."

"Please shut that thing up," the krate griffled, as everyone chickled. "Don't you understand? This is so much more than mere tweazle-pies. This is about how we all come together, about how we all face this together." He paused as eventually the laughter subsided, fixing them all with his most peffa-officious stare, "And most of all, good creatures of Winchett Dale, this is about how we all beat the 'something' together."

The three krates at the front of the hall all clapped enthusiastically, Serraptomus earnestly encouraging the creatures to all join in.

High above, Matlock watched as the peffa-important krate smiled. And he had to admit, it seemed a very convincing and genuine smile, as if he really cared about his griffling. Yet Matlock's Sisteraculous told him different. There was, Matlock suspected, the more he watched and listened, something deeply hidden and rather yechus about this particular krate.

"Who here, hasn't had something twizzly happen to them this very sun-turn?" the krate asked his bewildered audience. "You, Madam," he griffled, pointing to a large lullop-bear, struggling to keep her youngsters from wriggling too much, "what has happened to you this sun-turn that was twizzly and glopped?"

All eyes turned to the flustered lullop-bear.

"Well," she griffled, "I suppose I did drop a gribble-spoon this morn'up…"

"You see!" the krate triumphantly griffled. "She dropped a gribble-spoon! 'Tis a sure sign that the 'something' is coming to Winchett Dale!" He turned to a crested-throbb. "You, sir? What twizzly-strangeness might have happened to you?"

The crested-throbb thought for a snutch of moments, its brow creased in peffa-concentration. "I suppose…"

"Yes…yes…?" the krate encouraged.

"Well…"

"Spit those griffles out. We're all waiting…"

"Well, I did frumble my whammetts, and none of 'em was even partially dudged at the time."

A revelation that contrary to what Matlock had expected, seemed to galvanise the entire hall in much excrimbly twizzliness. Immediately, it was filled with griffles, as everyone began shouting out just how twizzly their sun-turns had all been, too. There were tales of lost neffle-hammers, wandering hydrazine problems, blurped-flidgers and much more, as all the while, the peffa-important krate looked as if he could hardly contain his relief.

"These are all signs!" he griffled above the noise, the other krates all appealing for calm. "All signs that the 'something' is coming! Nothing can stop it, so we must be ready!"

A ganticus thumping came from the back of the hall, vilishly silencing them all as Proftulous slowly stood.

"This isn't going to be about tweazle-pies, is it, dworp?" the krate asked rather sourly.

"No, it not be," Proftulous nervously griffled. "You just be griffling that nothing can stop the 'something'. Well, methinks that's where you're all wrong and glopped-up."

A brief scowl crossed the krate's face. "I *do* beg your pardon. I was not aware that a glopped-up, tweazle-pie eating, ganticus-eared dworp might know better than me about such peffa-important matters…"

"Matlock!" Proftulous suddenly cried, turning to all the others. "Matlock will save us from the twizzly 'something'! Just as he saves us all from everything twizzly and yechus. Matlock will keep us all crumlush and safe from the 'something'! He be the one to do it, not you, or us. Matlock be the one!"

Looking down from the window at all the creatures he'd known, helped, healed and guarded for so many sun-turns, Matlock's heart began beating with crumlushed pride, as everyone joined Proftulous in praising their saztaculous majickal-hare of Winchett Dale. It began to get so noisy that the krates were clearly getting nervous.

An urgent voice from outside also fought for Matlock's attention.

"Matlock!" Zhava griffled, lurching ever more dangerously against the side of the hall. "Get these yechus mirrits away from me, vilish! I really can't stand much more of this! They're everywhere!"

But Matlock was too busy listening to the commotion in the hall to hear the twizzly-tree's cries for help.

"So where," the peffa-important krate griffled, when order had finally been restored, "just where is this 'Matlock' right now? Look around you. Do you see your saztaculous majickal-hare anywhere amongst us?"

The creatures all looked then began slowly murmuring to each other as it slowly dawned on them that the krate was right; Matlock, majickal saviour of the dale for so many occasions and sun-turns past, simply wasn't there…

*"Matlock!" Zhava griffled, lurching ever more dangerously against the
side of the hall. "Get these yechus mirrits away from me, vilish!
I really can't stand much more of this! They're everywhere!"*

"Interesting, isn't it, good folk of Winchett Dale?" the krate griffled. "Here we all are, at a public-griffling, deciding on peffa-important changes to our lives that will affect us all, and your majickal-hare can't even be bothered to turn up."

"There'll be a peffa-good reason," Proftulous vilishly answered back. "He'll be out saving something, or making it all healthy and fuzzcheck again…or…or…"

"Or," the krate finished for him, "perhaps he's already *left* the dale, because he's too twizzly, and knows his majick would be absolutely useless against the 'something'."

Cries of 'No!' flew around the shocked hall, at the very same moment that a branch of elm smashed through the half-open window with a ganticus crash.

"Look!" pointed Proftulous, as his old friend fell from the branch and plunged straight down into a gasping group of disidulas below. "'Tis Matlock! He *do* be here, after all!"

Immediately the hall erupted into peffa-excrimbly griffling and chickling.

"Well," the krate griffled to Matlock after the pawplause and laughter had died down. "Some majickal creatures really do know how to make an entrance, don't they?"

Matlock, his head feeling glopped from the fall, just about managed to heave himself up from the groaning disidula pile and brush down his robes. "Mirrits may have a lot to answer for," he griffled.

"Mirrits?" the krate griffled. "I'm thinking that *you* may have a peffa-lot more to answer for, majickal-hare. Like, just why you couldn't use the doors, like everyone else?"

"They were locked," Matlock answered, turning to the others. "I was locked out."

"Indeed they were," the krate griffled back. "But I rather suspected that as majickal-hare, a mere lock shouldn't have prevented too much of a vrooshing problem for you? Not for the famous Matlock the hare, saviour of Winchett Dale, surely?"

"Why wasn't I invited?" Matlock griffled, slowly pid-padding towards the podium, the other three krates barring his way. "I'm always invited, along with everyone else. No one griffled to me about this public-griffling at all."

The krate smiled a thoroughly reasonable smile. "But if you are so majickal, then why didn't you already know? I must griffle, hare that you hardly appear to be very majickal to me."

An irate tricky-rickett stood, its leaves trembling in anger. "Matlock *is* majickal! He cured me of bludge once!"

The krate chickled icily. "My dear, deluded rickett, a common-frupper could cure you of bludge. 'Tis hardly the most excellent of proofs, is it?"

Proftulous was back up on his ganticus feet. "Matlock can be curing anything! One sun-turn, I be eating too many tweazle-pies, and be feeling all glubbstooled, so Matlock's gone and got a peffa-large norp-tube and stuck it right…"

"I've griffled you before," the krate warned, "no more of your tweazle-related spuddles, dworp!" He turned to Matlock. "What I'm griffling, majickal-hare, is that things in Winchett Dale are going to change. Going to *have* to change. And are most peffa-definitely going to change for the better. Your so-called 'majick' will be seen to be just what it is; simply common-cures and griffling, all designed to give you power in this honest, decent, krate-abiding community."

"That's not true!" Matlock angrily objected, peffa-russisculoffed at such an outrageous suggestion. "Ask anyone here. They'll griffle you how majickal I really am."

"Oh, I'm sure they will. I'm sure you have them exceptionally well trained to believe in your hokum. Just listen to your ganticus-eared dworp friend, for one."

"I haven't trained anyone," Matlock slowly insisted, grinding his teeth. "Who are you, anyway?"

The krate opened its eyes wide in mock surprise. "What, you need to know my name? You don't even have a name-finding vroosher up that wizard's sleeve of yours? Oh, my, this just gets even more disappointing by the moment, doesn't it?"

"You know perfectly well that there's no such vroosher," Matlock griffled. "I asked you your name."

"Well," he griffled, enjoying the humiliation, "if you'd got to the public-griffling on time, instead of destroying half the building with your peffa-dramatic entrance, then you'd already know my name very well, wouldn't you?"

A slightly dazed and glopped-up disidula whispgriffled something in Matlock's long brown ear. He listened, nodding, before looking back up at the krate. "Your name is…Coat?"

"No!" the krate griffled.

The disidula tried again.

"Boat?" Matlock griffled, becoming confused.

"Not boat, not coat!"

Matlock looked to the others for help, most of whom were now scratching their heads and various other parts of their sofutulousses, all trying their briftest to try and remember just what the peffa-important krate's name actually was. "Does anyone remember?" he asked them.

"It sounded a bit like 'coat'," Proftulous griffled, "but to be peffa-honest, Matlock, I was thinking about slurpilicious tweazles at the time. There be a whole bunch of them right down the front that would look saztaculous in a ganticus pie."

Matlock sighed, tried again. "Moat? Is your name 'Moat'?"

"No!" the krate griffled, becoming increasingly russisculoffed. "Not moat, not coat, not boat!"

"Well, your name doesn't really seem to matter, then, does it?" Matlock griffled. "Because everyone's already forgotten who you are, anyway!"

The largest round of pawplause so far broke out around the hall, followed by chants and griffle-calls of 'Can we go home, now?' and 'We're juzzpapped of this and just want to nifferduggle!'

"It's 'Note'!" the irate krate shouted above the chaos. "Frendeslene Note! First Officer of Officious Krating for all Districts of the Majickal Dales! And I'll beg you all to calm down and listen to me!"

Matlock pushed the other krates aside, mounting the small podium to stand beside Frendeslene Note. "Creatures of Winchett Dale," he griffled, as silence gradually returned to the hall. "I have been your majickal-hare for many years. I have listened to some of what Mr Note has griffled to you tonight, despite the fact that I wasn't even told of this public-griffling. And I can griffle to you here and now that all my extrapluffs and my Sisteraculous are telling me that something is peffa-definitely wrong here…"

He got no further. With the mere mention of the griffle 'something' the mood in the hall changed in a blinksnap. The mirth was gone, replaced by a growing twizzliness, dark-murmuring and hushed whispgriffles.

Note seized his chance. "You see? Even your not-very majickal-hare has sensed the arrival of the 'something'. His extrapluffs told him so! Now you will *have* to listen to me, and make the changes we need to make."

Matlock slowly turned to him. "But just what *is* the 'something'?"

"Are you totally clottabussed, hare?" Note griffled. "The 'something' is something, of course."

A voice from the front griffled out. "And it's something we should all be peffa-twizzly about, Matlock. Mr Coat be telling us all so."

"It's Note," Note sighed. "My name is Note."

"I'll try and make a note of it," the voice replied. "Only I can't be writing."

"Or reading," another creature added.

"None of us can," a third griffled. "Tis only Matlock that can be reading and writing in Winchett Dale. We all be clottbusses like that. He be reading all the griffles in his majickal driftolubb book things, because he needs them for all his vrooshing and curing."

Note suddenly reached out and pointed, his short claws just a mirrit's leg from Matlock's twitching nose. "This hare," he griffled to them all, "for all his vrooshing and majick, his books and cures, his robes and high office in your community; this hare doesn't even know what a 'something' is!"

"And neither do you," Matlock calmly replied.

"I know it's something we must all make changes for," Note replied defensively. "And I know that your 'majick' alone will not keep anyone in this hall safe from it. That much I do know." He took a breath, watching them all, then suddenly smiling once more. "But, I am a krate that also believes in giving everything a chance. Fair play, if you will. And as such, while I remain peffa-sceptical about your majickal-abilities, hare, I am still prepared to be convinced of them."

"Who's 'Note', then?" griffled a tweazle at the front.

"I beg your pardon?" Note replied, ambushed by the question.

"You griffled you were 'Note'. Now, apparently, you're Mr Prepared-To-Be-Convinced-Of-Them."

"T'was just an expression, not a name!" Note sighed heavily, turning to Matlock. "Are all the creatures in Winchett Dale really this clottabussed all the time?"

"Most of them," Matlock nodded. "But each and every one of them has the heart of Oramus, I can peffa-vouch for that."

"Then I'm beginning to see how easy it would be for you to convince them of your so-called 'majickal' skills," Note slyly concluded, before adding, "But I am not so easy to convince. Krates require proof, not tweazle-pies, or crackpot cures. If you are as majickal as you claim to be, hare, then I shall put you to the test tomorrow sun-turn. We shall all meet at the High Plateau in the morn'up, when you can dazzle us with your craft of majick. Only then will I concede that your ways of dealing with the 'something' could possibly be better than mine. 'Tis a fair test, and you would be fool not to take me up on it."

Cries and shouts of 'Matlock will do it!' and 'He's the most peffa-majickal-hare of all the dales!' rang out around the hall, as Note whispgriffled in Matlock's long, brown ear. "But beware, hare. Should you prove to be less than 'majickal' then I shall have no alternative but to ask you to leave the dale."

"You can't do that!" Matlock griffled.

"Oh, I assure you, hare, that as First Officer of Officious Krating for all Districts of the Majickal Dales, I most certainly peffa-definitely *can*. And you wouldn't have been the first hare to have been forced to leave and take your chances along Trefflepugga Path." Note waved his short arms in the air, signalling for silence. "Creatures of Winchett Dale, we meet tomorrow morn'up on the High Plateau! All are officially summoned to attend! Then we shall see just who would be better in dealing with the twizzly 'something' – me, or Matlock, your so-called 'majickal' hare!"

36

3.

Vrooshers, Driftolubbs and the High Pleateau

When the public-griffling had finally broken up, most creatures made their way back home to nifferduggle in their beds, excrimbly griffling to each other about the vrooshing saztacular to be held the following sun-turn on the High Plateau. With the exception, of course, of the grobbs, who regardless of whatever else might be happening in the village, somehow always found the time for a snutch of guzzworts at the Winchett Dale Inn most even'ups. With the sound of their distant, guzzworty sing-griffling drifting over the village, Matlock stood outside the empty Great Hall, trying to make sense of everything, when Proftulous joined him, a tweazle's tail still wriggling from the corner of his ganticus mouth.

"Proftulous," Matlock gently griffled, "take it out. That's Looper. He was one of your best friends at school, remember?"

Proftulous, frowned, removing the twizzly-tweazle, holding it by its tail and inspecting it closely. "Well, bless my cruckers, so it is! How be you, Looper?"

"Been better, frankly," the damp-tweazle replied. "And you really need to do something about your breath, Proftulous. It's peffa-yechus in there, it really is."

"See, that's from all the tweazles I's been eating," Protulous proudly griffled, before putting the twizzly creature gently back on the ground. "How be your brother, anyway? What was his name? Can't think…"

"Sterrick," the tweazle griffled, skrittling away as fast as he could, "and you ate him last moon-turn, you ganticus clottabus!"

Proftulous turned to Matlock. "Well, that be a mystery solved. I be remembering now. There was a tweazle got quite griffly when I be crunching on him. Turns out it be poor Sterrick. Why's he not be telling me?"

"I daresay he probably tried," Matlock griffled, wondering how much more crumlush things would be if all life's mysteries and complications could be solved so easily. Take, for instance, the arrival of Frendeslene Note in Winchett Dale. No one seemed to know why he was there, or how he had even got there, but seeing as he was a visiting krate in peffa-important robes, no one had even seen fit to ask. The rank of office and the officious manner had been enough. Certainly, Note and Winchett Dale's regular three krates had left the public Griffling as vilishly as they could, but exactly where they had gone was another mystery. As was the imminent arrival of the 'something', and why it was Note was trying to make Winchett Dale so twizzly with it. And why hadn't Matlock himself been invited to the public-griffling in the first place? All mysteries, which Matlock suspected would take an oidy bit longer to solve than Proftulous' tweazle-eating dilemma. He looked at his briftest friend, seeing yechus drool and oidy bits of stroffed tweazle caught in his yellowed teeth, realising that it was a shame that Frendeslene Note didn't resemble the most ganticus, slurpilicious tweazle Proftulous had ever seen. He'd have been crunched and swallowed whole in less than five mouthfuls.

"So what saztaculous vrooshers are you going to be vrooshing for us all tomorrow sun-turn?" Proftulous asked, as the two of them pid-padded round the side of the Great Hall to find Matlock's dropped wand. "Methinks, it'll have to be a peffa-shindinculous vroosher to be impressing that Mr Coat. I don't be liking him, Matlock."

"Indeed, good friend," Matlock griffled, groping on the ground for his dropped wand, then watching an eager group of mirrits scrittle forward from the darkness to bring the short, twisted hawthorn rod safely back to him. Zhava, had long gone, slowly returning on her roots to Wand Wood. Matlock thanked the mirrits, wondering just what it was about the oidy creatures that could cause such a ganticus tree to become quite so twizzly. But then he supposed everyone had some sort of twizzliness about another fellow creature – and for Matlock it was most probably the officious figure of Frendeslene Note. "I'm not sure that I like him too much either, Proftulous."

"We all have to be changing things in Winchett Dale though," Proftulous griffled, "or otherwise the yechus twizzly 'something' will be getting and stroffing us all. Mr Coat be telling us that."

Matlock reached up and patted his oldest friend's tummy. "But what if the 'something' is really the most peffa-ganticus tweazle pie?"

Proftulous' eyes widened, another slither of yechus drool running from his bulbous lips. "Well, then I be eating it, all slurpilicious and crunchy!"

"Exactly," Matlock griffled. "Which means you don't always *have* to change, do you?"

Proftulous thought about the griffles for a snutch of moments.

"Do you?" Matlock prompted.

"I still be thinking about that ganticus pie," Proftulous griffled. "I just can't seem to stop meself thinking about it."

And he didn't stop thinking, or griffling about it for one single pid-pad, as they made their way back through Wand Wood to Matlock's cottage, proving once again to Matlock that nothing ever really changes at all. At least, not with dworps, anyway.

But then something happened that really *did* change everything. As they turned the final corner of the path that led from the woods to the cottage, his dripple came bounding forward to greet them, quite twizzly and pointing at the cottage.

"Hey," Matlock griffled, scooping the excrimbly creature into his paw. "Now just what's got you all so flidgered, eh?"

The dripple pointed even more peffa-vilishly, the smallest of sounds trying to work its way out of its mouth. Matlock leant closer, trying to listen.

"Kr…Kr…" came the oidy sound.

"It be trying to griffle!" Proftulous gasped. "Well, I'll be a mupperwhapper! The dripple's trying to griffle!"

"Shush!" Matlock griffled. "You'll make him even twizzlier." He lifted the creature to his ear.

"Kr…Kr…" the dripple tried again, still pointing at the cottage.

"What's it be griffling about?" Proftulous asked.

"I'm not sure," Matlock griffled. "But I'm going to find out. Follow me, Proftulous, vilish!"

Together they pid-padded and lump-thumped to the cottage, finding the wooden front creaker wide open.

"You think there be someone inside?" Proftulous whispgriffled, getting more than the oidest bit twizzly. For despite his peffa-impressive size, he wasn't known as one of the braver creatures in the dale.

"Only one way to find out, isn't there?" Matlock griffled, heading inside, wand held firmly out in front of him, ready to vroosh any unwelcome guests. "You coming, Proftulous?"

"I probably be staying here for a while," Proftulous mumble-griffled. "Only, I gots meself this awful juzzpapped knee, and…"

Matlock emerged from the cottage a snutch of moments later.

"Well?" Proftulous griffled, "There be any yechus creatures inside that be needing much peffa-vroooshing?"

"No," Matlock quietly griffled.

Proftulous heaved a peffa-ganticus sigh of relief. "Saztaculous! My knee's not being so juzzpapped anymore. Let's go in and have ourselves a slurplicious-feasty."

Matlock sat on his hare's haunches.

"Why we not be going in and getting all feastied?" Proftulous asked.

"There's no food," was Matlock's hushed reply.

"No food?"

"No food, no table, no chairs, nothing. No potionary, no majickal driftolubbs. No nifferduggling bed, no cupboards, no wood for the piff-tosh…nothing." Matlock looked at his friend. "It's all gone, Proftulous. Everything's gone. My cottage is empty."

Proftulous frowned, trying to understand.

"See for yourself," Matlock griffled, as the dripple slipped inside the warm recesses of his crumlush hood. "There's nothing left. It's like I never even lived there."

Proftulous went inside, emerging a snutch of moments later, his face alive with shock. "It be all empty, Matlock! Everything be gone!"

"I know, Proftulous. I just griffled you that." Matlock let out a long hare's sigh, trying to extrapluff and make sense of everything. Someone, or some*thing*, or even a snutch of things had obviously been peffa-busy since he'd left the cottage earlier that even'up. A shudder coarsed through his entire softulous. Was this the 'something' Fendeslene Note had been warning everyone against? Had it come to his cottage and stolen everything while he'd been at the public-griffling?

"What's you going to do, Matlock?" Proftulous griffled, before adding," I know! You can vroosh your cottage all majicky again! Gets your wand out and vroosh everything back, then we can have a ganticus fuzzcheck feasty! You can be doing it because you be a saztaculous majickal-hare!"

"I'm afraid, my peffa-good friend, that it's not quite as simple as that." Matlock griffled, raising himself back up, and pid-padding back inside the empty cottage, Proftulous following closely behind.

"Why not?" Proftulous asked. "Just be doing a vroosher to make everything all be better again."

"Because," Matlock griffled, swinging open the wooden creaker to what had once been his potionary, "I don't even have a potionary anymore."

Proftulous poked his ganticus head around the creaker, gasping at the empty room. "Scaffercoggs! 'Tis all gone. 'Tis as empty as a krate's promise."

"And without my driftolubbs, I can't vroosh many vrooshers at all," Matlock sadly griffled, looking at the empty space where an old oak-shelf had stood, home to his set of majickal-driftolubbs; leather-bound volumes of majickal-wisdom hand scribed and recorded from all the ages, vital majickal lifelines for any majickal-hare, containing grillions of vrooshers and potion recipes. "It's hopeless," he whispgriffled, still in shock at the sight. "All my knowledge, everything I needed was in those driftolubbs. Without them, I am nothing. My wand may just as well be any other oidy twig."

"But surely you can be remembering some of the vrooshers, Matlock?" Proftulous griffled.

"Some, perhaps," Matlock conceded. "But certainly not one that's going to fill my cottage back up with all my things." He was thinking peffa-hard now, not of vrooshers he may remember, but of his dripple's first ever griffle to him. He closed his eyes and took a deep hare's breath. "Krates!" he suddenly griffled. "The dripple was trying to griffle the griffle 'Krates'! Don't you see, Proftulous? Without my driftolubbs and potions, there's no way in a fripp of Scruffsdays that I'll be able to vroosh anything peffa-saztaculous on the High Plateau tomorrow morn'up! I'll be made to look like…"

"A right clottabus?" Proftulous finished for him. "But you're not, Matlock. You're the briftest ever majickal-hare. Everybody be knowing that. And tomorrow morn'up, you'll be there, vrooshing the most peffa-saztaculous and fuzzcheck vroosher the dale has ever seen, won't you, Matlock?"

"But I need to have my driftolubbs so that I can find the right one," Matlock tried to explain. "I need to read all about it, and prepare with my potions and herbs. I need to learn the vroosher-chant, and wand position, and…"

Proftulous' shoulders sank a little. "But…but they're just books, Matlock," he griffled, frowning slightly. "Driftolubbs is just majickal-books. You're the real fuzzcheck majick, Matlock, you are, not the driftolubbs."

Matlock looked into the ganticus eyes of his oldest friend. "But the truth is, I can't do much majick without them, Proftulous." He tried to smile, his heart sinking as he watched the disappointment beginning to cloud Proftulous' face. He took a deep-hare's breath. "I suppose at the end of the sun-turn, I'm just a hare that learned to read."

Proftulous vislishly covered his ears. "No," he griffled, his voice an oidy bit sploinked. "Me not listening! And t'isn't true, not a griffle of it! You *is* majickal, Matlock. Not the driftolubbs. 'Tis you."

Matlock went to him, reached up and gently pulled Proftulous' paws back down. "But it's true," he griffled, seeing how each griffle was confusing and hurting his dear friend, yet also extrapluffing that this was something that Proftulous *had* to know and had to be aware of, no matter how much the ganticus dworp didn't want to hear the griffles.

Proftulous looked down, trying his briftest to understand. "And all these sun-turns that we've been briftest friends," he griffled, "and I've always been griffling up and defending you, Matlock, even though everyone knows I'm just a clottabussed dworp. Like tonight, when everyone is saying the 'something' is coming to gets us all, I's the one griffling that Matlock will be much saving us." He wiped away a small tear and sniffed a truly yechus sniff. "I's did that, Matlock. I did. For you, my briftest friend, because I believes him to be truly majickal, and not just a hare that be learning to read."

"I know," Matlock whispgriffled, remembering how proud he had felt when Proftulous had stood up and championed him, "and I'll always be peffa-grateful for that."

"Then do me a saztaculous vroosher tomorrow morn'up on the High Plateau, Matlock. You *can*, you knows you can. You's majick, Matlock, true and shindinculous majick, and you can be showing that Mr Coat and everyone else just how majickal you really be."

"Proftulous, without my driftolubbs…I…" he almost choked on the last griffles, "…don't really know that I can."

Proftulous looked at the ceiling, took a peffa-deep breath, slowly wiping his yechus nose again. "And all these sun-turns," he quietly griffled, "when we've always been the briftest of briftest friends, you never once be thinking that's you could be teaching me to read?"

Matlock looked away. "No, I didn't," he quietly griffled.

"Because that's would have been making me all majickal, too, wouldn't it?" Proftulous griffled, the hurt loud in his voice. "Making Proftulous all clever and vrooshy, instead of leaving me a glopped-up dworp?"

"Yes," Matlock admitted, "I suppose it might have done."

"And I could have been majicking myself ganticus tweazle-pies every sun-turn, couldn't I? And be making myself feel all proper fuzzcheck again whenever I gets too glopped-up?"

"Perhaps," Matlock griffled, feeling the worst he'd felt in a peffa, peffa-long time.

"And then everyone would be thinking I was a right majickal-dworp, wouldn't they, instead of always griffling about what a clottabus I am and chickling at me behind my back?"

"Proftulous…" Matlock tried to griffle.

"You could have done that for me, couldn't you, Matlock? You could have taught me how to be reading, couldn't you? To make me majickal and everyone-likey, just like you?" Proftulous shook his head. "I thought you were my briftest friend, Matlock, I really did, but I not be knowing about that anymore, I really don't."

"Proftulous, I will always be your briftest friend," Matlock tried, reaching up and trying to hug him. "I promise."

Proftulous gently pushed him away. "I's got to be going now, Matlock," he griffled. "I won't be at the High Plateau tomorrow morn'up, because it would make me too eyesplashy to watch you go glopped-up in front of everyone. Because I already be knowing what that feels like, Matlock, and I don't wants to be seeing you feeling the same way."

"Proftulous, don't go. Please."

Proftulous took a lump-thump towards the creaker then turned. "I got meself some extrapluffing to try and be doing, Matlock." He reached out a ganticus paw and gently stroked one of Matlock's long, soft ears. "Good-bye, friend who I was once thinking was truly majickal."

A snutch of moments later, he was gone.

The next morn'up everyone had dutifully gathered on the High Plateau, all peffa-excrimbly and waiting for Matlock the majickal-hare, the saviour of Winchett Dale, to arrive and conjure a saztaculous vroosher that would show the visiting officious, peffa-important krate just who was the briftest to deal with the imminent arrival and twizzly threat of the peffa-yechus 'something'.

Not that any creature really knew that the 'something' was peffa-yechus at all. None had even the oidiest idea of what it might actually be, but because an officious krate had told them it was coming – then it *had* to be on its way. And in the way of rumours and conjecture, there had been many hushed griffles during the night, as the creatures' twizzly imaginations began driving increasingly ganticus speculation over just how peffa-yechus the 'something' really was. Some griffled that its sole purpose would be to eat them all as they nifferduggled in their beds, others felt certain the 'something' would almost certainly destroy their homes first, whilst one lone creature feared it would set about to ruthlessly eliminate the dale's tweazle population, thus preventing any more slurpilicious pies. But seeing as this was Proftulous, no-one paid any attention to him, knowing full well that nearly all his griffles were even more peffa-clottabussed than theirs, anyway.

So, by the time Frendeslene Note, First Officer of Officious Krating for all Districts of the Majickal Dales, finally arrived and stood before them on the flat grassy top of the High Plateau, twizzly excitement ran through the assembled crowd more vilishly than a long, long-nosed krellit in a whupperstorm.

"Good creatures of Winchett Dale," he griffled, as his three fellow krates called for order. "Are we all assembled and ready to witness this show of majickal-saztaculousness?" He surveyed the crowd, their ranks swollen with every creature in the dale, from the oidiest wottler, to the Last Great Elm, her boughs full of flappers of every description, all eagerly watching and waiting. "Where's the one with the ganticus ears? The dworp thing?"

"Not seen 'im this morn'up," an old flusterbraggle with a pid-padding stick griffled back. "Let's get on with it. This damp's playing merry-jupps with me crifts, and I already suffer with 'em something chronic."

"Indeed we shall," Note griffled back. "Just as soon as your great and saztaculous majickal-hare deems to honour us with his presence and actually arrive. I wonder how he's going to make an entrance this time? Fall from the lid above, perhaps? Or burst from a rock? Either way, I'm sure it'll be quite shindinculous."

The creatures slowly began to chant Matlock's name, searching the lid above for any signs of a vilishly descending majickal-hare. Disidulas, wollumps, groks, drubs, everyone joined in, his name ringing out across the whole of Winchett Dale in the clear autumn morning light.

"Matlock! Matlock! Matlock!" they griffled in unison, a considerable achievement for one and all, especially the frozen-shrutts, who normally only griffled everything backwards.

"It seems," Note cried out above the noise, "that once again, your majickal-hare has chosen to excuse himself from his duties as saviour of this dale." He nodded and smiled at the other krates. "This has been far peffa-easier than even I would have thought."

But as he griffled, the crowd was quietening, slowly parting to allow the familiar figure of Matlock boldly striding through.

45

"Good morn'up, hare!" Note loudly griffled. "Peffa-nice of you to join us. I'm rather hoping you might have a vroosher up your long wizard's sleeve that could actually help you to turn up on time, as I peffa-much doubt the 'something' will want to glopp around for an age, simply waiting for you to arrive and vroosh it away."

Matlock stood before Note, the creatures of Winchett Dale backing away to give their majickal-hare an open grassy arena in which perform his saztaculous vroosher. Young and old were ushered to the front to get the briftest view, whilst the tallest made their way grumbling to the back, russisculoffed to be so far from the spectacle.

"Well," Note griffled, after everyone had settled, "You're looking an oidy bit glopped-up and juzzpapped, hare. Had a fuzzcheck nifferduggle, did we?"

Matlock looked the krate straight in its officious eye. "You know peffa-well, I didn't."

"Me?" Note griffled, pulling a theatrically hurt expression. "I know of no such thing."

Matlock frowned. "And you probably have no idea what happened to my cottage, my potions, and all my majickal-driftolubbs, either."

Note vilishly stabbed out a short, stubby paw. "Just what are you griffling about, hare?"

Matlock gave him a long look, before turning to the crowd. "Friends, creatures, dalesfolk. Lend me your ears for a snutch of moments…"

"You're not having *my* ears," an elderly thrabbwhipple griffled. "They're right fuzzcheck on the side of my head, and that's where they're staying."

"You could lend him a couple of them," a limping-sprettern called out. "You gots at least a dozen on each side, after all."

Matlock appealed for calm as a discussion quickly broke out amongst the crowd as to which creature was going to lend Matlock his ears for the vrooshing majick. "I meant, please listen to me," he griffled.

"Well how can we?" someone griffled, "If you've got all our ears?"

Note quietly griffled from behind, "I think this could well be a peffa-long morn'up, don't you, hare?"

"Please!" Matlock tried again, "Just listen to me."

The crowd eventually quietened; relieved they still all had their ears.

He took a deep hare's breath. "You have come here this morn'up to see me perform a saztaculous vroosher. It won't be easy, in fact, it will be peffa-difficult, but I hope that I can."

The creatures all looked at each other, murmuring low griffles amongst themselves.

"Last even'up, when I was at the public-griffling, someone broke into my cottage and stole all my driftolubbs. They stole everything. I don't have anything left. And the truth, my friends, is simply this, without them, it will be peffa-difficult for me to vroosh anything." He searched the sea of confused faces, looking for Proftulous' ganticus ears, but his briftest friend had been true to his griffles – he hadn't turned up to witness Matlock gobflopp in front of the entire dale.

He cleared his throat. "And whilst I have an oidy extrapluff who's behind this…"

"Careful what you're griffling, hare," Note warned from behind. "You need proof before making any accusations. You know full well that everyone from Winchett Dale was at the public-griffling. Whoever it was that stole your driftolubbs, it certainly wasn't any one of us."

A middle-aged leaning-flort called out, "When are you going to be starting the vrooshing, Matlock?"

Matlock reached into his robes and brandishing his hawthorn wand, an oidy shower of green sparks gently frizzing at its end. He turned to Note, full of the briftest intentions. "So what is it you want to see?"

"Something peffa-saztaculous, of course," Note griffled. "A vroosher that will stroff the 'something'. Shouldn't be too difficult, should it?"

Matlock narrowed his eyes in concentration, trying his briftest to remember any of the banishing-spells from his stolen driftolubbs. He looked to the lid above, waving the wand and griffling loudly:

By the powers of Oramus, and all you hold dear,
Be sure to banish the yechus 'something' if it dares to come near!

47

The wand splutted for a snutch of moments, seeming almost to cough as everyone watched in eager anticipation.

"Nothing's happening, hare," Note unhelpfully observed.

"Give it time," Matlock griffled through gritted teeth, before griffling the spell out loud once more, twirling and flicking the wand, a bright green vroosher suddenly shooting from its tip, arcing high into the air, then plummeting straight back to the ground by his feet.

"Need more time, hare?" Note gleefully offered, unable to conceal his enjoyment of the gobflopping spectacle. "Or perhaps you really need your driftolubbs?"

Matlock ignored him, trying the vroosher for a third time, this time sending it across the gasping heads of the crowd, then watching with a sinking heart as it turned in the air and vilishly returned, before landing with a heavy crump in the exact same spot at his feet as the previous one.

Note pid-padded over to the still fizzing grass, inspecting it closely. "Well," he griffled to the crowd, bending down and picking an oidy flower that had majickally appeared, before holding it high in the air for all to see, "it seems that your majickal-hare seems to think he'll be able to stroff the peffa-yechus 'something' by producing a moondaisy!" He took the tiny flower to the creatures at the front. "I don't confess to know much about the 'something', good friends, but I do wonder if it will be banished by an oidy moondaisy!" He turned to Matlock. "Is this *really* the briftest you've got, hare?"

Matlock set his jaw, griffling the spell again and firing off another vroosher, this time only managing to produce a flute-playing frianozz playing contentedly in the branches of a nearby tree.

"So that's the secret!" Note gasped, pretending to be impressed. "The crumlush music will lull it into nifferduggles, then we'll all simply pid-pad the 'something' away? Somehow, methinks it might not work. Any more, hare, or is that the lot?"

Matlock tried and tried, vrooshing as many vrooshers as he could remember, sending them streaking high into the lid, twirling his frizzing wand, yet managing to produce nothing more threatening than an oidy toadstool ring that mainly sat around griffling about the inconvenience of suddenly being vrooshed into such a spot in the first place.

The creatures were starting to get restless, unable to understand why it was that their majickal-hare was gobflopping so badly. One or two had begun griffling amongst themselves, shaking their heads. Other had their paws and wings to their faces, unable to watch just how hopeless it seemed, each and every one of them peffa-confused as to why none of the vrooshers was even the oidiest bit saztaculous.

In the end, Note called a halt to the proceedings, insisting Matlock stop. "You've had more than your fair share of time to impress us all, hare," he griffled, the frianozz still happily playing its flute in the background. "Admit it, you've gobflopped, and your majick will never be able to keep this dale safe."

Matlock, panting from his efforts, tried one last vroosh that simply dropped straight from his wand and singed the end of his shoe. "I need my driftolubbs!" he griffled.

"Because without them, you are useless?" Note teased. "Just a hare with a twig, whose briftest majick is to produce nothing of any real use, whatsoever? I'm beginning to think that these majickal books of yours are far more majickal than you'll *ever* be, hare." He looked at the hushed crowd. "And I suspect others of us are thinking the same thing, too."

A tilting-bloff slithered forwards. "Can't you do just *one* saztaculous vroosher, Matlock? Just one?"

Matlock slowly blew out his cheeks, trying to find the right griffles. "I'm not sure I can. I have no home anymore. Everything has gone." He dropped his hawthorn wand on the grass, turning to the rest of the hushed crowd. "Without my driftolubbs, this wand is glopped. Everything I needed to make saztaculous vooshers was in those old, majickal books. Without them," he felt something rise at the back of his throat, "perhaps I am just a hare. But I'll always be a hare that's here for each and every one of you."

Note began to slowly clap, his paws the only sound cutting the silence. "Congratulations, hare! Some peffa-fine griffling and High Plateau platitudes!" He turned to the crowd. "I think we've all seen more than enough, don't you? The hare has gobflopped, there is no more to see."

A young disidula, no more than three-moon turns old and wearing spectacles, pid-padded to Matlock's side, pulling at his robe.

"Thank you for being majickal, Mr Matlock," he griffled. "When I was peffa-peffa young, you took a yechus thorn from my paw and made it better for me."

Matlock looked down at the tiny-disidula's face, radiant from the morning. "I just…took it out, that's all," he quietly griffled.

Note was becoming increasingly russisculoffed at delays to proceedings. "Enough!" he griffled. "Let it be seen and remembered that the hare had his chance, but that he clearly isn't, and never really was the majickal-hare to save us all from the peffa-twizzly 'something'."

Matlock listened, watching the crowd, feeling their disappointment, wishing with all his hare's heart that he had been able to do more. And whilst he suspected Note was closely connected to his missing driftolubbs, without actual proof it was impossible to make any accusations, and to have done so to such a high-ranking krate might well have bought glopped-up consequences for all in Winchett Dale. He simply needed more time to try and make sense of everything that was going on.

"The hare's house," Note announced, "now stands empty on the edge of Wand Wood. It is, I suggest, rather like the many empty promises he made to you. By his own griffles he admits that without his driftolubbs then he is little more than a mere hare. As this is very apparently the case then I conclude that he has no place left in Winchett Dale, and I shall be issuing an order decreeing that he leaves by Trefflepugga Path this very sun-turn."

The creatures began to grow peffa-russisculoffed, surging forward as puffing krates struggled to control them.

"Anyone objecting to this ruling, or anyone found griffling to the hare from this moment forth, will be forced to suffer the same fate!" Note shouted. "Now get back to your homes and duties immediately!" He turned to Matlock, a thin smile creeping across his officious face. "You had your chance, hare, and you gobflopped. The time has come for you to pid-pad from Winchett Dale forever."

Matlock didn't griffle a griffle, his jaw set, watching as everyone reluctantly began leaving the plateau.

"Still here, hare?" Note griffled. "If I were you, I'd be pid-padding away as vilishly as I could. I'll be sending krates looking for

Enjoy your time pid-padding along Trefflepugga Path, won't you? I hear the long, long-nosed krellits are peffa-hungry at this time of year."

you all over the dale this even'up. I suggest that they don't find you. Enjoy your time pid-padding along Trefflepugga Path, won't you? I hear the long, long-nosed krellits are peffa-hungry at this time of year."

"I'm leaving," Matlock griffled, his mind made up. Not because even the oidiest part of him wanted to leave, but because he'd realised he had no other choices. An extrapluff coursed through him, confirming his decision as he ran recent events through his mind; his glopped morn'up on the plateau, the sudden arrival of Frendeslene Note, the robbery at the cottage – all these things, he was beginning to realise, were somehow fated and perhaps *meant* to be. Why? He didn't have the faintest extrapluff, save that no matter however sad and juzzpapped he felt, he was going to have to leave the only place he had ever really called home. If he didn't, it would only make matters worse for everyone. He would use his time on Trefflepugga Path to somehow find a way of making everything in Winchett Dale crumlush for everyone again.

He turned, took one final deep-hare's breath, feeling the autumn breeze gently playing around his whiskers, then pid-padded away, his hawthorn wand lying where he'd dropped it on the grass, the only sound the flute-playing frianozz playing contentedly in the tree.

4.

Goole, Drutts and Trefflepugga Path

Many moon-turns ago, when he was just an apprentice majickal-hare, Chatsworth, Matlock's old master, had once griffled to him, "No matter how glopped-up you feel, no matter how peffa-juzzpapped or twizzly, two things are always pid-padding with you; Oramus leading your way, and the Most Majelicus wisdom of the Sisteraculous by your side."

And being just a leveret, who frankly was finding it hard enough trying to learn griffles, vrooshers and reading the majickal-driftolubbs, young Matlock hadn't the oidiest idea what the old, wise hare was griffling about. In some senses, the notion troubled him, because like all hares, Matlock rather enjoyed being solitary, and to even think that there were now two peculiar strangers with him at all times was, frankly, rather perplexing.

"But what about when I'm in the bath, master?" he asked, trying not to blush.

The older hare lightly bliffed his young apprentice's downy ears. "If you even think that Oramus and the Sisteraculous would for one moment want to see you in the bath, then you've a lot to learn."

"But," Matlock griffled, still confused. "What if I'm feeling peffa-lonely and juzzpapped in the bath?"

At which point, Chatsworth had sighed, smiling slightly. The young leveret he had found in The Great Beyond was proving to be just as he had hoped; mindful, inquisitive and, in his own distinctive way, rather entertaining, too. "Then I suggest you put extra niff-bubble syrup in the water," he griffled, "to save you your modesty, Matlock."

Some conversations, for any number of explained and sometimes unexplained reasons just seem to stick with us through the years. Matlock found himself thinking of these very same griffles as he left the High-Plateau, making his way slowly back through Wand Wood to his empty cottage. He realised in that moment that he'd never really taken the griffles peffa-seriously at all. Of course he knew that Oramus kept Most Majelicus vigil over all creatures, and that the Sisteraculous sometimes provided extrapluffs and answers to the most peffa-sploinked problems, but somehow he'd never really felt either of them pid-padding by his side. Perhaps, he now realised, it was because he'd never actually *needed* them to. But this sun-turn, the sun-turn he had been ordered to leave Winchett Dale, was the one sun-turn in his life that he really needed to feel their Most Majelicus presence.

Instead, he merely felt alone.

Soon, he found himself in the very centre of the wood, looking up at Zhava, the Last Great Elm of the dale. "I know you're not allowed to griffle with me," he griffled.

"I'm not," she griffled, looking up into the lid above. "Can't griffle a griffle, Matlock. I'd be banished for griffling to you…" She suddenly slapped a large branch in front of her face. "I'm such a clottabus! I'm griffling to you now, aren't I?"

"Well, I suppose you are," Matlock griffled. "But I don't think anyone's going to hear you, Zhava."

She bent down very slowly, her large trunk creaking loudly in the ominous quiet of the surrounding woodland. "I suppose I could whispgriffle, couldn't I? No one griffled anything about not whispgriffling, did they?"

"You're right," Matlock whispgriffled back. "They didn't. And I think they'd have a peffa-difficult time getting you to leave the dale, wouldn't they? It would take a ganticus amount of creatures to move you, Zhava."

She lowered a little more, creaking all the while. "T'would merely take more of them yechus mirrits, Matlock," she whispgriffled. "They're everywhere, all around me. The krates know I can't stand the peffa-yechus oidy creatures. Those krates know everything. Serraptomus and his two fellow krates have been watching us, you see. Watching us for many sun-turns before this Note-krate arrived. Watching to find out what our most yechus fears are so they can be griffling them all to him. That way methinks Note can begin to control us, Matlock. 'Tis all most peffa-glubbstooled and wrong."

Matlock frowned, his mind digesting the whispgriffles. "How long has this been going on?"

"Serraptomus started in the early summer. You haven't noticed because you've always been in your cottage, reading your driftolubbs, or making vrooshers. But they were out here and in the village, watching us."

Matlock felt a bit stung by this, but he had to admit that Zhara's whispgriffles were mostly true. He couldn't deny that peculiar and strange things had been going on, all around him, right under his majickal-hare's nose, and he hadn't even caught the oidiest-snuffle of any of it.

"Just like last even'up, you didn't even know that mirrits make me peffa-twizzly. But the krates know, Matlock. They already know."

Matlock blinked. "But why didn't anyone griffle to me about this?"

Zhava leant down even closer; the leafy top of her canopy now just inches from Matlock's ears. "What would have been the point?" she whispgriffled. "What could you have done against the krates? They make the rules, Matlock, they've always made the rules. And your majick can't unmake a rule, can it? Or vroosh a krate into being unofficious? Everyone, every creature, every living thing in this dale now knows that, Matlock. Your majick just isn't enough anymore."

"But that's not true!" Matlock griffled, protesting as quietly as he could. "I would have tried. I would have…looked in my driftulubbs and found the brifftest ever vroosher ever to…"

"To what, Matlock? To what?"

"To…to…to…"

Zhava smiled, brushed him lightly with her leaves. "Matlock, you are so clottabussed for a majickal-hare. Look at me. I am the Last Great Elm of Winchett Dale. When my roots finally slip, when my leaves drop for the last time, there will be no more Elms that follow me. No amount of majick could make another of my kind. Some things simply end. Life as we knew it Winchett Dale is ending now, Matlock, and there be peffa-little we can be doing about it. 'Tis just the way of things, methinks, 'tis Oramus' will."

"No, Zhava!" Matlock insisted. "Don't griffle like that! You have many more sun-turns, many more moon-turns, many more…"

He was interrupted by a booming officious voice he immediately recognised as belonging to Serraptomus, leader of Winchett Dale's other two resident krates, and now, presumably chief spy for Frendeslene Note. "Matlock the Hare!" he roared, vilishly pidpadding through the woods towards them. "Stop griffling to that tree at once!"

"You must go!" Zhava urged, trying to bend and heave herself upright.

"But I can't leave you like this," Matlock griffled, trying to push, but knowing he was far too oidy for such a ganticus task. Zhava was stuck, simply too peffa-heavy to lift her canopy back to the lid.

"Go!" she urged, as Serraptomus neared . "Do as they griffle, Matlock. Leave the dale this sun-turn. It's the new way, Matlock, the new Winchett Dale. Majick won't stop it, and neither will you. You must leave, or you won't be safe!"

"Another griffle from either of you," Serraptomus barked as he arrived in the small clearing, panting slightly, "and I'll set the mirrits loose again, Zhava. And you know how much they like your bark, your juicy shoots, leaves and buds, don't you? Peffa-slurpilicious to mirrits, they are, aren't they, eh?"

"Please, Matlock," Zhava whispgriffled, "just go. I'll straighten myself in time. It's just age, you know. Makes things so peffa-difficult for an old tree like me, at times."

Matlock nodded, running a comforting paw through her leaves. "I'll be back," he whispgriffled. "I'll make everything majickal again, Zhava. Everything, I promise."

Serraptomus snorted. "Be gone, hare," he griffled menacingly. "Your time in this dale is over."

Matlock clenched his teeth and paws, trying peffa-hard to resist the overwhelming urge to fludge and bliff him in the swallops.

"What's happened here, Serraptomus?" he griffled, standing his ground. "Why has everything suddenly changed?"

Serraptomus began to chickle. "Suddenly changed? Listen to the hare! The change has been happening for many moon-turns – only you were too snuggly in your crumlush cottage, too far from the village to even begin to notice." His mouth glurped to a yechus sneer. "And now, it's all simply too peffa-late."

Matlock held his stare for what seemed like an eternity, his mind racing vilishly. How could he go, knowing what was happening to his crumlush Winchett Dale? Yet how could he stay, if it was going to make it even more peffa-glopped-up for everyone? He closed his eyes, hoping for an extrapluff. When one came, it was the same as before, telling him that for any number of unknown reasons, and despite his woes, worries and peffa-heavy heart, he must go. He had, he realised, no other choice.

"Bye, bye, hare," Serraptomus griffled after him, watching Matlock pid-padding slowly away into the woods. "Enjoy Trefflepugga Path! The long, long-nosed krellits'll have your bones!"

Mind churning more vilishly than a dilva-beetle in a windrushy, Matlock pid-padded through the woods on the path that took him back to his crumlush cottage. So many times before, this had been the sight that had cheered him at the end of a long, hard sun-turn; seeing his cottage, the thin blue welcoming smoke trail drifting lazily from the chimney, and Matlock knowing in that blinsknap that all was warm, crumlush and safe inside. But not now. Now, as he stood in-front of the empty cottage, it no longer felt like his home, or any home. Even his dripple wasn't there to greet him and bring him a cup of warm niff-nettle tea. It seemed for all the world to Matlock as if his cottage was as empty, cold and lonely as he was.

He waited a while, calling for his dripple, hoping it might be nifferduggling somewhere inside, but it didn't come. Then again, he reasoned, why would it have stayed in such a cold, uninviting place? He pid-padded round the side of the cottage and into the small walled-garden, looking at the majickal-plants and foliage he had tended so carefully as vital ingredients in his many potions and vrooshers. Again, he called for his dripple, hoping its oidy furry head might appear from a thropp-bush, or from beneath a wilting niff-plant. But nothing. Matlock's dripple, it seemed, had done exactly as the others in Winchett Dale had done, deserted him on the krate's instructions. He sat on a colley-rock, asking permission first. It shifted slightly, then sighed.

"How in Oramus' sake did this all happen?" he griffled. "Everything was peffa-perfect last sun-turn. But now, it's all gone glubbstool and glopped-up."

"Don't know," the colley-rock griffled. "I'm too busy spending each and every sun-turn just being a rock to notice. 'T'isn't as easy as it first appears, you know, being a rock."

"Really?"

"Well, it used to be. Used to be peffa-easy indeed. Just sort of sitting around. Course, that's all changed now." The colley-rock shifted again. "I hear tell that we're all going to be stroffed and garrumbloomed to make some sort of drutts."

"Drutts?" Matlock griffled. "What's a 'drutt'?"

"No idea. S'just what the other rocks and stones have been griffling about. S'pose we'll find out in time, though. Something to do with this new krate arriving here, is all I know."

"Seems this Frendeslene Note has been making all sorts of plans for Winchett Dale," Matlock quietly griffled, wondering about the 'drutts'. He'd never heard the griffle before, and had as much idea of what they were as the colley-rock did.

"You leaving then, are you?" it griffled.

Matlock nodded. "Not sure I have any real choice at the moment."

"Can't you majick it all better, then?"

Matlock stood, yawning. He did feel peffa-juzzpapped, and wanted nothing else than to walk back into his cottage and have a crumlush nifferduggle in his bed. "That's the problem," he griffled. "I'm just not sure I can. I'm not really sure if I ever *could*, really."

"Oh," the colley-rock griffled. "Well, my opinion, for what it's worth, is that I thought you was an oidy bit majickal *some* of the time. But now that I come to really think about it, I'm not sure I saw you doing anything majickal or shindinculous, at all. I mean, you made your wandy thing go all vrooshy sometimes, but mostly you were out here, gardening. I used to wonder why it was that you couldn't just vroosh the garden to be saztaculous. Probably know why, now."

Matlock didn't griffle a griffle, knowing it was time to leave. He took one last long hare's look around, hoping, perhaps, to see Proftulous' ganticus ears appearing over the back-wall, a snutch of stroffed tweazles in his paws, wanting to griffle the afternoon'up away with his friend. But just like the dripple, Proftulous seemed just a memory. Matlock would simply have to trust to his extrapluffs, his Sisteraculous and Oramus' Most Majelicus wisdom that leaving everything behind was the peffa-best thing to do. But then, he was forced to admit, in the glopped-up circumstances, it was also the *only* thing he could do…

Bidding the colley-rock farewell, he set off for Trefflepugga Path, the winding pathway that runs from the lands of The Great Beyond, right into the heart of Winchett Dale itself. Just the thought of it made Matlock feel an oidy bit twizzly, as he'd never followed the path beyond the entrance to Sacred Cave since Chatsworth had first bought him down into the dale.

"The Great Beyond," Chatsworth had griffled to him one evening in the cottage-potionary, "is no longer your home, Matlock. We were born there, were leverets there, but now we are here. Your memories of your time there will fade. And until such times as Oramus calls us, this is where you will stay, Matlock. Winchett Dale is your new home."

"Home," the young apprentice-hare had griffled, nodding peffa-earnestly.

"But one sun-turn, you will be called, just as I was, to journey back to The Great Beyond to find your own apprentice from all the other hares. And to do that, you will have to pid-pad right along Trefflepugga path, and deal with its peffa-twizzly dangers."

Matlock swallowed hard, not liking these griffles an oidy bit.

"But don't worry, little Matlock," Chatsworth griffled. "You will by then be a master of such saztaculous vrooshing majick, that no harm will come to you. Your wand, your skills and your learning will guide you safely every pid-pad of the way, just as it did with me." He pointed to his red-robes. "I wear these as a sign that I am Most Majelicus. Yours are the green robes of a mere majickal-hare. But if you work and study hard, one sun-turn you too could become Most Majelicus, like me. And when you do, it will be time for you to journey along Trefflepugga Path and find your own apprentice to teach and instruct in the ways of the ancient majick of the dales. Just as I did with you."

"Was it really, peffa-peffa-twizzly on the path?" Matlock had griffled. "With yechus monsters and long, long-nosed krellits waiting to stroff and eat you?"

Chatsworth smiled. "'Tis nothing that can't be dealt with using your majick, Matlock. Which is why we must continue our lessons and potionary studies peffa-vilishly. That way, when your time comes to make your journey along the path, you'll be the briftest majickal-hare ever to have pid-padded along it. And what do we always have to remember?"

Matlock frowned slightly, trying to remember, chasing his thoughts.

"That no matter how glopped-up we feel…?" Chatsworth prompted.

"The Sisteraculous is always by our side, and Oramus is pid-padding just in front," Matlock griffled, despite still being secretly baffled at just how Oramus could get so vilishly from his home on the moon, or be in so many places in the same blinksnap.

"Indeed, Matlock," Chatsworth had griffled, "indeed. Griffles that are peffa-worth remembering for any majickal-hare, methinks."

But now, as Matlock made his way slowly beside Thinking Lake towards the distant heights of Sacred Cave and the ominous beginnings of Trefflepugga Path, it didn't feel to him as if there was anyone either at his side, or pid-padding in front of him. One or two of the braver trees, plants and grasses, whispgriffled their hushed 'Good-byes' to him as he passed by, but mostly he just felt alone, trying not to think of the many times he and Proftulous had sat by the lake, waiting for extrapluffs, while the cool breeze troffled and lightly gruzzed their faces. Sun-turns that suddenly seemed such a peffa-long time ago…

But he had barely gone a snutch of pid-pads past the top of the lake, when there came a most ganticus flapping squawking and griffling, as at least a dozen chickling kraark-birds landed beside him, their black feathers gleaming in the fading sunlight.

"It's a hare," griffled one.

"Haven't seen of them for a peffa-long sun-turn," griffled another.

A third kraark was pecking at Matlock's robe, flapping and jiffling. "Quality material, this," it griffled. "Must be one of them majickal-hares from down in the dale."

Matlock felt himself becoming ever more russisculoffed. It had been a peffa-long sun-turn, and frankly, mostly glopped-up. The last thing he needed was to be surrounded and griffled at by a glopped-up snutch of chickling kraarks. "You'd do as well not to do that," he warned them, "or I'll…"

"Or you'll do what?" came the sudden booming griffles of a kraark quite unexpectedly dressed in a battered old tricorned hat and waistcoat, and shindinculous rings glinting on every flight feather. "Come on, Mr Hare, we're waiting. Just what *are* you going to do? Vroosh us all away? Majick us to another dale? We'd peffa-much like to be seeing that, we really would."

"Who are you?" Matlock griffled, noticing this kraark had one milky-white eye, the other as black and piercing as a lightning bolt from a stormy lid.

The kraark shook its wing at him, the rings chinkling. "Question is, hare, who are *you*? For I'm thinking that you must be Matlock the majickal-hare, of which so peffa-much has been griffled. 'Saviour of the dale', they griffles you, don't they? The hare that has Oramus in his very robed pocket." He turned to the other kraarks as they all pretended to bow. "Brother kraarks – we are most highly peffa-honoured to have such a saztaculous guest in our rather glopped-up and shabbily meagre company."

"What's he taste like?" a kraark griffled. "Not much on his softulous, we'd barely get a meal out of that."

"T'would make a good stew, though," another suggested, circling. "Slurpilicious with smelters, onions and niffs…"

"Silence!" the hatted kraark griffled, causing all to bow once more. He scrittled closer to Matlock, studying him intently with his one eye. "What we seem to be having here brothers, is something peffa-special indeed." He suddenly made several yechus noises from somewhere glopped in the back of his throat. "Methinks this hare's not for eating, or stewing…"

"Shame," a clottabussed kraark unwisely griffled, as he was immediately wing-bliffed on the beak by the hatted-Kraark.

"Methinks," he went on, "this hare has been sent to us lowly and peffa-humble Trefflepugga-kraarks for a *reason*." He held out a wing towards Matlock's paw. "I'm Goole," he griffled. "King of the Trefflepugga-kraarks. And whilst not exactly at your service, my ma-jickal-friend, you are now, unfortunately, most peffa-definitely at mine."

Matlock tried not to get twizzly as the other kraarks began skrittling towards him, their sharp talons and pointed black beaks getting far too close. "I suppose that I am, Mr Goole," he griffled, in a slightly cracked voice.

"Just Goole, not 'Mister'!" Goole snapped. "Trefflepugga-kraarks don't have no glopped-up titles. All excepting mine, of course," he puffed out his black-chest, his waistcoat straining so much a snutch of stitches plinged loose, "King of the Treffelpugga kraarks."

"Then I'm most peffa-pleased to meet you, your Highness," Matlock griffled, looking for a way past or through the encircling kraarks, but finding none. Even if he pid-padded as vilishly as he could, their speed in the air would soon catch him. Instead, he found himself griffling, "So what exactly is a Trefflepugga-kraark, then?" to the baying, swirling mob.

Silence descended more vilishly than a ganticus colley-boulder falling from the lid.

Goole scrittled closer as the others backed away, his one-eye beadily searching Matlock's face. "Did I just hear what you griffled to me?" he griffled, peffa-slowly, "Did you *honestly* have the nerve to be griffling 'what is a trefflepugga-kraark?'"

Matlock nodded, unable to deny the question, as all around him he noticed the other kraarks slowly covering their heads with their wings.

"The glopped-up hare's gone and done it," one whispgriffled. "There's no-way we can avoid a song now…"

Another nodded, its beak barely poking from behind black-flaxen wings, its griffles muffled by feathers. "It's the most gobflopped and peffa-clottabussed thing to do! We're all going to suffer, and it's his fault."

"Indeed, but he'll suffer far worse, brothers," a third whispgriffled. "Just look at the size of the ganticus ears on him!"

"Methinks," Goole griffled, his sharp beak plinging Matlock's whiskers, "that your ignorance of my most humble profession demands the invocation, explanation and peffa-saztaculation…of a song!"

The other kraarrks all groaned, Matlock watching in complete astonishment as a group of oidy ploffshrooms suddenly dashed from the undergrowth, complete with miniature harps, horns, bells and drums.

"Well, Matlock," Goole griffled, as the ploffshrooms began to strike a high-tempo beat that frankly, Matlock found just an oidy bit glopped. "'Tis a great pleasure to have you join us at Thinking Lake this afternoon'up. You pid-padded far?"

"Well…" Matlock griffled, finding himself distracted by the other kraarks, who had now formed themselves into a line and begun to scrittle around in somewhat reluctant unison, in what could only be very loosely described as some sort of peffa-clottabussed dance, "…just from my cottage, at the end of Wand Wood, really."

Goole backed away, his beak smiling broadly, wings open in a gesture of theatrical welcome, the ploffshrooms keeping up their musical beat all the while. "Then 'tis a peffa-pleasure to have you here for our Trefflepugging feast of musical entertainment that will bedazzle, shervazzle and skerpazzle you, my long-eared, majickal-friend." He suddenly held up a wing and everyone froze. "I used to do this for a living, you know, back in a little place called Sveag Dale. Played to packed woods and cliffs, caves and pastures every even'up. Met all the peffa-greats, you know, the legends; Gruppo the Twodd, Selimus Yullip, the Phleeks, all of 'em. Aah, those were the sun-turns, my friend, peffa-fuzzchecked and most proper saztaculous they were."

Matlock nodded, not really having the oidiest idea what the tricorned kraark was griffling about, and frankly, secretly rather glad he didn't either. "What happened?" he griffled. "How did you end up here?"

"Is a peffa-good question, good-hare!" Goole excrimbly griffled. "And one that I shall answer with a song of me own making and choosing." He winked at Matlock. "Every griffle's me own, by the way. And you can hire me for private functions on Yaaydays and Sluffsdays. Special rates if you want an afternoon show, you only has to ask."

"I'll bear that in mind," Matlock griffled, watching as Goole dramatically lifted then dropped his wing, and the ploffshroom band and reluctant kraark dancing chorus began their glopped-up skriffling once more.

A snutch of moments later, he began to sing:

> *Well, I's the most saztaculous kraark, like me there is no other,*
> *A truly peffa-fuzzcheck kraark, that became a Trefflepugga.*
> *We flaps ourselves from dale to dale,*
> *Thieving things and drinking ale,*
> *And we'd even rob an oidy mirrit from its weeping mother…*

He wrapped a wing around Matlock. "Feel free to join in the chorus, Mr Hare. It's peffa-easy."

"I probably won't," Matlock griffled as politely as he could, "if it's all the same to you."

"Suit yourself," Goole shrugged, raising both wings and urging the woeful kraarks to sing:

> *We're kraarks! We're kraarks! And we always sing and laugh!*
> *We're the thieving Trefflepuggas of Trefflepugga Path!*

Goole reached down and bliffed away an eager ploffshroom who was about to rush forward with a small harp. "We normally put a trinkulah solo in here, but frankly, as we're pressed for time, we'll just move on with verse two."

> *We flaps and croffs and scriffles around, let there be no ifs or buts,*
> *We only do the thieving lark to get ourselves more drutts,*
> *Then back to the wagon we all go,*
> *And puts on a crumlush-pugga show,*
> *'Cause we're all Trefflepuggas, right down to our peffa-guts!*

The backing kraarks unenthusiastically tried to form themselves into a juzzpapped pyramid over the final chorus, Goole urging them on with cries of "Tis the big-finish, Brothers!", as the puffshroom band lead the music to a soaring crescendo.

At the finish, there was just silence, save for just some rustling leaves on nearby trees.

"Well?" Goole griffled, anxious for Matlock's opinion, the kraark pyramid collapsing and tumbling into a glopped-up heap. "I mean, the ending still needs an oidy bit of working on, but it's a real showstopper, isn't it? You have to griffle us that."

Matlock cleared his throat. "It was," he slowly griffled, trying to choose his griffles as carefully as possible, "full of enthusiasm."

Goole nodded, turned to the others. "Yep, we'll take that. And?"

"You want me to griffle some more?"

Goole held his wings out wide. "Come on, Mr Hare, we've put on a peffa-good show for you. Oidy bit of encouragement doesn't go amiss."

Matlock thought about it. "Well, I thought the band were very good…"

Goole frowned then suddenly skrittled uncomfortably close, his breath quite yechus on Matlock's face. "But what," he griffled menacingly, "about *me*? Never mind about the band! Wasn't I the briftest of all of us?"

"Oh, most peffa-definitely," Matlock vilishly griffled, unable to avoid Goole's milky-eyed stare. "The briftest of the briftest, in quite the briftest kraark-pugging singing show thing I've ever seen."

Goole held his gaze for a snutch of moments, then suddenly broke away, turning back to the others. "You see, brothers? This hare knows talent when he sees it! Hear his griffles! I'm the briftest! Me – Goole, King of the Trefflepugga Kraarks is peffa-more briftest than any of you!" He began joyfully scrittling around, bliffing the other kraarks with his wings.

"But can I ask," Matlock griffled, "just what drutts are?"

Goole was back at his side in a blinksnap. "Whose been griffling about drutts?" he griffled, jabbing Matlock with the hard end of a broken flight-feather.

"Well, you have, just now – in your song."

Goole narrowed his one good eye, turning to the others. "Did I?" he asked them.

They all slowly nodded.

Goole thought for a while, silently mouthing the words of the song until he got to the relevant lyrics. "Well, jupple my blidgers in tweazle-jiuce, so's I did, Mr Hare!" he griffled. "I can see why you're asking now." He lifted a wing, pressing it lightly to the tip of his blackened beak. "But I've been sworn to secrecy, you see, over griffling about drutts. Could cost me dear if I starts griffling about drutts to anyone who asks."

Matlock took a hare's breath, seeing in an extrapluff exactly how to persuade Goole to reveal the truth about the mysterious drutts. Flattery would be the way, convincing the overblown kraark of his 'talents'. "But you see," he griffled, "while it was without doubt a peffa-saztaculous song…"

"That I was the briftest in," Goole vilishly cut in. "Your griffles, majickal-hare, not mine."

"Indeed," Matlock agreed, "but to make it *truly* peffa-saztaculous and shindinculous, I'd have to know what drutts are. Then I could griffle to everyone about your peffa-greatness. After all, I can hardly griffle anything without knowing about drutts, can I? They are an important part of the song, after all."

Matlock watched as the tricorned, waist coated kraark thought about what he'd said. He could almost see the thoughts crossing his oidy bird-brain; whether to let the hare know, and have him realise just how 'peffa-saztaculous' a singer he was – or to merely settle for being plain old 'saztaculous' without revealing a griffle about the mysterious drutts.

"And you'd griffle everyone that I was the briftest singer in all the dales?" Goole asked.

"The briftest of the briftest, your Highness," Matlock griffled. "The most yamamantally-spious and peffa-saztaculous singer in all the dales. I'd be able to understand the song completely, you see, if I actually knew what drutts were."

"Well," Goole slowly griffled, as Matlock sensed he could be winning. "I suppose I could. But you'd have to griffle not a griffle about drutts to anyone else, you hear?"

"Of course," Matlock griffled. "Not even the oidiest griffle to the oidiest creature, ever."

"Follow me, then," Goole griffled, wrapping a wing around Matlock's shoulder, and taking him further up the path, pid-padding straight past the darkened entrance to Sacred Cave, then suddenly veering off, heading deep into the undergrowth, eventually coming to a small clearing in and amongst a snutch of trees, the other kraarks scrittling and flapping along behind, all too glad the musical theatrics were over.

"This," Goole griffled, pointing to a large covered wagon in the centre of the clearing, "is me home, Mr Hare. The official-residence of all the Trefflepugga kings since Krilpvar Scrupe bought it here many years ago. Think yourself peffa-lucky, Mr Hare, very few souls have ever seen it, and of those that have, precious fewer have left here alive to griffle the tale of the Trefflepugga kraarks."

"Because we always stroffs 'em," a kraark added. "Then picks all the slurpilicious softulous from their bones!"

"And leaves the bones at the entrance to Trefflepugga Path," another griffled, flapping onto a low-branch just beside Matlock's head. "For the long, long-nosed krellits to be having. They loves them bones, you see. We sometimes hears 'em a'crunching on 'em at night, we do. Then they leaves us alone, you see, lets us get on with our business, as we let them get on with theirs. It's an offering. Always needing more bones to give them, we are, hare." He flew down and pecked at Matlock's leg. "Reckon you gots a nice few bones for the long, long-krellits in there, hare."

Sometimes, it is the peffa-oidiest things at the end of a long glopped-up sun-turn that finally cause our russisculoftulation to grubble over into true anger. And while Matlock wouldn't ever have considered himself to be an angry majickal-hare in a grillion sun-turns, the kraark's pecking at his leg was in some senses, the peck that broke his softulous. He'd lost his briftest friend, his home, all his belongings, his belief in just how majickal he'd ever really been, had been humiliated when he'd gobflopped in front of the entire dale, and been forced to endure the glopped-up song of a bloated, waist coated kraark – and was, to crown it all, now being pecked by one of his clottabussed flappers. It was, quite simply, all too peffa-much.

67

He vilishly bliffed the kraark away, angrily turning to Goole. "Let me griffle you this! King you may be, but frankly to little more than a court of clottabussed, dismally dancing kraarks, whose work in the chorus was mixed, to griffle the least. The trebles especially, need a lot more work in the more complex harmonies, and the baritone at the bottom of the pyramid only sounded the oidiest bit better than a murpworm emerging from the dale's most peffa-yechus and sticky pond!"

"I was trying, you know," the unfortunate baritone kraark griffled. "You have a go, with a mass of talons in your face. Could hardly breathe…"

"Silence!" Matlock cried. He turned back to Goole. "The only 'deal' you'll be making with me, is to griffle to me what drutts are. Then I'll be pid-padding right out of here, and I promise, as a majickal-hare of my griffles, that I'll let everyone know just what a yamamantally-spious, singing king you are."

Goole shrugged. "Seems fair, hare," he griffled. "Got to forgive the brothers, they sometimes get a bit carried away. Mind, you were right about the trebles, just don't do me any justice, really, especially not on a saztaculous showstopper." He motioned the other kraarks away, Matlock watching as they flew up into the branches to sit silently, scolded by both their king and a majickal-hare. It really hadn't been the most memorable of sun-turns for any of them.

"Come with me," Goole griffled, taking Matlock up the small wooden steps of the wagon, flapping open the heavy covers and motioning him inside.

If Matlock had been expecting any sort of saztaculous palace fit for a king, then he was peffa-soon disappointed. Inside the wagon smelt of damp, rotting canvas and any number of other glopped-up and peffa-yechus things, none of which seemed to even vaguely trouble Goole. It was cramped, too, so much that Matlock had to hold his ears down in order to stop them touching the roof. And in the middle, simply a large pile of pebbles and stones.

"These," Goole griffled triumphantly, "are drutts, Mr Hare. Shindinculous, ain't they?" He spread his wings and began digging the tips into the pile, lifting and dropping them. "They're the future of this here dale. The new way. The way of drutts."

"They're the future of this here dale. The new way. The way of drutts."

Matlock frowned, then griffled the obvious. "But they're just oidy stones and pebbles."

Goole wheeled on him in the confined space, holding a pebble from the pile up to Matlock's confused face. "This is no ordinary pebble, Mr Hare," he whispgriffled with great importance. "'Tis a drutt."

"Why?" Matlock griffled.

Goole blinked with his one good eye. "Because it is."

"Well, what does it do?" Matlock griffled, reaching deep into one of his robe pockets and finding a pebble. "How is it different to this?"

"Well, that's not a drutt," Goole griffled, shaking his head. "That's just an oidy pebble."

Matlock let out a small sigh, wondering how long he could stay in the yechus wagon debating the merits, or otherwise, of pebbles and stones.

"However, it would *become* a drutt," Goole whispgriffled, anxious to clear up the confusion, "if a krate had already given it to you first."

"A krate?"

"They're the ones, you see? The ones that can turn pebbles into drutts."

"But how?" Matlock insisted. "Your 'drutts' are just the same as my pebble. The same as any pebble I can pick up and find all over the dale! It's just another griffle for a pebble."

"Oh, but that's where you're *so* peffa-wrong, Mr Hare," Goole griffled, shaking his wing. "So peffa-peffa wrong." He pointed to the pile. "These drutts are worth something. Drutts gets you things, Mr Hare. Drutts can get you the most saztaculous things, the most peffa-shindinculous things." His eye gleamed in the glopped-up gloom. "And those that have them'll be fuzzcheck for ever; those that don't will be gobflopped for the rest of their lives. But not Goole, Mr Hare; Goole's got himself grillions of drutts, ahead of the rush. And when all the creatures of Winchett Dale runs out of their drutts, when the krates won't give them any more, who do you think they'll come pid-padding to, eh?"

Matlock saw it all too clearly. Although the very notion of 'drutts'

70

having any kind of value was utterly preposterous, clearly the krates had been working hard to convince Goole otherwise. Though, on reflection, Matlock realised, Goole was such a bird-brained clottabus he probably didn't take too much convincing. Most likely the krates had simply offered him the services of the ploffshroom band for a few sun-turns in exchange for whatever they wanted from him. Yet the whole sorry 'drutts' business was further proof to Matlock that the sudden arrival of Frendelsene Note in Winchett Dale had been peffa-well planned. And Matlock knew that if Goole could be convinced that a mere pebble was suddenly worth something simply because it had been given to them by a krate, then he really couldn't think of any other creature in Winchett Dale who would disbelieve it, either. For Matlock knew all too well that they were just as easy to convince as Goole.

Crouched in Goole's yechus wagon, holding his ears down, and finding just a pile of worthless pebbles, there seemed little doubt to Matlock that Note had spotted an opportunity in Winchett Dale – the simple fact that the creatures there wanted to believe in *something*. The glopped-up 'something' itself was a horrible but perfect proof of that. Just the oidiest mention of its arrival, delivered in sombre tones by Note, had sent them all into the most ganticus twizzle, even though not one of them had the oidiest idea what the 'something' actually was. Note must have known this, and further, to complete whatever plans he had, must have known he would have to humiliate and remove him, destroying his cottage and all his majickal driftolubbs in the process.

"I suppose all the creatures will have to come to you for their drutts," Matlock griffled. "You'll give them some in return for things they can do for you. Or make them give you even more drutts for the privilege of borrowing the drutts from you in the first place."

"S'exactly right, Mr Hare!" Goole griffled, quite peffa-excrimbly. "They will. All of 'em, begging Goole for more drutts. Shame you's just a hare, really, as you'd 'ave made a shindinculous Trefflepugga, you would've. Got brains, you see. And I hear tell you can extrapluff, too." He tapped the side of his black head with a wing. "Valuable commodities, is brains and extrapluffs. Not like that glopped-up lot out there. Bunch of clottabusses, they are."

"How did you get all these pebbles…I mean, drutts?"

Goole tapped the top of his long beak. "I has me ways, Mr Hare. Made a trip up Trefflepugga Path a few moon-turns ago. Went right up to the top of it. Know what I found there, Mr Hare?"

Matlock shook his head.

"Another dale, Mr Hare, another dale. But not one like Winchett Dale. This was a dale of opportunity, a dale of drutts, a dale of saztaculous houses and shindinculous halls, smooth stone pathways, and everywhere good and officious krates kept order, keeping everyone busy, kept working hard for their drutts."

"Then it sounds peffa-yechussly glubbstool," Matlock griffled, trying to imagine his own dale the same way. Not that he ever could, because the whole point of the Winchett Dale was that no creature ever really worked for anything. They simply worked for themselves and each other. The houses in the village may have been old, an oidy bit gob-flopped in places, juzzpapped even, but this was how everyone liked it, the way it had always been. The thought of smooth stone paths and ganticus buildings was as alien to Winchett Dale as it would have been for Proftulous to keep a tweazle farm just to watch the creatures merrily pid-padding around.

"Anyway," Goole griffled, "after I'd been there a snutch of sun-turns, and had got my head and wings around this whole drutts business, I begins to think to myself what a shindinculous idea t'would be to have 'em here, too. So I has a few griffles with a few krates, griffling them my idea, like. And they has a few griffles with some other krates, who has a few griffles with some other krates, who has a few gri—"

"Just how many krates are there in this other dale?" Matlock interrupted, anxious for Goole to get to the point.

The King of the Trefflepuggas shrugged. "No idea. Loads of 'em. Certainly more than the three gobflopped ones we has here. These were proper krates. Creatures gave them respect, because the krates has to supervise and administer all the drutts, you see?"

"Yes," Matlock quietly griffled, "I think I am."

"Couldn't do that with our lot, could we, eh? Serraptomus and his two clottabussed fools can't cope with a normal sun-turn in Winchett Dale, let alone when Mr Note introduces the new way of drutts tomorrow morn'up…" He suddenly slapped the end of his beak with both wings. "I've done too many griffles to you, Mr Hare. 'Tis all stuff you're not meant to be knowing."

Matlock seized his chance, vilishly reaching out and grabbing Goole by the wings, lifting him into the air. "I suggest you keep griffling, Goole, or I'll go straight to Note right now and griffle all I know about his plans, and exactly who it was that told me."

"Let me go, hare-brain!" Goole screeched. "Or I'll have them kraarky-flappers out there stroff you and clean your bones for the long, long-nosed krellits!"

But Matlock didn't let go. "You're forgetting that I'm a majickal-hare, Goole," he griffled, in what he hoped was his most peffa-menacing voice. "Right now I could vroosh you so that you'd never sing another note again in your miserable, greedy life."

"Not without your wand, you couldn't!" Goole protested, twisting and turning, trying to peck at Matlock's eyes with his beak. "Or your majickal-driftolubbs! You're nothing without those books, everyone knows that! Without the driftolubbs, you're just a hare from The Great Beyond that learned how to read!"

"Who told you?" Matlock griffled, forcing Goole's wings wider apart, sending more stitches of his waistcoat plinging into the side of the wagon.

"Note!" Goole screamed, alerting the other kraarks outside, who vilishly swooped from their branches and surrounded the wagon. "He griffled it to me me, hare!"

Matlock dropped the distressed krate which landed with a scrunch on the drutt pile. "Call the other kraarks off," he warned, "or it'll only get peffa-glopped-up for you, Goole."

"How?" Goole challenged. "You're not majickal anymore. You couldn't vroosh a freggitt with a bad cough better!"

Matlock narrowed his eyes. "I'm willing to bet that those flappers out there have no idea what these pebbles really are, do they? Because you haven't told them, have you? Because you don't trust them do you? And I very much doubt you've got any plans to share your drutts with them, have you? Call them away from me and this wagon right now, or I'll tell them everything."

Goole looked away, wiped his brow with a wing, then peffa-reluctantly did as asked, ordering the kraarks outside back up into the trees. Matlock helped adjust the distressed king's tricorn hat, and massaged his wings better, a part of him feeling an oidy bit guilty to have hurt the sulking bird. "You're not a bad kraark," he told him, "just a bit clottabussed, that's all. But then I suppose I am, too, for not seeing any of this. It's what I've been realising all sun-turn. Too much has been happening, and I've not seen any of it."

Goole sat quietly on his pile of pebbles. "Perhaps we're all clottabusses," he quietly griffled. "Every one of us."

"You bought Note here, didn't you?" Matlock griffled, trusting an extrapluff.

Goole nodded. He really didn't look like any sort of king anymore.

"Then he gave you all these drutts as a reward, I suppose?"

Goole looked Matlock in the eye, lowered his voice. "Note's just the first," he whispgriffled. "There'll be others, all here by morn'up. Coming down Trefflepugga Path while Winchett Dale is all nifferduggling."

Matlock tried not to think of the chaos more krates like Frendeslene Note would cause in his beloved dale. "You're their guide, aren't you? You show them the way along Trefflepugga path?"

Goole nodded a little shamefully. "But they gives me all these drutts, Mr Hare. Means one sun-turn, I won't have to be a Trefflepugga kraark, hiding in a wagon, living with glopped-up flappers. I'll be rich, and respected, and have things." His eye gradually began to glow again. "They're going to pull-down The Great Hall, and build a saztaculous new Hall of drutts, where the krates are all going to live. And Note griffled me that I'll even have my own stage there, with candles and bupple lanterns, and a proper band, and be able to do shows every even'up. I'll be…liked, Mr Hare. I'll be 'Goole the Peffa-Saztaculous' instead of…"

"Instead of…?" Matlock griffled, looking again at the pile of drutts, and wondering just how much of what was about to happen had been his fault. Most creatures' dreams and nifferduggles were really peffa-simple at heart – to be happy and fuzzcheck. No matter how glopped-up it really sounded, all Goole had ever wanted was to be a respected, singing kraark; and he had sold Winchett Dale for a pile of worthless pebbles in order to do so. Frendlesdene Note had spotted the kraark's clottabussed ambition, ruthlessly feeding it for his own ends.

"Instead of just being me, Mr Hare," Goole griffled, answering Matlock's question. "I'm peffa-juzzpapped with just being me. The krates, they can make me saztaculous. Peffa-saztaculous! They griffled me they would. All I have to do is show them the way into the dale. And is that really a glopped-up thing to do, Mr Hare? Haven't you always liked being saztaculous, with every creature, every tree, each and every plant and oidy blade of grass knowing you were the saztaculous majickal-hare of Winchett Dale?"

"Yes," Matlock quietly agreed, "perhaps in some oidy way, I did."

"And you did things, too, didn't you?" Goole persisted. "To keep yourself all saztaculous to folk. You learned your driftolubb vrooshing books, then kept yourself to yourself, being all mysterious at the end of Wand Wood. You got creatures thinking you be much more majickal than you really were, didn't you?"

Matlock didn't griffle a griffle.

"And now you think that these krates are just using Goole, don't you? Well, that's where you're peffa-wrong and gobflopped, Mr Hare. For really 'tis Goole what's using them, you see? I gets 'em into the dale, and they gets me to be all singy and saztaculous. I's the winner, Mr Hare, me."

"The other krates?" Matlock griffled after a long pause. "They're coming tonight?"

"I'll be away and fetching them as the sun sets over the dale while that lot of clottabussed flappers out there are nifferduggling on their branches. They won't know the oidiest thing about it."

"Then I'm coming with you."

Goole waved a wing, rings jangling. "Not a chance," he griffled, shaking his head. "Not even the oidest chance of all chances. Everything changes tomorrow sun'turn, Mr Hare. Mr Note has griffled me that his krates will fill me entire wagon with drutts when they're safely in. I's the only one they can trust to guide them safely through the dangers of the path, and I'm not risking me chance to be a saztaculous showstopping singer for any hare what used to be majickal, but now's all glopped and glubbstool, like the rest of the creatures in this dale."

"Fine," Matlock griffled. "Then, I'll simply tell your lot of 'clottabussed brothers' outside in those branches exactly what you're up to. I doubt they'll be too peffa-pleased to discover you'll be keeping all the drutts and making yourself saztaculous, while they simply skriffle around up here all sun-turn. I imagine they might get quite ruissisculoffed with that, Goole; their betrayal by their own king."

"You do that," Goole warned, "and they'll be the last griffles you griffle."

"Oh, I do peffa-doubt that," Matlock griffled, backing out of the wagon and down the steps, beckoning the other kraarks down to the ground. "I have an announcement to make," he loudly griffled, as Goole suddenly flapped from the wagon and vilishly wrapped a wing around Matlock's mouth.

"I could have this lot stroff you in a blinksnap," Goole whispgriffled in Matlock's long ear, as the kraarks began making yechus noises, drool running from their black, pointed beaks. "They may be glopped in a formation dance, Mr Hare, but they're pretty good at stripping a hare down to its bones. A lot more practised at that, they are, believe you me."

Matlock forced the wing from his mouth, gasping for breath. "Go ahead," he challenged. "Do it, go on. Give your order. But let me griffle you this; in the time it takes them to stroff me, I'll have told them all about your glopped-up pile of drutts, and what they really are."

The kraarks began looking at each other, wondering just what was going on.

"And then," Matlock warned, "When they've finished with me – they'll come looking for you."

A kraark skriffled forward. "What plans?" it griffled, as the others made similar suspicious noises.

Matlock turned to Goole. "Are you going to tell them, or am I? Or perhaps it would be better to take me with you up Trefflepugga Path this even'up?"

All eyes studied Goole, his brow furrowed in peffa-concentration. Eventually he cleared his throat. "Loyal brothers," he griffled, spreading his wings and trying his briftest to muster a smile. "The hare and I have just been playing around, that's all, developing a new showstopper about…about…" He looked to Matlock, pleading for inspiration.

"About," Matlock griffled, feeling for the peffa-first time that sun-turn that perhaps the Sisteraculous and Oramus were finally beginning to pid-pad with him, "the blossoming friendship and journey of a kraark and a majickal-hare, as they make their way up Trefflepugga Path. And in order to get it all peffa, peffa-right, your king and I shall be leaving you all this very even'up."

Goole gave Matlock a scowl.

"Isn't that right, your Highness?" Matlock griffled.

Goole nodded, peff-reluctantly. "I'spose," he griffled. Then purely because he was king, and therefore able to, began bliffing each of the other protesting kraarks on the head to vent his anger at being outsmarted by a mere hare.

For his part, Matlock simply watched the peffa-glopped scene, wondering all the while just what trials and twizzly dangers lay in wait on Trefflepugga path for a majickal-hare with no wand or vrooshers, and having a steadily growing feeling that he wouldn't have to wait much longer to find out.

Once again, Matlock's extrapluffs were about to prove him all too peffa-right…

5.

Note, Serraptomus and Dalelore

Sitting behind a large desk in the empty Great Hall, a twinkleabra of flickering brurf-wax candles above his head, Frendeslene Note rubbed his chin thoughtfully, idly playing with his whiskers. Even by his own officious standards, it had been quite the most saztaculous sun-turn he had known for a peffa-long time. He stood, then pid-padded the length of the hall, grimacing at the rows of glopped-up chairs and the general glopped state of the place. How anyone could ever use the griffle 'great' to describe the hall was simply beyond him. It seemed to him that the whole of Winchett Dale had gone glubbstool since his last visit many, many moon-turns ago. Not that any of the current clottabussed residents would ever have recognised him from those times. Some, he supposed, would have already made their final journey to Oramus, many others would have been born since – and the rest, those who might possibly have remembered him, were far too busy twizzling and griffling about the 'something', to give him even the oidiest thought.

Which was, of course, precisely the idea.

His thoughts were interrupted by an urgent knocking at the large oak-doors. "Enter," he griffled, pid-padding slowly back to sit behind his large desk once more.

"'Tis I, Your Officiousness," Serraptomus griffled, panting. "Here to griffle that Matlock the hare has left Winchett Dale as you ordered."

78

Note nodded, waiting. "Is that it?" he griffled. "You come here, bursting in like a gopflopped-trullock, merely to griffle me something I already knew? Of course the hare has gone. He had no choice but to leave."

"Well," Serraptomus griffled awkwardly, shifting from pid-pad to pid-pad. "There are one or two other matters."

"What is it, then?" Note snapped. "One? Or two?

Serraptomus, struggling with the question, reverted to an old tactic of his from krating school; looking up into the high vaulted ceiling for the answer he knew would never come.

Unfortunately, Note was made of slightly sterner stuff than his former teachers. "I meant," he griffled peffa-slowly. "Are there one, or *two* matters?"

Serraptomus began silently counting on his claws.

"Oh, for Oramus' sake!" Note exploded. "Just griffle me what you think you need to griffle me about!"

Griffles, which inevitably merely added to Serraptomus' panicked confusion, his eyes still studying the beamed roof above.

"Any time this even'up is fine by me…" Note griffled, drumming his claws on the desk in russisculoftulation.

Serraptomus swallowed hard and began to lower his gaze peffa slowly, wondering why it was that he always felt such a clottabus when dealing with superior krates. He was, after all, the most senior krate in Winchett Dale, and had been for more moon-turns than he cared to remember, yet none of this had ever rid him of the awful shrinking feeling he had when griffling to krates of more senior rank. The previous time had been when he was assigned Winchett Dale on his very last sun-turn at krating school, fully certified in Officiousness, the head handing him his official scroll of office and informing him of his new posting in front of hundreds of his fellow krating students, family and friends. It hadn't really helped when most of them had started chickling as soon as Winchett Dale was importantly announced as his new home, but then, as he'd tried so hard to convince himself over the years, it was probably just because they were all so peffa-pleased for him.

Eventually, Serraptomus' eyes met Note's. He cleared his throat, beginning to sweat a little under the candles. "Well, firstly, Your

Officiousness, I have to griffle that Matlock the hare left the dale with a Trefflepugga-kraark."

Note raised his eyebrows slightly. "I thought as much," he griffled. "It'll be that glopped-up fool, Goole. Gone and opened his beak too far about things. Where are they now?"

"Somewhere along Trefflepugga Path," Serraptomus griffled. "I followed them right to the stone archway at the entrance. Daren't have gone another pid-pad further, or the long, long-nosed krellits might have stroffed me."

Note rolled his eyes. "Did the hare and the bird see you?"

"Don't think so. They were too busy singing."

"Singing? Even the hare?"

"Indeed, Your Officiousness," Serraptomus griffled. "And pid-padding along beside them, they has this little band of musical ploffshrooms. Well, it's not going to be too peffa-long before the long, long-nosed krellits hear all that racket and stroffs them, is it?"

Note began lightly drumming the desktop with his claws again, eyes half-closed in thought. So, as he suspected, the hare had met Goole and had found the way into his beady-eyed affections; the glopped-up kraark's desire to sing. He shuddered briefly at the memory of having been exposed to it many times before. The final journey down Trefflepugga Path and into Winchett Dale had been truly yechus. At times, he'd wished he'd taken his chances negotiating the path alone, rather than having an eternally singing kraark leading the way. But unfortunately for him, using the clottabuseed bird as guide was the only way. The simple fact was that he needed Goole far more than the kraark king needed him. Hence the drutts, the promises of a new Great Hall to accommodate his ridiculous showstopping ambitions.

But, just as he had used Goole's misplaced dreams for his own ends, now it seemed the hare was doing the very same thing. Not that he hadn't expected him not to. The one thing Note hadn't ever done was to underestimate the hare in any way, whatsoever. But, Note knew, with no wand and no driftolubbs, his long-eared adversary was going to find the dangers of Trefflepugga Path peffa-difficult indeed. The hare might be thinking he could stop the inevitable arrival of the other krates, but he was going to find it far harder than he could ever, ever extrapluff.

Note stretched, yawned. "And the other 'matter', Serraptomus?" he griffled. "And before you do that aimless 'looking at the ceiling' thing again, please bear in mind that I still have a lot to do before tomorrow sun-turn, and my patience is already rather thin this even'up."

Serraptomus shifted slightly awkwardly, trying to choose his griffles with care. "Well…"

"Just griffle it out, for Oramus' sake! I'm peffa-juzzpapped, and frankly could do without all these constant glopped-up pauses!"

"'Tis about the drutts, Your Officiousness."

"What about them?"

Serraptomus cleared his throat, wondering why it suddenly felt so peffa-dry. "Last even'up, you griffled to me that if I emptied the hare's cottage and got you his majickal driftolubbs, then I'd get thirty of these new and saztaculous drutt things."

Note nodded. "I did. And?"

"Well," Seraptomus griffled, feeling suddenly far too peffa-hot under the candles. "I did what you griffled, Your Officiousness. And the hare has gone. So…"

"So you want your drutts, I take it?" Note griffled, reaching into a draw for a small bag of pebbles and emptying it onto the desk.

But as Serraptomus reached out a paw, Note slammed it down with his own. "Not so vilish, Serraptomus!" he griffled. "True, the hare has left, but I don't yet have the driftolubbs. No driftolubbs, no deal; no drutts."

"You've…" Serraptomus swallowed hard, "…not got the driftolubbs?"

Note answered with his eyes.

"But I organised everything so officiously," Serraptomus griffled, beginning to rub the palms of his paws, trying to stay calm, fighting a grillion twizzly feelings running right through him. "I griffled to the kraarks exactly what to do."

"Which was *what*, precisely?" Note griffled.

Serraptomus tried to remember. It wasn't one of his great strengths. "To go to the cottage and empty it when Matlock came to the public-griffling. Then to bring the driftolubbs to you in the middle of the night."

Note began inspecting his razor sharp claws. "You decided to use the Trefflepugga-kraarks for this task? You *actually* decided to use a glubbstooled bunch of singing flappers for this most peffa-important task?"

Serraptomus nodded, anxious to please. "Well, I had to Your Officiousness. Everyone else was here in the hall. I had no choice." He was sweating feely now, though more from the twizzly situation than the burning twinkleabra. "The kraarks never bother to turn up to any public-grifflings, you see? No one expects them to, no one wants them too. Only the oidiest pawful of creatures actually know where they live. Goole griffled me that they'd do it. He promised me it wouldn't be a problem, Your Officiousness. They'd empty the cottage, and he'd bring the driftolubbs straight to you."

"And like the most ganticus clottabus in this entire gob-flopped dale of clottabusses, you believed every griffle that fell from his sneaky, twisted beak, didn't you?"

"Well…I…er…"

"*Didn't you!*" Note ferociously barked. "For Oramus' sake! He's a singing fool, a self-styled made-up 'king', whose hunger for drutts is peffa-ganticus! He's got them, don't you see? He still has the driftolubbs! And as soon as the hare knows that, he'll easily find a way to get them back from the bird-brained fool! Which means…"

"He'll be able to do all his saztaculous, majickal vrooshers again?" Serraptomus interrupted, smiling, sheer relief coursing through him. "Then that's the most yamamantally-spious news! Once Matlock starts being all majickal again, he'll vroosh and stroff the peffa-twizzly 'something'. We'll all be saved!" He turned to leave, his whole softulous shaking and excrimbly. "I must go and tell the others of this most saztaculous good news!"

Note stood, his voice suddenly grave. "You'll do no such thing, Serraptomus."

"But why, Your Officiousness?" Serraptomus asked, confused. "Matlock will save us all, and Winchett Dale will be crumlush again."

"No," Note quietly griffled. "Winchett Dale will never be the glubbstooled dale it was before. What has started can't be stopped. Not even the briftest of the hare's vrooshers will stop it. The 'something' is more ganticus than, you, me, the hare's vrooshers, the whole of this glubbstooled dale. Do you understand?"

Serraptomus blinked a snutch of times, not quite believing the griffles. "But," he slowly griffled, "how are we going to be safe?"

"By following every griffled order that I and my fellow krates give you, Serraptomus. They arrive in the morn'up. The deluded and misguided hare will try and stop them, but he will fail. Only by doing exactly as I griffle will anyone be safe."

"More krates are coming?" Serraptomus griffled. "To my dale?"

Note chickled. "*Your* dale? You utter clottabus, can't you see? Your time as chief krate in Winchett Dale is over."

"But Your Officiousness, I…"

"You couldn't even get the hare's majickal driftolubbs to me, could you?" Note sneered. "A peffa, peffa-easy task, yet still you gobflopped. But then, perhaps that's what you've always been, Serraptomus; a peffa-ganticus gobflopper, you and your other two krates, allowing a hare and some clottabussed creatures to pid-pad rings around you. I've heard what they griffle about you, Serraptomus. They griffle that you're too peffa-fat, too lazy, too glubbstooled to be officious. And believe me, coming from this lot of gloppers, that really is griffling something."

Serraptomus tried to find some griffles, his jaw dropping slightly, face a perfect picture of awkward confusion. "They griffle that I'm…" he could hardly bring himself to griffle it, "…fat?"

Note nodded. "They all chickle behind your back, and frankly I'm not peffa-surprised, the size of it. Even the glopped-up, tweazle-eating dworp doesn't take a griffle of any notice of what you try so ineptly to griffle."

Serraptomus simply stood in the centre of The Great Hall, unable to believe how he'd just gone from feeling so elated at the news that the dale was safe, to now feeling so utterly wretched. The thought of Proftulous chickling at him behind his back was simply too much. "I'll eat less," he griffled, desperate to please. "And be more officious, and organise my other two krates to make everything peffa-better, and…"

Note silenced him with a single raised paw. "It's too late, Serraptomus. Just far too late. I am hereby, in my capacity as First Officer of Officious Krating for all Districts of the Majickal Dales, removing your office as Senior Krate of Winchett Dale."

"But…" Serraptomus tried.

"Stop griffling like an eye-splashy trilp!" Note griffled. "You will no longer issue any orders of officiousness in Winchett Dale from this sun-turn forth. You will return to your home and stay inside like the others, until you are griffled that it's safe to leave."

"Please, Your Officiousness," Serraptomus begged, cautiously pointing to the pile of pebbles on the desk. "Before I go, could I just have *some* of the drutts? After all, I did most of what you asked, and only really gob-flopped with the driftolubbs."

Note looked at the anxious krate, wondering for a moment if Serraptomus was about to get eyeplashy. He took a deep breath, sighing heavily. He didn't really like making creatures feel twizzly, even fellow krates, but sometimes there was no other choice in order to bring the changes that would make things so much peffa-better for everyone in the end. He looked at the puffed, sweating krate with the imploring eyes, its shaking claw still pointing at a worthless pile of stones, completely convinced they held some sort of key to a better future, and almost felt sorry for the begging, bloated creature. "Serraptomus," he softly griffled, "what are these?"

"Drutts," Serraptomus vilishly griffled, peffa-eager to please. "Drutts that'll make me all fuzzcheck, and safe from the 'something'."

"But," Note urged, "what are they *really*?"

Serraptomus blinked, lost in confusion.

Note tried his most encouraging voice. "Just tell me what they *are*."

"Drutts," Serraptomus answered. "Drutts, and they're saztaculous and…"

"They're pebbles, Serraptomus," Note quietly interrupted. "Just pebbles, that's all."

Serraptomus took a snutch of moments, working through the confusion, trying to remember what Note had told him about the stones. "Aha, yes," he griffled, peffa-pleased to have found the answer. "But when you give them to us, they become drutts, don't they? They change, don't they? You change them. And changing things is a peffa-good thing. Just like you griffled to me when you arrived, Your Officiousness, everything has to change, everything."

Note slowly rubbed his brow, looking into the eager face, and knowing in that instant just how easy the next few sun-turns would be, how ridiculously vilishly all the creatures of Winchett Dale would accept their new way of life, how easily generations of their traditional way of life would be trampled.

He sighed, pushing the pebbles towards Serraptomus, watching as he greedily filled his pockets, then eagerly thanked the very same krate that had glopped and ridiculed his entire life just a snutch of moments earlier, before pid-padding happily out of the hall. It was, Note thought, one of the saddest things he had seen in a peffa-long time.

"They're just pebbles," he quietly griffled, his mind turning to more pressing matters; the imminent arrival of the other krates and the many plans that had to be made. For if the changes were going to happen, much had to be officiously organised. Not even the oidiest part of the plan could be left to chance.

Outside the hall, the wind was getting up, bluffing and thworking against the windows and walls. It was going to be a stormy night along Trefflepugga Path. He closed his eyes, and for just the oidiest moment, wished the hare well on his journey.

Then, he began to prepare for change.

Majickal lore contains much about the dripples of the dales. Some is exaggerated myth and spuddles, some merely glopped-up nonsense, most probably written many moon-turns ago by a majickal-hare with a sense of humour and too much time on his paws. But some of it *is* true. Between the old hand-quilled pages of the drifftolub of *Majickjal Dalelore (Volume 68 – revised edition)* lies a host of truths regarding the creatures, that should be required reading for any apprentice majickal-hare. The sad truth is, however, that most apprentices much prefer to be practising vrooshers and preparing spells than actually reading, so peffa-rarely get past Volumes 1 -32, where the bulk of all the saztaculous vrooshy stuff can be found. Some apprentice-hares do read the entire canon of drifttolubbs, but they are mostly regarded with suspicion by their masters when they reveal this fact, as either being far too keen, studious or boastful – or a combination of all three.

Some peffa-wise and Most Majelicus hares have postulated the theory that Oramus himself had something of a 'helping-paw' with the original versions of the driftolubbs, and had them deliberately written to ensure that the really useful and most peffa-important stuff was hidden in the later volumes, most of which would never be read in the first place, including of course, dalelore connected to dripples. And if this seems an oidy bit harsh on dripples, then it's also as well to remember that although Oramus is noted for the constant Most Majelicus protection he gives to all the dales and The Great Beyond from the shindinculous moon above, he also has The Greater View Of Things – so really, at the end of the sun-turn, we have to griffle that how he does this is largely up to him.

However, if Matlock had ever taken the time to sit down and read *Majickjal Dalelore (Volume 68 – revised edition)* he wouldn't have been altogether surprised to discover that at the peffa-same time that he was pid-padding along Trefflepugga Path, the winds getting stronger, and with merely a singing kraark and a ploffshroom band for company – his dripple was making its own lonely way out into the gathering storm to the High Plateau, in order to try and find Matlock's abandoned hawthorn wand, and begin its own long journey to return it to its master as vilishly as possible.

Proving, perhaps, that the oidiest of things can sometimes make the most ganticus of all differences…

Along Trefflepugga Path...

6.

Laffrohn, Spuddles and Ursula Brifthaven Stoltz

"So," Goole griffled, as he and Matlock pid-padded along Trefflepugga Path, "How's about we have another song, eh, Mr Hare?"

They'd been travelling about an hour, but frankly hadn't made too much progress since leaving the ganticus stone archway at the beginning of the path. The way itself seemed straight and true, well pid-padded, Matlock thought, so progress shouldn't have been a problem. Except of course, if you're having to pid-pad at the speed of a marching ploffshroom band who were clearly already juzzpapped from the sun-turn's musical exertions, and a one-eyed, waist coated kraark who insisted on stopping every few pid-pads to sing another song.

"I think," Matlock diplomatically tried to suggest, "that perhaps the singing could attract the unwelcome attention of the long, long-nosed krellits." The wind was beginning to pick up, peffagusting, sending leaves dancing around them. And worse, Matlock could make out storm clouds gathering on the high-hills ahead.

"Well, that's where you're wrong, see?" Goole griffled. "On account of the fact that your long, long-nosed krellit's gots terrible hearing. Hardly hears a single sqwallop, does your long, long-nosed krellit. 'Tis fear he feeds from, Mr Hare. He closes in on the smell of fear. And the more we sings, and these oidy ploffshrooms keeps up their saztaculous rhythms, the less fearful and twizzly we'll all be, so the less likely we are to end up as a long, long-nosed krellit's supper."

"I'm fairly certain that there must be other ways not to be twizzly," Matlock griffled, stooping down and picking up the juzzpapped ploffshrooms, placing them carefully in his hood.

"Like what?" Goole griffled. "Spot of dancing? I could be teaching you some peffa-swell moves, Mr Hare. Then we could be dancing all the way to the end of the path."

"I think I'll give that one a miss, too," Matlock griffled, glad they were finally pid-padding and scrittling a little more vilishly along the path, now that the ploffshrooms were safely nifferduggling in his hood. Goole contented himself with trying to make up a song about Matlock, whilst Matlock tried his best to ignore it, wondering all the time just what he could do to save Winchett Dale from the imminent arrival of more krates. He supposed that in some oidy way that he *ought* to feel twizzly, and therefore be the peffa-perfect bait for roaming long, long nosed krellits, but the truth was that the more he pid-padded, the less twizzly he felt. It was as if something was calling him, an old memory perhaps, or simply a feeling from somewhere deep inside his own Sisteraculous. And although he didn't have even the oidiest extrapluff about what to do, he did know that somehow he was pid-padding in the right direction. Trefflepugga Path, for all its unknown dangers and mysterious twizzly myths and spuddles really didn't seem like much of a twizzly place at all. Just peffa-cold…

After another hour's journey, the path started to slowly drop, leading into a steep-sided valley echoing with the ghostly calls of curious flappers Matlock had never heard before. They stopped to rest. A small group of trees stood just off the path, offering respite from the wind and shelter, the only light just the shindinculous rays of the moon above, adding an eerie blue and white glow to the steep mountainsides.

"How much further?" Matlock griffled as they settled under the trees, their branches creaking and swaying in the winds above.

Goole shrugged unhelpfully. "No idea, Mr Hare."

"I mean, until we meet the krates?"

"Absolutely no peffa-idea of that, either."

"You don't know?" Matlock griffled, astonished. "You honestly don't know?"

Goole softly chickled. "Well, now, Mr Hare, there's a griffle to conjure with – 'honestly'. Can't really griffle that I's done anything 'honest' in me entire life." He flapped his wings slightly, the rings gently chinkling. "Each and every one of these here trinklets I've got dishonestly, Mr Hare." He picked out the smallest ring, looked at it, quietly sighing. "All except for this one. Used to belong to me mother, this."

"She gave it to you?" Matlock griffled, touched at the glopped-up kraark's fondness for the memory.

"No," Goole griffled. chickling. "I robbed it off her when she was nifferduggling. Still thinks she lost it to this very sun-turn, she does. Bit of a clottabus, me mother. Never think we were from the same stock."

A snutch of heavy raindrops began hitting the rustling leaves overhead. It really was turning into a yechus night. Matlock wrapped his robe tighter, trying not to think of similar nights he'd spent in the cottage, safe inside, his dripple on his lap, the piff-tosh blazing. "So you've not the oidiest idea how much further we have to go before we meet the other krates?"

"S'what I just griffled, Mr Hare, isn't it?" Goole griffled. "Crivens, you may have long ears, but they don't listen, do they?" He adjusted his tricorn hat. "Let me griffle you a question for once. How much do you really know about Trefflepugga Path? I mean, you're supposed to be all peffa-majickal, but it strikes me you wouldn't know a flummoxed dudge-whammett from a krettle-flapper, even if it was bliffing your brotts, Mr Hare."

Matlock tried not to take offence. "I'm far more of a majickal expert about what happens in Winchett Dale, rather than out of it."

Goole chickled again, as heavier rain began to drum the ground around them. "Then I don't be supposin' that you've ever heard of the riddle of Trefflepugga Path, either, then, Mr Hare?"

"For Oramus sake!" Matlock griffled, as a drop of rain fell from the leaves onto his whiskers. "Just griffle me what you know! And please, don't even think of making any kind of a song and dance about it, either. Just one more singing-griffle from that beak of yours, and I swear I'll…"

An opportune thunderous cracksplosion obscured the rest of Matlock's griffles, but even the peffa-clottabussed Goole knew what they most likely implied. "Alright, Mr Hare," he griffled as the thunder subsided, rolling away up the valley in a long garrumblooming echo. "Just keep your hares' hair on, and I'll griffle you all I knows about Trefflepugga Path. Just pin back your long ears, and shut your griffle-box for once."

Matlock listened peffa-carefully as Goole told him about the path, gleaned from his previous trips along it. The path, it seemed was majickally alive, directing the lives and fortunes of anyone bold enough to begin journeying along it.

"Thing is," Goole griffled, as another cracksplosion rent the lid above, sending down a ganticously heavy shower of rain, "the path has a mind of its own, Mr Hare. It simply takes you where it extrapluffs that you need to be. So no two journeys will ever be the same, just as no two sun-turns are ever the same, either. One sun-turn, you could be happily pid-padding along, and it'd take you to the most crumlushed dale you ever did see; the next, and it'd lead you to be stroffed by long, long nosed krellits, or right off the end of a cliff. It decides, you see, it controls everything." He pointed with a wing to the cracksploding lid above. "Even the weather, Mr Hare. This glopped-up storm is no peffa-coincidence. The path has made it happen. It knows exactly who we are, why we're here, and where it's going to take us. It's watching us all the time, Mr Hare, every pid-pad we make. The only reason we've been allowed to pid-pad this far, Mr Hare, is because the path wants us to."

Matlock shifted slightly closer to the trunk of the tree, trying to avoid heavy sploinks of rain.

"First time I took the path," Goole continued, "was when I was having meself a bit of a glopp-up in Sveag Dale. To griffle it bluntly, it all went gobflopped. One sun-turn I was singing me heart out to folk; the next I'm finding meself being chased out of the dale by a pack of hungry grudgers."

"Grudgers?" Matlock griffled, unaware of the griffle.

"Yechus creatures, Mr Hare. Real glubbstooled types. They was getting all russisculoffed, you see, because Goole was getting all their attention. They used to juggle tweazles for folk, and were peffa-popular until I's be stealing their limelight."

The mention of the griffle 'tweazle' made Matlock think of Proftulous, his oldest friend. "I know someone that would have liked to have seen that," he quietly griffled.

"Lots did, Mr Hare," Goole griffled. "Until, that is, I took to me natural vocation, and begins me singing. Well, them grudgers took offence, chasing me out of Svaeg Dale, right up onto Trefflepugga Path. So I took my chances and sets off along it."

"Which is what bought you to Winchett Dale?"

"Eventually," Goole confirmed. "But not before I hadn't had a peffa-bellyful of adventures and twizzliness along the way." He looked out into the pouring rain, unwilling it seemed, to detail the perils of his journey. "Save to griffle, I learns meself a lot, Mr Hare. One thing you can griffle about Goole is that he's always got his beak to the ground when it comes to looking after himself."

"I never thought for the oidiest moment that you hadn't," Matlock griffled, keen to hear more. For no matter how gobflopped his singing was, Matlock knew that Goole was also a survivor, a thieving-flapper of peffa-cunning and guile. And for those reasons alone, it was vital he learnt as much as he could from him. "So what happened?"

Goole cleaned a talon with his beak for a snutch of moments, enjoying keeping the hare waiting for his griffles. "When I gets to Winchet Dale," he griffled, "I keeps meself hidden to start with. Then I begins meeting the other kraarks. Well, they takes one look at me in all me Sveag Dale finery, and they thinks I'm some sort of king, don't they?" He tapped the side of his head with a wing. "And Goole's not the kraark to let 'em down, am I? So I declares meself their king, and that, Mr Hare, was that."

"Until you got bored with life in the dale," Matlock griffled, following the kraark's story, "and set off back up Trefflepugga Path, and found the dale of krates and drutts?"

Goole nodded, as more thunder cracksploded around. "Indeed, Mr Hare. Not because I wanted to, but because the path took me there. I was hoping to get back to Sveag Dale, see if them grudgers had gone – but the path had other ideas, other uses, for old Goole."

Matlock thought about the griffles. "So the path *wanted* you to meet Frendeslene Note?"

Goole shrugged. "Who knows, Mr Hare? All I'm griffling is that no two journeys will ever be the same. Who knows what the path has planned for you and I? I peffa-much doubt they'll be the same. We'll just have to wait and see, won't we?"

"I suppose we will," Matlock griffled, watching as the heavy rain thickened, soon becoming a ganticus wall of water out in the inky blackness of the valley beyond.

Goole scrittled over and sat by his side, the two of them leaning against the damp tree-trunk as lightning flashed overhead. "But for all its peffa-strangeness, Mr Hare, Trefflepugga Path does have rules. And once you know them, you've got a much brifter chance of not being stroffed, or lost for ever."

"What rules?" Matlock asked.

Goole adjusted his hat. "Well, see, it's peffa-easy for you to griffle me that, Mr Hare, and then just sit here expecting me to griffle you all the answers." He looked up at Matlock, showing his milky-white eye. "But them answers have already cost me dear, Mr Hare. Lost me eye, I did, finding out one of them. So I'm thinking that unless you can give me something peffa-saztaculous and shindinculous, maybe I'll be shutting my beak about what to expect along the path, Mr Hare. 'Tis brifter, methinks, to let you find out for yourself, rather than Goole making it all easy and giving you all the answers."

"And what about the riddle you griffled about?" Matlock griffled. "The riddle of Trefflepugga Path?"

Goole chickled. "Some griffle that 'tis merely a spuddle; a legend, Mr Hare. Others griffle that 'tis just a ganticus great chickler, put there by Oramus himself to cause him mirth as folks try to find it. And I don't think many has, Mr Hare, let alone try to solve it. But the spuddle has it that if you can find and solve the riddle, then you can pid-pad along the path wherever you want. It loses its power over your destiny, and sets you free to roam its length, and into any of the majickal dales that takes your fancy. But like I griffle, as far as old Goole knows, peffa-few have ever found it, or solved it. Though there's many who have been stroffed trying."

"And what do you believe?" Matlock griffled, raising his voice above the rain. "Is it a spuddle, or real? Does it exist, or not?"

"Haven't the oidiest idea, Mr Hare. In all my scrittles along the path, I've seen even the oidiest sight of it. I'm supposing that if it does exist, then Trefflepugga Path isn't that peffa-keen that anyone finds it." He shook out his wings as the rain suddenly began to slacken. "But enough of all this griffling. Methinks it's time to scrittle a little further along the way." He scrittled to edge of the trees, looked up at the dark twinkling lid, the storm almost gone now, leaving just distant rumbling round the valley. "But I will griffle you this, Mr Hare. One sun-turn on the path can last a blinksnap, or a grillion moon-turns. Time does peffa-twizzly things here. So, how long your journey will last, or how far you have to go, is up to the path, not you."

"Time changes?" Matlock griffled.

Goole nodded. "You'll find out, soon enough, Mr Hare. So when you's griffling to me about how much further we have to go to meet the krates, I griffles back to you that I don't know. And thems are the griffles of truth, Mr Hare, even if they are griffled by old Goole. If the path wants me to meet them, then I will. But I haven't the oidest idea when."

"And if it has other plans for you?" Matlock griffled.

"The I'll takes my chances, won't I? Three choices as I see it; one, I meets 'em, takes 'em back to Winchett Dale and gets all me drutts; two, the path takes me back to Sveag Dale this time…"

"And the third?"

Goole shivered slightly. "The path takes me somewhere else." He looked up at Matlock. "But the way I sees it, the first two choices aren't so peffa-glopped. And two out of three can't be bad, can it?"

Matlock was lost for griffles at Goole's clottabussed logic.

Goole winked at him with his one good eye. "Well, that's me away, Mr Hare," he griffled, scrittling back out onto the wet path. "I'm taking me chances, see what Trefflepugga Path has in store for old Goole this time. It'll be drutts, singing or stroffing; though Oramus only knows which one."

Matlock tried to pid-pad after him, astonished to see the ploffshroom-band now happily pid-padding beside Goole, striking up their tune with renewed vigour once again. The curious thing was, he hadn't even noticed them leaving the nifferduggling comfort of his hood.

"Shame, Mr Hare," Goole called back. "You never thought to ask me why I don't fly any more, did you? Or what them long, long-nosed krellits really look like? But Goole's guessing you're going to find out!"

Matlock's tried to follow him, but found to his sudden twizzly-horror that his legs just wouldn't work, refusing to take a single pid-pad after Goole. It was like he was stuck in the peffa-thickest niff soup in all the dales and The Great Beyond. No matter how peffa-hard he tried, he couldn't take another pid-pad in the kraark's direction. Instead he found himself being pulled another way entirely.

"I'm stuck!" he called out. "I can't get to you!"

Goole's distant chickles echoed off the steep mountainsides. "'Tis the path, Mr Hare. It's taking you where it wants you to go. Best advice is to let it, and take your chances like me."

The singing kraark-king's griffles were true. The more Matlock tried to follow Goole, the less he found he actually could. It was useless, peffa-glopped-up. He didn't have a choice. He turned slightly, feeling with a foot, searching where he hoped he would be allowed to pid-pad.

"Shindinculous good luck, Mr Hare!" Goole called, his voice getting fainter with each griffle. "You're going to need it! Oh, and one more peffa-important thing that you simply *have* to know…"

"What?" Matlock desperately griffled back into the dark night. "What do I need to know?"

But no answer came. Instead, as he stood waiting, he felt the ground begin to shake underneath his feet, as a ganticus rumbling garrumbloom began to fill the valley. Instinctively, he tried to pid-pad back to the safety of the trees, but again, his legs refused to move. He was stuck fast to the shaking ground, watching as it started to open up all around, the earth dropping away into steep dark crevices and caverns below.

"By Oramus and the Sisteraculous!" Matlock called out. "What the jitterflupps is going on?"

He felt the ground tilting and was knocked down, clinging to whatever he could to avoid falling into the black-depths. Never had he wanted his hawthorn wand so much in his life, his mind churning vilishly to try and remember a vroosher that would have kept him safe.

Then, in a rumbling din of scraping and creaking, to Matlock's peffa-astonishment, a building rose right out of the ground in front of him, complete with gardens and surrounded by a circle of trees, the whole peffa-strange sight floating just a few pid-pads in the air, as gradually the earth began to close again and a shocked quiet finally returned to the valley.

Peffa-cautiously, Matlock slowly stood, taking in the sight. In all his many years, he hadn't ever seen anything quite so saztaculous. The whole wooden building and gardens rocked slightly in the light breeze, and he became aware of a figure, pid-padding on the surface, armed with a long fire-pole, lighting beacons between each of the trees.

Cautiously, Matlock pid-padded towards the floating structure, standing underneath its edge, small trails of earth falling gently onto his head. "Hello?" he called out to the figure, as it lit the beacon closest to him.

The figure turned, looked down, allowing Matlock his first proper sight of it, its face lit by the flames. It had a long nose, tiny ears and peffa-ganticus paws. It was dressed in furs with wooden clogs, yet its griffles were quite the most crumlush Matlock had heard for many a sun-turn.

"Is that…is that a hare? A hare down there?" it griffled.

Matlock nodded.

"Hmm. Well, this is most peffa-irregular, but not all together unexpected, methinks." The figure disappeared, returning a snutch of moments later with a short rope that she tossed down, allowing Matlock to clumsily scramble up and onto the edge. "Oh, my drofflefripps!" she griffled, all peffa-excrimbly as Matlock stood and brushed himself down. "It *is* a hare! A hare from down there, that is now here. A here-hare!" She held out a ganticus paw, extending four sharply gleaming claws. "I'm Laffrohn," she griffled. "Keeper of The Vroffa-Tree Inn."

Matlock found the creature's manner so welcoming that he couldn't help but put his paw in hers, marvelling at just how oidy his looked compared to hers. "I'm Matlock," he griffled. "And, frankly I'm rather…"

"Lost?" Laffrohn griffled, pid-padding over to the next beacon and lighting it.

"Well, yes, I suppose I am."

She beckoned Matlock over; thrust the lighting pole in his paw, watching closely as he lit other beacons around the edge of the floating garden. "No one's ever lost, Matlock. Ever. You know peffa-well where you are; in the gardens of The Vroffa-Tree Inn, on Trefflepugga Path. I would have thought that that was peffa-obvious."

Matlock started a little, as suddenly the trees around him began to chickle.

Laffrohn hushed them. "Enough from you all!" she firmly griffled, turning to Matlock. "Forgive them, they don't mean to be rude. They're just peffa-excrimbly about their big night, that's all."

"Big night?"

Laffrohn leant back, eyes wide open. "You don't know?"

The vroffa-trees gasped, sharing Laffrohn's shock.

"Not…really, no," Matlock griffled, trying not to feel too embarrassed. "It's all rather strange to me."

"Your first pid-pad up the path, is it?"

"My second, though I was far too peffa-young to remember the first time," he griffled, briefly telling her about how Chatsworth had fetched him from The Great Beyond and they'd ended up in Winchett Dale.

Laffrohn's eyes widened in pleasant surprise. "Oh," she griffled, giving him a playful tug on his robes. "So you're one of those 'majickal-hares'. Well, this is most peffa-crumlush. I've heard tales of majickal-hares, but I always thought they were simply spuddles. But now, to meet one, well, let's just griffle that this is quite a moment for me." She quickly took out some spectacles, cleaning them on her long fur coat, before putting them on and taking a closer look at Matlock. "Well," she griffled, looking him up and down, "I must griffle that you don't really look that majickal to me. When was the last time those robes were cleaned? They look rather glopped to me. Don't you be having a vroosher to get yourself looking peffa-saztaculous and majickal?"

She beckoned Matlock over; thrust the lighting pole in his paw, watching closely as he lit other beacons around the edge of the floating garden.

Matlock shook his head. "Not at the moment," he griffled, griffling to her all that had happened with Frendeslene Note, Winchett Dale, his missing driftolubbs and the imminent arrival of more krates. "So, you see, I have to stop them. I must find them and stop them."

Laffrohn considered this. "But only if the path *wants* you to, Matlock. That's the point. You could be pid-padding along it for a peffa-different reason indeed, known only to Oramus himself. You might never even meet these other krates with their glubbstooled drutts. You also…" she looked kindly into his eyes for a moment, "…might never return to Winchett Dale, either. You simply have to pid-pad where the path wants you to go. Or, of course, you can learn to fly."

"Fly?"

Laffrohn studied Matlock's face peffa-carefully for a snutch of moments, as if somehow making up her mind. "Well," she griffled at last, "you don't seem like a twizzly hare, or a peffa-yechus hare, or even a glopped-up one, so I suppose I can be telling you."

Matlock waited, not really knowing what to griffle.

"Any time now, Matlock, we'll be having some visitors. Flying witches, a ganticus great kroffle of them." She pointed to the twinkling lid above. "Up there, Matlock, the path has no power over you. Those that can fly can see how it always changes, choose the places and dales they want to go to. All because they never, ever take a single pid-pad onto the path. It's why The Vroffa-Tree Inn floats. That way, the witches can land, and…"

"They never have to pid-pad on the path," Matlock finished for her, becoming suddenly excrimbly at the thought. "It's the riddle, the riddle of Trefflepugga Path, isn't it? The answer is that you have to fly!"

Laffrohn soflty chickled. "My dear Matlock, you don't believe in that old spuddle, do you?"

"Do you?" Matlock asked.

She shook her head, pointed to her spectacles. "'Tis merely a spuddle, a story, Matlock. I only believes in things that I can be seeing with my own eyes. And since no one's ever found the riddle, or solved it, then it must just be a spuddle."

Matlock frowned slightly. "But you just griffled that the witches can fly wherever they want above the path."

Laffrohn nodded. "Indeed, but they can't pid-pad anywhere along it, Matlock, remember that. For once you take a single pid-pad on the path, it has you in its power. A witch or a flapper who dares to pid-pad on the path is peffa-peffa gobflopped. I've seen flappers land, and never take to the lid again, ever. Instead they have to scrittle everywhere, trying to find the nearest dale for safety. 'Tis a most peffa-glopped-up sight."

Matlock thought of Goole, how the singing kraark-king never flapped, always scrittled. "But if I could fly," he griffled, "then I could see the whole path, find the krates, and stop them before they reach Winchett Dale."

Laffrohn lightly rested a ganticus paw on his shoulders. "Matlock, you've not been listening to single griffle I's been griffling. Because you have already pid-padded on the path, it will never, ever let you fly. That possibility ended with the very first steps you took along it."

"But I *must* stop them," Matlock insisted. "It's the only way."

"I think you'll find," Laffrohn griffled to him, "that Trefflepugga Path is the only way for you now, Matlock." She looked into the twinkling lid. "Won't be long. The beacons will attract them, and they'll all be here peffa-soon enough."

The vroffa-trees began to sway their branches, the leaves whispgriffling 'Witches! Witches!' over and over.

Laffrohn turned to Matlock. "'Tis the same, every year. Vroffa-trees always get excrimbly when they know The League of Lid Curving Witchery be coming to the inn." She turned and hushed the trees again. "They come for their branches, Matlock. Once a year, a witch has to change her flight branches on her broom. And, as every witch knows, the briftest flight-branches in all the dales are Laffrohn's vroffa-tree branches at The Vroffa-Tree Inn."

Matlock lit the last beacon, the blazing fires now forming a piff-toshing ring around the edge of the garden, saztaculoulsy lighting the trees and the large wooden inn at the centre. Laffrohn took him by the arm. "It's probably better we get inside now," she griffled, as they pid-padded towards the inn. "Believe me, it's all going to get witch-glopped peffa-soon."

"Witch-glopped?"

Laffrohn chickled, opening the large wooden creaker, leading Matlock inside. "Let's just say it sometimes goes a bit glubbstool when they're all after the briftest branches. We'll be safe in here until they calm down a bit. But it's peffa-fun to watch. Quite the briftest night of my year, this."

Matlock sat by a window with a view over the garden, as Laffrohn lit the piff-tosh and bought him a jug of guzzwort and plate of niffs with a cloff-beetle salad. He thanked her, wondering just how she knew it was his peffa-favourite supper, ever, then tucked in, realising just how hungry he was with each peffa-slurpilicious mouthful. And the more he ate, the better he felt; warm, safe and crumlushly cosy, his long shoes drying in front of the piff-tosh and a mug of guzzwort in his hand. His concerns and worries for Winchett Dale, finding and stopping the krates seemed to fade, become oidier with each mouthful. Indeed, he found it difficult to remember having felt quite so peffa-fuzzcheck for a long time. Perhaps it had been on Borascus Eve, back at the Winchett Dale Inn, all of the creatures drinking, singing, chickling and dancing, heralding in Borascus Day as only they knew how; Proftulous, endlessly griffling about how many tweazle pies he was going to be given, disidulas and clottabussed bloxers trying to dance on table tops, even Serraptomus the krate taking the even'up off from being officious to join in with the festivities.

Matlock shuddered slightly, wondering just what was happening in Winchett Dale that even'up. If anyone had even the oidiest idea what Frendeslene Note's plans were for their peffa-precious home, or if they simply nifferduggled on through the night, oblivious. He wondered if any of them missed him, too. He thought of his dripple and Proftulous, sending up a silent hare's prayer to Oramus, wishing them both safe from harm.

"You seem a grillion pid-pads away," Laffrohn suddenly griffled, breaking his thoughts, sitting at the table. "Niffs slurpilicious enough for you?"

"Yes," Matlock griffled, finishing the last one. "Just thinking about…"

"Home?"

"You always seem to be able to finish my griffles for me."

Laffrohn smiled, revealing two long, curved front teeth. "That's because I can see them in your face, Matlock. Can't read books, but I've always read faces." She stood, took away Matlock's empty plate. "And the way I see it, faces are far more fuzzcheck to read than books, anyway."

Matlock allowed himself a smile. "Yes, Laffrohn, you're probably right. But how did you know I like niffs?"

"Just an oidy hunch, Matlock. You see, you're not the only hare that's going to be in The Vroffa-Tree Inn tonight. There's another coming, and she's peffa-partial to niffs, too. So I always have some in." Laffrohn scratched the side of her face thoughtfully. "Mind, you'll have some explaining to do, Matlock. You've just eaten the last of them, and Ursula Brifthaven Stoltz isn't the sort of witch that takes too kindly to having her niffs guzzled by any other hare."

"I've just eaten someone else's supper?" Matlock griffled, shocked.

Laffrohn chickled. "Let's just griffle, it'll make all the other witches chickle. There's not many of them that really like Ursula. She's a solitary witch, you see, from the Land of the White Hares, far across the Icy Seas. And when they see she's flown all this way for new flight-branches, but has no niffs for her supper, I be thinking it'll get quite twizzly in here."

"But I had no idea," Matlock griffled. "If I'd have known, I'd…"

"Hush!" Laffrohn called from the fireplace, holding up a paw. "I can hear them coming. Enjoy the spectacle, Matlock, they're on their way."

And if Matlock had thought that the Vroffa-Tree Inn's saztaculous appearance was the most shindinculous thing he had ever seen, it was all too peffa-soon overshadowed by what followed. In a matter of just a snutch of blinksnaps, a great roaring filled the lid, as witches of every size, shape and description vilishly circled the gardens, sweeping by the windows of the inn; screaming, shouting and baying, their speeding, flying shapes lit goulish orange by the crackling beacons.

"How many of them are there?" Matlock griffled above the noise, watching in amazement as one truly ganticus witch riding a whole vroffa-tree swept low and uprooted an entire tree, casually discarding the old one, then sent it crashing to the ground with a garrumblooming thud that shook all four walls of the inn.

"There's more every year," Laffrohn griffled, stirring a large black soup-cauldron over the piff-tosh. "The griffles have spread about how Laffrohn's vroffa-branches are the briftest for witches." She joined Matlock by the window, pointing to the trees. "See how they all try and reach for the witches, Matlock? They're desperate to have their branches chosen."

Matlock watched as witches battled for the best branches, some producing short wands and vrooshing others away, or chasing and stealing vroffa-branches from witches on juzzpapped brooms. Oidy witches simply flew on one twig they were so small, occasionally startling Matlock by flying close to the window and hovering for a snutch of moments, studying him carefully before vilishly flying away.

He tried to recognise some of the creatures, yet most were completely new to him. Some had robes, some armour, some were simply in their own fur; but all had a black, wide-brimmed pointed hat, no matter how ganticus or oidy they were. Matlock had, of course, read about witches in his years as apprentice under Chatsworth's tuition. But to that sun-turn, he'd never actually seen one. Yet here he was now, in a floating inn, on Trefflepugga Path surrounded by what seemed grillions of them.

Laffrohn returned to the cauldron. "Get ready, Matlock," she griffled. "The first ones will be in for their soup and guzzworts in a moment. They're a good bunch, by and large, The League of Lid Curving Witchery, but sometimes it can go an oidy bit witch-glopped if they're still trying to steal each other's branches."

Matlock watched through the window as gradually the commotion began to subside. More and more witches were landing, pulling out their old branches, binding and tying the new ones to their brooms, before tossing the juzzpapped branches into the fiery beacons. The vroffa-trees looked much tidier now, stripped of their newest branches, one or two of them seeming almost to bow, as if thanking the witches for their annual pruning.

But a particular witch had caught Matlock's attention. Dressed in black robes, hat and long red shoes, it was unmistakeably a hare. A white hare. "Is that…?" he griffled, pointing.

"Ursula Brifthaven Stoltz?" Laffrohn griffled. "Indeed it is, Matlock. Indeed it is."

Matlock watched as the white hare-witch suddenly pid-padded to a far bigger witch, vrooshed her feet on fire, then calmly stole a large vroffa-branch, the bigger witch racing around the garden, cursing and frantically stamping the ground to put her feet out. Ursula watched for a moment, then sent out another vroosher, instantly extinguishing the fire, before expertly binding the stolen branch to her broom.

Matlock gulped at the spectacle, really beginning to wish he hadn't eaten the last of the white hare's niffs. She certainly could wield a wand, that was peffa-certain.

In a blinksnap, the creaker opened, ushering in the first of the witches; all excrimbly, griffling and loudly chickling, ladling themselves soup while Laffrohn served them ganticus jugs of guzzwort. Next came the battle for seats around the tables, as they all vied for the briftest places in a frenzy of witch-glopped squabbling and vrooshing.

Matlock watched the chaos, glad they didn't seem to pay him too much attention. His own table was empty, save for himself. Several of the peffa-oidy witches had thought to quietly settle on the window sill behind, but no one else had dared to come close. Then, for the first time that sun-turn, he had an extrapluff, and knew exactly why. Just as he had eaten the white hare's niffs, he was now sitting at her table! The creaker opened, and silence fell around the inn. Matlock looked at Laffrohn, who merely winked at him. And he knew in that instant that everything was going to go glubbstool and somehow, even more peffa-witch-glopped than it already was.

A second extrapluff vilishly told him that he should break the silence and take the griffling initiative. "Good even'up," he griffled, as the white hare pid-padded straight towards him. "My name's Matlock, and I'm peffa-much afraid that…"

"I don't care for your name," she griffled back, looking at him as if she'd just stepped in a throtted-blungheap. "I care for why you are sitting at my table and in my chair."

The creaker opened, and silence fell around the inn.

Matlock stepped from the table, the other witches watching, some beginning to softly chickle. "I apologise," he griffled, vilishy wiping a couple of wandering mirrits from the surface.

"And I don't care for your apologies, either," the white hare-witch griffled back. "I simply care for my plate of niffs." She sat, took off her hat, placed it on the table. "Laffrohn! Where are my niffs?"

Laffrohn made her way through the witches, standing at Matlock's side. As she did so, he felt a slight tugging on his long hood. "This hare ate them, Ursula," she griffled. "Every last one of them. Perhaps you can vroosh some more with your wand?"

The witches collectively gasped at the arrogance and glopped-up clottabussedness of the question.

Ursula Brifthaven Stoltz narrowed her eyes, pointing at Matlock accusingly. "You...you ate my niffs?"

Matlock nodded. "By mistake, not deliberately. I mean...I did eat them, but I didn't know they were yours, I just..."

Ursula stood, her fizzing wand sparking blue at its tip. "You *ate* my niffs?"

Laffrohn stood between them. "But Ursula," she griffled, "this one's a majickal-hare. That's why he's all robed and in his fineries. He could vroosh you some more niffs...that is, if you can't."

Ursula turned to the other witches. "Tell them," she ordered. "Tell them there are no vrooshers to majick niffs!"

The other witches vilishly did so, all shaking their heads and agreeing.

"But this hare is so peffa-majickal, Ursula," Laffrohn insisted, "that he can majick niffs anywhere. He griffled me so, didn't you, hare?"

The witches began murmuring amongst themselves, curiosity pricked by the thought of a niff-majicking, majickal-hare.

Matlock looked at Laffrohn, as she made just the oidiest nod in the direction of his hood. "Indeed I did, good Innkeeper," he griffled, thankfully finally realising just what Laffrohn was up to. "And indeed I can."

Cries, shouts and griffles of 'Prove it, hare!' and 'Majick the niffs!' vilishly began to fill the inn, as witches pressed forward from all sides, eagerly straining to see the saztaculous niff-vroosh.

"Everybody back!" Matlock griffled, calmly looking Ursula Brifthaven Stoltz in the eye. "This is a peffa-shindinculous vroosher, and peffa-complicated. If it goes glopped-up, we could all end up stroffed!" He seized Ursula's wand and began twirling it in the air, weaving trails of blue-sparks all around him.

"Give that back at once!" Ursula protested, watching as Matlock twirled the wand even more, pulling his hood over his long ears, before vilishly shaking his head in the middle of the vrooshing, blue-sparking storm, looking like a ganticus November garrumbloom exploding high into the twinkling lid.

Then, from the midst of it all, he called out:

By powers given to me as majickal-hare,
I call upon more niffs to be there!

He vilishly bent towards the table, sending the niffs Laffrohn had dropped into his hood shooting across the surface.

"You see?" Lafrrohn cried out. "He is truly-peffa majickal! He majicked the niffs from thin air!"

The inn erupted in a chaos of pawplause and excrimbly whooping, as Matlock handed back the wand. "I'm Matlock," he griffled.

The white hare-witch nodded slightly. "And I'm Ursula," she reluctantly griffled, examining one of niffs carefully. "Sit with me."

Matlock sat back down at the table, watching as Ursula delicately ate the niff. "Sorry for stealing your wand," he griffled.

She looked up. "Don't take me for one of those other splurks," she griffled. "That would be your worst mistake."

"Splurks?"

She smiled slightly. "I think in your dale you might call them 'clottabusses', or 'glopped-up fools'. In the Land of White hares, we call them 'splurks'. And let me griffle you this, I'm *not* one of them."

Matlock rubbed his paws, feeling all too awkward under her penetrating gaze. "I never, for even a moment, thought that…"

Ursula waved her wand at the others. "You might think it's easy to fool all these guzzwort-guzzling splurks with your so-called majickal-tricks, Matlock. But believe me, I'm not so peffa-easy to convince. And producing a snutch of niffs from your hood in a shower of blue vroosh is far, far from majickal."

"I'm sorry," Matlock genuinely griffled.

"Tchoh!" Ursula clicked. "Your apologies are as peffa-glopped as your majick!" She leant slightly closer, lowering her voice so that Matlock had to struggle to hear above the cackling chaos all around. "Just because we are both hares, don't for the oidiest moment think that it makes a gruhplstaad of difference with me. What bothers me more is why Laffrohn would think that I would be being even vaguely impressed with such a pathetically glubbstooled trick."

Matlock cleared his throat, knowing that honesty had always been the briftest way, and quietly explained how he had eaten the last of the niffs without realising they were for someone else.

"But don't you see?" Ursula insisted. "They obviously *weren't* the last of them, were they? Otherwise, I wouldn't be eating these." She began eating another niff thoughtfully. "So why does she put us both through this game?"

Matlock shrugged, as uncertain as Ursula of Laffrohn's motives for the impromptu majickal-niff show. "I guess we'll have to ask her," he suggested.

Ursula leant back, still scrutinising him peffa-closely. "Why are you here?"

"You really want to know?"

"It's why I ask you the question, you splurk."

Matlock took a breath, then told the icy-cool white hare-witch all he knew, right from the moment he had gone to the public-griffling, fallen through the window of The Great Hall, had met Frendeslene Note then being expelled from Winchett Dale to begin his journey along Trefflepugga Path, with a singing kraark king and a ploffshroom band for company. "And the next I knew," he griffled, "was that the inn rose from the path, Laffrohn helped me up into the gardens, I ended up in here eating your niffs. I'm peffa-sorry for trying to deceive you."

Ursula took a snutch of moments to take it all in, slowly finishing her last niff as she considered all she had heard. "So now you plan to stop these krates and their drutts entering your dale?"

Matlock nodded. "And find my driftolubbs. Without those majickal-books…" He tailed off, not wanting to hear himself griffle the actual griffles out loud, as the truth was that the longer he spent with Ursula, the more gobflopped he felt.

A hint of a smile played around Ursula's soft, white face. "Without those books, you couldn't even convince a true tzorkly-witch that you can vroosh niffs from thin air?"

Matlock nodded again, not wanting to meet her brown eyes, instead looking around at the other witches, chickling and griffling, still noisily squabbling over soup and guzzworts.

Ursula broke the silence between them. "You're really quite lost aren't you?"

Matlock turned back to her. "The path is leading me somewhere, but I've not the oidiest extrapluff where."

"Because extrapluffs are useless on the path," she griffled. "None will happen when you pid-pad along it. Trefflepugga Path forbids them. You simply have to go where it takes you."

"Or you can fly," Matlock griffled, "and beat the path that way."

"But only if you've never taken a pid-pad along it," Ursula insisted. "It's why we witches never set a single paw along it."

"But you can see the whole path when you're flying above it, can't you? You could see the krates, griffle me where they are, take me to them." He instinctively tried to reach for her paw, which she quickly withdrew from the table, shaking her head and putting her black hat back on.

"Nothing will guide you, except the path," she griffled, standing and making ready to go.

"The riddle?" Matlock griffled, anxious she didn't leave. "If I solve the riddle of Trefflepugga Path, then I'll be able to find them, won't I?"

Ursula pushed past him. "Your griffles are peffa-glopped-up, hare. You're just another splurk, like all the rest of them." She stopped, turned, looked him once more in the eye. "There is no 'riddle', no majickal solution to the path. It's just an ancient spuddle, a glubbstooled myth that many have been stroffed trying to find."

"But…" Matlock hesitated, "…what if it isn't a spuddle? What if the riddle exists, and it's simply that no-one's ever solved it?"

"And I don't believe anyone's ever found it, either," Ursula vilishly griffled back. "You'd do as well as to remember that. You've begun your journey on the path. You have no choice but to pid-pad on." She shook out her robes, tying them around her neck. "And I have my journey, too. I must be back in my lands before morn'up. I wish you well."

"Please," Matlock tried. "Just take me up on your broom, let me see if I can see the krates? I must stop them."

Ursula shook her head. "To fly over the path with one who has already pid-padded upon it would be like stroffing us both. This problem you have with your home is yours, Matlock, not mine. As a solitary witch, I must remain solitary. Other creatures' problems are theirs. I ask no-one to help with mine, and I expect none in return, either. Already, I have griffled with you for too long. I'm leaving."

"Please," Matlock insisted one more time, as Laffrohn joined him at his side. "Just stay a while longer."

"Let her go," Laffrohn griffled. "She has her own path, and whether it crosses yours again be up to far greater wills than ours."

Ursula nodded to Laffrohn, turned to go, then stopped, reached into her robes and took out an oidy leather potion bottle. "Take this," she quietly griffled to Matlock, anxious the others didn't see. "It's for your journey. You'll know when the time is right and tzorkly to use it."

Matlock took the bottle, but before he could even ask her what was in it, she had left the inn. He watched through the window as she collected her broom and set off peffa-vilishly into the twinkling lid, never looking back for even the oidiest blinksnap. It was a signal that started the unceremonious exit of all the other witches, as they loudly finished their guzzworts and began shuffling, scrittling pid-padding and, in some cases, lump-thumping towards the creaker, Laffrohn wisely deciding that she'd supervise the collection of their newly-vroffa'd brooms outside.

When the last of them had gone, Laffrohn joined Matlock at the table, the inn strangely quiet now, just the splutting piff-tosh keeping them both company, a crumlush contrast to the chaotic scene just a snutch of moments earlier.

"So," she griffled. "That be that for another year, then."

Matlock was still looking at the bottle, uncorking the oidy lid and sniffing at it, trying to fathom just what on earth it could be. He poured an oidy amount on his paw. The liquid itself was odourless and colourless and simply looked like water. Nothing moved in it, no vapours rose from the surface. He lifted his paw to his mouth, keen to taste it.

Laffrohn stopped him with her own ganticus paw. "I wouldn't, Matlock," Laffrohn warned. "Solitary witches are peffa-tzorkly. They give nothing away without a reason, and sometimes it's not very crumlush." She wiped Matlock's paw with a cloth. "Remember, Matlock, you have to be peffa, peffa careful now you're on the path. It plays all sorts of tricks."

Matlock frowned slightly. "But you already know Ursula," he griffled. "She seemed fuzzcheck to me."

"No one ever really *knows* a solitary witch," Laffrohn explained. "Ever. If a creature gets too close to them, they lose all their tzorkly powers. So they stay on their own. They're safer that way."

"Why did you griffle to me that you had no more niffs?"

Laffrohn paused, considering Matlock's griffles. "I'll griffle you why another time," she yawned, but in such a way that Matlock didn't really think she was juzzpapped at all. "But right now, I need some nifferduggles. There'll be a lot of cleaning up to do in the morn'up." She stood, gave Matlock a long look. "You look peffa-juzzpapped, too. I suggest you nifferduggle now. There be nothing else you can do this even'up. You'll be safe from the path upstairs, and there be peffa-crumlush bed waiting for you."

"But I feel fine," Matlock insisted, "and I need to get on and find the krates before the morn'up…" He didn't finish his griffles, suddenly finding himself almost exactly as Laffrohn had described; peffa-juzzpapped and in real need of some crumlush nifferduggles.

She gently took him by the paw, and led him to a small creaker by the piff-tosh, opening it and pointing up the wooden stairway beyond it. "Your room's at the top," she griffled. "Get a good night's nifferduggles, Matlock."

He watched as she pid-padded around the inn, blowing out candles and collecting empty guzzwort jugs. "Thank you," he griffled, barely able to keep his hare's eyes open. "I think I will."

He made his way slowly up the wooden staircase, opening the creaker at the top to find a truly peffa-crumlush bedroom waiting for him. Yawning one final time, too tired to take off his robes, he lay on the bed as his heavily-juzzpapped eyes closed…

…and it was only then that the floor opened up beneath him and he was sent plunging down into the inky-black depths below…

7.

Note, Proftulous and
the Ganticus Tweazle-Pie

Frendelsene Note stood outside the glopped-up creaker and sent a silent prayer to Oramus above. The moon was barely a slither, making it impossible to see the Most Majelicus Hare that looked over all the dales and The Great Beyond from the yellowed calmness of its drifting surface. Yet even so, Note knew Oramus would be there, and perhaps worse, was watching every pid-pad he took, every change he sought to bring. But someone, he kept reminding himself, *had* to do it...

After a snutch of moments, he opened his eyes, took a peffa-deep breath and knocked on the door, part of him hoping that the ganticus occupant would be nifferduggling and unable to hear. He knew in his Sisteraculous that this would be one of the peffa-worst parts of his time in Winchett Dale, but as all had gone to plan so saztaculoulsy well so far, the next part was unavoidable. The hare was gone, Serraptomus dismissed, the entire dale twizzly about the 'something' and all completely unaware of the rest of the krates arrival in the morn'up. Even though he felt juzzpapped and desperately wanted to nifferduggle himself, Note knew he couldn't. Being officious didn't allow for tiredness. Being officious demanded total concentration for every moment of the sun-turn. It was simply how it was for a krate, the life that he'd chosen.

The creaker opened, and a bleary eyed dworp with ganticus ears peered out.

"May I come in?" Note asked. "I think we need to griffle."

Proftulous tried to close the door, Note jamming it painfully open with a foot. "If you persist in denying me entry," he hissed, trying to ignore the sudden, shooting pains, "then I shall be forced to return in the morn'up with more krates than you've eaten tweazle-pies, dworp!"

"I wants you to be pid-padding away, Mr Coat," Proftulous griffled. "I don't wants you to be coming into me house. I's be needing me nifferduggles, and 'tis peffa-late."

"Open the creaker," Note warned in a peffa-squeaky voice, truly worried his foot would never be the same again. "Now, dworp! Or life will get peffa, peffa-glopped for you!"

Proftulous hesitated, completely unsure what to do. "But I don't wants you coming in."

Note seized his chance, pushing violently with all his strength against the creaker, allowing just the oidiest gap for him to finally to stumble through and into the house, his foot throbbing in pain.

"I's be asking you peffa-nicely to leave," Proftulous griffled, panicking. "I's not be wanting you here, Mr Coat. I's not liking you, not an oidy bit."

Note tried his briftest to ignore the protest and the pain, looking around the darkened room. He'd been in lots of houses in his time, but truly, never one as completely glopped-up as this. The smell was surely the most peffa-yechus to have ever shlopped and glopped its way into his officious nostrils. Broken furniture filled the room, and the curtains, such as they were, seemed to be made from badly stitched tweazle-pelts, their decaying claws and noses still horribly visible. At the far end, the only source of light came from a ganticus fireplace, and set above it, hanging in soot-blackened chains, was the largest pie-tin Note had ever seen, yechus gloop oozing down its sides, frizzing and splutting into the fire below. Note hadn't felt so ill for a peffa-long time.

"I'll keep this short, dworp," he griffled, not wanting to take another pid-pad on the buckling stone floor covered in murp-worms and half-eaten tweazle-pies. "You know very well what I'm here for. Hand them over now, and it doesn't have to get any more glopped-up for you. I'll even ignore your frankly rather ludicrous charade and foot-assault at the creaker, so consider yourself peffa, peffa-lucky indeed."

Proftulous dropped to one knee with a ganticus crash, begging with his paws. "Please, Mr Coat, I knows nothing about what you're griffling about. I don't be having no majickal driftolubby book-things." He shook his head as earnestly as possibly, his ganticus ears almost flapping in Note's face. "I don't be having none of them at all…" He suddenly stopped, realising the enormity of what he'd just griffled, what he'd so easily and clottabussedly given away. He took a deep dworp's breath, stood then lump-thumped to the door. "So's you's gots to be leaving, now, Mr Coat. Gots to be going back to your own home, now."

Note sighed. "Just get the driftolubbs, dworp. The sooner we're done, the sooner I'm gone." He cautiously limped to the blazing piff-tosh, peering into the ganticus pie-tray, trying hard not to herreuch at the yechus sight of stroffed and skinned tweazles boiling in their own glopped juices.

"But 'tis just like I just griffles to you, Mr Coat," Proftulous pleaded. "'T's not be having no majickal-bookies. Especially not behinds that big tweazle curtain over there."

Note followed the ganticus pointing paw, went to the curtain and holding his nose, pulled it back. There, in a glopped-up pile were all the hare's majickal-driftolubbs; ancient books full of majickal dalelore, written and added to for the benefit and learning of all majickal-hares through the ages. It seemed almost a travesty to see them in such a gobflopped mess, behind a yechus tweazle curtain, in a peffa-clottabussed dworp's home. "And just how," he slowly griffled, trying to savour the moment, "did these come into your possession?"

Proftulous folded his arms defiantly, shaking his head and sending a snutch of slidgers from his ears flying across the darkened room. "Don't know," he griffled. "Proftulous never sees them before."

Note sighed, turned. "Then let me griffle what happened, dworp, as your memory appears to be as peffa-glopped as your yechus little home. You weren't up at the High Plateau, to see your former hare-friend gobflopp so spectacularly, were you?"

Proftulous started to blink, becoming panicked again. "I was,"

116

he earnestly griffled. "I was being there, Mr Coat, honest!"

"Oh, for Oramus sake!" Note exploded. "It's hardly difficult to miss a ganticus pair of ears like yours! You weren't there, dworp, because you were stealing these driftolubbs!"

"No!" Proftulous protested. "I's nots be stealing 'em, Mr Coat. I's be…" Proftulous struggled for the griffles, "…finding 'em."

"Where, exactly?"

Beads of sweat started to break from Proftulous' forehead. "Somewhere up near Trefflepugga Path," he confessed, his voice cracking with each griffle.

"And just what were you doing there, when you had specific instructions to attend the hare's majickal vrooshing on the High Plateau?"

Proftulous looked away, mumbled something.

"I didn't hear that, dworp!"

"I was trying to extrapluff," he quietly griffled. "By Thinking Lake. S'what Matlock and me used to do. We goes there to extrapluff about things when everything goes glopped."

"But dworps *can't* extrapluff," Note griffled menacingly. "Only majickal-hares can extrapluff. Every fool of a creature knows that."

Proftulous looked into the krate's beady eyes. "But I was trying," he quietly moaned. "I's be needing to know what to do to be helping my briftest friend."

"Pathetic," Note griffled. "Peffa-pathetic!"

"What be so wrong with trying?"

Note tried to stay as calm as possible. "So what happened?"

Proftulous eyes became slightly brighter as he remembered. "I's sitting by the lake, when over the wind, I be hearing all the noises and griffles at the plateau, and my mind is doing all sorts of twizzly pictures of Matlock gobflopping because he can't do a saztaculous vroosher. I gets a bit eye-splashy, but then suddenly I's getting another feeling, and it's making me feel sort of twizzly and shindinculous all at the same time."

"Go on," Note griffled, eyes narrowing, watching him peffa-carefully.

"Then I hears a voice, Mr Coat, griffling to me as clearly as your griffling to me now. And it's griffling me to go round the lake,

117

up towards Trefflepugga Path. Well, I's be shaking me ganticus ears, and looking all around, but there's no other creature there – just Proftulous, sat by Thinking Lake."

"And you went towards the path?"

Proftulous nodded. "And all the while these griffles are telling me where I must go. So I follows them, heads into these trees and sees all Matlock's things, right there in the wood."

"Did you see anyone else?" Note griffled.

Proftulous shook his ganticus head. "In the distance, there's a wagon, with some kraarks, and they was looking like they all trying to sing-griffle and do some scrittly, flappy dancing."

"Kraarks," Note quietly griffled, seeing the scene in his mind's eye. The fool Goole was too distracted with his own clottabussed singing ambitions to even notice when a ganticus dworp had blundered into the woods and stolen the driftolubbs right from under his own thieving beak.

"So I's be gathering up the majickal-books and bringing them back here, Mr Coat."

"To give them back to your hare-friend?"

Proftulous nodded eagerly, keen to explain the wisdom of his plan. "S'right. Because when he has them back, he can be vrooshing a peffa-saztaculous vroosher to save us all from the twizzly 'something', can't he?" Proftulous' excitement was growing. "Can't he, Mr Coat? Matlock can pid-pad back and save us all, because Proftulous had an extrapluff and saved all the driftolubbs for him. And no-one will ever griffle that Proftulous is a ganticus clottabus ever again! And Matlock and me will be back to being the briftest of briftest of friends, and being all majickal and extrapluffy! That's why I be doing it, Mr Coat. "

Note looked into the excrimbly face. "Only he's not coming back, dworp."

"Oh, but he is!" Proftulous insisted. "Matlock always saves Winchett Dale."

"Not this time," Note griffled. "It would take a grillion majickal-hares to vroosh the 'something' away."

Proftulous thought for a moment, frowning slightly, before suddenly raising his arms in triumph. "And that must be what he's doing! Don't you see, Mr Coat? Matlock's gone to be fetching grillions of the most peffa-majickal-hares from all the dales! It's why he's on Trefflepugga Path! And he's going to be pid-padding back with them all, to stroff the 'something' and make us feel all excrimbly and fuzzcheck again!" His face broke into a ganticus smile. "Matlock's the briftest majickal-hare, ever, Mr Coat."

Note calmly walked to the pile of books, selected one and simply threw it into the piff-tosh. "I think this tweazle-pie needs a little more cooking, don't you, dworp?"

Proftulous stood, his mouth wide open, unable to believe what he'd just seen. "What's you be doing, Mr Coat?" he griffled, voice breaking a little. "Why you be doing that?"

Note took another book, threw it into the flames. "These driftolubbs are as gobflopped as you are, dworp," he coldly griffled. "Nothing will save us from the 'something' except me and my krates."

"But…" Proftulous griffled, starting to tremble. "You can't be doing that, Mr Coat! Those be Matlock's majickal-driftolubbs, and…"

"And *what*, dworp?" Note hissed, as another book joined the others on the flames. "I suggest you shut your griffle-box and begin making some pastry, peffa-vilishly! Unless, that is, you want to be locked up for a grillion sun-turns for stealing these books, lying to me, and assaulting the foot of a First Officer of Official Krating!"

"But you can't be locking creatures up," Proftulous moaned, become ever more twizzly with each book Note casually tossed to the flames. "Locking up creatures be peffa-wrong and glopped-up!"

Note wagged a sharply pointed claw at him. "I think you'll find stealing and lying are the peffa-wrong things to be caught doing, dworp. And from tomorrow sun-turn, anyone in this dale found doing so, will be subject to the new ways of Winchett Dale." He looked Proftulous straight in his confused eyes. "And locking them up will be one of them. So I suggest you stop acting quite so clottabussed and eye-splashy, do as I griffle and start making pastry."

"But…"

"No 'buts', dworp!" Note barked. "Do it, now, or you'll never see the light of another sun-turn, or taste a tweazle-pie ever again!"

Proftulous ears started to fall, already sensing that despite everything, he was beaten. The krate was too strong, too officious, too clever. He really, really had wanted to help his briftest friend, more than anything he'd done in his life, but the thought of being locked-up forever was too strong. He knew he had tried his briftest, but at the end of the sun-turn, he also knew he was just a ganticus, peffa-glopped-up and clottabussed dworp. What possible use was he in trying and stop officious krates like Note?

Another book was thrown into the fire, the piff-tosh roaring now with brightly coloured flames, forged from the many majickal inks used to inscribe the griffles over the centuries. The pie-tin angrily bubbled and splutted, tweazle-gloop running over the sides and hissing into the dancing flames below.

Note grabbed a large ladle from the wall, and began stirring the contents. "Time for the pastry, dworp!" he shouted above the roaring fire. "I have the feeling this is going to be the most slurpilicious tweazle-pie you've ever tasted!"

Despondently, and with a peffa-heavy heart, trying not to get too much eye-splashy in the mixing bowl, Proftulous set about making a ganticus yellow blanket of pastry, placing on the top of the splutting tin when he had finished.

"My, that does look crumlush," Note griffled. "Now, let's really stoke this piff-tosh up." He threw Proftulous a book. "You do it," he insisted. "They're nothing but griffles, anyway. Just useless, gobflopped griffles!"

Proftulous' paws shook, as he reverentially laid the driftolubb on the flames; blue, purple and green flames singeing his furry arms. It was almost too much for him to bear, feeling as if he was burning the last ever connection with his briftest friend. He thought briefly of Matlock, wondering just where he was, how far he had gone along Trefflepugga Path to find the grillions of other majickal-hares to stroff the 'something'. He only hoped that he was safe, and that one sun-turn, somewhere in his hare's heart, he would find it in him to forgive him.

"Now we're cooking!" Note enthused, passing more books over. "Nothing wrong with change, is there, dworp? Out goes the old, and in comes the new – the way of krates, and drutts, and officiousness."

He reached out a paw, resting it on Proftulous' shoulder. "You'll be remembered for this, dworp. And rewarded, I promise. You'll have as many tweazle-pies as you wish to eat."

Proftulous shook his head. "They's not be tasting the same any more after this, Mr Coat. They's will be making me feel all glopped and gobfloppy."

The pliff-tosh spluttered ferociously all the while, the ganticus pie cooking from the roaring heat of the burning driftolubbs.

"Oh, I'm sure that will pass peffa-soon," Note griffled. "Most clottabussed creatures like yourself forget things all too peffa-easily. And frankly, you're, the most clottabussed I've ever met."

"Thank-you," Proftulous quietly griffled, watching the flames, his watery eyes following the trails of smoking griffles swirling around the pie-tin. He wished he could read, and know what all the strange symbols meant, discover their meanings. "Do you be reading?" he asked Note.

"What possible use is it?"

"To make things majicky."

Note slowly nodded, watching the griffles leaving the burning pages to dance around the edge of the tin. "But remember," he griffled, "reading is bad. The majickal-hares that read and write use it for their own ends. It isn't majickal power they want, it's real power, over all the creatures in all the dales. And by keeping their secrets safe in these books, and not allowing anyone else to learn how to read, so they keep their power, dworp." He shook his head sadly. "So what we're doing is a peffa, peffa-good and saztaculous thing. You must remember that. And Oramus will thank us both for it one sun-turn."

They watched for a while longer, burning the last of the books from the pile. Eventually, the dancing majickal-griffles began to fade, merging into just a single column of thick black smoke rising steadily into the chimney.

"There," Note griffled, after the blaze had died down to just a pile of blackened pages with orange glowing edges. "I think that's one ganticus tweazle-pie's that's peffa-ready to eat." He began searching through glopped cupboards, eventually finding a large wooden plate, setting it on a leaning table covered with murpworms

The pliff-tosh splutted ferociously all the while, the ganticus pie cooking from the roaring heat of the burning driftolubbs.

and skrittling mirrits. "Sit, my new dworp friend," he quietly instructed. "Tis time to enjoy your slurpilicious late-night supper."

Proftulous slowly lump-thumped to the table, sitting on an old creaking barrel, watching as Note ladled him a steaming portion of tweazle-pie onto the plate.

"And now," Note griffled, "you're going to prove to me just how much you really like tweazle-pies, dworp. Because I'm not leaving, until you've finished every last oidy bit."

Proftulous looked at the krate, then at the pie; warm, inviting and slupilicious. Thick drool began to fall from either side of his mouth, and his paws began to shake again at the anticipation of the first peffa-crumlush mouthful.

A snutch of moments later, he had cleaned the plate, all too eager for more…

Of all the ancient majickal-driftolubbs, *Majickjal Dalelore (Volume 68 – revised edition)* is perhaps the least read. But not because of its size. In fact of all the driftolubbs, it is the slimmest, a mere seventy pages or so, depending on the translation, and which creature painstakingly copied and scribed the griffles. But regardless, most majickal-hares agree that it is the least 'majickal' of all the driftolubbs. The spells and vrooshers contained therein are peffa-few and far between and mostly concern themselves with the more mundane instances of majicking, such as grarrpelling an irate kurrawocka, or thwarting a creeping-zill. There's a small section on the merits and life-cycles of mirrits, alongside several ancient recipes for various crumlush leaf brews. Thus, for most majickal-hare apprentices, a peffa-quick skim of the pages suffices, with perhaps a little idle note-taking done as 'proof' to their masters that the volume has been read.

However, for those driftolubb purists (of which, it has to be griffled, there are peffa-few) *Majickjal Dalelore (Volume 68 – revised edition)* does stand out from its companions, and not only for its smaller size. The interest for the serious student of majick lies in the revisions themselves, making it quite a different edition from the original, unrevised version.

One such revision, scribed by Baselott, a Most Majelicus hare many moon-turns past, deals with observations he made as a mere majickal-hare of his dripple. The faithful companion, it seemed, had begun to learn to griffle, starting with just small guttural noises, before eventually progressing to actual griffles themselves. Baselott, being at that stage a majickal-hare concerned with ancient rites of alchemy, decided that this extraordinary occurrence should immediately be investigated according to his own majickal-scientific principles, and set about devising a series of experiments in his potionary to try and discover just why it was that his dripple was griffling.

His theory was peffa-simple, and far from unique to the approach of many a majickal-hare. Instead of trying to find the answer himself, he would try and teach his dripple as many griffles as possible, so that in time, it would inform him of just why it was that it alone, of all the dripples, was griffling. Was it simply a one-off twizzly occurrence, or did every dripple share this ability? And if so, just what had caused it? The dripple itself, Baselott assumed, was best placed to provide the answer.

Fearful of ridicule by other majickal-hares, Baselott kept his experiments and research a secret, as each and every sun-turn, he endeavoured to teach his dripple new griffles. Some it picked up almost immediately, others it clearly hadn't the oidiest idea what they meant at all. Aware that he could be merely accused of training his dripple to respond to certain items with corresponding griffles, and noticing a steady decline in the health of his companion, Baselott abandoned his research, sensing in his Sisteraculous that he was venturing into forbidden majickal-territory with his experiments.

He fully expected his dripple to make a recovery, and indeed nursed it every sun-turn with potions and cures of every description. But none worked. All too aware that the dripple of a majickal-hare passes to Oramus' Most Majelicus Eternal Care at the same moment, and on the peffa-same sun-turn as its master, Baselott began fearing for the premature end of his own life. If his dripple were to pass – then so, inevitably, would he.

But when the dripple's time came, he went alone, peacefully as he nifferduggled. Baselott was left alive, completely confused as to why this central majickal premise had been overlooked. All he could conclude that was by griffling, the dripple had somehow shortened his own pid-pads on the dale immeasurably, and broken the bond between them. Nevertheless, Baselott was left with the lingering and dreadful thought that by encouraging his dripple to griffle, he had contributed to its sad decline significantly.

Baselott never mentioned a single griffle of the peffa-strange episode, griffling to those who asked about his absent dripple that the oidy creature was simply busy on chores, or sorting things out elsewhere. Eventually, creatures stopped asking, accepting Baselott's griffled excuses. Why shouldn't they? He was a majickal-hare, after all, and everyone knew they wouldn't ever, ever lie.

However, to make amends, when he sensed his own passing was close, Baselott sat down and scribed the tale of his griffling-dripple. It was found on the desk, exactly as he had left it by the creatures of his dale. Unable to read the parchment pages, they dutifully passed them on to the Most Majelicus High Council For All Majickal-Hare Driftolubbs. Upon reading the Baselott's intended revision, and immediately realising its extremely majickal significance, they made the peffa-vilish decision to include it in the smallest driftolubb that was also the least likely to be read – *Majickjal Dalelore (Volume 68)* – becoming as it did in that instance, the revised edition; hoping and praying to Oramus that Baselott's account of the griffling dripple should never be found.

And, of course, not before they had made some 'revisions' of their own, reducing Baselott's thirteen page manuscript to a mere paragraph, with instructions that it only appeared in the peffa-oidiest print in any future copies.

The actual revision reads:

Whilst there have been spuddles of dripples griffling in some peffa-extreme instances, these are largely to be ignored, as none have been available for majickal study at this time. Dripples are silent, ungriffling creatures, and to ever encourage them to be otherwise would endanger your own life significantly.

In a bizarre, but pleasing footnote to the story, it's worth knowing that when Baselott finally left the dale and passed to Oramus' Most Majelicus Eternal Care, one of the first things he did was to sit down and have a right good griffle with his own dripple, who told him all the answers he had been so desperately striving for.

And when Baselott heard them, and everything finally made the most saztaculous sense, he merely nodded his head, tucked his dripple lovingly back into the hood of his robes, and smiled the most crumlush smile…

8.

Sylphas, Dreggs and the Cove of Choices

Matlock gradually came awake, his hare's eyes slowly adjusting to the clear blue autumnal morning light. He sat up, remembering parts of drifting dreams, the last one featuring Goole the Trefflepugga-kraark, singing one of his peffa-annoying songs.

He rubbed his face with his paws, as memories of his witch-glopped even'up at The Vroffa-Tree Inn came flooding back. He wondered if he'd had too many guzzworts, as his head felt fuzzy and his Sisteraculous was telling him to lie back down in the crumlush bed for a while. He did so, then began to wonder just why it was he could still hear Goole's singing, and the ceiling in his room looked for all the world like a clear blue morn'up lid.

A leaf drifted down, and underneath, lightly clinging to the underside, was quite the most crumlushly wispy sprite Matlock had ever seen, as frail as a trail of mist, but with a saztaculoulsy curved tail that it gracefully used to guide the leaf gently onto his pillow.

"Morn'up," she cheerfully griffled, drifting slightly in the breeze. "And a shindinculous welcome to the Vale of Dreggs."

Matlock raised himself up again, taking his first proper look around. The bedroom at The Vroffa-Tree Inn was gone. Instead he found himself lying on the same bed just a snutch of pid-pads from a small brook that slowly meandered through a saztaculous low-sided rolling valley. Quite what had happened in the night, he

A leaf drifted down, and underneath, lightly clinging to the underside, was quite the most crumlushly wispy sprite Matlock had ever seen, as frail as a trail of mist.

hadn't even the oidiest idea, yet somehow he felt warm, calm and safe. With the exception of just one thing – the persistently annoying sound of Goole's singing, coming, he now realised, from underneath the very bed itself. He rolled over, peering under.

"Goole?" he griffled.

"The peffa-same, Mr Hare," the waist coated kraark replied, breaking off from his singing. "Crivens and scrimples, I was beginning to wonder just how much longer I 'as to be singing to ever wake you up!"

"What are you doing there?"

"Oh, that's peffa-fine, I must griffle! Coming from you! The question, Mr Hare, is just what the Balfastulous are *you* doing here?" He tried to scrittle, clearly stuck. "There I was, waiting in the vale, minding me own business, doing a bit of the old singy-songy, then – wallopers! – you's go and falls out of the lid and crashes right on top of me with that bed of yours." He adjusted his tricorn hat. "Could've had me bloomin' beak off!"

Matlock gradually climbed from the bed, feeling the sun-warmed grass under his bare feet. He looked for his long purple shoes, remembering he'd left them drying by the piff-tosh back at the inn. "I fell?" he griffled, looking up at the lid.

"And don't you be griffling to me that it wasn't no accident, either!" Goole angrily griffled. "I reckon you be aiming that thing deliberately!"

"No, no," Matlock griffled, moving the bed and releasing Goole's trapped foot. "I was simply nifferduggling and ended up here." He told Goole about his even'up at the inn with The League of Lid Curving Witchery. "So you could griffle that the only reason I ended up landing on you was because the path *wanted* me to. It does decide where we go, after all."

Goole puffed up his chest, waistcoat straining. "Just how peffa-glopped-up are you, Mr Hare? You was in a place *above* the path in your witchy-inn, weren't you? So it wouldn't have had no hold over you. Then only reason you ended up nearly stroffing me was because someone else wanted you to." He scrittled away, dipping his beak in the brook and drinking from the clear waters.

"So you've not found the krates, then?" Matlock asked.

Goole turned, touched the side of his head with a wing. "Just how splonked in the boncey are you, Mr Hare? Don't you remember nothing what goes in those gobflopped long ears of yours? Time on the path has no meaning. It's different from time in the dales. It could take me a grillion sun-turns until I meets 'em. But when we finally arrive back in Winchett Dale, it'll still be the morn'up after we left." He turned back to the brook, shaking his head. "Goole's thinking that all me griffles of wisdom are lost on you, Mr Hare, I really am."

Matlock pid-padded over, enjoying the warm sensation of grass under his bare feet, suddenly reminding him of his time as a normal hare in The Great Beyond before Chatsworth had found him. He honestly couldn't remember the last time he'd pid-padded barefoot in Winchett Dale.

"I'm sorry," he griffled, lightly bliffing Goole's hat, "about your foot."

Goole looked at the lid, blinked, nodded slightly. "Accepted, Mr Hare. Casualty of the path, I'spose. I mean, no one expects to scrittle along here without getting glopped at some point. Already lost me eye, I can't flap or fly no more, so what's a gobflopped foot, eh?" He turned to Matlock. "Besides, when I be getting me talons on all those crumlush drutts, I'll be getting someone to makes me a new foot, eh? A peffa-saztaculous foot that everyone'll look at and griffle about how shindinculous and fuzzcheck it is." He shook out his feathers. "That's right, that is. Peffa-right, Mr Hare. Drutts'll make everything better."

"And I daresay there'll be a saztaculous song to be had from it."

Goole's one good eye brightened. "Well, now we're griffling, aren't we! Me own saztaculous foot song! I'll have the brother-kraarks working on their routine the moment I gets back, don't you worry. It'll bring the house down, will that!"

"It'll be a real showstopper, I'm sure," Matlock griffled, pid-padding back to the bed, the gliding leaf-sprite still lazily drifting above it. He sat on the edge, trying to make sense of everything. The last thing he remembered was going to bed, the next waking up in this crumlush vale. Nothing in between. He'd nifferduggled as soundly as he ever had, and had awoken feeling refreshed, with more energy, younger almost than he'd felt in some time. He remembered the potion bottle Ursula the white hare-witch had given him, reaching into his robe pockets, rolling it in his paw, checking that it was actually real, proof that he *had* been at The Vroffa-Tree Inn in the first place.

The sprite darted in front of his face. "So many things," she griffled, "are peffa-confusing, aren't they?"

Matlock looked into the translucent face, which although changing constantly, had at its centre quite the most shindinculous smile. "Yes," he griffled. "I suppose they are."

"It's better that way," she griffled.

"Who are you?"

The sprite performed a loop in the air. "I am, but I am not; I was, but am no longer." She surveyed him curiously. "You have such crumlush long ears. Can I touch them?"

Which she had done even before Matlock had time to answer, feeling just the faintest touch somewhere above his head, like the oidiest breath of his dripple on the side of his face as he'd carried it in his hood back in Winchett Dale.

The sprite glided back in front of him. "Yet the kraark griffles that you don't listen to anything in your crumlush ears. I think it's better that way, too."

"What's your name?"

"I have none," she griffled. "But I am a sylpha. There are many of us. In autumn, we ride the leaves. Look."

Matlock looked towards the lid, watching other leaves drifting slowly through the clear blue, borne by the breeze, squinting at those that came close, glimpsing similar sprites also holding tight to the edges. "Looks like fun," he griffled, watching the tiny sprites soar back up into the lid to ride more leaves, gliding from one to another in a looping dance.

"It is," the sprite griffled.

"But you don't have a name?"

The sprite tipped onto its back, looking back up into the lid, as if lying on an invisible bed. "You can name me, if you like."

"Name you?"

She turned to face him. "What would like to call me?"

131

"I don't know," Matlock griffled, caught by the question, and realising that he'd never really named anything before. Everything already had names, or, like his dripple, simply didn't need one.

"Think of one," the sprite griffled, gliding and twirling in front of him.

"Flyer?"

The sprite pulled a face, chickling. "Flyer?"

"Well, it's what you do," Matlock tried to explain. "You fly, and so I thought…"

"But that's not a name though, is it?" She pointed a delicate arm at Goole. "It would be like naming the kraark 'Scrittler', because that's all he does. Think of something you'd *like* to call me."

Matlock tried to think, rather stuck.

"What's *your* name?" the sprite asked, breaking the awkward silence.

"Matlock."

She smiled. "It is a crumlush name that suits you. I like it. I like you, Matlock. Give me a crumlush name like yours."

Matlock's mind raced, trying to think. "How about…"

"Yes?"

A name flew into his mind, and Matlock grabbed at it, relieved to have finally come up with something. "How about Plusa?"

"Plusa?"

He watched as she mulled it over, mouthing the griffle to herself a snutch of times.

"Why 'Plusa'?" she griffled.

"Because I think it sounds nice."

"And crumlush?" she asked.

Matlock nodded, relieved that at least she seemed to like it. "Peffa-crumlush. Saztaculously crumlush."

"Then you can call me Plusa," she griffled, chickling and trying her name again as she span and turned in the air. "It's better that way."

Matlock watched for a snutch of moments before pid-padding back over to Goole, with other more pressing matters on his mind. "You griffled that you were waiting here before I fell from the lid?"

Goole nodded. "S'right, Mr Hare. I was."

132

"Waiting for the krates?"

Goole chickled, shook his head. "No."

"Well what, then?"

Goole pointed with a wing, its stolen rings jangling. "Just you try pid-padding over there, Mr Hare. Go on."

Matlock set off, pid-padding along the side of the brook, then suddenly stopping, his legs unable to move another pid-pad. He was blocked, completely unable to go any further forwards. Trefflepugga Path was playing its games again. He took a few pid-pads to the side, trying to walk forwards, becoming just as stuck.

"S'like that all the way round here," Goole called out. "It's got us trapped. We can't move nowhere, Mr Hare. We're stuck here, in the Vale of Dreggs, and all we can do is be waiting."

"For what?" Matlock griffled, still trying to find the edges of what appeared to be an invisible wall.

"Until the path decides what it wants to be doing with us," Goole griffled, scrittling over to the bed, climbing up and lying down, wings behind his head, staring up contentedly at the bright blue lid. "Still, there's worse places to be stuck, I s'pose. Least we're not stroffed, eh?"

"But how long is it going to take?" Matlock griffled, finding absolutely no way past the invisible wall. He'd pid-padded a complete circle, the bed stuck hopelessly in the centre.

"No idea," Goole griffled, playing with Plusa as she danced and drifted around his tricorn hat. "My betting though is that sometime soon, there'll be a parade of them peffa-yechus dreggs."

"Dreggs?" Matlock griffled, pid-padding back to join them.

"S'what I'm griffling, Mr Hare," Goole griffled, watching as Plusa, landed on his wing and began playfully tugging on his rings. "Careful, sprite! That was me mother's; her pride an' joy, it was."

"My name is Plusa," she griffled back, "not 'sprite'."

"Well, keep your thieving wispy hands off of 'em, Plusa! Taking peffa-liberties, you are." He turned to Matlock. "So you've never heard of a dregg before?"

Matlock shook his head.

"Not even in those majickally driftolubby book things of yours? The ones you used to keep in that back room in your cottage?"

Matlock instantly narrowed his eyes. "Just what would you know about where I kept my driftolubbs?"

Goole paused, blinked, caught, trying desperately to think his way out of his glopped-up griffling blunder. "Just…just that I heard that you…being all majickal an' that…"

"Yes?" Matlock pressed, keen to know just how it was that a singing-kraark who had supposedly spent most of his life in Winchett Dale hidden from all the other creatures, knew anything about his books or their location in his potionary.

"Well…" Goole griffled, making a big thing of clearing his throat, then suddenly pointing high into the lid and crying out. "Just look at that up there! Well, I'll be moffled! It's a flying shickle-flapper! Now you don't be seeing many of them around here."

"Oh, for Oramus' sake!" Matlock angrily griffled. "You stole them, didn't you? You ransacked my cottage and stole my driftolubbs while I was at the public griffling. It was you, wasn't it? And all this time you haven't griffled a griffle about it, because you're too interested in a worthless pile of glopped-up pebbles!"

Goole sat upright, placed a wing over his chest, adopting a theatrically pained and hurt expression, before slowly closing both eyes. "How your griffles have hurt me, Mr Hare. Cuts me to the peffa-quick, they has, like ganticus swords piercing me very…"

"Hush!" Plusa suddenly interrupted, pointing towards the brook. "See the splashy! It's changing and beginning to dance. 'Tis nearly time for the parade – the twizzly parade of the dreggs."

Matlock jumped from the bed, pid-padding over to the water's edge, Plusa gliding behind.

"Only when the parade has passed by on the other side of this brook, will Trefflepugga Path let you continue on your way," she griffled, drifting and looping over the water that was already beginning to spluttle and mist before Matlock's very eyes.

"I'd move away from that fog, if I was you, Mr Hare!" Goole called out.

Matlock took a couple of pid-pads back from the edge, as a thick wall of fog began rising from the churning water. "What's happening?" he griffled.

"'Tis the beginning of the parade," Plusa griffled. "Soon, the dreggs will be here. Listen carefully, Matlock, and you'll hear their pid-pads; grillions of them, making their twizzly way to us down the vale."

A distant rumbling began to build as the mist continued to swirl and surround them, the vale now echoing with distant sounds of pipes, trunkulahs and drums. Matlock felt a powerful force at his back, moving him forwards, pid-pad by pid-pad.

"Don't fight it, Matlock," Plusa warned. "You cannot beat the will of the path. Let it take you."

Matlock felt his pid-pads quicken, looking down and seeing Goole breathlessly scrittling next to him. "Where is it taking us?"

"Further up the vale. Right to the water's edge," Goole panted. "It's Trefflepugga Path. Every time a creature pid-pads or scrittles along it, it remembers and keeps a memory of their journey as a dregg – a phantom of how you were on that journey. A likeness of you, but not you. A ghost, if you will. A peffa glopped-up thing to ever see, Mr Hare. 'Tis like looking back through time itself. This is my fourth time along Trefflepugga Path, so right now there's three twizzly dreggs of me coming to meet me."

The noise was building, garrumblooming around the vale, together with grillions of approaching pid-pads and lump-thumps, slowly marching in time to the macabre music. Matlock peered through the mist, halting by the edge of the brook, seeing nothing, but feeling the ground begin to shake under his feet. "There must be grillions of them," he quietly griffled, trying to level his breathing, calm his twizzles.

"S'right, Mr Hare," Goole quietly griffled, his voice shaking a little. "Dreggs of those that made the journey, and dreggs of those that got stroffed along the way; from the very beginnings of time, when there was nothing in all of The Great Beyond but Trefflepugga Path itself."

Matlock swallowed. "But I've already made the journey once," he griffled. "When I was first bought to Winchett Dale."

Goole nodded. "S'right, Mr Hare, and that's the reason you're here. The path knows, it remembers everything. Somewhere, in and amongst this glopped nightmare, there'll be a dregg of you on its yechus way to meet you. The only advice I have, is if you sees it, then never, ever look it in the eye." He looked up at Matlock with his milky eye. "First time I was stood here, I was foolish enough to do just that. Second trip up the path it was, and the mists came down, right where we are now. Then, in the crowd, I sees meself, just as I was, making me first trip out from Sveag Dale, all those moon-turns ago. And then I goes and makes the most peffa-gobflopped mistake."

"What?" Matlock griffled, his breath quickening as the commotion grew in the shrouding mist.

"I looked it in the eye, Mr Hare," Goole griffled. "Just for the oidiest blinksnap, I looked it in the eye. And that's what did for me peeper. Took him right out. Just the oidiest look in the eye."

Plusa wisped in front of Matlock's face. "Just let them pass," she griffled. "Don't look, don't distract them. It's better that way."

The fog was starting to thin, allowing Matlock occasional oidy glimpses across the brook. There were figures everywhere, of all shapes and sizes, slowly marching, pid-pad, scrittling and lump-thumping by, some slowly turning to look at him as they passed, their eyes just black, empty, yechus holes.

"Remember, if you see yourself," Goole griffled, "just look away. They'll have your peepers out, drag you across the water and swallow you whole. Come the next parade, it'll be you that's joining 'em."

One or two dreggs had stopped, now pointing across the brook at Matlock and Goole, moaning, their mouths opening horribly, oozing peffa-yechus drool.

"They've seen us," Goole quietly griffled. "But they can't get across. The water stops 'em, see. They can't cross it, unless you looks into the eyes of your own dregg."

"But they don't have eyes," Matlock griffled, never having felt so twizzly in all his life. "Just…"

"Holes," Goole griffled, his breathing coming faster now, rings shaking on his twizzly-wings. "If they want to touch you, let 'em. 'Tis the only way they'll eventually move on."

"Touch us?" Matlock griffled, becoming truly alarmed at just the thought. "But how? They can't reach us, the brook's too wide."

"Is it?" Goole griffled. "Just watch, Mr Hare. Trefflepugga Path always has its ways."

Matlock looked down into the brook, seeing it begin to shrink before his widening eyes, bringing the outstretched arms, paws and claws of the peffa-yechus dreggs closer and closer. He felt faint with the twizzliness, and knew that if the path hadn't held him firm to the ground, he'd have collapsed in shock there and then.

"Get them away!" he cried out, as glopped-up, yechus paws began tugging at his robes and stroking his face.

"Hush!" Plusa whispgriffled, hiding in one of his long ears. "Be still, and they will go. It's better that way."

"Stop them!" he yelled. "It's too yechus, I can't stand it! By the Most Majelicus powers of Oramus, get them off me, now!"

And in that moment, the drums, trinkulahs and pipes all stopped. The marching army of dreggs came to a rambling halt, all stopping to slowly turn and look across the tiny trickle of brown, yechus water that had previously been such a saztaculoulsy clear, meandering brook. The fog too, was clearing, allowing Matlock to see just how many of these twizzly, peffa-yechus visions there were; grillions and grillions, stretching as far as he could see, filing the vale, all now eerily quiet in the slight autumnal breeze.

Goole sighed, quietly whispgriffling, "Well, now you've gone and done for us, Mr Hare. Thanking you for that, you twizzly great clottabus!"

"It got too much for me," Matlock whispgriffled back.

"That's nothing to what's going to happen now, Mr Hare. Just you wait. We should have just let them pass."

The crowd of dreggs was slowly parting, a long pathway opening up between them. A tall dregg dressed in ripped rags with a drum tied to its body began slowly beating it with an old skull held loosely in its claws. Then, from further down, Matlock made out a kraark that looked for all the world just like Goole, complete with hat and waistcoat, rings on its wings, skrittling forward towards them.

"It's you," he whispgriffled to Goole, heart racing.

Goole was staring intently at the ground by his feet. "T'isn't me, Mr Hare. 'Tis one of me dreggs. Chances are it's the same fella what's I 'm looking at last time I was here, and you won't catch me looking at him again, either."

Goole's dregg, its eyes just blackened pits, started to chickle,

137

pointing to a chain hanging round its neck, holding it out for Matlock to see. He gasped, seeing the small black eye hanging from the end of it.

"It's got your eye," Matlock whispgriffled to Goole. "On the end of a chain."

Goole still stared at his feet. "Well, he ain't getting me other one, Mr Hare, that's for sure."

A second dregg of Goole scrittled forward as the brook thinned even more, soon joined by another, all staring ahead intently, holes where their eyes should have been.

"There's two more," Matlock griffled, watching as all three kraark-dreggs stood inches from Goole, only separated by the merest trickle of water.

"Tell me when they're gone," Goole griffled, covering his face with his tricorn hat. "Tell me when they've scrittled off. You's can look right at them, Mr Hare, but I can't."

The three empty-eyed dreggs scrittled around, cawing and bending, trying desperately to look under Goole's hat and meet his one remaining eye. They bliffed him with their wings and hats, rings jangling in the stilled quiet, trying anything they could to catch the vital glimpse, as all the while Matlock watched in complete twizzly terror, rooted to the spot by the power of the path.

Thankfully, to Matlock's ganticus relief, they gradually began to slowly lose interest, as if somehow sensing the cause was lost and Goole was never going to face them from behind his hat. All three began backing away in rhythm to the beating drum, their black sockets staring at Goole every skrittle of the way in case he was foolish and clottabussed enough to take even the oidest peak. A ganticus moan broke from the glopped-up crowd as the three kraarks finally rejoined the other dreggs, shattering the overwhelming silence in the vale.

"I think," Matlock griffled, letting out a huge breath, "they're gone."

"You sure?" Goole griffled from under his hat.

"Fairly, yes."

"Fairly sure, or peffa-sure?"

"Erm…peffa-sure…I think."

Goole cautiously tipped back his hat, slowly peering out from under it and looking down the clear pathway between the dreggs. "Methinks you're right, Mr Hare," he griffled, his beak breaking into a broad smile. "They've gone and skrittled off, 'cause old Goole's not been looking at 'em!" He punched the air with both wings. "That showed, 'em, didn't it, Mr Hare! Goole's too peffa-clever to let 'em have his other eye and then swallow him all up!"

All the while the drum kept on beating, the grillions of dreggs refusing to move, now all staring straight at Matlock, instead.

Goole passed his tricorn hat. "Reckon two things, Mr Hare. First, it's going to be your turn. And second, you're going to be needing this."

Matlock took the hat, paws shaking, as two figures began to make their way slowly down the path towards him, the drum beating steadily in time to their pid-pads. Matlock instantly recognised the red-robes of Chatsworth, his old master, and behind him, hopping and playfully boxing nearby dreggs as it passed by – a young brown hare.

"Crivens!" Goole griffled. "That's you! When you was all peffa-young and crumlush. One of them…oidy hare things."

"Leveret," Matlock quickly corrected him, raising the hat so that all he could see was Chatsworth's head and shoulders approaching. He felt twizzly and faint again, looking at the dregg, recognising the familiar smile, but seeing no eyes in his old master's face…

It stopped just inches from him. "Matlock!" it beamed, in a voice that bought back so many crumlush memories. "So peffa, peffa-pleased to see you again!"

"I…I…" Matlock tried, completely unable to griffle, the feelings far too strong.

Goole nudged him in the elbows with his beak. "It can't see nothing, Mr Hare. Remember that. It's just a dregg, a glopped-up phantom memory of a journey he once made. It's not who you think it is."

The dregg smiled again. "You won't remember, Matlock, when you and I made our journey along this path together, many moon-turns ago. But I do." The griffles were soft and kind. "It was always one of the peffa-briftest things I did, Matlock. And it is with you

139

that also I have some of my briftest memories, too; our trip across this path, seeing you grow and become majickal in the potionary. In fact, all our time in Winchett Dale together. And when, at last you had completed your apprenticeship and it was time for me to leave, it was with a peffa-heavy heart."

Matlock closed his eyes, not wanting to hear any more griffles.

"But now I'm asking you to remove that hat and open your eyes, Matlock," the dregg griffled. "You're safe with me, just as you were all those moon-turns ago. Together we can sort everything out, Matlock, everything. We can find our way back to Winchett Dale, and make everything saztaculous and peffa-shindinculous again. All you have to do is look down at the hare at my feet and into its eyes. Just look, Matlock. Remove the hat and see yourself as you were. You're here, with me now, by my feet, waiting so peffa-patiently for you to simply look."

"I can't," Matlock griffled, his heart pounding with peffa-twizzliness . "You're not Chatsworth. You're not him. And I'm not looking at that hare. It's not me!"

"But *it is*, Matlock," the dregg calmly griffled. "Look and see."

To his horror, Matlock felt himself being forced down to his knees, as if a ganticus weight was slowly pushing down on his head. "No!" he cried out. "It's a trick!"

Goole clung on to his robes. "Keep breathing, Mr Hare. Deep and easy. 'Tis just the path that's pushing you down. Breathe, Mr Hare. That's the way. Deep and easy, and it'll be gone."

The dregg reached across the trickle of water, softly rubbing Matlock's ears. "Matlock, we don't have much time. If you want to save Winchett Dale, then you must look. *You must.*"

"I am Matlock the Hare," Matlock griffled, removing the hat and staring up intently into the dregg's black empty sockets. "And you *aren't* Chatsworth, my crumlush and saztaculous old master. You never will be! I have no majick to vroosh you away, but a wise and shindinculous majickal-hare once told me that wherever I am, the Sisteraculous pid-pads by my side, and Oramus always leads the way." He looked into the lid, holding out his arms and shutting his eyes with peffa-concentration. "And I now call upon them both to save me from this!"

He kept his eyes tightly shut, hoping with all his will that something would happen, that somehow, despite the overwhelming odds that neither Oramus nor the Sisteraculous would answer his call, they would be able to find a way…

"Oh, Matlock," the dregg griffled disappointedly. "Such a glopped-up thing to ask! Such peffa-gobflopped griffles to griffle! Now just why would you suppose that either Oramus or the Most Majelicus Sisteraculous would be even an oidy bit concerned with the eye-splashy griffllings of a mere hare? A hare that visited this path of his own freewill, that pid-padded along it voluntarily, running as he was, from all his troubles in Winchett Dale? I'm sure they have far brifter things to worry about than you, Matlock." It leant down, its twizzly blind face inches from Matlock's. "The path decides your destiny now, Matlock. Not you, not me, not your unhearing gods. Just Trefflepugga Path."

"No!" Matlock cried out, the grim beating of the drum quickening all the time.

"You have been forgotten, Matlock, right from the very first pid-pad you took along this path. All you once had and held so dear is gone. All you knew is no more. All you hope for is lost."

Matlock took his deepest hare's breath, desperate for rescue from the abomination in front of him, but knowing none was coming. There was only one thing to do, no matter how twizzly it was. "If your griffles are true, and I am to be stroffed along this glopped-up path, then I would rather do it here. I would rather do it now." He calmly reached across the trickle of water and held onto the dregg's yechus red robe.

"Mr Hare!" Goole cried. "Don't! We'll both be stroffed!"

Matlock nodded, staring back into the dregg's black empty eyes. "That's as may be, Goole," he griffled, determination coursing through him. "And if we are, then you'll never meet the krates and take them back to Winchett Dale and ruin my crumlush homelands for ever, will you? So you see, if we're stroffed – then so are all your plans."

"Don't be such a ganticus clottabus!" Goole pleaded. "Let go of it, now!"

"I think," Matlock calmly griffled, "that it's simply better this way." Using all his strength, he vilishly pulled on the robes, the dregg crying out in twizzly-fear. He pulled again, this time managing to haul it over the oidy trickle of water, hurling it onto the ground behind, as the smaller hare-dregg screamed in high pitched rage.

"Time to move, Mr Hare!" Goole griffled, vilishly scrittling away from the trickle that was now rapidly widening with every blinksnap, turning into a raging torrent that threatened to drown them all. "See what you've gone and started with your hare-brained heroics? 'Tis a bloomin' flood! To the bed, vilish!"

Matlock raced towards the bed, water swirling around his knees, the whole vale turning into a dark churning river, engulfing and sweeping away grillions of fleeing dreggs in its wake. He leapt onto the spinning bed, turning in the dangerously swirling current.

"Save me!" Goole desperately cried from the water, reaching out a wing for Matlock to pull him up onto the bed. "Grillion thank you's, Mr Hare. Thinking old Goole was a stroffed-gonna, there, I really was."

"I'd like to griffle that it was a pleasure," Matlock cried, as a powerful wave crashed over them, "but I'm really not so sure." He shook out his ears, Plusa darting for safety inside his long wet hood. "And I have no idea where it's taking us."

The bed was picking up speed, tossing and turning in the churning waters, the tide hurtling it vilishly along the fast disappearing vale. Trees were being swept into the waters, and the whole roaring mass was filled with grillions of dreggs, their yechus arms, paws and talons desperately reaching out for the bed as it crashed by.

"I'm no seafaring-flapper," Goole cried out, staring straight ahead. "But it looks like it just stops, Mr Hare!"

Matlock wiped the spray from his face and eyes, trying to peer through the raging surf, making out a ganticus tree up ahead, being swept towards a horizon. However, as it reached the edge, it appeared to momentarily stand as if waving one final time, before plunging straight over into a roaring abyss.

"Waterfall!" Matlock cried. "Stop this thing, or we'll be going over!"

Plusa flew from the safety of his hood, whispriffling into his ear. "Go where it takes you, Matlock. It's better that way."

"It's not better at all!" Matlock screamed, as they crashed and hurtled towards the thundering edge. "We're going to be stroffed!"

They were his last griffles before the front of the bed suddenly lurched and tipped, throwing them all straight down into a ganticus falling wall of water, then plunging into swirling mists far below. The bed smashed into a grillion pieces, Matlock, Goole and Plusa all swept vilishly downstream over rocks and roaring rapids.

Matlock urgently fought for breath, struggling to stay afloat, his robes heavy in the water, weighting him down. Twice he thought he might drown, thankfully finding submerged rocks and trees from which to frantically push back up to the surface, lungs bursting from the effort, struggling for breath. The third time he went under, he closed his eyes, waiting to be sucked down deep into the blackened depths below, too juzzpapped to even try and swim anymore, on his inevitable way to his final watery grave in this peffa-glopped place – drowned and stroffed on Trefflepugga Path.

But the black never came. Instead, to his saztaculous relief, he felt the waters calm, realised he was somehow floating back to the surface, gratefully breaking the waters and taking a ganticus, spluttering breath.

"Hurry up, Mr Hare," Gooole's voice called from somewhere close. "Over this way, come on. Shift yourself out of there. It's right proper crumlush over here."

Matlock made one final effort, turning in the water, seeing Goole and Plusa waiting for him on a shallow grassy bank a short distance away. His paws and every muscle in his softulous aching, he took a final few strokes towards the water's edge, this time allowing Goole to return the favour and help him out of the water and onto the bank.

"Right saztaculous, it is here, Mr Hare," Goole happily griffled. "Fair takes me old breath away whenever I sees it."

Matlock lay on the grass, panting heavily, totally peffa-juzzpapped. A warm sun beat down on his face, orange on his closed eyelids. He took more deep breaths before slowly opening them, seeing Goole staring right back down at him.

"Fear not, Mr Hare, we're in a good place, the right place, the briftest place we could ever be. It's all going to be peffa-fuzzcheck from now on, you'll see."

143

"Where are we?" Matlock asked, painfully raising his head and looking round.

Goole helped him fully upright, Plusa issuing calming instructions and cooing over him all the while. "S'called The Cove of Choices, Mr Hare," Goole explained, pointing at the sheer cliff faces that surrounded them on all sides. "And while it might not look much, believe me, this is where the fun really begins."

Matlock looked, eyes gradually clearing and coming back into focus after the swirling waters. The cove was ganticus, completely enclosed by a circle of cliffs, the waterfall they had all plunged over barely visible at the distant far end. In front of him, the water was now still and flat, curiously inviting. Cries of nesting flappers echoed around the high cliff walls. It was, to all extents and purposes, a truly crumlush and peaceful place. "You've been here before?" he griffled.

Goole nodded. "All three times, Mr Hare. So this is me fourth. Mind, I've not always had to nearly stroff meself coming over that glopped-up waterfall. That's a new one on me, that really is. All sorts of ways of getting into here, there are. But every time I've made the trip up the path, sooner or later I've always end up here, in The Cove of Choices."

"Choices?"

"Look around you, Mr Hare, look at the bottom of the cliffs."

Matlock did so, beginning to make out faint outlines of stone arches set into them, with one in particular catching his eye. "It's the arch at the beginning of Trefflepugga Path in Winchett Dale!" he weakly cried, struggling to stand and taking a few pid-pads over to it, pressing the sun-warmed stone with his paws. "It's home, isn't it?" he griffled. "Home's through here, just on the other side!" He began chickling with relief, running his paws all over the blocked stone archway. "It must move, or open somehow."

"Indeed, it does," Goole griffled. "They all do. All these arches open, and each leads to a different dale." He scrittled over to another blocked archway. "This one here leads to Sveag Dale. If this opens, then I'm scrittling back there as vilishly as me glopped-up legs will take me, I can griffle you that, Mr Hare."

Matlock watched as Goole scrittled to yet another archway, his griffles echoing around the quietened cove. "And this one," he griffled, tapping the rock with a wing, "leads to Alfisc Dale – or the dale of drutts, as I griffles it. Goole's hoping that this one'll open, too, so's I can be meeting all the krates. Then Winchett Dale'll open, and I'll be leading 'em all back down. Either way, your old Goole's a peffa-happy Trefflepugga kraark king, because we made it this far without getting stroffed."

"And I suppose," Matlock griffled, "the choice of which arch opens isn't really ours to make, is it?"

Goole clapped his wings. "S'right, Mr Hare, now you're gettin' it! The path'll decide which arch to open, where old Goole's going to be scrittling off to next. Just as it will with you, too."

"But not if you find and answer the riddle," Matlock griffled, anxiously looking for anything unusual in the rocky cliff face; some writing, or and ancient carved tablet whose griffles would only make sense to a majickal-hare. "If you know the answer to the riddle, then Trefflepugga Path has no power over you."

"You're not still believing in that old spuddle, are you?" Goole mocked.

"It must be here somewhere," Matlock griffled, still searching. "We just have to find it. Help me."

Goole scrittled back over to the water's edge, dipping his feet in, holding his face up to the sun. "You're on your own with that one, Mr Hare," he griffled. "I'll take me chances with going wherever the path chooses. 'Tis simply a matter of waiting until it decides."

"But we could find the riddle," Matlock insisted. "Remember, I can read. What would look like a glopped-up mess of old griffly-symbols to you would make peffa-perfect sense to me." He pid-padded over. "Listen, Goole. If we find and solve the riddle…"

"Which has never been found, and never been solved," Goole vilishly corrected him.

Matlock ignored the interruption. "Then *we'd* be the ones who made the choices. Don't you see? You wouldn't have to wait. You could simply scrittle off down to Sveag Dale in a blinksnap." He turned, pointed to the many other archways. "What happens if one of those opens? What happens if you have to go to some totally different dale you've never even seen before, full of twizzly dangers and glopped-up things?"

Goole nodded, slowly turning his soaking wet hat with his wing-tips, chickling softly. "And what makes you think that old Goole would get glopped in a different dale, Mr Hare, eh? Wouldn't hold no twizzles for me, would that. Old Goole's been around too much, always finds a way to keep himself saztaculous at all times, don't you be fretting your hare's head about that." He met Matlock with his one good eye. "I'll take me chances with what the path decides."

"But why?" Matlock griffled, becoming russisculoffed. "When you could take your destiny into your own wings, beat the path and go exactly where you wanted to?"

Goole didn't answer, just sighing, then tipping his tricorn hat over his face and lying down, wings under his head, enjoying the crumlush sun.

"Well, I'm not about to give up!" Matlock angrily griffled, pid-padding back to the cliffs, ignoring Goole's chickles. "I'm going to find this riddle and…"

"And what?" Plusa suddenly griffled, gliding between him and the rock face.

"And solve it, of course" Matlock griffled. "Now please, out of my way, I need to see. It could be ganticus, or even, peffa, peffa-oidy."

"Why would it be here?" she griffled.

"Because this is obviously the centre of the path, Plusa," Matlock griffled as calmly as he could, trying not to become more russisculoffed than he already was. Goole's apathy was glopped-up enough, the peffa-last thing he needed was a sylpha's constant interruptions. "These arches lead to all the dales, so it follows that if you know the answer to the riddle, you could open any one of them. Therefore, the riddle has to be here somewhere."

Plusa considered this. "It could be," she griffled. "And I suppose it would be better for you if it was here."

"It would," Matlock vilishly agreed, searching every crevice with his paws.

"Instead of where it really is, of course."

He stopped, slowly turning to the floating sprite. "Just…griffle that again?"

Her sprite's eyes widened. "I griffled that it would be better for you if the riddle was here, instead of where it really is."

Matlock swallowed hard, wondering if he could believe his long hare's ears. He held out a paw to catch her, but she was too quick at the game, darting from his grip and vilishly rising beyond his reach, turning circles and chickling at him. "Tell me!" Matlock griffled. "You know where the riddle is?"

"I know where it isn't," she griffled. "The reason it's never been found on the path is because…" she waited for him to finish the griffles, watching him all the while.

"Is because," Matlock slowly griffled, mind churning as he gradually worked it out, "it isn't on Trefflepugga Path!"

Plusa looped twice in the air. "Peffa much more fun, and so much better that way. All these creatures looking in the very place they'll never, ever find it." She lowered her voice to a whispgriffle. "The path prefers it that way. 'Tis better for it."

"So where is it, then?" Matlock urgently griffled. "Plusa, you must help me! I need to…"

But before he could finish griffling, an ominous low garrumbloom echoed round the cove, sending panicking flappers screeching and wheeling high into the lid above.

"Hey-ho, here we go!" Goole called excitedly from the water's edge. "It's happening, Mr Hare! The path's made up its mind and the archways are opening!"

Matlock vilishly backed away from the cliffs, shards of sharpened stone falling all around, the ground rumbling and shaking under his feet, churning the stilled waters as gradually the centre one of the arches began to open.

"'Tis Alfisc Dale!" Goole cried out above the ganticus noise. "It's opening!"

Matlock watched the stone centre of the arch slowly slide to one side, seeing an approaching column of wagons, each pulled by puffing and panting krates, their heavy wheels rumbling and skrunching over the stony ground.

"'Tis all me krating pals of drutts!" Goole griffled, his voice peffa-excrimbly in the chaos. "I knew they'd come, Mr Hare! Just knew they would!"

Matlock backed further away as more and more wagons began

to slowly fill the cove. He'd never seen so many krates, their breath shot from the effort of pulling the wagons. He turned to Goole imploringly. "You can't let them do this!" he desperately griffled. "Goole, I'm begging you, please don't let them into Winchett Dale!"

Goole vilishly scrittled over to the wagons. "T'isn't me that has the power to decide that, Mr Hare, 'tis Trefflepugga Path, and no other. It's all out of our paws and wings now." He pointed to the Winchett Dale archway, as it began to shake and rumble, chippings falling as it too slowly slid open. "Looks like I'm away, Mr Hare! Love you to join us, but somehow I think the path may have other plans for you!"

Matlock tried to pid-pad to the wagons, but couldn't move, his legs once again as solid as the surrounding cliffs. He watched in desperation as the archway finished opening, and the first of the wagons began crunching and trundling their way down into Winchett Dale, catching occasional tantalising, cruelly teasing glimpses of the all too familiar landscape, its trees thrashing in the rising winds, as if they seemed to be willing him to try and stop the invasion.

"Goole!" He roared. "Don't do this! It'll be the end for everyone!"

Goole chickled, then triumphantly called out,. "No, Mr hare, 'tis the beginning for Winchett Dale. A new beginning. A time of drutts, and work and saztaculous things. Way I sees it, this is a chance for all of Winchett Dale to improve themselves, be less glopped-up and clottabussed like they normally are. Because you never seemed to bother how clottabussed they were before, did you, Mr Hare, eh? Folk is griffling that it suited you that way, everyone believing in all your majicky-nonsense. These may look like wagons full of old pebbles to you, Mr Hare, but this…this is progress!"

More and more wagons began leaving the cove, heading out under the stone archway. Matlock strained with all his might, trying to move just the oidiest bit, but was utterly stuck fast. He raged, screamed and yelled at Goole, who calmly sat on the last wagon in the line, waiting his turn, chickling at Matlock with the other krates.

Plusa glided in front of him.

"Please, Plusa," he griffled, "now is peffa-definitely *not* the time to griffle me that everything is better this way. Just griffle me the riddle, please! Then I'll be able to stop this!"

"But how do I griffle to you about myself?" she asked.

Matlock blinked twice, taking a short breath and wondering if he'd heard her right amongst the noise and confusion. "You'... *you're* the riddle?"

She twisted in the air. "I am, but I am not. I was, but am no longer."

"Plusa, please," Matlock urged, "for Oramus' sake, just griffle me the riddle!"

"The riddle can't be griffled or read. It has to be found."

"But you just griffled that *you* were the riddle!"

She nodded. "I am, but I am not. I was, but am no more."

"And that's it, is it?" Matlock griffled, as the final wagons began rumbling towards the archway to Winchett Dale. "That's the riddle? 'I am, but I am not. I was, but am no more?'" His mind raced, urgently trying to work it out. "A snowflake!" he griffled. "It's a snowflake! They are, but they're not, because they come from clouds. Then they melt, so they become no more. It's a snowflake, isn't it, Plusa? The answer's got to be a snowflake!"

Plusa shook her head. "It is the right answer, Matlock. But also the wrong answer." She turned to the leaving wagons. "I'm so glad they're all going. Far too peffa-noisy for such a crumlush place like this."

"Plusa!" Matlock begged, "You have to help me! If you're the riddle, then you must know the answer!"

"I am, but I am not…"

"Oh, for Oramus' sake! Please! They'll be gone in a snutch of moments!"

"Good," she griffled. "They're too noisy, and smell peffa-yechus."

"Just griffle me the answer, Plusa!" He anxiously glanced across at the last two wagons, Goole still sitting contentedly on the back of the final one.

"But I *am* the answer, Matlock," Plusa griffled. "I am, and I am not. I was, but am no more. And to find me, you mustn't ever think. It's better that way."

Matlock felt his heart begin to sink, knowing that despite all his briftest efforts, it was going to be too late, Goole's wagon was almost at the archway. "I just don't know what you're griffling about, Plusa."

She nodded. "It's better that way."

"No, it isn't!" Matlock angrily insisted, his whole softulous crying out in rage and frustration. "There's nothing more glopped-up than this, Plusa! Nothing! My crumlush Winchett Dale is about to be overrun with hundreds of krates, and I can't do oidiest thing to stop it!"

She darted down, put a spritely finger across his lips. "Hush, Matlock. You think too much, when you don't need to. To find the answer, you mustn't think. From the briftest of things come the smallest things that visit the darkest places. I am, but I am not."

Goole had dismounted his wagon, now standing under the archway as it trundled through, the ganticus heavy rock-doorway already beginning to slowly slide shut behind him. "Well, I'll be griffling me good-byes, Mr Hare!" he called across, not noticing a small, panting creature vilishly race past him, under the archway, and out into the cove. "And if the path ever lets you return here, and you be needing some drutts, please don't hesitate to look up old Goole. I may even do a special rate for you, Mr Hare! How's that for old friends, eh?"

Goole waved his hat one final time before vilishly scrittling down into Winchett Dale, just a blinksnap before the archway closed with a ganticus rumble that shook the surrounding cliffs.

Matlock cried out, sinking to his knees, finally able to move, freed from the will of the path. He closed his eyes, splashers of rage and frustration streaming down his cheeks. He'd gobflopped, let everyone down, just as surely as he had on the High Plateau. He'd tried and tried, but in the end his peffa-briftest simply wasn't good enough. Trefflepugga Path had beaten him, every pid-pad of the way. It was hopeless, he was hopeless, all was lost.

But then, as he opened his eyes, he became aware of a small creature still vilishly pid-padding towards him across the grass. An oidy, furry and saztaculoulsy familiar creature, getting ever closer, panting heavily, carrying a hawthorn wand in its paw...

"Dripple!" he cried, as the creature finally flung himself at his juzzpapped master, nuzzling its nose in his face, dropping the wand

150

An oidy, furry and saztaculoulsy familiar creature, getting ever closer, panting heavily, carrying a hawthorn wand in its paw…

in his lap. "You found me!" Matlock fell onto his back, beginning to chickle as the excrimbly creature pid-padded all over him. "You pid-padded through the archway!" he griffled, stroking its head. "Surely, you must be the peffa-cleverest dripple in all the dales."

The dripple eagerly nodded , then pointed at the wand in Matlock's lap, ganticussly pleased with itself, a smile bigger and more crumlush than Oramus in the moon breaking out all over its face.

Matlock picked up his old wand, turning it in his paw. "You bought this all the way from the High Plateau?"

The dripple blinked, nodded. "For…you."

Matlock's mouth dropped in shock. "You griffle now?" he griffled, scarcely believing his long hare's ears. "You can *griffle*?"

The dripple nodded again, before turning to pid-pad after Plusa, chasing her around the cove as the two of them played together in the warm sunshine.

Matlock watched for a snutch of moments, turning his wand in his paws, trying out the occasional vroosher he could remember, but getting them wrong. It was as if his memory had gone completely, the griffles for his spells simply not coming at all. The tip of his wand never even began to glow, let alone fizz and hum. He let out a long sigh. Without his driftolubbs the wand was simply just a piece of hawthorn, and while he couldn't quite believe his dripple had gone to such lengths to bring it to him, it may as well have bought Matlock a stroffed tweazle, for all the use it was. However, he still tucked it into his robes alongside Ursula's potion bottle, not wanting to disappoint the loyal little creature, then called them both back over.

"Plusa," he griffled. "I have to griffle this to you one more time. What is the answer to the riddle of Trefflepugga Path? I must know so that I can get back to Winchett Dale."

"But the path wants you to go through that archway," she griffled, pointing to the open archway leading to Alfisc Dale. "You see? It's still open for you, Matlock. It's waiting for you."

The dripple nodded his head earnestly, pointing at the archway. "For…you."

"And is that where I'll find the riddle?" Matlock griffled. "Or even, the answer to the riddle?"

Plusa considered the question carefully. "The answer is

152

everywhere," she griffled. "It comes from everything, because everything has it in it. And the less that you think, the more you'll find it. It lies peffa-close to the path, but not along it. As long as you pid-pad on Trefflepugga Path, you will never find the riddle, or the answer. Leave the path, Matlock. Pid-pad under the archway, begin a new journey. Stop thinking, and see how the briftest, Most Majelicus things become small things joined in darkness. Only then will you have found the answer – but not the riddle."

Matlock shook his head. "I really have no idea what you're griffling about, Plusa."

"I know," she cheerfully griffled. "It's better this way." She vilishly rose into the air. "The previous journey you took along this path changed your destiny from just a normal hare from The Great Beyond to a majickal-hare of the dales. I too, have changed, but not as you did, Matlock. I came from darkness, but now I know light. I was, but am no longer. I wish you well, Matlock."

"Come back!" Matlock called into the lid, watching as she suddenly span three times then darted up and away over the top of the looming cliffs. He took a deep hare's breath, softly griffling "Please, I don't know any of the answers."

His dripple climbed up his robes, hugging his neck before settling in his familiar place in his hood.

"I take it," Matlock griffled, looking over his shoulder, "that means we're going, does it?"

The dripple nodded, pointing to the open stone archway.

"Well, I suppose that at least it gets us off this glopped-up path. Who knows, we might even find the riddle in this Alfisc Dale place, eh?"

The dripple made a short gurgling noise.

"And you can explain to me to just how you learned to griffle along the way."

The dripple held on tight to Matlock's neck, closing its eyes. "For…you."

Matlock tried his briftest to smile, stretching his aching softulous, and after looking around the silent cove one final time, briskly set off under the open stone archway and down towards whatever lay in wait for him in Alfisc Dale.

Fragus, Colley-Rocks
and Zhava

Proftulous wasn't an early riser, ever. Indeed, very few dworps are, preferring instead to sleep off their tweazle-pie excesses for as long as possible, nifferduggling in peffa-yechus beds that most other creatures would pid-pad several dales from, rather than even having to sit on. As such, dalelore history only records one dworp who actually enjoyed getting up early, often to be sighted lump-thumping around, looking to stroff more tweazles most morn'ups. But as he was called Blopple the dworp, his name alone was enough for him to be ignored and largely despised by the rest of the dworping community, let alone his shameful predilection for early rising.

Proftulous, it has to be griffled, led no such life, preferring instead to indulge himself in the time-honoured dworp tradition of nifferduggling in his bed for as long as was feasibly possible under a thick pile of tweazle-pelted blankets, before eventually getting up some time in the afternoon and setting off to find a snutch of the unfortunate creatures for his supper.

So it was with a glopped degree of russisculoftulation that he was awoken the next sun-turn by a loud and insistent hammering on his creaker. Being a dworp, he found it easy to ignore at first, suspecting that someone had the wrong house and would eventually lose interest. But they didn't. The hammering went on, and just wouldn't stop. Curiously, as Proftulous lay in his bed, he became gradually aware that the hammering wasn't purely at his creaker alone, sounding to him as if the whole of the village was being woken up at the same time.

"Scuffling cafferdoggles!" he griffled, lazily lump-thumping out of bed and crossing to the window to peer outside. "What the Balfastulous be going on?" It was bad enough that he hadn't really nifferduggled properly, his crimple having grumbled throughout the night after eating the ganticus tweazle pie cooked by Matlock's majickal driftolubbs, but to be rudely awoken from his glopped-up slumbers was almost intolerable. He wiped away some yechus gloop on the window, peering through the smeared glass.

"This is being most peffa-gobflopped," he griffled, looking out and seeing more krates than he'd ever seen in his tweazle-pie eating life, hammering at what looked like all the creakers of all the houses in Winchett Dale. "'Tis most peffa-gloppflopped and glubbstooled, indeed."

He opened the window, hung out his ganticus head, calling down to the group of krates knocking urgently at his creaker. "You's be making too much hammering noisey stuff!" he griffled. "I's be asking you to leave now. Mr Coat be griffling to me that he's my friend, so if you're not being going, then I'll be griffling to him that's you've all been much waking me up far too peffa-early."

The krates stopped, looking up.

"Out of your sorry glopped-up house!" one griffled. "Now dworp! We have orders to lock up any creature that refuses!"

Proftulous frowned, confused. "What's 'orders', then?"

The krate frowned. "Orders are things you have to obey!"

"What's 'obey'?" Proftulous griffled.

The krate rolled his beady eyes, took a breath. "It means 'do'. To obey is 'to do'. I griffle an order, and you do it – you obey it."

Proftulous considered this. "Like when I orders you to all be going and leaving me alone? And you's not be doing it?"

"I order you not to get smart with me, dworp!" the krate griffled, becoming rapidly russisculoffed. "Leave this house now, and get to the public-griffling in The Great Hall!"

"Why's would I be doing that, when I don't be wanting to?"

"Because it's an order, you dworped-up clottabus!"

"Seems to me," Proftulous observed, "that all this ordering and obeying is just making everyone peffa-russisculoffed. I'm not knowing why you be doing it, I'm really not."

The krate pointed a stubby paw up at the window. "If you refuse to leave your house, dworp, then I shall be forced to break down this glopped-up creaker and take you away to be locked-up for a peffa-long time."

"Well, I don't be wanting that to be happening, either, do I?" Proftulous replied. "Not peffa-much at all, I don't. So why would you be doing that to my creaker? Don't be making even the oidiest sense, you don't."

A small crowd had begun to gather, as creatures and krates vied to see what was going on. Proftulous cheerfully waved to the villagers he knew. "What's be going on?" he called to them.

"We're being made to go to The Great Hall," a wandering-spullitt called back. "Dragged us out of our nifferduggles, these krates have."

"There's a peffa-lot of them," Proftulous griffled. "Where they all be coming from?"

"Trefflepugga Path," the wandering-spullitt griffled. "While we be all nifferduggling last night. They've got wagons, too."

"Wagons? What's them, then?"

"Like houses on wheels, and they moves 'em. Only now they've moved 'em all here, and they're making us do things."

Proftulous closed his window, lump-thumped downstairs and stood, hands on his hips, surveying the glopped-up mess from the previous night. The fire was out now, the majickal driftolubbs just black flaked ashes, the smell of burnt paper and cooked tweazles hanging in the air, filling the small room.

"Oh, Matlock," he softly griffled. "I be being so sorry."

And then he had a sudden thought that appeared to tingle right through his ganticus softulous, much like the extrapluff he'd had at Thinking Lake. He looked behind the curtain where he had so woefully tried to hide the driftolubbs. "All the majicky book things be gone, because I likes to be eating tweazle-pies too much."

The pounding on the creaker started up with renewed vigour. "Out now, Dworp!"

"I's be coming," Proftulous griffled, suddenly noticing something

156

small and flat on the floor, almost lost in the darkness behind the curtain. He stooped down, examining it closely, picking it up, a smile spreading over his ganticus face. "Well, I'll be floured and pastried! 'Tis an oidy driftolubb!" He turned the unexpected find in his paws, wiping away a mirrit from the front cover. "I's be having an extrapluffy something was here, and I's be right."

Ignoring the creaker starting to splinter under constant pounding from outside, Proftulous opened the book, squinting at the mass of written griffles, trying to make just the oidiest sense of any of them. He knew the griffles themselves were on lines, and that the spaces between them divided them into meanings. But short of that, he was completely stuck. But then, as he looked more closely, he very gradually began to see patterns in the griffles, starting to match repeated symbols and shapes. Some griffles were peffa-oidy with just one or two symbols, others contained lots, but it seemed to Proftulous that there were only really a limited number of symbols, simply repeated and then put together in different combinations.

"So that's how Matlock be doing it," he whispgriffled to himself. "That's how he be reading." A mirrit dropped from his ear onto the pages. "I's just be needing to know what these symbols be sounding like, then I's can put them together, muchly." He quickly stuffed the small book into his leather tweazle bag, tied it round his ganticus waist, then lump-thumped to the door, finally opening it.

"Seen sense at last, have we dworp?" the krate asked.

"Don't know," Proftulous griffled. "Has you lost it?"

The krate smiled icily.

"All I can see," Proftulous griffled, "is that there is being far too many krates in Winchett Dale banging on our creakers and making everyone do things."

The assembled crowd of waiting creatures outside cheered and chickled. Proftulous bowed to them, flourishing a ganticus paw.

"Enough of this!" The krate griffled, struggling to keep some sort of order. He pointed to a disidula, caged on the back of a nearby wagon. "Anyone disobeying orders from now on will be locked up like that unfortunate creature over there."

Proftulous waved at the disidula, who waved back. "Morn'up, Fragus," he griffled. "What's you be doing in that cage, then?"

The disidula shrugged. "Nothing much, really. Just thought I'd try it."

"Any good?" Proftulous asked.

"Reasonable," the disidula griffled. "Could be doing with a chair, if I'm honest."

Proftulous turned to the krate, who looked for all the world as if he was about to cracksplode. "Fragus griffles he could be much doing with a chair in there."

The krate began rapidly puffing out his cheeks, as a rising chant of 'Fragus wants a chair!' broke out all round. "Silence!" he screamed at the top of his most officious voice. "You are all to pid-pad to your glopped-up Great Hall this very instant!"

Eventually the chants died down, but only after the krates had been reluctantly forced to fetch a chair, a bowl of niff-soup and a large guzzwort for Fragus, who contentedly and peffa-politely thanked them for being so kind.

The creatures then made their way traditionally slowly into The Great Hall, despite urgent orders barked at them by krates. Once inside, and the all too predictable squabbles about seats, blocked views and why it was that the tweazles always got to sit right at the front were over, Frendeslene Note, robed in his officious finery made his way imperiously up onto the podium that had been set next to a ganticus pile of drutts.

"Creatures of Winchett Dale," he addressed them in his calmest, most reasonable tone. "Welcome to the morn'up of a brand new way of life for us all. A better way. The peffa-briftest way." He shot a warning look at some jart-flappers who were already bored and starting to bliff each other with their wings.

"He started it," one of them moaned.

Note ignored them, indicating the pile of drutts. "This dawn, this new age, this new life, begins with these."

"What, pebbles?" someone griffled from the back. "Don't seem very new to me."

"No, not pebbles," Note corrected. "These are drutts, my good friends."

A stitled-jotta stood. "Are you sure, Mr Boat? They be looking like pebbles to me."

Krates quickly moved in, forcing the stilted-jotta to sit back down.

Note addressed the creature after the krates had returned to their places at the edge of the hall. "Please, just what is it that you do?"

"Do?" the stilted-jotta griffled.

"I mean," Note pressed, "Do you grow anything, or make anything?"

The stilted-jotta thought for a snutch of moments. "I sometimes grows brottle-leaves. Then picks 'em for a crumlush brew by the piff-tosh."

"Good," Note griffled, feeling encouraged. "Peffa-good. And just suppose I knocked on your creaker, and wanted some of your brottle-leaves, what would you do?"

The stilted-jotta looked confused. "Well then, I'd be giving you some, of course, Mr Boat."

"Just give them away?" Note griffled. "And ask for nothing back by return?"

"What's I want 'em back for? I just be giving them to you, didn't I?" The stilted-jotta looked around, seeing everyone equally confused by Note's bizarre griffles. "I'd be a peffa-clottabus to ask for 'em back, wouldn't I? T'would be a glopped-up waste of time."

The creatures in the hall all nodded their heads in agreement.

"But," Note griffled, pointing once more at the pile of drutts, "just imagine I gave you one of these for your brottle-leaves."

Which really threw the stilted-jotta. "What's I be wanting a pebble for? I've got grillions of 'em in me garden already. Honestly, Mr Boat, I not be following your pebbly-griffles one iody bit."

Note took a breath, folded his arms. "I can see that perhaps that I might be going an oidy bit too vilishly for you." He turned to rest of the hall. "Does anyone else understand what I'm griffling about?"

All eyes stared back in unblinking silence.

"Then let me try and explain this peffa, peffa-simply. These," he pointed again at the pile, "are drutts. Not pebbles. Drutts. Pebbles can *become* drutts, but only if they are personally and officiously given to you by a krate. Now, I really don't see what could be at all confusing about that."

Just complete uncomprehending silence from the hall.

Note pressed on, regardless. "From this sun-turn, you will all work for drutts. The more work you do, the more drutts you will be given. Then you can use the drutts to get you things."

"Like what?" someone called out.

"Like brottle leaves," Note griffled, keen to make the point. "Instead of merely giving them away, you can now get a drutt in exchange for them."

"Well that's me out, then," the voice shot back. "Don't like brottle-leaf brew. Never has. Yechus stuff."

"But not *just* brottle-leaves," Note urged, not quite believing just how peffa-difficult explaining a relatively simple concept had become. "Other things. When you make and grow things from now on, people will give you drutts for them, so you can get other things with those drutts." He turned to a bloated-vellup which was trying its peffa-briftest not to fall back into nifferduggles. "You sir, do you grow anything?"

"It's 'Miss', actually," she griffled, yawning. "I'm big boned and I'm bloated, what do you expect?"

"My peffa-apologies," Note vilishly griffled. "Do you grow anything, Miss?"

"No."

"Nothing?"

"No."

"Nothing at all? You grow absolutely nothing?"

"S'right."

Note cleared his throat, nervously scratching at his whiskers, trying to think. "Well, do you make anything, then?"

"Like what?"

"Anything? Something?"

"Anything, something like what?"

Note grimaced slightly, mind-racing for an example. "Cakes or pies?"

"No."

"Guzzwort?"

"No."

"Niff-soup?"

"No."

"*Anything* food related at all? Just even the oidest, oidiest thing?"

The bloated-vellup shook her head.

"Chairs, tables, candles, clothes, shoes?"

"No."

"So, what you're griffling is that you don't actually make or do anything at all?"

She held up a bloated paw, signalling for silence and shutting her eyes while she thought peffa-carefully about the question for quite some time. Eventually, she turned back to Note. "Yes."

Note seized on the admission, relieved. "You *do* do something?"

"No," she griffled. "I mean 'yes', as in agreeing to your question about me *not* making or doing anything."

Chickles rippled around the hall, immediately hushed by the officious attention of the watching krates.

Note waited for silence, cleared his throat and adopted a more officious tone. "I think we're becoming rather distracted and confused this morn'up. The plain facts of the matter are these. From now on, everyone will work for drutts. You will exchange things for drutts. Everything, no matter what it is, will cost you drutts. And the harder you work, the more drutts you will have. So it follows – I would assume, even to the most peffa-clottabussed amongst us – the harder you work, the more things you will be able to get." He took a deep breath, then griffled, peffa-slowly, "Now, does everyone understand?"

"So, what's all them pebbles for?" a lone voice griffled out.

It took far longer than Frendeslene Note had anticipated for the drutt to finally drop with the clottabussed residents of Winchett Dale. Endless examples had to be given, countless explanations gone over, time and time again. It seemed to him that of all the dales he had visited, Winchett Dale had suffered the most peffa-ganticus brain drain of them all. He found it almost incomprehensible that they'd somehow managed to live their lives fairly contentedly up until this point, merely by giving things to each other for no rewards whatsoever. Indeed, the very concept of a reward for doing things had glubbstooled the whole hall completely; with creatures totally unable to see the merit of being given anything in return for things they had done well, or merely given to others. And yet, he was forced to admit, somehow they *had* got by for countless generations, simply by living without rewards or wealth. He thanked all his lucky stars in Oramus' twinkling-lid that at least Goole and Serraptomus had quickly seen the opportunity in drutts. And whilst an oidy part of him despised them both for their greed (and indeed, applauded Winchett Dale for its glopped-up apathy) their drutt-hungry ambitions were vitally necessary for his plans. He *would* change Winchett Dale for the better. It was his chosen duty, and a most officious one, at that. The way of drutts would simply take time. Note knew all too well that in a snutch of moon-turns, the old ways would be gone, and a new dale of honest labour would rise to take its place. It was change, and nothing could ever pid-pad in its way.

Finally, with the drutts explained as best as he could, Frendeslene Note moved on. "I now want to griffle to you all about another peffa-important matter." He ignored the moans and complaints, knowing that the longer he kept them all in the hall, the more they'd all want to leave, hence his officious logic in leaving his most controversial change until last, knowing full well they'd be more likely to agree to anything, simply to get back to their houses. "Tis the matter of this Great Hall."

"Excuse me, but what's them big pile of pebbles for?" someone called out.

Note pressed on, trying his briftest to insert some cheerful urgency in his voice. "I won't keep you long, as I know most of you will be peffa-keen to get out there and start earning all your drutts…"

"What for?" another voice griffled.

Note sighed. "Look, whoever it is, please stop these glopped-up interruptions! If it continues, you'll be locked up like the disidula was this morn'up!"

"He's got a chair!" someone griffled.

"And niff soup! And guzzworts!" another added. "Living the life of Oramus in there, he is. Least he's not stuck in here."

Note turned to his krates, as once again commotion broke out in the hall. "Is this true?" he hissed to the nearest. "The disidula has a chair, niffs and guzzworts?"

The unfortunate krate stepped forward, bowing awkwardly. "It was the only way we could get them to come here, Your Officiousness. The big-eared dworp was making it all peffa-unpleasant for us."

"I'll have griffles with you later," Note warned, as the other krates gradually restored order. He cleared his throat in what he hoped would be his most officious and important manner, addressing the rest of the hall. "Now this may come as something of a shock to you all. It may even make you feel an oidy bit twizzly."

"Is it about the 'something'?" a spotted-pelter in the third row asked.

"In a manner of griffling, yes, it is. My krates have arrived in Winchett Dale with two peffa-important jobs to do. The first is to introduce the way of drutts that will make us all a hard-working and caring community…"

"What's 'drutts', then?"

Note ignored the griffles pressing on. "…and the second thing is to protect us all from the peffa-twizzly 'something'."

A bald-hullitt shot up a paw. "I know!" he eagerly suggested. "We could all be throwing them pebble things at it! That why you bought them all here, is it? We be chucking them all at it!"

Note counted to five inside his head before continuing. "Friends, it would take more than pebbles to stop it."

"But you griffled they was 'drutts' just now," the stilted-jotta griffled. "Honestly, I haven't been as confused as this in all my sun-turns."

"Please," Note pleaded, desperation clearly audible in his griffles. "Peffa, peffa-please, just listen to me. The drutts can help us. We need to pull down this glopped-up hall and build a new one in its place. A bigger hall, a greater Great Hall – a safer Great Hall. A place where the whole of Winchett Dale can hide when the 'something' makes its yechus way here. A hall of stone, not wood. A stronger hall, capable of withstanding a grillion 'somethings' for a grillion moon-turns." He took a breath. "Now I know this will come as a twizzly shock. No doubt you all have shindinculous and excrimbly memories of many saztaculous times in this hall…"

"Not really," the bloated-vellup griffled out.

"Well, maybe not you, Miss," Note griffled. "But I'm sure many of us here have some." He paused for a snutch of moments, surveying the sea of blank faces. "Not even…one of you?"

"Methinks that we's all thinking that 'tis a crumlush idea, this new hall of yours," the bloated-vellup griffled. "Better than your glopped-up pebble one, anyway. Was proper glubbstool, that."

Note looked at the faces, stunned. He hadn't expected their compliance for a moment. Here they were, a supposedly happy community of creatures, without the first idea about trade or wealth – and worse, seemed to have no problems in letting go of the past, either. The hall obviously meant nothing to them, and held no special places in any of their hearts. It simply seemed absolutely incomprehensible.

"So there's no one here who objects?" he asked incredulously.

A short-winged flifthropp raised its wing.

"You have an objection?" Note asked, heartened that even if it was the only creature who had the oidiest sense of the importance of preserving the past, at least there was one.

"Can we go now?" it griffled, a suggestion immediately seized on by all the other creatures.

"But surely there must be things to cherish in here?" Note called out above the commotion. "Memories and traditions, reminders of times past and with loved ones?"

The bloated-vellup confirmed his worst fears. "Just get on and build us a new hall," she griffled. "Sounds crumlush to us."

"Ah, but that's where you're not quite understanding," Note griffled. "When you griffle 'build us a new hall', what's actually going to happen is this; *you're* going to build the new hall, each and every one of *you*, by all working peffa-hard. There'll be lots to do; breaking down this old hall, fetching stone and building the new one. And at the end of each sun-turn, I will personally and officiously give you each a drutt for all your hard work."

"What's a 'drutt', then?" someone griffled.

At which point, pushed beyond the utmost limits of all his peffa-officiousness, Note finally lost his temper. "No one is to griffle another griffle!" he barked, silencing the entire hall. "Never in all my time as First Officer of Officious Krating for all Districts of the Majickal Dales have I encountered such a glopped-up and peffa-clottabussed collection of imbecilic fools! From now on, there will be drutts. There will be hard work. No more lying around nifferduggling all morn'up. No more giving things away. Winchett Dale will change, and you will all just have to get used to it. Anyone clottabussed enough to disobey will be locked up. And there will peffa-definitely be no more chairs if you are!" He scanned the hall, waiting for oidiest response. "You have this sun-turn to return to your houses and get them cleaned peffa-thoroughly. My krates will inspect them all this even'up. Then you will each be given jobs to do building the new Great Hall. Do I make myself clear?"

A welted-spottle raised its paw.

Note sighed. "Has this got anything to with drutts? Only I'm not going through it all again."

The welted-spottle shook its head. "No, Mr Boat, 'tis not be being about the drutts, I's be understanding all that."

"Thank Oramus for that," Note griffled. "At least one of you has finally got the point."

"I was just wondering, though," the welted-spottle griffled, "what the ganticus pile of pebbles be for?"

It didn't take more than a snutch of moments to empty The Great Hall, the creatures practically stampeding through the large creaker, knocking chairs and krates flying as they did so. Note watched in utter dismay, knowing all too well that the last thing on their glopped-up, clottabussed minds was to return home and vilishly begin cleaning them – they simply wanted to get out. And yet whilst the drutt situation was one they couldn't even begin to grasp, at least his plans to build a new Great Hall had gone seemingly without the oidiest hitch or objection, though he fully anticipated griffling-moans and grumbles when the creatures were actually forced to begin working on the process the following morn'up. He wondered if he shouldn't have his krates prepare more cages, as he feared it wouldn't be long before locking creatures away was the only way for them to see sense and obey.

The ganticus-eared dworp was becoming something of a problem, too. Popular with the other creatures, and responsible for the glopped-up locking up of the disidula, Note wondered if caging the dworp as soon as possible would be sufficient enough to discourage the others from such futile acts of defiance. He would give it some thought, more time to decide.

"Some things," he quietly griffled to himself, "simply take time. To put a paw wrong at this stage, to take the wrong pid-pads, could be peffa glubbstooled, indeed." He turned to the remaining krates in the hall and began barking orders at them. "Bring the rest of the drutts in here! Organise a guarding rota. The rest of you, scour the area for all the colley-rocks you can possibly find. We're going to garrumbloom the lot of them into grillions of oidy pieces! We're going to need more drutts!"

Proftulous lump-thumped from The Great Hall and encountered for the first time in a peffa long time something unusual – the morn'up. Unused to being awake at such an hour, his immediate reaction after the public-griffling was to go straight back to his glopped-up bed for more nifferduggles. However, he also realised that he'd got to the point where even if he'd wanted to, lying under a tweazle-pelted blanket just wouldn't allow him to get back to nifferduggles. He was too awake, and also far too excrimbly to be secretly carrying the last remaining majickal driftolubb around with him in his leather tweazle bag. There was, he half-reluctantly admitted to himself, little point in returning home.

As he watched the others leave the hall, he saw that some were pid-padding straight to the Winchett Dale Inn on the opposite side of the square. There were times, he griffled to himself, when a morn'up guzzwort or two were probably required, and after the glubbstooled public-griffling about pebbles and new halls, this was peffa-definitely one of them.

Fragus the caged disidula had been wheeled into the square, there to be guarded by four officious krates.

"Morn'up, Fragus," Proftulous griffled. "Still there, then?"

"Where else would I be?" Fragus griffled. "Did I miss much?"

Proftulous shook his head. "Something about pebbles, Fragus."

"Pebbles?"

"S'right. And how having them is going to be making ourselves a saztaculous new Great Hall."

Fragus scratched the side of his face. "Well, that's a peffa-new one on me, Proftulous. Never heard such glopped-up griffles. You off to the inn for a guzzwort?" He passed his mug through the bars above the guarding krates heads. "I'd get one meself, but these here krates are being all too officious about keeping me in here."

Proftulous took the mug, turning to the nearest krate, who was already looking an oidy bit uncomfortable. "P'raps you could be thinking about letting Fragus out to gets himself a guzzwort, Mr Krate."

The krate looked at his companions, all beginning to get twizzly at the thought of an irate dworp being so close to them. He cleared his throat. "Will he come straight back?"

Proftulous looked at Fragus. "You be wanting to coming straight back here, Fragus?"

Fragus shrugged. "Might do. Depends."

"He griffles," Proftulous unnecessarily informed the krate, "that it be a 'depending' situation."

"I know," the krate griffled, grinding his teeth, "I heard every griffle."

"Well, why you's be asking me, then?" Protfulous griffled, confused.

The krate had a hushed conversation with the others, whispgriffling and nodding their heads. While there was no way they wanted to upset the dworp, they couldn't possibly risk letting the disidula go, leaving Note to discover an empty cage. In all their many moon-turns of locking up hundreds of creatures in many dales, they'd never quite encountered a situation as gobflopped as this before.

It took an extrapluff from Proftulous to resolve matters. He cleared his throat, feeling suddenly rather important and clever, as an oidy mirrit dropped from the end of his sleeve into Fragus' waiting guzzwort mug. "I's be having a suggestion to be putting forward to you's all," he importantly griffled.

The krates broke from their huddle, turned and listened.

"I's be thinking," Proftulous griffled, "that if you's be wheeling this wagon right up next to the window of the inn, then I's can be passing Fragus his guzzwort straights to him, so he's not be having to be getting off his chair and out of your cagey-thing, which methinks he quite likes to be in, anyways."

Fragus nodded. "Fuzzcheck griffles, Proftulous. Everyone's be happy with that. Now let's get this wagon shifted to the inn!"

Which duly happened, the krates having no solution of their own. So it was that with Fragus happily in position by the window, Proftulous bowed his ganticus head and entered the inn. Though it was far from the expected scene of guzzworty merriment that greeted him inside. Indeed, it seemed to Proftulous that it all felt rather glubbstool, and worse, he noticed that no one even had a guzzwort. Undeterred, he lump-thumped to the bar. Even Slivert Jutt, the normally jovial, ever-smiling and chickling landlord seemed rather glopped-up.

"Morn'up, Slivert," Proftulous loudly announced. "I'll be having two of the guzzworts, please. One's for me, and one be for Fragus. But we needs to be passing it to him through the window, so's he can be drinking it on his chair in the cagey-thing."

Slivert Jutt shook his head and shrugged his hairy shoulders. "Got's ourselves a problem with the guzzworts, my friend," he replied. "I's not allowed to just give it away anymore. You has to be giving me a drutt for it."

Proftulous thought for a snutch of moments, trying to remember what a drutt was. "One of those pebbles?" he griffled. "I has to be giving you a pebble for it?"

"Well, two, actually, Proftulous, on account of the fact that you's be wanting two guzzworts, you see."

Proftulous frowned. "Two pebbles?" It simply didn't begin to make even the oidiest bit of sense. "And do you really be wanting two pebbles, Slivert?"

"No. I gots enough pebbles at home, methinks."

"Well then, 'tis all being peffa-glopped up, methinks," Proftulous griffled. He turned to the others. "That be why you all not be drinking of the crumlush guzzworts, is it? Because you don't be having any pebbles?"

The others nodded, mumbling and groaning.

"But we never had to gives anything for guzzworts," Proftulous griffled. "Never in much evernesss, ever, has we had to be doing that."

Slivert Jutt nodded. "I know, Proftulous, but 'tis this new way

168

of Mr Coat. I can't be giving any guzzworts to anyone unless they gives me a drutt first. 'Tis simply how it is from this sun-turn. It's all changed."

"Then change," Proftulous griffled, beginning to get russisculoffed, "is peffa-clotabussy, methinks. And me also thinks we should all be getting together and stroffing it!" He banged a ganticus fist on the bar, turning to the others and raising his voice. "Then when it be stroffed, we's all going to cook and eat a ganticus change-pie, so it's all be gone, and we won't be needing pebbles and change ever again!"

"I think," came some officious griffles from somewhere behind, "that perhaps I could be of some assistance, good creatures?"

All turned to see Serraptomus, dressed in tweeds and scarf in the far corner of the darkened inn, the only creature who was actually drinking a guzzwort.

Proftulous peered into the corner. "Serraptomus? What's you be doing in here? Especially when you's should be doing all your officious duties with the other krates?"

Serraptomus sighed. "Alas, good creatures, I am no longer your most peffa-important and officious krate. Mr Frendeslene Note has seen fit to relieve me of my krating responsibilities."

"I not being surprised," Proftulous griffled. "You was being so gobflopped at it."

Serraptomus tried his briftest not too look too crestfallen by the ganticus dworp's griffles. "'Tis a cruel blow," he griffled, "when one gives one's whole life to the servitude of a community, and then is cast out in a single sun-turn without the oidiest thought given to my welfare."

Proftulous considered this, then nodded. "Yep," he griffled, turning his back. "You probably be right."

"But good creatures," Serraptomus griffled, an oidy edge of desperation breaking in his voice. "We can all still be friends, can't we? Just because I'm no longer officious, doesn't mean we can't be friends, does it? Look," he indicated the neatly stacked pile of drutts on the table in front of him, "I can exchange these for guzzworts for you all. I can be doing that. Then you can all be my friends. *We* can all be friends, can't we?"

"But I just be wanting two guzzworts," Proftulous griffled. "Don't knows I want another friend."

"Then I'll get you three, or four guzzworts," Serraptomus eagerly offered. "All of you. You just have to sit here and drink them with me, as friends; my saztaculous and crumlush new friends."

Proftulous turned to the other creatures, lowered his griffles. "I's be thinking 'tis the only way we'll be getting any guzzworts."

Serraptomus played his trump card. "And I can also be griffling to you all about the 'something'. For I know exactly what it is. Frendeslene Note griffled me all about it. If you have guzzworts with me, I'll griffle you all I know about it."

The creatures reluctantly agreed, sitting at the table, as Slivert fetched them their guzzworts in exchange for Serraptomus' drutts, the pile beginning to go down rather vilishly as he regaled them with all his description of the peffa-twizzly 'something'.

"It has grillions of yechus eyes," he enthusiastically griffled, making shadows on the wall, "and two ganticus paws with a glopped up mouth on each end. It never nifferduggles, either, so it can come for you whenever it wants. It's stroffed grillions of creatures across all the majickal dales, and it can live for a moon-turn of all eternities."

Proftulous and the others finished their drinks as one. "Well, thanks for that, Serraptomus," he griffled. "We's all be going, now."

Serraptomus' mouth hung open. "You're not…you're not all twizzly about the 'something'?"

Proftulous shrugged his ganticus shoulders. "Don't rightly think we are, Serraptomus, no. Thanking you for the guzzworts, though."

"But I don't understand," Serraptomus griffled. "When Frendeslene Note griffled to you about the 'something' the other even'up, you were all most peffa-twizzly."

Proftulous nodded. "Well, see, that's because Mr Coat's being an officious krate, isn't it? Whereas you's not being one anymore, Serraptomus. So's we don't gets twizzly about anything you griffle anymore, do we?"

The others all agreed, standing to leave; a chorus of chairs scraping loudly on the stone floor.

"Please," Serraptomus griffled, trying his briftest not to sound as lonely as he felt. "You can't go. You have to stay. We're friends,

"It has grillions of yechus eyes," he enthusiastically griffled, making shadows on the wall, "and two ganticus paws with a glopped up mouth on each end.

that's what we agreed. We'd all be friends while we sat here. Here," he called Slivert over, vilishly ordering more guzzworts from his depleted pile of drutts, "Sit back down, and I'll tell you something else that's peffa, peffa-secret."

The creatures sat, cheerfully accepting another free guzzwort.

"So what's being your peffa-secrety thing?" Proftulous griffled, after passing Fragus his drink through the open window.

Serraptomus lightly bliffed the side of his nose. "Something really saztaculoulsy peffa, peffa-secret that I can only really griffle to…friends."

Proftulous and the others looked around the inn. "Well, they don't appear to be any here, Serraptomus."

"You!" Serraptomus griffled, trying to rein in his russisculoftulation. "You're my friends, all of you!"

"Are we?" Proftulous replied, confused. "Well, what's being the peffa-secrety thing, then?"

"Only if you griffle that you're all my briftest friends," Serraptomus griffled, arms folded, looking them each in the eye. "And that I'm the briftest ex-officious krate, ever. And that everyone was wrong to chickle at me at krating-school when I became officious, because actually I am saztaculous, and they were all wrong and peffa-glopped-up to think that way. And that Frendeslene Note is glopped-up, too, and you'd rather have me back as your officious krate, and not him, and if anything, I should be made First Officer for Officious Krating in all the Dales, and not him, because I am much brifter. Only if you griffle all that, will I tell you the secret."

There was a pause as Serraptomus searched their faces for just the oidiest sign of compliance or understanding.

"Tis a muchly peffa-lot to be remembering," Proftulous confessed. "I thinks I've forgotten most of it already. What be right at the beginning of it?"

It took another two guzzworts each before the creatures had all slowly repeated the griffles, and although Serraptomus' drutts pile had disappeared, he thought the bargain to be a most saztaculous one, as finally he had heard the griffles he had so desperately craved and wanted to hear for so many years. Perhaps, for all his life. It didn't really even matter that it was only a guzzworted snutch of glopped-up creatures griffling them, the point for Serraptomus was that they were griffling them. His krate's heart swelled with pride at each of the mumbled griffles, and he almost felt an oidy bit eyesplashy, wishing in all the world that his mahpa and pahpa, brothers and sisters, together with every creature and krate that had ever thought of him as clottabussed and glopped-up were there to hear them, too. Finally, Serraptomus knew that he had succeeded, and if only for the oidiest moment in his lifetime, some creatures were prepared to griffle that he was the briftest krate, ever…

"So what be the secrety-thing?" Proftulous asked after they'd finished.

"Aha, my peffa-dearest new friends, let me griffle all to you. But remember, not a griffle of this must leave this inn."

"You might 'ave to shut the window, then," Fragus called from outside. "I can hear every griffle from here. Peffa-entertaining it is, too. Had a right chickleful, I have."

The window was duly closed, and Serraptomus beckoned them all closer, lowering his voice to just a whispgriffle. "When Frendeslene Note first arrived, he was bought to this dale by a glopped-up singing Trefflepugga-kraark. The first thing Note did was to come straight to me, tell me of the changes he had planned for Winchett Dale, then ask me to call the public-griffling, but under no circumstances was I to let Matlock know."

"Tis why he wasn't there!" Proftulous griffled, probably far too loudly, as the others round the table quickly hushed him.

Serraptomus continued. "Note told me that he was going to griffle to you all about the arrival of the twizzly 'something', then make Matlock leave Winchett Dale, so that all the other krates could come down Trefflepugga Path unopposed, bringing their drutts with them."

"But that's not all secrety," Proftulous complained, looking round. "That's being what's already happened."

"True," Serraptomus agreed, "but here's the secret bit," he beckoned the creatures in closer, their faces less than a mirrit's leg from his. "Some of those wagons are loaded with Trikulum, and he's going to get all the colley-rocks in Winchett Dale and garrumbloom them all up into grillions of drutts."

173

"But why's he going to be doing that?" Proftulous whispgriffled, Serraptomus recoiling from the peffablast of Proftulous' yechus breath. "Sorry," he apologised. "Ates meself a ganticus tweazle-pie last even'up, and it be making me griffle-hole all glopped."

"I don't know why he's going to garrumbloom all the colley-rocks. All he would griffle to me is that they're too dangerous, and would make his plans go gobflopped."

"Colley-rocks?" Proftulous griffled. "Are you sure? They's just being rocks what griffles a bit. I can't be seeing what makes them be dangerous and twizzly."

Serraptomus shrugged. "And I haven't the oidiest idea, either, good friend. T'was simply what Note griffled to me. Colley-rocks are dangerous, and they're all soon be stroffed and garrumbloomed into a grillion pieces, never to griffle again."

With guzzworts finished, no more secrets to be heard, and all the drutts spent, it was time to leave, Proftulous lump-thumping outside, waving good-bye to Fragus. He noticed that the caged and contented disidula was now wearing slippers, and an oidy table had been put into the cage too, complete with a rather fetching pot-plant on top.

"Be starting to look right crumlush in there, Fragus," he griffled through the bars, the guarding krates stepping aside to avoid any unpleasantness with a potentially guzzworted dworp.

Fragus nodded. "Everyone's been tidying their homes and finding things they not really be needing, then bringing 'em to me. I think Mrs Barchspruttle be bringing me some curtains soon. Where you off to now, then?"

"Might gets meself some tweazles," Proftulous griffled. "Heard there's being a new nest of them up in Wand Woods. Grillions of them up there, I reckons."

"Well you has yourself a peffa-crumlushed sun-turn, Proftulous," Fragus griffled, thanking a young whillup who had just passed him a side-handled gergle-brush through the bars.

"I will," Proftulous griffled, lump-thumping away. He left the village, crossing the River Winchett and heading along the wooden walkway over Grifflop Marshes. The morn'up was cold, but bright. Wading fliffthropps broke from the watery reeds, greeping at the intruder, before flying into the lid to play with drifting leaves above.

At the end of the walkway he entered Wand Wood, finding to his quiet surprise that he could move more quickly, feeling lighter on his ganticus feet. He wondered if the guzzworts had helped, or his softulous was finally over its crimple-grumbling after eating the ganticus tweazle-pie. Whatever the reason, the more he lump-thumped through the wood, the more shindincous he felt.

He had, of course, a plan. And even that surprised him, as for the first time in his life it had nothing to do with tweazles whatsoever. He was going to Matlock's garden to rescue the colley-rocks before Note and his krates could garrumbloom them all into grillions of drutts, feeling it was the peffa-least he could do to make amends with his briftest friend after burning all the majickal driftolubbs. He didn't know when Matlock would return, or even if he ever would, but one thing in Proftulous' mind was certain, he would save those colley-rocks.

When he finally lump-thumped into the walled garden, he was peffa-relieved to see the rocks still there. There were four, each in separate corners of the garden, gently sunning themselves in the autumn light, utterly at peace with the world. Proftulous went to Matlock's old potting-shed, finding a large sack, before vilishly gathered the protesting colley-rocks together and putting the first three inside.

"Steady on, dworp!" the final colley-rock griffled. "What in Balfastulous do you think you're up to?"

"If I don't be hiding you, you're all going to be garrumbloomed," Proftulous griffled. "Some krates have come with houses on wheels full of cracksplosey stuff."

"That'll be Trikulum," the colley-rock griffled. "Peffa-dangerous, that is."

"I knows," Proftulous agreed. "But what's you don't know is that you'll be stroffed into drutts."

"Of course we know," the rock griffled. "I griffles it all to the majickal-hare before he went pid-padding up Trefflepugga Path. Us stones and rocks have been griffling about it for many moon-turns."

"Matlock knew?" Proftulous griffled.

The colley-rock sniffed. "Don't think he was really listening, dworp. He seemed to have too much other gloppedness on his mind. Kept on griffling on about how he wasn't really that majickal. And that wasn't really news to us, either. Sits out here, he does, right on top of me, griffling on about how juzzpapped he is, and how he's gone and gobflopped with his vrooshers in front of everyone. Well, there's only so much a rock can really griffle, isn't there? All got an oidy bit dull in the end."

"But he's Matlock," Proftulous griffled, anxious to protect his friend. "He's the briftest majickal-hare, ever."

"Really?" the colley-rock sighed. "Then where is he now, then? Listen dworp, what you've got to get your ganticussly clottabussed head around is this; I've been in this garden for grillions of moon-turns, and in that time, I've seen more majickal-hares come and go than you've had tweazle-pies. One more, or one less, don't make a difference to me."

"But Matlock makes a peffa-ganticus difference to me," Proftulous insisted.

"That's as maybe, but not to us. See, after a while, they all seem to blend into one. Can't even remember their names any more. It's just the same routine, over and over. Majickal hare arrives with hare from The Great Beyond, hare becomes an apprentice, hare becomes a majickal-hare, hangs around doing a few vrooshers, hare gets old, hare disappears, new majickal-hare arrives with another hare from The Great Beyond. It's the peffa-ultimate hare-circle of endless tedium for a colley-rock like me. Nothing ever changes, you see? Just the hare thing, over and over. I mean, just how many times do you think I've had to sit out here, listening to the majickal-hare trying to teach the apprentice how to read? Honestly, dworp, it'd do your fissures in."

Proftulous almost gasped. "So's you know how to be reading?"

"Of course," the colley-rock replied, yawning. "Heard it done that many times, I could save the majickal-hare the bother, teach the apprenctice myself in half the time."

Proftulous seized his chance, vilishly taken the iody driftolubb from his pouch, rubbing glopped-up tweazle gloop from the cover and showing it to the rock. "Then could you be teaching me how to be reading this?"

The colley-rock looked at the driftolubb. "Well, well," he griffled.

"Now how's you been coming about this, dworp?"

Proftulous pointed to the scribed griffles on the cover. "What's it be saying?"

"*Majickal Dalelore (Volume 68 – revised edition)*" The colley-rock took a rumbling breath. "The oidiest driftolubb of them all, and some griffle that's it's also the most peffa-important. I haven't seen one of these in a peffa-long time. I don't know much about driftolubbs, dworp, just the things what I've overheard when majickal-hares have been griffling out here. But what I do know is this, that the driftolubbs themselves are rumoured to reflect the ways of all the dales, and sometimes it's the smallest things that can make the most ganticus differences. Open it, show me. I've never had meself the chance to read one of these."

But before Proftulous could even show the colley-rock the first page, he heard the officious voices of krates approaching from the woods. "I's be extrapluffing that we needs not to be here, Mr Rock," he griffled.

"But I thought only majickal-hares can extrapluff?" the colley-rock griffled.

"Not anymore," Proftulous griffled, stuffing the rock into the sack with the others and heading out of the garden as vilishly as he could. "Not anymore."

He lump-thumped around the edge of the woods, the sack of muffled and protesting colley-rocks over his shoulder, stooping down and hiding behind bushes, trees and shrubs to avoid the party of krates sweeping the woods in a line, making their way slowly and inevitably towards Matlock's cottage.

"Looks like I'd be getting to you all just in time," he whispgriffled, waiting until the krates had passed, then cutting back into the woods behind them, realising that for all he was doing, he didn't feel twizzly at all. Not the oidiest bit. If anything, he felt suddenly saztaculous, more than able to cope to with outsmarting a snutch of krates, part of him even enjoying the game.

A while later, as the krates began making their way back after their fruitless search of the cottage gardens, Proftulous simply climbed a large oak tree, sitting in the heavy branches, watching the oblivious krates pass by underneath. A snutch of moments later, he opened the sack and set the colley-rocks beside him in the crook of the tree.

"Oh my fissures!" one gasped, looking down. "How did we get up here?"

"I climbs it," Proftulous proudly griffled. "To be escaping of all them krates, and keeps you all safe. I never been climbing a tree before, have I?"

"But…you're too ganticus and glopped-up to climb anything!" the rock griffled, getting peffa-twizzly.

"I know," Proftulous griffled. "But I must be doing it, or else we wouldn't all be being up here, would we?"

"So this is the 'big-plan', is it?" the colley-rock Proftulous had griffled to in the garden asked. "We're going to hide halfway up an oak with a tree-climbing dworp for the rest of our stony lives? Probably would have preferred to have been garrumbloomed into drutts, personally. I mean, at least it'd be a change, wouldn't it?"

"But isn't being up a tree a change?" Proftulous griffled. "There be lots of different and crumlush things to be looking all around at."

"Still just sitting though, isn't it? Just on a lump of wood in the air, that's all."

"Well," Proftulous griffled, "I's be peffa-sorry if that's how you be feeling about it, but that's what we're doing until it gets dark, and I can find you all a safe place for hideys. But in the meantime," he reached back into the tweazle-pouch and bought out the driftolubb, "you can be teaching me just how to be reading this."

So it was that Proftulous the dworp, the most clottabussed creature in the most peffa-clottabussed of all the dales began to learn how to read, the colley-rock teaching him the sound for each of the symbols, Proftulous gradually putting them together to form the griffles. The colley-rock found the situation peffa-extraordinary, and not just the fact of being halfway up an oak-tree with a dworp, more it was the sheer vilishness with which his ganticus, eager student appeared to be learning. Proftulous only had to be told a sound once to remember it. As soon as he had griffled the griffle out loud, he remembered that too, his face peffa-excrimbly as he vilishly found the same griffle on other pages.

"You're learning things that it takes your average majickal-hare apprentice many, many moon-turns, dworp," the colley-rock griffled.

Proftulous gave the rock a hug. "I's be thinking that's because I be having the briftest teacher, ever."

"Well, it's peffa-kind of you to be griffling that," the rock griffled, "but I honestly not be knowing any creature that has learned to read so vilishly. Even your hare friend, the last one, took peffa-ages to learn."

Proftulous' eyes widened. "Then I's be beating Matlock?" he griffled. "Maybe's I can be learning how to be all majickal, too, and do saztaculous vrooshers and be the only majickal-dworp in all the dales?"

"Well, let's take it one pid-pad at a time," the colley-rock griffled, turning Proftulous' attention back to the book, watching impressed as the ganticus dworp followed each line with his glopped-up paw, clearly reading from the ancient pages, his mouth silently moving to the rhythm of the griffles upon them.

Proftulous had read the first nine pages by the time it got dark. As dusk settled in the woods, it was time to move on. He carefully put the driftolubb back in his pouch, before gently placing each rock back in the sack and cautiously making his way back down the old oak, not forgetting to thank it for its patience and protection.

Once on the ground his immediate priority was to find a hiding place for the colley-rocks, and this being Wand Woods, he already knew there would be no shortage of those. He carefully lump-thumped to the centre of the wood, finding Zhava, the Last Great Elm, bent double and still unable to raise herself upright.

"Zhava?" he griffled. "You be being alright?"

She shifted, her trunk creaking as she turned. "Proftulous?" she griffled in the gloom. "Is that you?"

"Tis being the very same. What's you be doing, all fally-over like that?"

"Had a bit of a glop-up whispgriffling to Matlock," she explained. "Think I've gone and snapped a few things I shouldn't have. All a bit embarrassing for a lady, really."

Proftulous lump-thumped around the base of her trunk. "All your roots be coming out round the back, Zhava. And there's

179

a ganticus hole, too." He peered closer, making out oidy moving shapes scrittling all around the edges.

"Tis those mirrits, Proftulous," Zhava griffled. "The moment I fell, they all began scraping around peffa-vilishly."

"There must be peffa-grillions of them," Proftulous observed, seeing the oidy creatures everywhere, scrittling through the leafy woodland floor and making their way straight into the hole. "Methinks they be making some sort of tunnel, Zhava, right under your roots."

"Tis a blessed and most saztaculous relief not to have the oidy creatures all over me, for once," Zhava confessed. "I don't care what they're doing, as long as they're not scrittling up my trunk, or along my branches and under my bark."

The extrapluff came to Proftulous as clearly as a wottle-thrupp greeping on a summer's even'up. "I be going in," he griffled. "For this surely be the most peffa-perfect place for me to be hiding these colley-rocks."

"Are you sure?" Zhava asked, turning right round to see Proftulous already making his way into the inky-blackness. "I mean, if it's a tunnel, you don't know how safe it is. Or even where it leads."

"I know," Proftulous called out, as a mirrit dropped from his nose onto the damp earth of the tunnel floor. "But I's be a dworp what's can read and extrapluff, Zhava. So's now I's be going to have myself a saztaculous adventure."

A snutch of moments after he had disappeared, quite the strangest thing happened to Zhava. Slowly at first, she found herself able to move, her branches straightening and repairing themselves, pulling her upright as they gratefully reached up and out for the twinkling lid, as if somehow wanting to touch the face of Oramus in the moon himself. Next, her roots found their crumlush foothold of the forest floor, gratefully burying themselves back into the soft, rich earth.

Within moments, she was totally restored, with nothing to show of the tunnel beneath her trunk, the remaining mirrits seemingly quite content to encircle her trunk, almost as if they were guarding her, waiting expectantly for the time when the tunnel would open again.

"Are you sure?" Zhava asked, turning right round to see Proftulous already making his way into the inky-blackness. "I mean, if it's a tunnel, you don't know how safe it is. Or even where it leads."

10.

Alfisc Dale, the Nifferie and The Great Beyond...

Alfisc Dale, of all the majickal-dales, is most often regarded as the least clottabussed, especially by the resident creatures themselves. All, it has to be griffled, take great pride in this fact, and were you ever to somehow fetch up there, they'd spend many a sun-turn griffling to you just how un-clottabussed, more sophisticated and civilised they all are compared to creatures in other dales. And while you may think that in reality this constant bragging makes them more clottabussed than say, the residents of Winchett Dale, who somehow manage to take a glopped-up sense of pride in being peffa-clottabussed, those in Alfisc Dale would be the absolute last to see it this way.

The dale itself is kept immaculately tidy at all times. Trees, bushes, vegetables and shrubs are all planted in exact rows, as curves are seen as a sign of slovenliness. All the pathways are utterly straight, meeting at crossroads to form perfect corners with brilliantly sharp edges. The village is made entirely of stone, home to perfect rows of saztaculous houses with neatly trimmed and tended gardens.

The way of drutts has been embraced for many generations in Alfisc Dale, its residents completely at ease with the acquisition and distribution of wealth by officious krates in exchange for hard work. All creatures are clothed, even flappers in the lid, as the display of unnecessary fur or feathers is considered quite vulgar and unnecessary. And in truth, it has to be griffled, the saztaculous costumes make for quite a sight, though some visitors to Alfisc Dale have griffled that the clothing is merely an excuse to display your drutt wealth and peffa-little else.

A large library stands in the middle of the village, alongside the equally impressive stone Great Hall. Inside there are rows and rows of neatly stacked books which villagers are allowed to borrow for a snutch of sun-turns in exchange for drutts. As no creature can read, however, the acquisition of a book might at first seem rather pointless, but here you'd be wrong, as the volumes themselves merely contain blank pages and all that's really important is the colour of the cover, and whether it complements the clothing of the creature who borrows it. The last creature capable of reading was a majickal-hare named Baselott, and since his hurried departure from Alfisc Dale many years previously, none has ever read since – or, in fact ever needed to try to, so confident and assured are the creatures of their own peffa-clever thinking, that they are utterly convinced that there is nothing in a book that could ever teach them anything.

Come the even'up, most creatures put their young offspring to nifferduggles, and dress in their most crumlush clothes to carry their books around the village, hoping to bump into other creatures with duller clothes and badly-chosen books, or better still, less drutts. Some might then join others for a meal at The Nifferie, a peffa-crumlush but saztaculoulsy expensive restaurant at the edge of the square, intent on getting seats to be next to the windows, anxious they be spotted and acknowledged by other villagers who don't have enough drutts to eat there. Once inside, discussions will vary, but mostly they griffle about just how shindinculous it feels to be so saztaculoulsy admired by all the other dales.

Afterwards, they might pid-pad slowly back to their houses, passing by 'the Trefflepuggas' (those that have pid-padded into Alfisc Dale by way of Trefflepugga Path) griffling in peffa-loud voices just how lucky they are not to be as gobflopped as them. You might wonder just why it is that creatures as lowly as Trefflepuggas are tolerated in the pristine surroundings of Alfisc Dale, but the truth is that they form a vitally important function; by seeing such gobflopped creatures, it allows the residents of Alfisc Dale to assume

Trefflepugga Path had bought them there specifically to be the peffa-perfect glubbstooled comparison to their own sheer saztaculousness. And since it was the path's will that the Trefflepuggas be bought to Alfisc Dale in the first place, then clearly Trefflepugga Path must hold the same views about their inferiority as everyone else.

The Trefflepuggas themselves are few and far between in comparison to the other creatures and can be spotted almost immediately. Some wear just their fur and no clothes, or (perhaps worse) bad clothes. They don't carry books because they aren't allowed to join the library, and are mostly to be found begging for drutts, or doing the sort of yechus tasks that no other creature really wants to. They are forced to live in a large stone hut at the far end of the village, hidden behind a row of trees, their hard earned or begged drutts just being enough to pay for what passes as a bed for the night.

One time, it had been griffled that if ever the stone hut became full, then the krates of Alfisc Dale would find a way to block the entrance to Trefflepugga Path, in order to stop the unwanted arrival of any more Trefflepuggas. But when it was pointed out that the task itself would be so big that it would need lots more Trefflepuggas to actually complete it, thereby leaving the residents effectively walled-in with more Trefflepuggas than before, this rather ambitious plan was dropped. And besides, most Trefflepuggas didn't stay too long in Alfisc Dale, preferring instead to take their chances back along Trefflepugga Path to find another dale, rather than stay in such a place for a sun-turn longer than was absolutely necessary.

Complaints about Trefflepuggas were always top of the agenda in any public-griffling in Alfisc Dale. Here they would be discussed and griffled about, have decisions taken concerning where they were allowed to beg, or how many hours in each sun-turn they would have to work for their lone drutt, all without a single voice of their own to represent their minimal rights and interests. The only way a Trefflepugga ever got into The Great Hall was if he or she was having to clean up the half-chewed niffs and cups of trupplejuice after the public-griffling itself.

Once, a group of residents had proposed that every Trefflepugga should be forced to leave Alfisc Dale, as they were glubbstool to look at and glopped-up all the straight lines. And whilst many were in favour, it took the krates some time to convince them that without Trefflepuggas, they'd all have to do a lot of the yechus work in the village themselves. An idea greeted with stunned disgust by the book-carrying, saztaculously dressed residents.

So it was that the Trefflepuggas were tolerated, mainly because even the most peffa-glopped up residents of Alfisc Dale could always consider themselves above a Trefflepugga, regardless of just how gobflopped they were themselves.

Matlock had, of course, discovered all this within just a snutch of moments of his pid-padding down the path into the dale, there to be greeted by two officious krates barring his way into the village.

"Trefflepugga?" one asked him.

Matlock didn't know what to griffle.

The other krate was touching and inspecting his green robes. "You one of them majickal-hare things?" he griffled suspiciously. "Only we don't be allowing any of that vrooshing nonsense here. We've orders to lock up any majickal-hares."

"Well, I'm not really sure," Matlock griffled. "I mean, I used to be majickal, I've come from Winchett Dale and…"

He got no further, the mere mention of Winchett Dale causing the krates to collapse into chickles.

"What's so funny?" he griffled.

The krates tried to compose themselves. "Sorry, hare. 'Tis just the thought of the place. Gets us every time, it does. Everyone so's clottabussed there."

The other krate nodded. "I bet the creatures there even believed all your majickal nonsense, eh? They'd believe anything over there, they would."

Matlock tried not to get too russisculoffed. "And have you ever been to Winchett Dale?"

The krate shook his head. "Don't have to, do I, to know what it's like? Everyone knows. A bunch of our lot left a while back to be going to Winchett Dale, try and make it more civilised. Glad I wasn't one of 'em, I can griffle you that. Never going to work in a grillion moon-turns that, is it? Just too clottabussed your lot, always have been, always will be. Anyway, enough of this griffling, I'm making it my officious duty to griffle to you that as you's most likely be coming into Alfisc Dale by way of pid-padding from the path, then you most definitely be being a Trefflepugga."

Both krates studied Matlock, waiting for his response.

"For…you," the dripple suddenly griffled from Matlock's hood.

"Hold on a blinksnap, hare," the krate griffled, inspecting the creature closely. "Looks like you've been trying to smuggle another 'pugga in!"

"No, no, no," Matlock vilishly griffled. "It's my dripple. It goes everywhere with me. It's my familiar. It's perfectly harmless."

The krate narrowed its beady eyes. "But I heard tell, hare, that them dripple things what you majickal-hares have, never, ever griffle a single oidy griffle. Yet your one does."

"Exactly," Matlock griffled, seeing a way round what could well become a rather glubbstooled situation. "A griffling-dripple must surely prove that I'm *not* a majickal-hare, and so not really worth the bother of locking up, am I?"

The krate quickly reached into Matlock's hood, roughly grabbing the wriggling dripple. "Cute oidy thing, isn't it?"

"Please, put it back, only it gets peffa-twizzly with strangers and…"

"Do it again!" the krate ordered at the dripple. "Make your griffles. And if you don't, then I's be knowing your master really *is* a majickal-hare, then I's can be locking you both up for a drutt apiece!"

The dripple looked at Matlock, completely twizzled.

"It's not doing nothing, now," the other krate griffled. "Gives it to me." He roughly grabbed the dripple. "Oh, you're right, it's peffa-crumlush, ain't it? Sort of makes you want to really squeeze it."

"Please don't," Matlock griffled, trying not to panic as his dripple fought for breath.

"What else does it do?" the krate griffled. "Can it fly?" He threw the dripple high into the air, catching it in his other paw. "S'cute, but a bit rubbish, really. Can't griffle, can't fly. Can't do nothing, can it?"

The other krate grabbed Matlock by the robe. "Well, seeing as your dripple doesn't griffle, then I'm assuming that it makes you a real majickal-hare, so now we're left with no other alternative but to be locking you up."

"No, please, wait," Matlock griffled. "He *can* griffle. You're just squeezing him too tightly."

The krate slightly relaxed his grip, watching the dripple all the while.

Matlock looked into its eyes. "Please," he griffled. "Please, just griffle for them."

The dripple slowly opened its mouth, taking its most ganticus breath.

"I's getting peffa-bored waiting for this," the krate griffled.

"Just wait," Matlock griffled, urging the twizzly creature on with his eyes. "Please." He held out his paw. "Perhaps if you let me have it, it'll griffle." He took the dripple, stroking its ears, calming it with whispgriffles.

"I still don't be hearing no griffles," the krate griffled, leaning closer. "Methinks we're wasting our time waiting for such nonsense, when we should be locking you both up."

"For…you," the dripple finally griffled. "For…you."

The astonished krates took a pid-pad back. "Well I'll be a blappert's uncle!" one gasped. "It *did* griffle! The oidy dripple-thing actually griffled!"

Both krates had a short hushed conversation as Matlock tucked the dripple safely back into his hood.

"Right," the krate griffled. "Well, seeing as your griffling-dripple allows you to be able to support yourself and earn your own drutts without taking drutt-earning opportunities away from other griffling-dripples…"

"Of which there are no others currently griffling in Alfisc Dale," the other krate griffled.

"Indeed," the first krate griffled, nodding at his guard partner. "Good point. Well made." He cleared his throat. "Then I am officiously letting you into this here dale for the purposes of being a begging Trefflepugga with a griffling-dripple novelty act." He lowered his voice, addressing Matlock. "Between you and I, methinks there's a few drutts to be made from the oidy creature, hare. My advice is to get yourself a spot in the square. Outside The Nifferie is always pretty fuzzcheck for begging. Get the oidy creature to do a little dance or something, maybe sing a song or two, and you'll soon be rolling in drutts. Off you pid-pad, and have a crumlush sun-turn."

"And thank all the stars in Oramus' twinkling-lid you're here, and not back in Winchett Dale!" the other krate called out, as Matlock began slowly pid-padding down towards the village.

If his reception at the top of Trefflepugga Path caught Matlock off-guard, then nothing could have prepared him for the village of Alfisc Dale itself. In all his many moon-turns, he'd never experienced anything even remotely like it. The first thing that struck him was just how grey, straight and painstakingly even everything was. Falling leaves were vilishly swept up the moment they dared touch the neatly flagged stone pathways. The only colours seemed to come from the brightly dressed, book-carrying residents themselves, all turning to look and point at him, but none seemingly bothered to even griffle 'Morn'up' back to him.

Juzzpapped and hungry, he made the mistake of knocking on someone's creaker and politely asking for some niffs and a crumlush brew. The ensuing commotion was completely incomprehensible to Matlock, with the owner pulling her intrigued youngsters from the creaker and vilishly summoning more krates.

"This Trefflepugga has just had the glopped-up nerve to actually knock on my creaker!" she bellowed, angrily pointing at Matlock. "And look, he even has no shoes! He'll give my cherished ones yechus nifferduggles for life!"

Matlock was led away through the village, the krates explaining to him what he could or couldn't do as a Trefflepugga in Alfisc Dale, which it seemed didn't amount to very much, apart from working for the village, begging and staying in the stone hut with the other Trefflepuggas.

"And you'll be needing one drutt to stay there each night," the krate griffled. "No drutt, no bed. We simply lock you up." He indicated a neatly stacked row of cages at the back of the village square, each with a glopped-up creature inside.

"But that's completely peffa-glubbstool," Matlock griffled.

"No, hare," the krate helpfully explained. "That's the rules."

There were, in Matlock's opinion far too many 'rules' in Alfisc Dale, together with far too many krates to enforce them. He estimated that nearly half the population must be krates, the rest being book-carrying, saztaculoulsy dressed creatures who seemed to spend most of their sun-turn simply pid-padding around, waiting to be noticed. Trefflepuggas, on the other hand, worked everywhere, cleaning the village, working the machines and looms in the clothing shops, cooking, preparing and serving food. And also, begging. For as Matlock vilishly discovered, life without drutts in Alfisc Dale soon became peffa, peffa-glopped.

After griffles with several of the other Trefflepuggas, he decided to take their advice and sit outside The Nifferie in the town square most even'ups, entertaining passing residents with his griffling-dripple. And for a while, things went well. Although he had no idea why Trefflepugga Path had chosen Alfisc Dale as his destiny, Matlock knew full well it must be for a reason, if only to point out to him just how peffa-glopped things would be becoming back in Winchett Dale. So he resolved to stay, to try and find out as much as he could about the strange dale, before trying to make his journey back home. He could even perhaps try and find the elusive riddle, too, suspecting that the answer might be locked away somewhere in the village's ganticus library.

But in the short term, it was drutts that he needed for food and a bed, so the pavement outside The Nifferie became his chosen begging spot, entertaining passing residents with his griffling-dripple as best as he could.

"Oh, my!" they would griffle, as the dripple duly delivered its two griffles. "It griffles! I always thought they never griffled. Are you supposed to be one of those majickal-hare things? Your robes are quite convincing, but you have no shoes. Don't they wear shoes?"

"They do," Matlock would honestly reply. "I simply left mine at an inn along Trefflepugga Path."

And then they might chickle, thinking it was all part of the act, or take pity on him, or want to stroke the dripple and hear it griffle again. But most would leave a drutt, sometimes two. By the end of the even'up, especially if it was a Yaayday, Matlock might have a pocketful of drutts, which he always quietly slipped to the caged Trefflepuggas, pressing them into their eager paws through the bars when the guarding krates weren't watching, in order that they would be released to nifferduggle safely back in the stone hut.

189

Each morn'up they were woken at dawn by krates, ordering them out of their beds and setting them to work. But because Matlock was earning his own drutts begging, he wasn't assigned village chores, and was largely left to his own devices provided he didn't break any rules. Mostly, he spent his sun-turns away from the village, in and amongst rows of trees in the immaculately planted woodland, watching the last of the leaves fall, searching for sylphas gliding on the underside, and thinking of home. Occasionally he might catch one in his paw, asking them if they'd seen Plusa, whereupon they'd give him a puzzled look before twirling away.

His dripple meanwhile, seemed to be getting more and more tired, its appetite diminishing sun-turn by sun-turn, despite Matlock's earnest encouragement. Sometimes it would nifferduggle all sun-turn in his hood, only waking when they had settled in front of The Nifferie to begin their griffling-dripple turn, when it would slowly climb out and sit in Matlock's paws, griffling 'For…you…' on demand to whoever was willing to pay a mere drutt for the privilege. Even the slurpilicious and crumlush cooking smells from the restaurant wouldn't persuade it to eat anything but just the oidiest scraps. Matlock tried everything he could think of; berries, nettles and leaves from the woods, all of the dripple's favourite woodland feasts, but to no avail. His dripple was sick, wasting away. He simply hoped Oramus would see fit to lend a Most Majelicus curing paw from above, as he knew full well that when a dripple passes on, it is on the exact same sun-turn as its master. It had always been this way, right back through the generations of majickal-hares. If his dripple passed, then so would he. His dripple, Matlock fully realised, mustn't get any more glopped-up.

He even began to wonder if the constant griffling of 'For… you…' was the cause for the dripple's illness, as if by somehow acting so ganticusly out of dalelore and character, his dripple had unwittingly broken some hidden majickal-law that had cursed them both. But as Matlock knew of no previous example of a griffling-dripple, it was impossible to make any comparison, and with there being no one to griffle the problem over with, he merely had to trust and surrender himself to Oramus' Most Majelicus will.

And, of course, as the dripple became even more glopped,

residents no longer wanted to hear it griffle. They'd become bored of the pretend, shoeless majickal-hare and his griffling creature. Besides, most had already heard all that it had to griffle. Why pay another drutt for something you'd already heard? It wasn't even as if the hare could make it griffle anything else. The whole thing, they began to assume, was probably little more than a glopped-up trick. The hare most likely moved the dripple's mouth in some way, squeezing it to make the sounds. And it looked ill, too. So frankly who would pay a drutt to watch a sick dripple with only two griffles to griffle?

Matters came to a head one even-up as Matlock arrived outside The Nifferie, only to find his place on the pavement already filled by a lolloped-glurp playing a jattflute through its nostrils to a large appreciative crowd of saztaculoulsy-dressed, book-carrying residents.

Matlock pid-padded through, his feet sore from the stone flags, his robes more tattered and glopped-up than they'd ever been. "I think," he griffled, as most peffa-politely as he could, "that you're in my place."

The glurp stopped playing. "Listen," he griffled, pulling the jattflute painfully from his nose. "I've only just arrived in this place. The krates told me to get meself here to earn a few drutts. Apparently, there used to be some sort of majickal-hare with a griffling thing, but he's gone all gobflopped now…" He stopped, looked Matlock up and down. "Oh, sorry, hare. It's you, isn't it?"

Matlock nodded, his dripple lightly clinging to his neck as the residents pushed him aside, eagerly urging the glurp to re-insert the jattflute and resume playing. With nothing else to do, Matlock pid-padded to the other side of the square, trying to find a different place to beg by the walls of the library. But no one came, no one stopped. The dripple had fallen into exhausted nifferduggles, deep in his hood. Everything just seemed peffa, peffa-hopeless. He wondered if he could have done anything differently, anything at all, but somehow it all seemed to destined to end in this glubstooled place, glopped-up and begging by a library wall, from the very first moment Chatsworth had pid-padded into his life many, many moon-turns ago. It felt as if every pid-pad he'd taken, everything he'd done since, every path had simply led him to this miserable spot.

He sighed, looked to the twinkling lid, the distant, shadowed figure of Oramus clear in the bright full moon above. "I just don't know what to do," he whispgriffled. "My dripple is ill, if he is stroffed, then I will be, too. I have no drutts, my clothes are peffa-glopped, I've never been this juzzpapped." He took a deep hare's breath. "I don't even have any shoes…"

"Well now, just look at you," came a crumlush voice that he instantly recognised, a pair of purple shoes suddenly landing on his lap. "You're a peffa-difficult hare to find, Matlock. Just don't be leaving your shoes in my inn again, will you?"

"Laffrohn?" he griffled, breaking into the broadest smile he'd had since arriving in Alfisc Dale. "Is that really you?"

"No, it's a wobbling-fettle, perfectly disguised as me, who happens to sound exactly like me, that somehow has your shoes from when you came to the Vroffa-Tree Inn." She pulled him to his feet. "'Course it's me, you clottabus! Now get these shoes on, for starters. They're all washed, peffa-clean and crumlush. Your feet must be ice-blasting on that stone."

Matlock slipped his juzzpapped, aching feet back into his shoes, almost gasping with the joyful comfort of the moment. "New laces, too?" he griffled, tying them.

"Of course," Laffrohn griffled. "Can't have you looking all gobflopped now, can we?"

"How did you find me?" Matlock griffled. "How did you get here?"

"I has me ways," she whispgriffled, tapping the side of her nose with a ganticus paw, its claw gleaming under the moonlight.

"You took the path, didn't you? I mean, you had to, didn't you?"

"Hush, Matlock, you're getting all peffa-excrimbly. I'm not too peffa-keen to be spotted by krates in this glopped-up dale. Let's just griffle that I wanted you to have your shoes back, so's I be finding myself a way."

"But…" Matlock griffled, his mind racing faster than a vilish scrittling-beetle, "…how did you know I'd be here? How did you get here?" He thought for a snutch of moments, suddenly snapped his paw-fingers. "You *flew*, didn't you? You flew over the path to find me!" He felt like yelping out loud. He took several deep-hare's breaths. "Which means you could take me with you, couldn't you? You could take me out of here, and back home to Winchett Dale!" He gave her the most peffa-ganticus hare's hug, eyes tightly shut in shindinculous delight. "You can finally take me home!"

Laffrohn chickled softly. "You're not going anywhere until you've had a peffa-good meal, Matlock." She peered into his hood, becoming suddenly concerned. "Your dripple's peffa-ill."

Matlock nodded. "It's getting worse each sun-turn, ever since it started griffling. It's another reason why I have to get back to Winchett Dale, Laffrohn. It'll get better there, I just know it."

Laffrohn raised her eyes. "It griffles? Now this is peffa-interesting." She lightly stroked the creature's nifferduggling head. "I have heard of this before, a long time ago, from another majickal-hare who once made his way along Trefflepugga Path. He stopped to the inn and perhaps had one too many guzzworts, griffling me a similar tale of his dripple that had once griffled."

"What was his name?" Matlock asked, intrigued.

"I can't remember," Laffrohn griffled. "Besides, I thought the whole thing was just a spuddle, anyways. He just sat there in my inn, all sad and glopped-up by the memory. His dripple had eventually passed, but the peffa-curious thing was that he had lived on, then spent the rest of his life blaming himself for the poor creature's demise, almost as if he'd stroffed it himself by forcing it to griffle in the first place."

"But he lived?" Matlock griffled. "He outlived his dripple?"

Laffrohn nodded. "But it was as if something inside him had been stroffed, Matlock. I gave him more guzzworts, and he resolved there and then that he would make a revision to one of the majickal-driftolubbs when the time was right, to let every other majickal-hare know just what had happened."

Matlock racked his hare's brain. "But I've read the driftolubbs," he griffled. "There's nothing in any of them about griffling-dripples. They're silent and they pass when we do, that's all there is."

"Ah," Laffrohn nodded, "but have you read *all* of them, Matlock? Each and every one? Or were you like most other apprentice majickal-hares, far too eager to start vrooshing your saztaculous spells without reading everything you should have done first?"

Matlock sighed. "Perhaps, but it was such a long time ago…"

"And since then," Laffrohn griffled, "in the peffa-long even'ups as you sit in front of the piff-tosh, how often did you read your driftolubbs, Matlock? Or did you use them simply to find spells, potions and vrooshers when a creature asked you to? Because there's so much more in them, Matlock, than mere majickery. So much more."

Matlock looked around the cold square, watching the residents of Alfisc Dale pid-padding, griffling and chickling, carrying their books and waiting to be noticed. "You're right," he quietly confessed. "I've never read them all. I just…"

"Didn't have the time?" Laffrohn griffled. She waved a paw at him and clicked her tongue. "No, no, Matlock. That's an excuse that's too easily griffled. You didn't read them because you didn't *want* to. You have to be honest. You took what you wanted from the driftolubbs, and found little else besides."

He turned to her, his tone insistent and pressing. "But if you take me back to Winchett Dale, I'll find them again Laffrohn. I'll really, really read them all, from cover to cover, over and over. I'll…"

Laffrohn put a paw on his shoulder. "I can't take you back to Winchett Dale, Matlock. Only you can; just you. It's not up to me, it never has been." She fixed him in the eyes. "You still think that the path decides the destiny of your journey? Then you haven't even begun to realise the real truth of any of this. It doesn't. *You* decide it, Matlock; you. You ended up here, because you never knew where you really needed to go. You chose Alfisc Dale, and all Trefflepugga Path did was lead you here. Find where you need to go, Matlock, and let the path take you there."

"But I already know!" Matlock protested. "I need to go back home, to be in Winchett Dale."

"What for?" Laffrohn griffled. "To begin again? To put everything right and start all over? To read your driftolubbs properly and learn all your vrooshers, rather than spending your time in your garden, or your potionary, or sitting by Thinking Lake, or in front of your piff-tosh?"

"Yes," Matlock vilishly agreed. "Exactly that! To be better, saztaculoulsy better, so none of this would ever happen again!"

Laffrohn smiled. "And what journey could ever do that for you, Matlock? How can we ever go back and start all over again? All Trefflepugga Path did was to take you where it thought you needed to be."

Matlock looked about, his voice rising. "But I don't *need* to be here!" he griffled. "I don't need to be here at all!"

"Then leave," Laffrohn calmly griffled. "Leave this even'up, take Trefflepugga Path again. But it will simply bring you back here no matter how many times you try. And every time you do, there will be more and more of your dreggs waiting for you, Matlock."

"Yes, but if I knew the answer to the riddle," Matlock insisted, "then I could go wherever I wanted to. I could get back to Winchett Dale and really begin all over again. I just need the answer to the riddle, Laffrohn, don't you see?"

Laffrohn smiled. "All I see, Matlock," she quietly griffled, "is a glopped-up majickal-hare who can't even beg for drutts with a sick dripple. A majickal-hare who wants to wipe away the past and make everything better. That's not pid-padding forwards on your journey, that's going backwards. It's why you've ended here with creatures who can't read, yet want to be admired in their robes. Look at them, Matlock. Can't you *see*? They *are* you. Just as you are them. Your dripple sickens because it has no place here. It be paining me to be griffling this to you, Matlock, but the truth is that your dripple weakens every sun-turn because it has no place with you as you now are, the hare you've become." She looked him straight in his shocked orange eyes. "Or perhaps, the hare you always really were. And maybe, methinks, this journey was only really all about finding that hare, Matlock, and nothing else."

Matlock looked around, his breathing coming in short breaths. His softulous began to shake, and he felt suddenly panicked and peffa-twizzly. Creatures passed by, pid-padding and chickling, ignoring the curious hare by the library wall. "It's a nightmare, isn't it?" he griffled, his voice cracking slightly, reaching for any sort of answers. "I know what's really happening, Laffrohn. I'm still nifferduggling in the bed at the Vroffa-Tree Inn, aren't I? None of this real, or true, or…"

"Or just how long do you intend to make a glopped-up exhibition of yourself like this?" snapped another voice Matlock instantly recognised. "It's all most peffa-untzorkly, and I expected more of you, hare."

He turned, facing the white hare-witch, her narrowed eyes searching his face accusingly. "Ursula?" he griffled, looking all round for Laffrohn, who seemed to have simply vanished. "What's going on? Where's Laffrohn? What's happening to me?"

Ursula Brifthaven Stoltz narrowed her eyes. "I have no idea what's happening to you, hare," she griffled. "And as for Laffrohn, I suspect she's tending to The Vroffa-Tree Inn, just like she always does."

Matlock shook his head, desperate to explain. "But she was here just a blinksnap ago. Right here, right next to me, by my side."

"I think," Ursula slowly griffled, "that perhaps you have some sort of griffle-fever. You are making no sense whatsoever."

"Aha! That proves it, then, doesn't it? It's all a dream!" Matlock started chickling out loud in the small square, completely unconcerned at anyone's reaction . "All of it! It's all a dream, everyone! And really, I'm safe and crumlush and nifferduggling and…"

"And if you don't shut up," Ursula urgently hissed, "you'll have us both locked up in cages!" She gave him a hard bliff around the cheek. "That hurt?"

Matlock nodded, shocked and stung, feeling the side of his face, completely unprepared for the even harder bliff that followed to his other cheek.

"That hurt, too?"

"Peffa-definitely," Matlock griffled, flinching and expecting a third.

"Good," Ursula snapped. "Then at least you know this is no dream. Progress, at least." She looked around, spotting an advancing guard of krates. "You're clottabussed behaviour has been noticed. Take deep breaths and calm down, or they will have us caged."

Matlock nodded feeling sore and embarrased, doing as Ursula griffled.

"This Trefflepugga causing you problems, madam?" a krate officiously asked.

"Nothing that I can't handle, thank you," Ursula politely griffled, reaching into her robes and passing each of the krates a drutt. "Please, be on your way now. We'll be fine."

The satisfied krates vilishly pocketed the drutts, turned and left, marching away over the square.

"When was being the last time you ate a crumlush meal?" Ursula griffled.

Matlock rubbed the side of his stinging cheeks. "Probably when I ate your niffs in The Vroffa-Tree Inn."

"Tchh," Ursula clicked. "That is so un-tzorkly. To be on a journey you must be eating to be healthy for all the pid-padding you will have to do. Be following me."

She set off across the square for The Nifferie, determination in every pid-pad, Matlock lagging slightly behind. "We can't go in there," he urgently whispgriffled. "They'll never let a Trefflepugga in."

She instantly stopped, turning slowly, scrutinising his face. "And is that what you *really* think you are?" She screwed her face in disgust. "A Trefflepugga?"

"Well…I…No, I don't," Matlock replied, swallowing. "Although I am, but I'm not, I'm…a majickal-hare…although I'm not really… because…"

"Oh, for Oramus' sake!" Ursula griffled. "Just how much more russisculoffed do you want to be making me? More bliffs? Is that it, you want to be having more bliffs?"

"No!" Matlock griffled a little too noisily, causing heads to turn nearby. He lowered his griffles. "I mean, no, I don't want that."

"Fine," Ursula griffled. "At least you know that much. A start, I suppose. Now follow me. You have shoes, and are with me. Your robes may be glopped-up, but they can't refuse you."

Matlock followed Ursula to the saztaculous creaker of The Nifferie, watching as she passed the creakerman a handful of drutts before they were duly let inside and shown to a table with great, but largely unnecessary ceremony.

"How did you do that?" he whispgriffled once they'd sat and the table had been laid with fresh linen and a shindinculous candlestick.

"In this dale," Ursual griffled, "Drutts griffle, Matlock. It's as simple as that."

Matlock leaned closer, whispgriffling. "But where did you get them all from?"

Ursula waved the question aside with an elegant flourish of her white paw. "What do you mean? For Oramus' sake, Matlock, they're just pebbles. There's nothing saztaculous or tzorkly about them. You can find them anywhere."

He looked around the restaurant, watching the Alfisc Dale residents eating their food, fascinated by just how small the plates were and how little they actually ate, preferring instead to aimlessly push their food around, griffling loudly about how saztaculous and crumlush they all looked. The meals themselves were served by vilishly scrittling Trefflepuggas, some of whom Matlock recognised from the stone-hut. The floors and tables were immaculately clean, divided by large white stone pillars that rose into a high arched ceiling decorated with elaborate mosaics made from painted drutts. He'd never been in such an expensive looking place, let alone ever tried to eat with a knife and fork – a wooden bowl and spoon being his normal preference.

"I used to do that," he griffled to Ursula, pointing to the window at the lolloped glurp outside.

Ursula looked, pulled a face. "What? Put a flute up your nose?"

"No," Matlock tried to explain. "The dripple and I, we had this thing where it would griffle, and I'd get drutts."

Her eyes widened. "Your dripple griffles? What would it griffle?"

"Just 'For…you…'"

Ursula frowned. "Well, that's hardly peffa-tzorkly is it?"

"The point is," Matlock tried to explain, "dripples *don't* griffle. They just don't. But my one does." He reached behind him, pulled the nifferduggling dripple from his hood, laid it gently on the table.

"It looks much peffa-glubbstooled," Ursula observed, poking it slightly with her paw. "I not want it on our table, thank you."

Matlock laid the dripple in his lap, lightly stroking its head. "So how did you find me?"

Ursula clicked her teeth. "What makes you think I was even looking for you?"

"Because you're here?"

"And so are you," she griffled. "'Tis all just coincidence, and

"I used to do that," he griffled to Ursula, pointing to the window at the lolloped glurp outside. Ursula looked, pulled a face. "What? Put a flute up your nose?"

nothing peffa-tzorkly at all. I sometimes fly over The Icy Seas and come here with some pebbles if I can't be bothered to be much cooking in my cauldron at home." She vilishly held up a paw to stop Matlock's griffles. "And before you ask me to fly you back to your Winchett Dale, let me stop you. You have pid-padded along Trefflepugga Path, surrendered your will to it. To have you on my broom would be to defy the path. It would stroff us both."

Matlock nodded, lowering his griffles. "Yes, I know that, Ursula. But do you know about the riddle?" he asked. "The riddle of Trefflepugga Path? Ursula, if you know the answer, please griffle it to me, then I can go wherever I want. At the moment I'm trapped here, it won't let me leave."

"But why would I wish to know of any such thing?" Ursula griffled, puzzled. "I have no need of riddles. The path has no power over me, as long as I fly above it, and never take a pid-pad along it." A Trefflepugga arrived with two glasses, filling them each with trupplejuice. "A riddle is only useful if you need to know the answer, and I have no such need of them."

The Trefflepugga still waited by the table, looking at them both. "Matlock? Is that you, friend?"

Matlock looked up, recognising the short-kruttle immediately. "Yes, Shriggs, it is."

The short-kruttle vilishly put a stubby finger to his lips, wincing. "Shhh! You can't be calling me that in here, Matlock. I has to be Shriggalovsky in here."

"Why?" Matlock asked, as the dripple stirred a little on his lap.

"It's what the residents want, proper saztaculous sounding names, not glopped-up ones like Shriggs. Sort of makes them forget we're Trefflepuggas and we should really be out there, and not in here with them. It makes us more saztaculous for them, I suppose, less glopped. If you ever have to do chores in here, Matlock, the krates'll be changing your name to Matlovsky, I reckon."

"Well, that would be glubbstool," Matlock admitted.

"I don't know," Ursula griffled. "I am thinking it would be a saztaculoulsy tzorkly improvement. Matlock sounds so dull and peffa-ordinary."

"Thanks," Matlock mumbled. "It's the name I was born with,

and it's the one I'll keep, if it's all the same to you."

"Aha," Ursula griffled, shaking her head at him. "But once again, you are being so peffa-wrong and splurked."

"I am?"

She nodded. "You were simply born a hare, with no name, in The Great Beyond. Your master would have named you, Matlock, not your mahpa or pahpa. You are simply called what your master chose for you, what suited his purposes. It's no different from being him." She pointed at the Trefflepugga, "He becomes something else to suit his masters and changes for them, just as you do."

Shriggs nudged Matlock in the ribs, gently chickling. "Guess this could be a peffa-long dinner, friend."

Matlock sat, not really listening, stroking his dripple as Shriggs griffled out a ganticus list of ridiculously complicated menu-choices, most of which merely seemed to involve niffs in various different cuts and combinations. Instead he thought of Ursula's griffles, and those of Laffrohn before her – if he'd even really seen the crumlush landlady of The Vroffa-Tree Inn at all. But regardless of who was really where, why he was, or where he was, Matlock felt a growing sense of something lost stirring deep inside his Sisteraculous. He realised that he hadn't had many extrapluffs since arriving in Alfisc Dale, despite no longer being under the influence of Trefflepugga Path, as if his once majickal powers were choosing to leave him, deny him who he was – if he really knew himself any more. He wondered just what it was that had once persuaded him to follow the upright hare in redrobes that had pid-padded so saztaculously into his field, or what he might have done if he'd chosen not to and simply carried on living the life of a normal hare out in The Great Beyond. He fought hard, trying to remember those times, what it must have felt like not to griffle, to hop, not to have to wear robes and live in a cottage doing spells, potions and vrooshers, having just strange creatures for friends…

"I griffled," Ursula asked, cutting across his thoughts, "what will you have? We're waiting."

Matlock looked up, mumbled an apology. "I wasn't listening."

Ursula sighed. "Let me make this peffa-simple for you. The crushed niff in a welt-brottle sauce, slowly roasted over a lightly-glaggotined piff-tosh? Or the soup?"

"What's the soup?"

"That'll be niffs," Shriggs helpfully griffled. "Only it's done with a delicate fluverte of moist wulps for the peffa-discerning palate."

"Fine," Matlock griffled, not really bothered. "I'll have that."

"How many whulps with it?"

"What?"

"How many? Only they are rather moist, and some residents prefer less, but made an oidy bit crispy in a dulled kettle-bennion."

Matlock hesitated, lost. "Er…three?"

Shriggs took instant offence. "What, only three?"

"Well, I'm not really sure what they are, am I?"

Shriggs looked to Ursula. "Are you peffa-sure you really want to eat with this clottabus?"

"Well do *you* know what they are?" she calmly griffled back.

"'Course I do," Shriggs griffled, looking uncomfortable under Ursula's gaze. "Sort of moist whulpy things, aren't they?"

"Then why are you asking us?" she griffled. "If you already know?"

Shriggs sighed, turning back to Matlock. "How about I put you down for six? I'll have the 'puggas out the back cook 'em in yorple-fat over a slowly smouldering bed of dulled meadow grasses."

"Sounds fine," Matlock wearily griffled, relieved his Trefflepugga friend was finally gone. Even ordering a humble niff-soup in a place like this could soon turn into a ganticus ordeal. He turned to Ursula. "So how did you get your name?"

She smiled for the first time since they'd sat. "It was given to me by my mahpa. We white hare-witches are born majickal – or tzorkly, as we griffle in our lands. We know no other life but the tzorkly one, from the peffa-first time we open our eyes as leverets. We are taught everything by our mahpas and pahpas, from learning vrooshers, potions and spells, even to flying. We have no master to teach us, and none of your driftolubbs to rely on. Everything is taught by griffles and example. Nothing is written down, so there is no need to read or write. When we are old enough, we leave to become solitary witches, to find our own homes and follow the ways of witchery by ourselves."

"It must be lonely," Matlock griffled.

She nodded. "At times. But other times it is peffa-tzorkly. Look around you, here I am now, buying a crumlush meal for a few pebbles and enjoying your company with all these other creatures. I don't think that makes me lonely, do you?"

"Gosh," Matlock griffled, taken aback.

"What?"

He squirmed a little. "I'm just pleased to hear that you're enjoying my company, I suppose."

She looked at him. "What's not to enjoy? When I am with you looking so glopped-up, glubbstooled, juzzpapped and gobflopped, then it must be making me feel brifter."

"Oh," Matlock griffled. "I see. I just thought…"

She suddenly reached across the table, looked him straight in the eye and set a delicate white-paw across his lips. "Hush, Matlock. It does not do to think all the time. This is your gloppedness, to think, think, think too much. Much too peffa-much." She leant right over, stunning Matlock with a kiss on his cheek. "Now, less thinking, more eating, drinking and griffling. Tell me all your adventures since I last saw you at the inn."

So he did exactly that, griffling to her all that had happened; falling from the sky in the peffa-crumlush bed, waking in the Vale of Dreggs, the twizzly parade, the waterfall, The Cove of Choices and his time in Alfisc Dale. And more besides, finding himself griffling about life in Winchett Dale, his adventures there, the creatures and buildings, even describing his potionary down to the smallest detail, as Ursula nodded all the while, listening intently.

Before he knew it, they had finished their meal. As the table was being cleared, Ursula leant across once again. "Listen, Matlock," she griffled, "there's something I must ask you."

"Of course," Matlock griffled. "Anything."

"The bottle I gave you in The Vroffa-Tree Inn? I want it back."

"Oh," Matlock griffled, feeling suddenly bought back down to earth, but nonetheless reaching into his robe pocket and placing the oidy leather potion bottle on the table between them. "I've kept it safely."

She smiled. "I was hoping that you would be doing that." She slowly turned the bottle in her paw, lost in thought for a snutch of moments. "You never used it?"

Matlock shook his head. "You griffled to me that I'd know when the moment was right. I'm sorry, I just didn't ever feel that moment."

She nodded thoughtfully, looking distracted. "Then…then that's how it is, Matlock."

"But I always made sure to keep it safe for you," he insisted, wondering if he'd done anything wrong, or upset her in any way.

"Why?" she griffled.

"Because," he slowly griffled, "because…"

"Yes?"

"Because I wanted it to be peffa-perfect when I…" he tailed off.

"When you what, Matlock?"

He cleared his throat. "For when I saw you again."

Ursula sat back in her chair, nodding, then placing the potion-bottle back in Matlock's paw. "Then you must look after it again."

"I don't understand."

She smiled. "The tzorkly majick of a white hare-witch is peffa-different to yours, Matlock. It works on feelings, not griffles from a book. This bottle is a potion of my feelings, and only someone who wanted to protect them and keep them safe from all harm would never have opened and used it." She closed his paw around the small bottle. "Keep them safe, Matlock. And keep me safe, too."

"I'll try," Matlock griffled, still not totally sure what she was griffling about.

Ursula made to leave, standing. "It's time for me to be flying back," she griffled, taking his paw in hers. "It has been a pleasant even'up in your company, Matlock. I have learnt much about you."

"Please," Matlock griffled. "Don't go, Ursula."

She flinched slightly. "You're squeezing my paw."

He let go. "Sorry. I just…I just don't want you to go. I don't know what to do here, and I don't know when I'll see you again, and…"

"This is you with all your thinking again, Matlock," she griffled, lightly tapping the side of his head. "Like I griffled before, you think too much." She held his eyes for a moment. "I am thinking that you are stuck here because of all this thinking you do. Now is the time for no more thinking, now is the time to be doing."

"But do what?" he griffled. "I don't know what to do."

"You wish to leave this place?"

Matlock vilishly nodded. "More than ever, Ursula."

"How much?"

"Peffa-ganticus muchly," he griffled. "The most peffa-ganticus muchly that's ever been muchly peffa-ganticus, ever. I swear on my dripple's life. I swear on *my* life."

Ursula closed her eyes, deep in thought, occasionally nodding to herself, as if trying to persuade herself of something peffa, peffa-important. Eventually, she opened her eyes. "There is *one* way I can fly you home, Matlock," she griffled. "But you *must* trust me. The journey will be shorter than you think, but so much longer than you think, also."

It sounded like the briftest, most saztaculous music to Matlock's long hare's ears. "Home?" he griffled, all peffa-excrimbly and trying not to hug her. "You can fly me there?"

She nodded. "And you will trust me?"

"Of course!" Matlock griffled. He reached out and eagerly shook her paw in gratitude. "Ursula, you have no idea how excrimbly this has made me! Truly, you are the most saztaculous and peffa-crumlush tzorkly white hare-witch!"

"*Solitary* white hare-witch," she vilishly corrected him, removing her paw. "Just follow me. Do exactly as I say, and when you are on the broom, make no unnecessary movements. You've ever ridden one before?"

Matlock shook his head. "No, but I'll be fine. I'll do everything you griffle."

She left some drutts on the table for the meal, as Matlock followed her out through the kitchen to the back-creaker, a Trefflepugga opening it for them both and getting a drutt for his troubles.

"Crumlush thanks, Miss Stoltz," he griffled, pocketing the pebble. "Your broom's as safe as when you left it."

Ursula nodded, beckoning Matlock to follow her into the small yard, her waiting broomstick leaning against the far wall.

"Ursula," Matlock griffled. "I just can't thank you enough. I know how peffa-dangerous this will be for you to fly me over the path."

She grabbed the broom handle, spinning it expertly and checking the vroffa-branches. "We're not going over Trefflepugga Path."

"We're not?"

"I met a friend of yours the other sun-turn. She had travelled a long way to see me. She told me of another way to get you home. A sylpha, she was, and quite a charming one at that."

"Plusa? You've met Plusa?"

Ursula chickled. "Plusa is your name for her, Matlock. She has always answered to Rihaana to me." She paused, smiled, saying both names silently a snutch of times. "How peffa-clever. I can see that now, yes. She's truly tzorkly, that oidy sylpha. And as she would griffle, perhaps it's better that way."

"So there's another route?" Matlock griffled. "Did Plusa give you the answer to the riddle of Trefflepugga Path?"

Ursula mounted the broom, gripping it firmly. "Matlock, I have no need for the riddle, but even I know the answer. Now it's your time to find it out, too. Get on, hold tight to my robes. Keep your dripple safe. In the unlikely event of anything going gobflopped, be sure of one thing."

"What?" Matlock asked.

"Keep my potion safe. That's all I ask of you in return."

Then, before Matlock could griffle another griffle, they set off vilishly into the twinkling-lid, rising steeply from the small backyard as The Nifferie's Trefflepuggas watched and cheered from below. In a snutch of moments, Ursula had levelled the broom, and Matlock was able to catch a welcome breath, the tips of the roaring vroffa-branches behind him glowing red hot in the night-sky.

In what seemed like just a snutch of blinksnaps, they had left the village completely, the stone buildings and houses disappearing into the dark surrounding countryside, Matlock clinging to Ursula's robe, trying to stay level and not lurch or tip the broom, his long ears trailing behind him, hoping his dripple was still safe in his flapping hood. He closed his eyes, realising just how absolutely juzzpapped he felt, but also so peffa-relieved to be leaving Alfisc Dale, and finally on his way back home. It didn't matter what awaited him in Winchett Dale, it was purely the yamamantally-spious thought of being back there that made him want to eyesplash and chickle at the same time. He resolved with all his hare's heart to find his driftolubbs, read

He was going home, and for Matlock, asleep on a white hare-witch's broom high in the twinkling lid, nothing had ever felt quite this saztaculous…

them, vroosh his dripple better, beat Frendeslene Note and all his glopped-up krates and drutts, then make everything shindinculously better again.

He was going home, and for Matlock, asleep on a white hare-witch's broom high in the twinkling lid, nothing had ever felt quite this saztaculous…

When he awoke, he was lying on damp grass, cold and shivering from an unwelcome covering of morning dew. He rubbed both eyes, trying to place where he was, where Ursula had left him. Nothing looked like Winchett Dale at all, yet the surroundings were still familiar in an oidy way he couldn't begin to ever explain. He thought back, trying to remember the final few moments before he had fallen into nifferduggles on the back of the broom, trying to see if he had any other memories of arriving in what simply looked like a ganticus field, bordered by hedgerows with a single elm tree in its centre.

A bird flew close by, Matlock immediately calling to it and asking for help, the startled creature quickly flying away into the cold grey sky. The last of the autumn leaves blew around the field, some becoming caught in the longer grasses, or impaled in dense hedgerows at the edges. Above, a weak sun tried to break through thickening skies, its rays denied by dark rolling rainclouds, sweeping in on a strengthening wind.

He pulled his damp robes tighter around him, feeling a slight stirring in his hood. "Dripple?" he griffled, craning his neck to see the small creature groggily peeping from the top. "I think we've come to the wrong place. I think we're lost on Trefflepugga Path again. We must have crashed, or fallen."

The dripple slowly pointed to the elm tree, as the first few rain-drops fell from the leaden sky.

"Fuzzcheck idea," Matlock griffled. "We'll shelter there until the lid-splashy stops."

He stood, his body aching in unfamiliar ways, trying to take a snutch of pid-pads, but finding his back legs far too heavy, too stiff for the task. "We must be on the path," he murmured. "It's stopping me from pid-padding again, not letting me get to the tree."

As he tried to wipe the rain from his face, a sudden gust of wind raced across the field, blowing his cap clean over his ears and sending it high into the air, eventually landing amongst a tangle of swaying bare branches in the elm. He tried more pid-pads, each becoming harder and harder, the effort of standing almost too much. He felt truly peffa-glopped and wondered if he'd broken anything in his softulous during the fall. He looked around, searching for any signs of Ursula or the downed broomstick, but couldn't see any. He resolved to search later, after the rain had passed, hoping the path would weaken and let him move more freely. His searched his robe pockets, glad to find his wand and the potion-bottle still safe and unbroken inside.

It took too long to reach the shelter of the elm, each pid-pad more painful than the last, as if he was being pressed down, just as he had been in the Vale of Dreggs. He cried out with each few steps, falling down onto all fours, the dripple jolting round in his wet hood.

"We'll get there," he griffled, gritting his teeth. "We'll get there, my friend. Just hang on."

He crawled the last few steps, the effort of standing too much to bear, both back legs now working as one, slowly pushing him forwards to the base of the elm's trunk. And there he lay, on his front, panting heavily, watching the thick heavy raindrops falling all around, too tired to even think anymore, and falling into another deep sleep.

The dripple slowly climbed from its hood to lie beside its master for what it already knew would be the last time. It gingerly pressed a paw against Matlock's cheek, moving closer to his long, wet, flat ears.

"My…name…is…Ayaani…" she whispgriffled, wrapping her short arms around Matlock's neck and hugging him with the very last of her fading strength. "For…you…"

Then she closed her soft and tired eyes, her paws falling to the ground, taking her final breath beside the master she had always loved and been loyal to, knowing that it was, for her, the briftest and most shindinculous way to pass to Oramus above.

The hare awoke in a panic almost the instant the rain had stopped, struggling to free itself from the wet green robes, its powerful back legs bucking and tearing at the material, fighting to find a way out, its body frantically twisting and racking on the ground. Its feet were trapped too, thick purple material somehow covering each one. With just a few more powerful kicks it was free, sitting upright, its bright orange eyes completely alert, scanning the field for any intruders or danger. It noticed something at the ground by its side, sniffing at a small dead creature with long ears, all its instincts telling the hare to bound away before crows came from the clearing skies to peck and devour it. Instead, it did a curious thing, finding leaves and pushing them with its nose to cover the body, before settling down and sitting quite still by the trunk of the elm once more, looking for the slightest movements in its keen-eyed field of vision, caught by just the smallest swishing of the wind-swept grasses, the tiniest distant call from a passing bird above.

And next, the hare did a second curious thing; taking the torn wet green and red material and suddenly bounding with it over the wet grass to the furthest hedgerow, before seeming to almost deliberately hang it with its nose on a branch leaden with sloes. After, the hare sat quite still, staring straight ahead, alert and intent in its new home. A sudden rustling just a short distance away caused it to startle, the hare immediately pressing itself low to the ground, wary of other hares now slowly leaving the safety and protection of their forms, revealing themselves to him from a cautious distance.

The hare gradually sat back upright, ready to bolt as the other hares moved closer to inspect the stranger. At twenty yards apart, they stopped, as if waiting for some collective signal to approach any nearer. The stand-off lasted a full five minutes or more, each hare as still and silent as a statue, simply watching, the only movement just the tiniest twitching of their noses, keen to catch the stranger's scent on the breeze.

When he had waited long enough, the hare gradually began to move, slowly turning its body, its head remaining completely still, staring straight ahead at the others. At the last moment, it turned itself completely, then bounded quickly back across the field to the safety of the elm, settling once more by the small pile of leaves, watching as the distant hares slowly approached the damp rags it had left on the other side. Finally, it gathered some nearby grasses, chewing the moist ends and pulling at the tougher stems to begin making its own form for sleeping.

After, the hare sat quite still, staring straight ahead, alert and intent in its new home.

As the days passed, the hare began to leave its sanctuary under the elm more frequently, exploring its new territory, always wary of the other hares but unhindered by them, each seeming to tolerate the other.

One day, however, was different. It was an early December morning, and the hare was startled awake by a rustling nearby. An elderly female hare was approaching, carrying the weathered remains of the green material in her mouth. She stopped a few yards from the hare, who cautiously approached, looking all round for danger, but seemingly sensing none. The elderly hare dropped her burden, sniffing the material, before hopping slowly to the hare, their faces now just inches apart, and rubbed the side of his face with her nose as he sat perfectly still. Whatever it was that had once been between them had been restored in that single moment and solitary gesture.

Over the next few weeks, the hare gradually joined the others in the drove, moving its form alongside others already under the protection of the wintered hedgerows. They played together in the short evenings, before sitting in the stilled moonlight, or sheltering closely as icy snows whipped and crossed the field. His coat grew thicker and he soon learnt which were the choicest berries to be had, together with the best, most succulent grasses to eat.

As spring finally drove the biting winter from the fields, the hare was as accepted by the drove as any of the others, the elderly female hare especially seeming to always make time for it, sometimes to be joined by an elderly male, the three of them bounding across the field together, playfully chased by the rest of the drove.

One morning, however, just before dawn, things changed in the field, the sleeping drove quickly awakened by a sudden, unexpectedly large crash from the elm, peering through the half-light to see that it had fallen, its roots high now in the air, the trunk completely on its side. A strange lumpen figure seemed to somehow emerge from underneath, walking upright and making peculiar noises as it roamed the fields, clearly looking for something in particular.

The hares scrambled further under the hedgerow, their bodies pressed flat to the earth, motionless, hearts beating rapidly in silent terror as the threatening figure approached.

A large paw suddenly shot under the hedgerow, and a face

appeared, topped by two large ears. The hand swept along the ground reaching out for the hares. It found one, roughly pulled it out, holding its protesting body by the scruff, turning it from side to side and inspecting it closely, before putting it back with the others and reaching for another.

The elderly female hopped close to protect the hare, the elderly male rushing forward to bite the invading paw, the strange creature letting out a sudden cry, but not giving up his efforts for even a moment, eventually finding the hare and pulling it out, peering at it just as closely as the others before it.

"Well, hare," Proftulous griffled. "You's most peffa-definitely be Matlock, and we be briftest friends, so's none of your bitey-bitey trickery, please."

The hare violently struggled, held by the scruff, twisting and turning and savagely kicking out with its back legs. Proftulous looked under the hedgerow again. "Sorry to be all twizzlyfying you, but has anyone of you's been a'seein' his robes? He had a cap, too, and the most crumlush boots."

Sensing perhaps, that the strange creature wasn't as dangerous as she'd previously thought, the elderly hare crept very cautiously forward.

"You's be knowing where they are?" Proftulous griffled to her, holding the struggling hare close to his chest, trying his best to calm it with strokes from his huge paws. "I'd be being most peffa-shindinculously grateful if you did."

The elderly hare stared into the creature's eyes for a long time, as if making an important decision, and not quite fully knowing what to do. Then, finally, she slowly set off across the field towards the downed great elm, the first shaft of dawn settling on the ragged green material still lying where she had dropped it months earlier.

Proftulous reached down, picked it up, watching as the elderly hare hopped onto the trunk, then along the branches to where Matlock's green hat lay, just inches from her nose.

"You's be being most kindly, Mrs Matlock," Proftulous griffled, taking the cap. "And you knows that I be taking the briftest care of him, don't you, when I be making him all majicky again? Because I knows mahpas likes to be thinking that, I does."

The elderly hare hopped from the trunk to a small pile of rotten leaves, moving them with her nose to reveal a tiny frozen body underneath.

Proftulous took a breath. "'Tis the dripple," he gasped. "And it be stroffed."

The elderly hare began rolling and moving the body towards him.

"You wants me to be taking it?" Proftulous looked around nervously. "I don't know," he griffled. "I just don'ts be knowing about that, I don't." He looked into her eyes, watching as they held his intently. "But I suppose I gots to, when you's be looking at me like that, Mrs Matlock." He picked up the frozen body and dropped it into his tweazle pouch, before following the hare once more, this time to find Matlock's purple shoes just a short distance away.

The other hares had moved across the field under the careful guidance of the elderly male, as more and more of dawn's early light continued to flood the field.

"Morn'up, Mr Matlock!" Proftulous griffled, waving to him. He turned to the female, reached down and gently stroked her head, his other paw holding Matlock tight and safe. "I'm afraid we's got to be going now, Mrs Matlock," he griffled. "And I don't wants you to be getting all eye-splashy, because I be making you this promise – one sun-turn Matlock and I will pid-pad back here, and we'll take you all along the tunnels so's you can be seeing Winchett Dale and where he be living and being all majickal. That's a Proftulous promise, that is, and I always be as good as my griffles."

The elderly hare closed her eyes, then slowly turned and hopped away to join the others, leaving Proftulous to wonder if she had understood a single griffle, but hoping somewhere deep in his ganticus dworp's heart that she had.

"Right, Matlock," he griffled, holding the hare, the small robes, shoes and hat. "We's be going on a saztaculous adventure to make everything all peffa-majicky and shindinculous again." He held the hare up to his face. "And I's going to be teaching you, because I's been learning to read."

The hares watched as the strange creature disappeared back under the elm, then scattered in panic over all four corners of the field as the tree slowly re-rooted and righted itself to greet the new day.

All except the two elderly hares, who simply sat and watched.

The Majickal
Apprenctice

11.

Oramus, Chatsworth and the Purpose of Dworps

Much had changed in the months since Frendeslene Note's arrival in Winchett Dale, though in some senses he was forced to admit, very little had changed at all, most notably the glopped-up resident's resistance to any sort of change of which they didn't all entirely approve. The former wooden hall had been swiftly demolished, though inevitably the bulk of the work was done by the krates themselves, the residents proving so peffa-glopped-up, dangerous and incapable of operating even the crudest piece of machinery without some sort of easily predictable disaster. Over the moon-turns, they had become used to waking earlier, though only to assemble in the square and watch the krates hard at work, criticising or just wandering aimlessly around and getting in the way.

Initially, Frendeslene Note had ordered his krates to show no mercy, locking up all creatures who behaved in such a lazy fashion. However, it soon became apparent that a sun-turn spent in a cage proved to be little or no deterrent at all, and if anything the clottabussed creatures of Winchett Dale often treated the experience as something new to do, or 'a change'. Some morn'ups, the creatures would even pid-pad enthusiastically to the cages themselves, each determined to try one they hadn't been in before, some becoming quite russisculoffed if they were already full.

Fragus was the longest serving cage resident, and had become so used to his life behind wooden bars that he now refused to leave, despite repeated pleas from the krates, griffling that he would only consider a move to a larger cage in order to properly house the many items of furniture the other creatures had willingly given to him, as his original cage was now barely recognisable, resplendent as it now was with curtain, its very own roof, and plants growing round its door. Note hoped the foolish disidula's insistence to stay put would be thwarted by the coming snows of winter, and it would soon be begging to be released to be back inside by a warm piff-tosh. But here, once again, Note was wrong, Fragus helpfully suggesting that the krates made a much bigger entrance to the Winchett Dale Inn instead, in order to allow his saztaculous and crumlush cage inside for the cold winter even'ups. Fearing the peffa-annoying creature might be stroffed in the freezing nights, Note had little choice but to agree. The last thing he wanted was any other creatures rising up against him and his officious krates, who he duly set to work removing a large part of the front wall of the inn, and replacing it with Fragus' very own wagon-sized creaker entrance, which they then had to heave and haul him inside every nightfall.

The drutts, too, provided much confusion, the creatures of Winchett Dale still freely giving each other everything they wanted the moment a krate's back was turned. And with so few creatures actually doing anything to rebuild the new stone Great Hall, most had no drutts at all, so knew no value in them whatsoever. The only place they were used was at the inn, where landlord Slivert Jutt still had the thirty original drutts given to him by Serraptomus after the public-griffling on the morn'up the krates had arrived. Now whenever creatures popped in for a guzzwort, they would simply ask him for a drutt, whereupon Jutt would give them one, allowing them to pay for their guzzwort, then promptly take the drutt back, before giving it to someone else. When questioned about this by Note, Jutt griffled that by doing so he was adhering to the rule of 'one-drutt; one-guzzwort', and also in his opinion, helping the krates out, so they weren't wasting valuable officious time by having to give any more drutts out, when they should be working peffa-hard to build the new stone hall. Such logic, Note was vilishly discovering, was hard to argue with, especially as Jutt informed him that he was quite looking forward to his time in a cage, as everyone else had mostly already had a go, and he felt an oidy bit russisculoffed to be left out. He would, Jutt griffled, be more than happy to pid-pad to one right there and then if he'd done anything wrong.

However, in and amongst the chaos of most things going glopped-up, one plan did appear to be working reasonably well, the garrumblooming of the colley-rocks into grillions of drutts. Though in retrospect, perhaps 'reasonably' was an oidy bit optimistic. True, the protesting colley-rocks had been gathered from all four corners of Winchett Dale then taken to the base of Foffle Mountain to be garrumbloomed with Trikulum powder bought by the krates in large barrels. However, as the task was so peffa-dangerous, only the most officious and proficient krates were put in charge of the operation, thereby leaving the rest of the dale guarded and managed by less competent krates, resulting in much of the ensuing chaos.

A further discovery was made after the rocks had been garrumbloomed. Whilst they were now in grillions of pieces, none had lost their ability to griffle, resulting in Note being taken and shown a ganticus pile of noisy drutts, all busily protesting about their treatment. Note had the griffling drutts scattered throughout the dale, ordering the krates to knock at every creature's door and inform them that under no circumstances should a griffling-drutt be used instead of a normal one, and that anyone found doing so would be *forbidden* from being locked up for at least three moon-turns. It was, he felt, the peffa-best he could do in the circumstances, ordering his krates back to work on the stone hall immediately afterwards.

Another thing bothering Note in relation to the colley-rock glopp-up, was the news that none had been found in the majickal-hare's garden. This, he instantly knew, was evidence of foul-play at work, right under his very officious nose. With no way of moving on their own, someone or some*thing* had deliberately taken them, and of all the colley-rocks in the dale, these were the ones he wanted more than any others. He thought back to his previous time in the dale under another guise completely, remembering the four colley-rocks in Matlock's garden, and knowing just how much information they must still have about the driftolubbs.

The ganticus-eared dworp was another looming problem, Note

noticing its absence at any further public-grifflings, or indeed, its glopped-up presence anywhere in the rest of the village. He'd had his krates force the dworp's creaker to search his yechus home in case it was hiding inside, but no sign was found, the search-party vilishly complaining about their ordeal inside the glubbstooled house, griffling that they would never be persuaded to undergo such a yechus task ever again. Of the six who bravely entered the cottage, four were ill for nearly a moon-turn afterwards, and the other two hadn't stopped shaking since.

Note had the entire dale swept dozens of times for the dworp, but again no sign was ever found. Other creatures had no information on the disappearance, and really didn't seem too bothered by it in the first place, griffling that he'd most likely 'come back when he felt ready'. Nevertheless, as the sun-turns rolled by and still no sign of it was found, Note began to worry more and more about the dworp's disappearance.

He summoned Goole, accusing him directly of stealing the colley-rocks from Matlock's garden, a charge Goole vehemently denied. Although Note suspected the Trefflepugga-kraark was most probably lying, he still couldn't be absolutely sure, so he set him to work with Serraptomus, whose only duty since being demoted was to guard the old timbers that had once stood proudly as the former Great Hall, now to be found in a glopped-pile in Chiming Meadows on the outskirts of the village. He also sent one of his briftest krates to quietly spy on them both, hoping he might find out just what they were griffling about each sun-turn, as the two of them had become increasingly friendly; Goole driven by his lust for drutts, Serraptomus simply far too desperate for any kind of friend. When Note's spying-krate reported back at the even'ups however, it was merely to inform him that he'd overheard nothing to do with either the missing dworp, or the colley-rocks.

"Then just what *do* they griffle about all sun-turn?" Note had asked the krate after a particularly glubbstooled sun-turn.

The krate cleared his throat, anxious Note wouldn't get too russisculoffed with him. "Well, Your Officiousness, 'tis mostly about the Trefflepugga-kraark's leg."

"His leg?"

"Indeed. Apparently it got badly bliffed on the path. A bed fell on him. He just griffles on and on about it, all sun-turn." The krate paused.

"And?" Note griffled.

"And he sings about it, too."

Note sighed. "But nothing about the dworp or the rocks? Just singing about his glopped-up leg?"

The krate shifted uneasily. "He also griffles on about singing the song at the grand opening of the new Great Hall, Your Officiousness. Apparently, you promised him that he could."

Note nodded. " I did. It was part of his payment for bringing us here."

"But he's so gobflopped at singing, Your Officiousness. Really peffa-glubbstool. I've never heard anything worse. It'll make a mockery of our new Great Hall…"

Note vilishly held up a paw, immediately silencing the krate, revealing his sharpened claws. "Are you daring to question my judgement, krate?"

The krate flinched. "No, Your Officiousness, never! I was simply griffling…"

"Well perhaps it would pay to keep your griffle-hole shut in future!" Note snapped. "The kraark will sing at the opening, do you understand? The other creatures in this gobflopped dale will like it and everyone will have a saztaculous even'up. That way they will finally begin to appreciate their new way of life under us. Anything else to report?"

"Well, there's Serraptomus. He's taken to carving these last few sun-turns."

"Carving?" Note griffled, puzzled.

The krate nodded. "He goes through the woodpile looking for oidy bits to carve. The kraark has even persuaded him to make a new leg for him."

Note's eyes widened in disbelief. "A new leg? Are you peffa sure?"

The krate nodded. "He thinks his glopped-up one is going to drop off, and wants Serraptomus to make him a wooden one when it happens. I thought it was peffa-glubbstool when I first heard it, but he does seem to be having some trouble scrittling around lately. He griffles that it's the price he had to pay for taking Trefflepugga Path too many times."

Note spent a snutch of moments absorbing it all, nodding slightly before turning to the krate. "You may go."

The krate hesitated slightly. "How…how much longer do I have to keep spying on them, Your Officiousness? Only it's peffa-boring, and the singing is driving me clottabussed. Can't I just go back to the others and work on the Great Hall, only there's still so much to be done, and…"

"You'll do what I griffle you to do, krate," Note griffled, flexing his paw once again.

Once his spy had gone, Note poured himself a glass of trupplejuice then sat in front of his piff-tosh, trying not to think too much about dworps, driftolubbs, colley-rocks, caged-disidulas, wooden-legs, singing kraarks and majickal-hares.

Proftulous, however, in his time underground, had discovered a whole new way of life, from the very first moment he had first entered the mirrit-tunnel under Zhava. He had been looking for a saztaculous adventure, and he had most peffa-certainly found it.

Initially, he was simply intrigued to see where the tunnel led in order to find a hiding place for the sack of colley-rocks. But the further he lump-thrumped along in the damp, earthen pitch-black, the less he found himself wanting to turn back.

Mirrits were everywhere, and although he couldn't see them, he felt them all around, dropping from the tunnel roof and vilishly scattering from his path, seeking the walls for safety. He'd stopped for a while, simply listening to curious sound of grillions of mirrits, chewing away at the earth, tunnelling further down. There were times when he had to almost bend double, forcing himself through narrow gaps, his body pressed against the walls, inching further until the tunnel suddenly widened again, allowing him to lump-thump on, unhindered.

He didn't feel the oidiest bit twizzly either, just excrimbly, which surprised Proftulous. Not normally known for any form of bravery (indeed, his 'glopped-up knee' was a regular excuse for avoiding any sort of twizzly situation) now he didn't feel even the peffa-oidiest twizzle at all. If anything, he felt rather crumlushly safe underground.

Another peculiar thing began to happen the further Proftulous lump-thumped into the gloom. He began to make out the pale bodies of the mirrits, vilishly scrittling over the tunnel walls. Next he saw tree roots pushing through the burrowed earth above his head, and could clearly make out his ganticus paw in front of his face. For some saztaculous and unexplained majickal reason, Proftulous was slowly beginning to see in the total darkness. He stopped for a while, letting whatever it was that was happening to his eyes take full majickal effect. A snutch of moments later, he was off again, seeing everything as clearly as the daylight far above him, totally accustomed to the tunnels, and now able to make out smaller ones at the sides, ascending and descending all around.

He stuck to the main tunnel, lump-thumping on until it suddenly branched into two. An extrapluff told Proftulous to take the one on the right, and he followed it, descending deeper and deeper into the ground, using more extrapluffs with each choice of tunnels he reached, until finally he emerged into a truly saztaculous and ganticus cavern that made him gasp at its complete unexpectedness and sheer, shindinculous beauty.

In the middle was a vast lake, and floating above it what looked like some sort of inn, surrounded by a crumlush garden with vroffa-trees and flaming torches at its edges. His eyes gradually readjusted to the lit cavern, seeing the many tunnel entrances leading to this crumlush place, some set high in the cavern walls with long ladders dangling below. A wooden bridge crossed the lake to the inn, and Proftulous duly lump-thumped across, there to be greeted by a kindly and crumlush creature who called herself Laffrohn, and if anything, seemed to almost have been expecting him, leading him inside to a large tweazle-pie already set and steaming on one of the welcoming wooden tables.

So it was that Proftulous the dworp came to stay at the Vroffa-Tree Inn, right under the very beating heart of Trefflepugga Path, safe and secure, throughout the harsh winter months. Laffrohn set him to work tending the garden in exchange for his bed and constant supply of tweazle-pies. He never once thought to ask her where she got them from, too busy in the garden, griffling to the colley-rocks,

223

learning to read, and caring for the many crumlush plants. There were guzzworts every Yaayday, and visitors would arrive, strange creatures from other dales that Proftulous could never have even imagined, with tales to griffle by the roaring piff-tosh of all their adventures. Proftulous would frequently ask them if any had ever seen a majickal-hare by the name of Matlock, but none ever had, which would often make him feel sad.

"Methinks he's been stroffed on Trefflepugga Path," he'd moan to Laffrohn.

Whereupon she'd put her ganticus paw on his shoulder, and tell Proftulous of the night Matlock had stayed at the inn, reassuring the sullen dworp that the Matlock she knew was so saztaculous that she felt certain he'd be all fuzzcheck. "And one sun-turn, you'll see him again," she'd griffle. "'Tis simply that the time isn't right at the moment. In the meantime we must wait, Proftulous, while you carry on with your reading."

Proftulous did as Laffrohn asked, sensing somewhere deep inside that she was right, he would simply have to wait. He set to the task of reading with renewed energy, devouring *Majickal Dalelore (Volume 68 – revised edition)* from cover to cover in the garden. Occasionally, he would lump-thump back into the inn, as peffa-excrimbly as a youngster, to griffle to Laffrohn just what he had learnt, his ganticus paw urgently pointing to the scribed griffles.

"It griffles here," he'd griffle, "that mirrits are born from extrapluffs, Laffrohn. And that every time you's be having one, it makes an oidy mirrit to be born. So all these tunnels be here because of all the extrapluffing by majickal-hares over grillions of moon-turns. 'Tis amazing to be thinking of such a thing, isn't it?"

Laffrohn would smile. "Well, I can't be saying you should be believing *everything* you be reading in that driftolubb, Proftulous. Sounds peffa-glopped to me, that does."

"But it's in the driftolubb," Proftulous would keenly insist. "So it must be being true, mustn't it?"

And then he would lump-thump back outside to read some more, griffling to the colley-rocks about other things he'd read, or asking them what else they knew about majick from their time spent listening to Chatsworth teaching Matlock in his cottage garden.

It was only when Proftulous read the revisions section on the very final page of the driftolubb that he became peffa-twizzly. "Oh, my scruffling-cafferdoggles!" he suddenly griffled, causing Laffrohn to come pid-padding outside.

"What's being the matter?" she griffled, drying her paws on her apron. "You be looking as white as a mirrit's underbelly."

Proftulous slowly read out the griffles. "*Whilst there have been spuddles of dripples griffling in some peffa-extreme instances, these are largely to be ignored, as none have been available for majickal study at this time. Dripples are silent, ungriffling creatures, and to ever encourage them to be otherwise would endanger your own life significantly.*"

"So why be that making you all shakey and twizzly?" Laffrohn asked him. "Everyone knows dripples don't griffle. Why, it must be the first bit of something sensible in that driftolubb thing of yours that I can actually agree with, methinks."

"But Matlock's dripple was starting to griffle," Proftulous insisted, his griffles coming more and more vilishly. "It was making all noisily things and starting to griffle. But now I knows that griffling-dripples are peffa-twizzly and dangerous, Laffrohn. And if his dripple is stroffed, then so is he, because Matlock used to griffle to me that a majickal-hare and its dripple both go to see Oramus on the very same sun-turn." He fought for a breath. "I must be lump-thumping away to find Matlock. I must. Can't be doing no more of this waitey-rounding any longer. He could be stroffing somewhere right now, while I be here doing nothing about it."

Laffrohn slowly sat by his side. "Proftulous," she gently griffled, "just how much do you want to find Matlock again?"

Proftulous vilishly threw both paws out as peffa-widely as possible. "This much! A grillion this-muchness! You be's having any extrapluffs where he is?"

She shook her head, chickling softly. "No, Proftulous, I don't be doing extrapluffs. Only majickal-hares be doing them. Well, and sometimes a ganticus dworp who can even read the driftolubbs."

Proftulous stood, began anxiously lump-thumping around the garden, his voice bouncing and echoing off the cavern walls. "But what use is reading and extrapluffing, Laffrohn, if I can't even be using them to be finding my briftest friend?" He angrily threw the driftolubb into the lake, watching as it vilishly sank into the deep, silent waters. "Just griffles on a page, is all it was. Just peffa-glopped-up griffles what only tells you things you don't be needing to know, or things you don't be wanting to be knowing!" He turned to her. "I be peffa-russisculoffed about all this, Laffrohn. And I be getting right twizzly for Matlock, too."

She stood, went to him, gave him a hug then leant back, holding both his elbows in her paws, searching his face intently. "Proftulous, I want you to listen to me, peffa-peffa carefully. I needs to be going away for a while this even'up, and I wants you to be staying here and looking after the inn, do you understand?"

"But where you be going to?" Proftulous griffled.

"To a place called Alfisc Dale."

"I never be hearing of it," Proftulous griffled. His face suddenly brightened. "Is that where you be thinking Matlock might be? 'Cause if he is being there, then I's be needing to lump-thump along, too."

She shook her head. "No, you can't, Proftulous. If Matlock is there, then it would far too dangerous and twizzly if he saw you. Everything could go peffa-glubbstooled and gobflopped."

"But why?" Proftulous protested.

Laffrohn took a deep breath. "Because Matlock is on a peffa, peffa-long journey. Alfisc Dale is just the beginning, Proftulous. And on this journey, there are some things he simply has to do and learn on his own. That's all I can griffle to you."

Proftulous was nifferduggling in front of the piff-tosh when Laffrohn returned, not that he'd even noticed her leave. One moment she was there, the next she had gone, just vanished, leaving him with little to do but wait and tend the inn as she'd asked. Not that any creature had pid-padded along the tunnels to stop for a guzzwort. The whole cavern was as silent as a nifferduggling flummer, who of all the silent creatures, are the most peffa-silent of them all. Eventually he'd drifted into nifferduggles himself, his dreams full of finding Matlock and having saztaculous adventures with him.

Laffrohn woke him gently. "He's fine," she griffled. "Matlock's fine."

Proftulous rubbed some yechus gloop from his eyes. "And you be bringing him back?"

She shook her head. "No, Proftulous. But when the time is right *you* will be. 'Tis just like cooking a tweazle-pie, you needs to be waiting until the pastry is all brown and crusty-slurpilicious before you be eating it. So for now, you simply have to wait and know that Matlock is fine, fuzzcheck and in just the place he needs to be."

Which is exactly what Proftulous did, reassured by Laffrohn that all was well with his briftest friend, and going back to spending his time in the garden, or eating tweazle-pies in front of the piff-tosh and doing whatever he could about the inn to help, until at last the sun-turn came when Laffrohn griffled to him that the time had finally arrived; he was to find Matlock and bring him back to the inn.

Proftulous punched the air with a ganticus fist. "This be the most peffa-yamamantally spious sun-turn, ever!" he griffled, then suddenly stopped, his face becoming confused. "But how is I s'posed to be finding him?"

Laffrohn chickled. "Same way you found me, you ganticus clottabus. By following your extrapluffs. I'll be betting that's you starts getting 'em pretty soon, now that the time's exactly right."

"But he could be being anywhere." He looked all around the ganticus cavern at the many tunnel entrances. "There's too many ways and directions to choose from."

"You don't have to see a tweazle-pie to know there's one cooking, do you?" Laffrohn griffled. "You just be following your ganticus nosey. So that's what you be doing now. Follow your extrapluffs and you'll find him."

She pid-padded with him to the bridge. "There's something you might just be needing," she griffled, opening his leather tweazle pouch and slipping the driftolubb inside.

Seeing the book, Proftulous had a sharp intake of breath. "How's you be finding that from the bottom of the lake?"

She tapped the side of her nose and winked. "Let's just griffle that I be following this, Proftulous, and I suggest you be doing the same."

Proftulous tried his most un-yechus smile, then set off across the bridge, vilishly lump-thumping along the many tunnels that his extrapluffs griffled to him to take, until finally rising steeply up and out into the daylight of a spring dawn in a ganticus field. More extrapluffs drove him to the very far side, where a twizzly drove of hares cowered under a hedgerow. He waited for a snutch of moments for more extrapluffs, but none came. This was it, he was at the end of his journey. Incredible, strange and peffa-glopped-up as it appeared, there was no other conclusion – one of these hares *must* be Matlock.

He reached in, risking their anger and getting bitten for his troubles, eagerly searching for his old friend. One that appeared to be being closely guarded by an older hare caught his attention. He grabbed it, pulling it from the undergrowth, staring straight into its eyes. The most saztaculoulsy ganticus extrapluff coursed through his softulous – knowing in that blinksnap that it *was* Matlock. He'd found him!

After gathering Matlock's tattered clothes and thanking the other hares, Proftulous vilishly lump-thrumped back down into the tunnel as the tree closed the entrance behind.

If he thought squeezing his ganticus softulous through the narrower tunnels was hard enough on his own, then it was nothing compared to having to take a twizzly, bucking and biting hare with him, let alone its clothes when it had once been majickal. Proftulous tried everything he could to calm the hare, but nothing seemed to work, it was so clearly peffa-twizzled by the pitch-black journey. It struggled so hard that at times Proftulous found it difficult to extrapluff which of the many tunnels to take.

"You's got to be being all still now, Matlock," he griffled, trying not to get too russisculoffed as it took another bite at his paw. "Otherwise we'll be getting muchly lost and never be finding our way back."

Eventually the hare seemed to tire, allowing Proftulous to receive the guiding extrapluffs that finally took him back towards the ganticus cavern. Light from the beacons flooded the tunnel and then he saw it, the wooden bridge leading back to the warm welcome of The Vroffa-Tree Inn.

"We be home," he griffled, holding the hare by the ears. "And a right peffa-crumlush home it be, too."

"We be home," he griffled, holding the hare by the ears. "And a right
peffa-crumlush home it be, too."

Laffrohn was waiting by the piff-tosh when they arrived, quickly taking Matlock in her arms and settling him on top of a nearby table. "Oh, just be looking at him," she griffled. "He's all twizzly, glopped-up and juzzpapped." She peered closer into the hare's bright orange eyes. "Hello again, Matlock."

"It does be him, doesn't it?" Proftulous proudly griffled. "Only I has meself the most ganticus extrapluff when I sees him, so it has to be him."

Laffrohn stroked the hare's ears with a calming paw. "It be Matlock alright. He has his eyes. You be getting his clothes, too?"

Proftulous dropped them on the table. "What's be happening to him, Laffrohn? He's gone all glopped. He not be griffling anymore. I's be finding him out in The Great Beyond, and he was with all his family. Why's he not being Matlock anymore?"

Laffrohn sat, settling the hare beside her. "There's only two types of creatures that can cross from the dales to The Great Beyond; hares and Most Majelicus majickal-creatures. All others get stroffed if they stay too long."

"Then I's be lucky not to get stroffed," Proftulous griffled. "For I's not be a hare, or Most Majelicus."

Laffrohn nodded. "Well, whatever happened out there, I'm just peffa-glad you're both well."

Proftulous sighed, reached into his leather tweazle-pouch and took out the dripple, laying it gently on the table. "Matlock's dripple did get stroffed, though," he quietly griffled.

Laffrohn looked at the oidy creature for a long time, griffling nothing, but in the peffa-deepest thought. "Proftulous," she eventually griffled, "I really be wanting you to try and understand this. Everything that's happened so far has happened for a reason. I know that it's making us an oidy bit eye-splashy, but I also be thinking that if the dripple is stroffed, then Matlock should be, too. But he's still very much alive, isn't he?"

Proftulous face brightened. "You be being peffa-right!" he griffled. "Matlock hasn't gone to Oramus like his dripple has."

"Which makes me wonder," Laffrohn griffled, "if this sad thing hasn't happened for a reason, too." She put the nifferduggling hare into Proftulous' lap. "Look after Matlock," she griffled, taking the dripple from the table. "Now, give me your tweazle-pouch."

Proftulous did as asked, his attention fully taken with stroking the hare and gently whispgriffling to it as Laffrohn opened the pouch, removed the majicjkal-driftolubb and took both the book and the dripple upstairs, before returning a little later with a tweazle-pie for Proftulous.

"I suppose we be having to get Matlock a new dripple, do we?" he asked, tucking into a yechus mouthful of pie. "After we gets him all back to being majickal again?"

Laffrohn nodded. "One thing at a time, methinks," she griffled, gently waking the hare and setting a steaming bowl under its nose. "First thing we got to be doing is seeing if your briftest friend Matlock remembers just what niff-soup is."

To their ganticus surprise and relief, the hare seemed to enjoy the soup, so much so that Proftulous insisted it have another bowlful, something Laffrohn gently persuaded him wasn't such a good idea. Afterwards the hare quietly explored the inn, as Proftulous and Laffrohn griffled by the piff-tosh.

"Laffrohn," Proftulous asked, watching the flames dance and sprockle, "I's been thinking about things."

"Has you, indeed?" she griffled. "Don't always pay to be doing all that thinking-stuff, Proftulous. Especially what with you's being a dworp, an' all."

"I know," Proftulous nodded, "but I have things on my mind, and they just won't be going away. I even tries thinking about tweazles, and they still be there."

"What sort of things?" Laffrohn asked, pouring herself a guzzwort from a large jug.

"Well," Proftulous griffled, "why does Matlock not be being all majickal anymore?"

Laffrohn smiled. "Because he spent time out in The Great Beyond. His powers have all been lost, alongside all the memories he ever had of his life in these dales. He became just a normal hare out in The Great Beyond. But one sun-turn, if he becomes Most Majelicus, then he will return in safety in all his Most Majelicus red robes to be finding his own apprentice hare to become the new majickal-hare of Winchett Dale. 'Tis the way of things, Proftulous, the cycle of majickal-hares."

Proftulous turned to her, trying to understand. "So he won't be being in Winchett Dale anymore?" he griffled, trying not to sound sad. "He won't be being with Proftulous, his briftest friend?"

She reached out and took his ganticus paw in hers, squeezing it gently. "Proftulous, what you has to be understanding is that the journey of a majickal-hare is a truly saztaculous one that mere creatures like you and I will never fully understand. Why, Oramus himself who looks over us all from his home in the moon, was once a majickal-hare, the first majickal-hare in all the dales. All hares have majick inside them, Proftulous, but those chosen by their masters to be majickal-hares are the most peffa-majickal of them all. And from that moment their life becomes a journey, a ganticus pid-pad in which they have to do many things to prove to Oramus that one sun-turn they will be truly worthy of being Most Majelicus. Matlock is on that journey right now, right at the very beginnings of it."

Proftulous looked over at the hare, hopping between chairs and table legs. "But he don't be looking Most Majelicus. Not one oidy bit."

Laffrohn chickled. "Tis the way of Oramus. Any majickal-hare that is chosen to become Most Majelicus must complete three peffa-special and difficult challenges. The first is to lose everything; majick, driftolubbs, home and friends, and be returned back into The Great Beyond to live the life of a normal hare, then to return and solve the riddle of Trefflepugga Path."

"But I don't be seeing why."

"By going back to the field of its birth, its family can choose whether to let it go a second time. Some don't, guarding their hares closely and never letting them go. Others let them return to the dale, and 'tis a peffa-important pid-pad in the journey to becoming Most Majelicus. Your family must approve, despite all the risks and peffa-twizzly dangers."

Proftulous nodded. "Matlock's mahpa helped me be finding his robes for him."

"Because all hares are majickal, Proftulous, even out in The Great Beyond. Somewhere in her Sisteraculous, she would have sensed Matlock had to go, that his journey was only really just beginning."

"But how you be knowing all this?" Proftulous asked.

Laffrohn chickled. "I's be the landlady of The Vroffa-Tree Inn, Proftulous, so I's be hearing all sorts of strange spuddles and griffles, especially after a few guzzworts has been had by all." She poured Proftulous a guzzwort. "Those that come to this inn are powerful creatures, Proftulous. They may look like normal clottabussed creatures, but all are in some oidy sense Most Majelicus, as they have found the way to move freely from dale to dale. Trefflepugga Path lies just above us, Proftulous, and on it right now will be creatures thinking they're peffa-glopped-up and lost, but really 'tis simply the path taking them where they need to be." She took a long sip of guzzwort, watching the flames. "But once you solve the riddle of Trefflepugga Path, then the tunnels reveal themselves to you, and you can begin to learn how to use the tunnels to go anywhere you want to."

Proftulous frowned, struggling to understand. "But I be lump-thumping along tunnels, Laffrohn, and I never be solving no riddle. I be too clottabussed to solve any riddles, me."

She smiled, nodded her head. "Clottabussed you may be, Proftulous, but believe me, you've already solved the riddle. Otherwise you wouldn't be here."

"But I don't be knowing of any such riddling," Proftulous insisted. "I not heard of it, and I not be seeing it."

"Of course you've seen it," Laffrohn griffled. "And heard it. And tasted it. And smelt it. And felt it. It's everywhere, Proftulous, all around us."

"I's not be understanding any of this one oidy bit," Proftulous griffled, scratching a ganticus ear.

"Because you don't have to," Laffrohn griffled, ducking as a murp-worm flew close to her head. "You already have the answer, so why should you be getting russisculoffed about not knowing the question? Somehow, without you even knowing it, you've solved the riddle of Trefflepugga Path, and that is enough. Now Matlock has to do the same. But first he has to become majickal again. Once he has done that, and solved the riddle, then he will have completed the first of the three tasks to becoming Most Majelicus." Her eyes gleamed in the firelight. "T'will be a peffa-excrimbly and most shindinculous adventure for him, Proftulous, and methinks he will be needing the help of a saztaculous friend, too."

Proftulous brightened at this, following her griffles. "I's can be teaching him how to read, can't I? And how's to be griffling. And how to be pid-padding properly, not all hoppy like he is now."

"You can," Laffrohn griffled, nodding. "But not here, Proftulous. Matlock will only become majickal again in the dale where he first became a majickal-hare. He has to learn again, but this time not from his master, from someone else. 'Tis why you have been chosen to teach him, Proftulous."

"I's be having to take him back to Winchett Dale like that?" Proftulous griffled, pointing to the hare, now soundly nifferduggling on the cool stone floor. "But the dale be full of krates and they's not be liking Matlock one oidy bit. They's be locking him away and doing glopped-up things with him if they finds him."

Laffrohn nodded. "Indeed, it will be a peffa-twizzly task, Proftulous."

"I don't know I's be liking this," Proftulous suddenly griffled, beginning to frown. "Why I's be chosen to do this? Why not someone else? And who's be choosing me for this?"

Laffrohn gave his paw another squeeze. "There's be some things I knows, and grillions of things that I don't, and this, quite simply, be one of those."

"But what happens if I gobflops?"

"Then use the tunnels, Proftulous. Come back to me. The krates can't be following you as they're not Most Majelicus." She gave him a long look. "I have no idea why it's happened, but for some reason you are already Most Majelicus. But be warned, it may not last. Your extrapluffs might suddenly stop, or you could be realising you can't be seeing in the dark anymore, or be finding you can't read. So you must hurry, and take Matlock back to Winchett Dale and begin his apprenticeship all over again. It's all you can do."

Proftulous thought hard, trying to make up his mind. "It all be making me feel twizzly."

Laffrohn nodded. "But at the moment you have luck and Oramus at your side. You must be doing this for Matlock."

Proftulous looked into the flames for a long time. "I's be beginning to wonder where all the tweazle-pies be coming from," he slowly griffled, turning to her. "Tis because you be being Most Majelicus, too, Laffrohn, isn't it? That's why you be down here, using all the tunnels, and going to find Matlock when he be in Alfisc Dale that night."

Laffrohn chickled, shaking her head. "No, Proftulous, I not's be being Most Majelicus for a peffa, peffa-long time. I was once, many moon-turns ago, but no longer." She stood, stretching and yawning. "But that's another story you'll discover in time. For now, I'm juzzpappd, and be needing my nifferduggles. And you, good-friend, need to be taking this hare back home. It'll be night-time in Winchett Dale now, so's you'll be able to find somewhere to hide him that no one would be thinking to look." She bent down and lightly bliffed his ears. "But that's one problem I'll be leaving up to you."

Proftulous watched as she gathered the nifferduggling hare in her arms, whispgriffling in its ears before passing him over.

"Leave the driftolubb and his clothes with me," she griffled. "He'll not be needing them for a while, and you'll have enough on your paws simply teaching him how to griffle and pid-pad properly."

"I really not be sure about this," Proftulous griffled, moaning slightly. "I's be getting all my twizzly thoughts back again."

"Just extrapluff," she griffled to him. "Be patient, and all will be fuzzcheck."

Laffrohn opened the wooden creaker, watching as he slowly lump-thumped over the wooden bridge, stopping in front of several tunnels before deciding which one to take, giving her one last wave before disappearing into the black.

A blinksnap after he had gone, she pid-padded back inside, upstairs to her bedroom, opening a small wooden box on top of her dressing table, peering inside at the furry body lying on the majickal-driftolubb.

Well," she quietly griffled, stroking the top of its head and noticing that the fur didn't seem quite as matted and glopped as it was before, "those crows out in The Great Beyond have peffa-definitely left your stroffed body for a reason, crumlush creature. Methinks 'tis about time Oramus and his majickal-driftolubbs did some proper Most Majelicus majick."

*

235

It was easier with the hare in the tunnels the second time. Mostly it nifferduggled contentedly, juzzpapped from the exertions of its peculiar day, Proftulous following his extrapluffs until finally he found the ascending tunnel leading under Zhava, her roots wriggling above his head as he approached, then slowly opening the entrance back into Wand Wood.

Proftulous stepped out, thanking the Last Great Elm for the inconvenience as she righted herself again.

"What in Oramus' name have you got there?" Zhava griffled, curious as to the small bundle in Proftulous' arms. "And where have you been, Proftulous? You've been gone so long."

"It be Matlock," he whispgriffled. "But it be peffa-secrety, so you mustn't be griffling to anyone that I's been and found him."

Zhava leant closer, examining the hare. "This be Matlock? Are you sure?"

"Peffa-sure," he proudly griffled. "And I's been solving the riddle of Trefflepugga Path, too, even though I not be knowing what I'm doing."

Zhava frowned. "Have you been drinking too many guzzworts, Proftulous? You're not making any sense."

Proftulous shook his head. "That's because I be being Most Majelicus, Zhava. 'Tis making my head spinny and glopping-up all my griffles."

Zhava sighed. "Of all the creatures in this dale, I never thought you'd be the one to turn to the guzzworts, Proftulous, I really didn't."

Proftulous frowned, realising his griffles would be wasted on the shocked elm-tree, but wished Zhava well and made his way steadily through the woods, listening carefully for any unexpected noises. His immediate problem was where to hide the hare for long enough so he could teach it how to be majickal again. He needed a place that no one would possibly find, either krates or creatures, in order to keep everything peffa-secrety. He stopped, closed his eyes and waited for an extrapluff. A blinksnap later he knew exactly where to go, the place where Matlock's second apprenticeship would begin – in his very own peffa-yechus and glubstooled house. For apart from Frendeslene Note forcing him to eat the ganticus tweazle-pie, Proftulous couldn't remember the last time anyone had dared to pid-pad beyond the front creaker, such was the glopped-up state of the place. It would be ideal, Proftulous realised. He would train the hare during the sun-turns, and in the darkened even'ups it could accompany him into the woods, hunting tweazles.

Pleased at his extrapluffing, Proftulous slipped quietly back into the nifferduggling village, amazed to see The Great Hall had disappeared completely, replaced by ganticus piles of stone, set by high walls defining the beginnings of the new hall. A roof had been completed, and he saw candlelight glowing from inside.

"Them krates be getting on with all sorts while we's been away, Matlock," he whispgriffled to the sleeping hare. "I just be hoping my crumlush cottage still be there."

Proftulous needn't have worried, his cottage standing just as he'd left it. Indeed, with the exception of a long row of cages at the far end of the village square, he was relieved to notice that nothing else had really changed in Winchett Dale at all. He quietly slipped inside his cottage and closed the creaker behind him, the hare instantly waking as its sensitive nose was immediately assaulted by a barrage of appallingly yechus smells.

"You's be all calming down, Matlock," he whispgriffled, setting the panicked creature gently down on the mirrit infested floor. "Welcome to your new home."

The hare immediately bolted back towards the creaker, pawing at it desperately. Proftulous picked it up, being bitten again for his troubles, this time putting it on the table. Again, it bolted, and for the next few minutes both hare and dworp chased each other all over the hideous house, until Proftulous slumped into a chair, peffa-juzzpapped and wheezing, but feeling that somehow the hare had rather enjoyed every leap, hop and bound.

It was a game they were to play regularly over the next few sun-turns, racing round the house, sometimes the hare turning to bound after Proftulous as he chickled and lump-thumped away. By days they stayed concealed, and by nights Proftulous led the hare on a piece of glopped-up twine out into Wand-Wood to collect tweazles and niffs, returning in the dead of night when the rest of the village nifferduggled.

By the end of the first moon-turn however, Proftulous was

becoming rather juzzpapped of the same routine. By contrast, the hare seemed perfectly content, but totally unwilling to learn anything Proftulous was trying to teach it. Proftulous would wait until the hare tired, then try griffling to it, over and over, repeating 'My name be Matlock' hoping for just the oidiest noise or griffle back, but the hare simply watched, confused, its bright orange eyes staring blankly back.

Undaunted, he tried teaching the hare to stand and pid-pad, lifting it by both paws and shuffling it forwards, whereupon the hare would vilishly twist and bound away, growling if he tried again. The only things it seemed to like were playing, being out in the woods and eating a constant supply of niffs.

One even'up, things became too glopped, even for Proftulous. He was tired of the hare now, tired of being stuck inside his cottage hiding away from all the other creatures behind his yechus tweazle-skin curtains. It was the middle of spring, and with the lighter even'ups, the other creatures of Winchett Dale were venturing outside more often; griffling, chickling and visiting the inn for guzzworts. Proftulous wanted to join them and be with his friends again. It was, he thought, far worse hiding in his house than it would have been outside in one of the cages. At least he'd have had company to griffle with nearby.

The hare, perhaps sensing his increasing russisculoftulation, watched cautiously from a darkened corner of the room as Proftulous made a gobflopped attempt to eat a tweazle-pie, before pushing the half-empty plate aside and suddenly banging the table with his ganticus fist.

"Tis no good, Matlock!" he griffled. "This teaching is going all peffa-glopped, and you not be learning anything properly!" He peered under the table into the far corner, pointing accusingly at the cowering hare. "I be thinking lately that's you not even *being* Matlock in the first place! You's more like a clottabussed normal hare that just looks an oidy bit like him." He banged the table again, harder this time. "I's be having enough of this! I's Proftulous the Dworp, and I's be able to extrapluff and be reading and be Most Majelucussy, and you's be keeping me here in the dark, just like a murp-worm! You's not be learning anything, just eating niffs and glubbstooling around.

Well, I's be reaching my limit with you, so's I be taking you back to where I's be finding you, so's I can be forgetting about all this!" He stood, angrily lump-thumped to the corner, reaching out and grabbing the protesting hare roughly by the ears, then raising it to his face. "You be clottabussed, glopped-up and glubbstooled, hare, and I is done with you!"

A calming voice suddenly came from behind. "They can be so peffa-tiring, can't they?"

Proftulous spun round, beaming at the familiar figure in the bright red robes of a Most Majelicus majickal-hare. "Chatsworth!" he griffled, dropping the hare and giving Matlock's old master a ganticus hug. "That be you? Really you?"

Chatsworth nodded. "And you've grown, Proftulous," he griffled. "The last time I saw you was on the High-Plateau, when Matlock tried his very first vroosher."

"And it all went glubbstool!" Proftulous griffled, peffa-excrimbly. "He tried to make the lid all splashy, and gobflopped four disidulas into Chiming Meadows instead!" He gave the elderly-hare another hug. "Oh, I be so peffa-pleased to be seeing you, Chatsworth, so peffa, peffa-pleased, indeed so."

"And you too, Proftulous," Chatsworth griffled, closing his eyes and whispgriffling for a snutch of moments, his nose and whiskers twitching, as gradually a bright yellow ball of flashing light grew above his head, Proftulous standing back and gasping as it roamed and floated around the cottage, cleaning and mending everything it touched. Eventually, the entire cottage looked as pristine and crumlush as the day it was built. A warming fire burst into flame in the piff-tosh, and the ball of light disappeared.

"That be most peffa-shindinculous!" Proftulous griffled, marvelling how saztaculous everything looked. Not a single mirrit scrittled across the peffa-perfectly clean floor, broken tables and chairs had been majickally restored, and the ganticus tweazle-pie tin shone bright silver over the gently-splutting piff-tosh.

Chatsworth sat in an armchair. "Sorry about that, Proftulous," he griffled. "Only t'was far too peffa-glopped-up in here."

"Tis all the hare's fault," Proftulous griffled, watching as it sniffed around at Chatsworth's feet. "I's been so busy trying to be

239

teaching it that I's not been having any time to be doing me tidying."

Chatsworth stroked the hare's ears as it settled beside him. "And from what I overheard just now," he griffled, "it doesn't seem to be going very well."

Proftulous nodded. "He not be learning anything at all. I's be trying my peffa-hardest, but he's just being glopped and clottabussed, and I's be so russiculoffed with it that I's be having my crimpleful of it and don't wants to be doing it any more. So I's be taking him back to where he belongs, 'cause he's just not being majickal, not an oidy bit."

Chatsworth tickled the hare under its chin. "And how do you learn things, Proftulous?"

Proftulous thought for a snutch of moments. "I just be learning, don't I?" He slowly stood, looking around the small room. "I just be doing it."

"I heard you learnt how to read."

"How's you be knowing that?"

"A friend of ours griffled me."

"What friend be this?" Proftulous griffled, watching as Chatsworth stood and reached into one of his long pockets, pulling out a long green robe, purple slippers, a green cap, an oidy leather potion-bottle and a hawthorn-wand. "Laffrohn?"

Chatsworth nodded. "She has repaired Matlock's clothes. She wanted me to give them to you."

Proftulous took the clothes, all beautifully clean and crumlush, as immaculate as when Matlock first tried them on, many moon-turns previously.

"She told me of your time at The Vroffa-Tree Inn," Chatsworth griffled. "I was hoping you'd find your way there." He chickled. "She griffled to me that she's never had to make so many tweazle-pies in her many, many lives. She was quite taken with you, Proftulous, as indeed, I hoped she would be."

Proftulous' eyes widened. "'Tis *you*, isn't it?" he griffled. "You's been the one behind all this glopping, haven't you?"

"Partly," Chatsworth admitted. "But only the oidiest, most peffa-humble part. There are others, many others, all far more important and superior to a mere Most Majelicus majickal-hare like

Proftulous took the clothes, all beautifully clean and crumlush, as immaculate as when Matlock first tried them on, many moon-turns previously.

me, Proftulous. I am simply playing my oidy part in the beginnings of Matlock's most saztaculous and shindinculous journey to become Most Majelicus."

"And then he'll be like you?" Proftulous griffled. "Able to be all majickal and do clean-uppy vrooshers?"

Chatsworth smiled. "And peffa-many more things besides, Proftulous."

"And why you's be griffling me all this?"

Chatsworth took a breath, rubbed at his own chin thoughtfully. "Because, and I'm sorry to have to griffle you this, you will soon forget everything I griffled."

"What's you mean?"

"It's why you were chosen, Proftulous. From the very first moment I pid-padded into Winchett Dale with Matlock, I was also looking for the creature that would be able to help him on the first part of his adventure when his time came. And it had to be a peffa-clottabussed creature, Proftulous, a most completely glopped-up, hopelessly gobflopped creature."

"So you's be choosing Proftulous?" Proftulous griffled, trying not to sound too hurt.

Chatsworth nodded. "I thought it would be difficult considering how clottabussed everyone in Winchett Dale is. But when I saw you, a yechus gloopy-faced, young dworp, I just *knew* you were the one."

"Oh," Proftulous quietly griffled. "So's that be the reason why you let me be friends with Matlock, was it? I thought that perhaps it was because you might be thinking that I wasn't so clottabussed as everyone else was always griffling."

"Oh, for Oramus' sake, don't get upset," Chatsworth griffled. "Why can't you just be excrimbly about being chosen?"

"Because," Proftulous griffled, trying to keep calm and not begin banging tables again, "abouts the only thing I can see to be excrimbly about is that you've cleaned up my tweazle-tin! I's been used by you, Chatsworth, and you still be using me now. I may be a yechus gloopy-faced dworp, but I still has bits that be hurted inside, and that's what your griffles is doing to me."

"What do you know about dworps?" Chatsworth griffled, his voice calm and steady.

Proftulous frowned, caught by the question. "Well, I be one."

"Do you know any other dworps?"

Another long pause. "No."

"What's your earliest memory?"

An easier question for Proftulous. "Chasing my first tweazle! It be right peffa-crumlush!"

"You remember your mahpa? Your pahpa?"

Proftulous shook his ganticus head.

"Any brothers, or sisters?"

Proftulous was beginning to frown again, confused by the speed of the questions. "I not's be knowing why you's be asking me all this, Chatsworth."

Chatsworth nodded. "Let me griffle an oidy bit about the purpose of dworps, Proftulous, seeing as you know so little about your own kind. It is the job of a Most Majelicus hare to travel into The Great Beyond and find a hare to become its apprentice in any dale Trefflepugga Path chooses to send them both to. Once in the dale, training must begin. Some hares are rather glubbstool, and have to be returned. Others are brifter and become majickal-hares. But there are some that are destined one sun-turn to undertake the three tasks to become Most Majelicus." He looked directly at Proftulous. "And these hares make friends with a dworp, one of the rarest and most peffa-clottabussed creatures in all the dales. So when I saw you lump-thumping around in Winchett Dale, I knew that it was my job to force you two together, in order that when he was ready, Matlock would be ready to make that journey. You were a sign, Proftulous, a sign that one sun-turn, Matlock could become a Most Majelicus hare."

"But you's not be forcing us," Proftulous protested. "We's becoming briftest friends because we's always be peffa-liking each other."

Chatsworth shook his head. "It was because he had no other friends. Don't you see? I made sure of that. A majickal-hare apprentice will befriend a dworp because they both live solitary lives; the hare on the edges of villages, and the dworp because he is so yechus and clottabussed that all the other creatures chickle at it, glad it isn't their glopped-up friend." He paused, sighing. "T'isn't my

243

duty to upset you, Proftulous, 'tis simply my duty to griffle you the truth. In a while you will have to make a peffa-important decision, one that you can choose to undertake, or to lump-thump away from, as some dworps do when they understand exactly what they are expected to do."

Proftulous swallowed, his yechus eyes beginning to glisten. "I don't knows I wants to be hearing anymore," he griffled.

"You must, I'm afraid," Chatsworth griffled, moving the hare gently onto Proftulous' lap. "Oramus grants that the purpose of a dworp is to help a majickal-hare solve the riddle of Trefflepugga Path. In this journey the dworp will receive majickal powers to help him with his task. He must be prepared to journey into The Great Beyond and find the hare, bring it back and teach it to be majickal."

"But I already be doing all that," Proftulous quietly griffled. "All except the teaching."

"Indeed, Proftulous. And you have done well. But you task isn't over, far from it. Matlock needs to learn again. And in order to teach him, you must first be prepared to lose all that you yourself have ever learnt."

"I not's be understanding what you're griffling about," Proftulous griffled.

"Proftulous, please try. Your majickal powers of extrapluffing, reading and even the ability to lump-thump so vilishly and climb trees, are all soon to be Matlock's, and not yours, ever again. You have simply been keeping them safe for him."

Proftulous' heavy brow creased into a deep frown. "I's not be able to be reading again?"

Chatsworth slowly shook his head. "Every griffle you teach Matlock will be lost from your memory. So too, will be your part in his journey, your time at the The Vroffa-Tree Inn, our griffles together, everything. Even the memory of Matlock himself. When the time comes for him to become a majickal-hare, you will never see, or remember him, ever again."

"But he will still be remembering me?" Proftulous asked. "He will be coming to find me and taking me to Thinking Lake to griffle about extrapluffs?"

Chatsworth shook his head. "Just as I have no memory of the

dworp that helped me, so I'm afraid Matlock will have no memory of you, either. Your time together will be done."

Proftulous scratched a ganticus ear, trying not to get too upset. "This seems to be being peffa-wrong," he moaned, his voice beginning to crack a little. "So peffa, peffa-wrong. What's I be doing to be upsetting Oramus like this? I never even be seeing him, and I've been a good dworp and always done good things and only tried to make creatures chickle and be fuzzcheck."

"Proftulous," Chatsworth griffled. "The time has come. You know the truth about your destiny. Oramus grants you the right to choose what to do. You must decide either to teach Matlock, or not. If you choose not to, then I am dutifully bound to return him to The Great Beyond, and you can live the rest of your life in peace."

Proftulous began to panic, scratching at both his ears. "But I not's be knowing what to do!"

"Just choose."

"I can't, Chatsworth! 'Tis too glopped a choice to be making! I don't wants him to be going back, but I don't wants him to be all forgetting about me, either!"

Chatsworth reached out a paw, placing it gently on Proftulous' shoulders, the ganticus dworp's head bowed now, a single eye-splashy running down his yechus face. "Proftulous," he griffled. "Although I have no memory of the dworp who helped me, I am forever grateful to it, and I will never, ever forget that. Matlock will be the same, I promise you."

Proftulous slowly lifted his head and took the deepest dworp's breath he'd ever taken in his glopped-up and clottabussed lifetime. "I don't be believing in 'promises'," he quietly griffled. "Only thing I really ever believes in was Matlock. Promises is just griffles, and I not be knowing if I be liking them anymore. So I don't be wanting no more of your promises, Chatsworth." He met Chatsworth in the eye, jaw set and determined. "All I be wanting from you is some proper griffles telling me just how I goes about teaching and majicking this hare back into being Matlock again."

12.

Thinking Lake, the Dripple Fair and Niff-Soup

There are no 'rules', as such, for training a majickal hare. Over the generations, Most Majelicus hares have trained their apprentices in whatever way they thought best. However, by contrast, dworps in charge of the re-training process generally tend to opt for one proven approach; carrot and stick – or, as in Matlock's case – niffs and hawthorn wand. Not that Proftulous was ever tempted to use the wand to bliff Matlock, he didn't have to, and besides he hated bliffing anything except tweazles. But by stabbing a fresh niff on the end of the wand, Proftulous found he was able to encourage Matlock enough to stand on his hind legs for short periods of time. Gradually, he began to take one or two faltering pid-pads, until the sun-turn came when he was able to pid-pad from one end of the cottage to the other, Proftulous gleefully leading the way, holding the crumlush niff just in front of Matlock's ever-twitching nose.

Getting Matlock used to wearing clothes however, was quite a different problem. Chatsworth had advised Proftulous to try the green cap first, preferably while Matlock was nifferduggling. However, a dworp's ganticus paws are clumsy at the briftest of times, and the task proved trickier than it sounded, Matlock waking up and bolting the moment Proftulous tried to push his long ears through the cap. However, with perseverance and more niff-treats, the task was eventually accomplished more or less satisfactorily.

Chatsworth would occasionally drop by to review Proftulous' progress, letting himself in through the back door in the dead of night, griffling with the weary dworp, offering hints and advice of what to do next. A moon-turn passed, and Matlock was now pid-padding quite freely and able to more or less dress himself, only really needing help with the buttons on his robe, after which he'd give Proftulous a ganticus hug to thank him.

"Now you's not to be doing that, Matlock," Proftulous would griffle, gently pushing him away. "Only I's not going to be here for too much longer. Once you be all learned how to griffle, I's won't be allowed to be seeing you again, and you'll be needing to find another creature to be hugging."

Griffling was the next challenge. Chatsworth suggested Proftulous start at the most obvious place, with the griffle 'niff', using the crumlush vegetable as reward. Next came 'soup', then 'crumlush', 'fuzzcheck', 'bowl', 'please' and 'thank you'. When Chatsworth next returned Matlock had learnt nearly twenty griffles, and seemed eager for more.

"You have a saztaculous way with him," Chatsworth observed. "You are a patient and kindly dworp."

"I's be peffa-juzzpapped, though," Proftulous griffled, passing Chatsworth a steaming brottle-leaf brew and slumping into a chair.

"Indeed," Chatsworth griffled. "But it's working, Proftulous. All your peffa-hard work is paying off. However, I strongly advise you not to get too close to him. It will only be harder for you in the end. Be sure Matlock only refers to you as 'Master' from now on. He is never to learn your name. It will be easier for you both that way."

Proftulous looked confused. "So he can't be calling me by my proper name, then? I's not sure I be liking this 'Master' business. I just be his friend, Proftulous. 'Tis hard enough as it is, without him having to call me 'Master'."

"But it's how it's done, Proftulous, how it's always been done."

"Well then, I be thinking that p'raps it's always being done glopped, then."

Chatsworth sipped at his brew. "Proftulous," he griffled, "how did you think you got *your* name?"

The juzzpapped dworp scratched his cheek, trying to think. "I not really be knowing."

"Think, Proftulous. You have no mahpa or pahpa, or family. I found you lump-thumping in the dale."

Proftulous slowly turned, looking the Most Majelicus hare in the eyes. "*You* be naming me?"

Chatsworth nodded. "I did."

"I not sure I be liking the thought of that, either."

"It's the truth, Proftulous," Chatsworth griffled. "I named you. Just as I named Matlock, too; from a place way out in The Great Beyond, near to where he was born."

"So I's been there?" Proftulous griffled. "I goes to the real Matlock when I goes to be getting him and bringing him back?"

Chatsworth nodded again. "A place close enough to it, yes."

"And I'd be named after a place, too?"

"I named you after a star," Chatsworth griffled. "One of the briftest, brightest and most shindinculous stars in the twinkling-lid; the star of Proftulous." He stood, went to the window, pulled back the tweazle curtain and pointed high into the night sky. "Look to the moon," he griffled, as Proftulous awkwardly lump-thumped to his side. "There, just above it, is the Most Majelicus star of Proftulous, thought to be the oldest in all the twinkling-lid."

Proftulous squinted at the star. "That be me? But it looks so close to the moon, like it's almost touching it."

Chatsworth chickled. "Tis a trick of the lid," he griffled. "The star of Proftulous lies far, far away. Yet from here, it appears to be the closest to the moon."

Proftulous frowned. "But if I's be on the moon, I thinks I would be able to reach out and put it right in my tweazle-pouch."

"Perhaps," Chatsworth slowly griffled, "one sun-turn, you will." He closed the curtain, watching as Proftulous painfully lump-thumped back to his chair. "You're having trouble getting around?"

Proftulous winced, wheezing as he eventually sat back down.

"Tis because you have taught Matlock how to pid-pad. Remember, everything you teach him to do, you will no longer be able to do yourself. Don't fight it, Proftulous. You must accept that your lump-thumping sun-turns are nearly over. It is time for you to walk on all fours. You will find it easier that way."

But Proftulous shook his head. "I's be lump-thumping for as peffa-long as I can lump-thump, thank you. I not be wanting to be on me all fours. Would be glopped."

Chatsworth sighed. "Do it your way, Proftulous."

"I will," Proftulous proudly griffled. "That's why I be the most peffa-clottabussed creature in the most peffa-clottabussed of all the dales. 'Tis because I don't be listening to nobody that griffles me clever things to be doing. I always be doing things my own way."

"But Proftulous," Chatsworth warned, "the longer this goes on, and the more you teach Matlock, the less you will be able to do *anything* your way. It's how it is, how it's written, and every dworp who has undertaken to train a majickal-hare has gone through exactly the peffa-same."

"But I's not be like every other dworp," Proftulous griffled, wincing as a sudden shot of pain coursed through his legs. "I be Proftulous, named after a star, and that be making me muchly different and brifter than all the other dworps."

But as the sun-turns passed, Proftulous inevitably found it harder and harder to lump-thump and was eventually forced to begin walking on all fours, just as Chatsworth had predicted. Matlock, however, continued to make steady progress with his griffles and was now able to ask for things and be taught small chores around the house. Proftulous showed him how to make niff-soup and tweazle-pie, the pair of them chickling and griffling, all excrimbly as they frequently glopped the entire kitchen making pastry.

Matlock duly referred to Proftulous as 'Master', as he knew no other name for him, but as his grifflecabulary grew, so did the complexity of his questions, some of which Proftulous now knew had absolutely no hope of answering in a grillion sun-turns.

"What makes rain, Master?" Matlock would ask, as Proftulous tried desperately hard to find the right griffles, realising that he had forgotten far too many already.

"I not's be sure, Matlock," Proftulous mostly griffled to the questions, wondering just how long it would be before he wouldn't be able to griffle any longer.

Matlock would be nifferduggling upstairs when Chatsworth

came to visit, leaving Proftulous and the Most Majelicus hare to review the eager apprentice's progress. Proftulous was finding everything increasingly difficult, especially having to stay indoors every sun-turn. Matlock was getting bored too, and wanted to explore, meet the other creatures he saw pid-padding around when he peeped through the curtains. He wanted to know why he was being kept a secret, why he wasn't allowed outside, why it was that they could only leave the house when everyone else was already nifferduggling.

"It be wearing me right through," Proftulous confessed to Chatsworth, late one even-up. "I be done with it all. He be getting too much for me. I be forgetting griffles all the time."

Chatsworth reached into his robes and placed a small book on the table. "You remember this, though?"

Proftulous juzzpapped eyes brightened a little. "'Tis me driftoloubb." He picked it up, flicking through the pages. "*Majickal Dalelore, (Volume 68 – revised edition.)*"

"I collected it from Laffrohn earlier. She has finished with it now." Chatsworth put a paw round the tired dworp's shoulder. "You must teach Matlock how to read, while you still have enough griffles left. Then there is just extrapluffing. After that, you are done, I can collect Matlock and he can become a majickal-hare once more."

Proftulous simply stared at the driftolubb, too juzzpapped to griffle another griffle.

Matlock didn't really take to reading at all, regardless of how much Proftulous tried to explain how important it would be to him. "But Master," he would griffle, "it's just so peffa-boring and glopped-up! And I don't really know if I *want* to be a majickal-hare anyway. It all sounds glubbstool, and there's far too much peffa-hard work. Why can't I just be like all the other creatures I see outside?"

Proftulous would try to explain just how shindinculous it was going to feel to do saztaculous vrooshers with his hawthorn wand, but Matlock would simply pull a face, asking to go outside and explore instead.

"I've told you before," Proftulous would griffle, "there be krates out there that don't be wanting you here. They'd be locking you up for a peffa-long time if they be finding you. You must stay here and learn how to be reading. Once you can read, and be doing the extrapluffing, then you can be being a majickal-hare doing saztaculous vrooshers to drive the krates away, and be getting your own crumlush cottage at the end of Wand Wood, and be going wherever you want, griffling and chickling with all the creatures here in Winchett Dale, growing niffs and be being peffa-happy."

And then they would try some more, until Matlock became bored again, and Proftulous would have to explain it all over, trying harder and harder to remember the griffles which seemed to be fleeing from his mind quicker than a limping-bligger chased by a peffa-hungry krefflefox.

But gradually, as the days of spring began to lengthen and give way to early summer, Matlock started to apply himself to the task. The more griffles and sounds he recognised, the easier it became, as he began slowly reading through *Majickal Dalelore (Volume 68 – revised edition)* and asking Proftulous to explain as best as he could just what it all meant.

One even'up, he bought his master a tweazle-pie for his supper, noticing just how gobflopped he looked. "Master, are you well?"

Proftulous shifted slightly, slowly rubbing his face. "What's 'well'?" he griffled. "I don't be knowing that griffle."

Matlock frowned. "It means fuzzcheck, Master. You taught me that yourself."

"I did? I don't be remembering, I really don't."

"Are you juzzpapped?" Matlock griffled, concerned. "Perhaps you should nifferduggle."

"No, Matlock," Proftulous sighed. "I'll be…"

"Fuzzcheck?"

"That's the griffle, fuzzcheck, yes." He patted Matlock's head with a ganticus paw. "Now, don't you be worrying about your master, I'll be fuzzcheck."

Later, after Matlock had washed up and was finally nifferduggling, Chatsworth came to the house, finding Proftulous staring into the piff-tosh, its flames slowly dying into a pile of glowing red embers. He turned his ganticus head painfully towards the red-robed figure. "It be time, isn't it?"

251

Chatsworth nodded. "Early tomorrow morn-up, before anyone has woken. Take him to Thinking Lake. I'll meet you both there. Teach him to extrapluff and your job will be done."

"T'will be the last I sees of him?"

"I'm afraid so. I'll be there to take him when it's over."

Proftulous stared into the piff-tosh for a peffa-long time, Chatsworth lightly stroking his weary dworp's head all the while.

"Master," Matlock griffled, as he sat by the shindinculously still waters of Thinking Lake, peffa-early the next morn'up, Proftulous slumped on all fours by his side. "What is it that makes 'extrapluffing' so different from 'thinking'?"

Proftulous slowly raised his head. "Someone saztaculous and crumlush once griffled to me that it's an oidy bit like listening, only you be using your insides, Matlock."

Matlock's bright orange eyes widened. "Like when my crimple goes all grumbly when I want some niff-soup, and then afterwards I'm feeling all fuzzcheck again?"

Proftulous couldn't help but smile at his own distant memory. "In a manner of griffling, Matlock, then yes, it be so."

Matlock closed his eyes. "Master, I'm thinking peffa-hard about being hungry, but nothing's happening."

"Matlock," Proftulous griffled, his dworp's mind desperately struggling to find the griffles. "In a snutch of moments, a great hare will come for you. He will be Most Majelicus and peffa-shindinculous. When you will be seeing him, you will have an extrapluff, and it will be griffling you exactly what you have to do. He will be your new master, and you will go with him."

Matlock suddenly shivered. "New master?"

Proftulous nodded. "You be having no need of me anymore, Matlock."

Matlock threw his arms around Proftulous. "No!" he cried, his griffles rising to a twizzly panic. "I'm not going anywhere with anyone else! I want to be here with you, forever!"

"Matlock," Proftulous tried to explain. "I'm changing. I'm not how I used to be when I first gets you out in The Great Beyond. I can't be stopping what's happening to me, and I can't be stopping

252

what's going to be happening to you, either. I'm just a clottabussed dworp who's simply trying to be helping you on your journey."

Matlock vilishly shook his head. "But I'm not going on any journey without you!"

Proftulous looked into Matlock's determined eyes and slowly, painfully smiled. "The extrapluff will griffle to you that you must go, and you will have no choice but to follow it."

"Then I'm never having any glopped-up extrapluffs! I don't want them!" Matlock buried his head in Proftulous' deep fur, hugging him as peffa-tightly as he could. "I'm not having a new master! I'm not being a majickal-hare! I'm not..."

"Matlock," came a sudden voice from behind. "It's time."

Matlock turned, seeing an elderly red-robed hare standing with a paw outstretched towards him. His whole softulous coursed with the most saztaculous, shindinculous and peffa-crumlushed feeling he'd ever had. Memories and dreams tumbled and churned in his mind; faces, places and grillions of things long forgotten. He let out a gasp, recognising the stranger immediately, running to him and giving him a ganticus hug, eyesplashers of joy running down his cheeks, and the briftest smile breaking all over his face.

"Chatsworth!" he cried, completely peffa-excrimbly. "It's really you?"

"Indeed, Matlock, it is."

"But this is the most yamamantally-spious thing! The most yamamantally-spious thing of all the grillions of yamamantally-spious things, ever!"

Chatsworth nodded, turning to see a lonely dworp walking slowly away by the edge of the lake. "We don't have long," he griffled. "The krates are coming. We must leave, or they will find us."

Matlock was still looking at the lake, more memories revealing themselves every blinksnap. "This..." he slowly griffled, pointing. "This is Thinking Lake! I used to come here with you." He bliffed the side of his head, looking all around. "And this is Winchett Dale! My home! Chatsworth, what's been going on? Why are you here? Where have I been?"

"I'll griffle everything to you later, Matlock," Chatsworth griffled, as a large party of hunting krates moved quickly over the horizon, closing in fast. "For now, we must pid-pad as vilishly as we can. There are friends coming to help us, but we musn't be caught. Hopefully, the krates will merely take the dworp, and we can be safe. Follow me."

"What's a dworp?" Matlock asked.

"Nothing," Chatsworth griffled, as they both began pid-padding vilishly around the far side of the lake, then up towards the entrance to Trefflepugga Path. "A dworp is nothing but a dworp."

They stopped, breathless behind a large bush by the stone archway entrance to the path, looking back at the lakeside as the hunting krates vilishly surrounded the dworp, which roared and protested as they roughly pushed it into a large cage wagon, before finally heaving it slowly away.

"Looks like they've done a peffa-good job," Matlock griffled. "That dworp looked most glopped-up."

Chatsworth didn't griffled another griffle about the dworp. "There's more krates on the way," he griffled, pointing to a second, larger group of approaching krates. "They know we're here."

"But why do they want us? They've got the glubbstooled dworp." Matlock griffled. "We've done nothing wrong."

"Do you trust me, Matlock?" Chatsworth asked as a distant roaring began to fill the skies.

"Of course," Matlock griffled. "With my life."

"Then just do exactly as I griffle, when I griffle it."

The roaring grew closer, Matlock looking up and suddenly seeing hundreds of witches of all shapes and sizes come racing over the archway, their vroffa-brooms loudly streaking through the lid.

"'Tis The League of Lid Curving Witchery!" Chatsworth shouted over the noise. "Right on time, just as they promised! They'll see off the krates for us! Follow me, vilish!"

Together, they broke from the bush, as two witches expertly landed their brooms just in front of them, dust flying all around.

"Get on!" Chatsworth griffled.

"Get on?" Matlock griffled. "But it's a witch!"

"Just do it!" Chatsworth ordered. "Trust me, you already know her, she's safe. I'll explain everything later!"

Matlock vilishly pid-padded to a waiting broom driven by

a white hare-witch, hesitantly climbing onto the back.

"This is the point," the witch griffled to him, "where you're supposed to griffle something like 'we must stop meeting like this'."

"We've met before?"

"Let's just griffle that you already owe me two bowls of niff-soup, hare," Ursula griffled, firing up the vroffa-branches to bright red, before vilishly streaking back up into the skies.

Matlock held on as tightly as he could, his mind totally gobflopped by everything, as Ursula expertly banked the broom back around Thinking Lake, Matlock watching the other witches swooping low over the scattering, peffa-twizzly krates, shooting bright green wand vrooshers at them, chickling and cackling at their helpless prey.

"We haven't had this much peffa-tzorkly fun in many moon-turns!" Ursula called back. "The krates will live, but their softulousses will feel peffa-glopped for a while!"

Matlock looked ahead, seeing Chatsworth on another broom driven by a much larger witch who seemed to be having trouble keeping it in a straight line. "Is he safe?" Matlock shouted over the roaring of the broom, the wind pulling at his cheeks.

Ursula chickled. "Tis simply Agrelia. She always has a few guzzworts before take-off. Your master will have to hold on tight!"

The four of them flew on, right over Trefflepugga Path, Matlock watching in total amazement at the continually shifting landscape below, memories flooding back all the while. "I've been there!" he managed to yell, pointing down.

"Indeed," Ursula called back. "Last time we met I couldn't fly you over here, as you'd already pid-padded along Trefflepugga Path. But since you have been to The Great Beyond, its memories of you are forgotten. It's why the path lets us fly above it, now. Before, and we would have both been stroffed."

Matlock stared down at the changing mountains and dales, rivers re-twisting, ganticus cliffs crumbling and moving all the time. "You took me, didn't you?" he cried. "You took me out to The Great Beyond! I've been on this broom before. I remember!"

Ursula nodded. "What choice did I have? You cannot begin the journey to becoming Most Majelicus without first revisiting your original home. And I have no wish to be being stroffed with just a mere majickal-hare. It really wouldn't be peffa-tzorkly at all. Now, no more griffles, just hang on."

Matlock did as Ursula ordered, clinging to her flapping robe as more memories slowly began to reveal themselves; Zhava, Frendeslene Note, the krates, a glopped-up singing Trefflepugga-kraark king, The Vroffa-Tree Inn, Lafrohn – all fighting for space in his mind. He felt as if he had woken from the longest ever nifferduggle to find himself in a place that he somehow knew, yet at the same time, couldn't really recognise at all. A fleeting image of his smiling mahpa appeared, disappearing just as quickly, replaced with the twizzly feeling of being led down a long dark tunnel by his ears. Everything felt glopped-up, nothing felt real.

After a while, both brooms banked steeply to the side, flying away from the ever-changing landscape of Trefflepugga Path, before eventually beginning to descend. Matlock looked ahead as they slowed, making out a series of brightly coloured tents in the distance, adorned with ganticus flags flapping in the breeze. It was the perfect summer's day, the crumlush and warming sun high in the lid.

"Welcome to Currick Dale," Ursula griffled, landing the broom on the edge of a wood that overlooked a large field full of tents below. "I believe my job is done with you now."

"Where are you going?"

"Away," she griffled. "What, you think rescuing hares is all I have to be doing with my life?"

"No, it's not that," he griffled, looking into her eyes. "It's just… I *do* remember who you are. You're Ursula." He reached into his robe, pulling out the oidy leather potion bottle, its stopper still neatly attached. "You gave me this, didn't you? When we had niffs at Alfisc Dale?"

She nodded. "But do you remember what's in it?"

Matlock frowned, desperately trying to find the memory, but it was no good, there were too many jostling for attention in his mind, pulling him a grillion ways at once.

"You don't remember, do you?" Ursula griffled.

"I…can't. I'm sorry."

"Then that is also why I am going now, Matlock." She fired up the vroffa-branches once more as the other broom landed close by, Chatsworth pid-padding over to join Matlock at the edge of the trees. She looked him in the eyes. "Perhaps one sun-turn, you will remember, Matlock. But that is your destiny, not mine."

Matlock watched as both witches quickly took off, flying back into the lid, following Ursula's broom as it gradually became the oidiest dot, before finally disappearing over the horizon. He felt a hand on his shoulder. "Sit down, Matlock," Chatsworth griffled. "There's peffa-much I have to griffle to you."

They both sat on the edge of the wood, former apprentice majickal-hare reunited with his old Most Majelicus master, Chatsworth griffling to Matlock exactly what had happened in order for to him to be here in this most crumlush place, overlooking the saztaculous tents and festivities below. He griffled of first finding Matlock out in The Great Beyond, teaching him, then leaving him as a majickal-hare. He griffled of their first journey together along Trefflepugga Path, and how it had chosen Winchett Dale as Matlock's home. Chatsworth griffled for a long time, asking Matlock simply to listen, accept and trust the truth in each and every griffle. The only part of Matlock's story Chatsworth never griffled about was a dworp named Proftulous.

"And one sun-turn," he griffled. "I was called before the Most Majelicus Council for all Majickal-Hares and asked who I would choose to become a Most Majelicus majickal-hare. Now, I have taught many majickal-hares in my time, Matlock, in many different dales, but there was only one I could ever think of as being the briftest to undergo the three tasks to become Most Majelicus."

"Me?" Matlock griffled, finally beginning to make sense of the chaos of glopped-up memories slowly ordering themselves in his mind. "But I'm not even that majickal. I remember having to try a saztaculous vroosher on the High Plateau. But my driftolubbs had been stolen, and without them, I gobflopped. I'm just a hare, Chatsworth, which you taught to dress, and pid-pad and read." He thought for a snutch of moments, frowning, a fresh thought occuring. "And you've had to do that twice, haven't you?"

Chatsworth cleared his throat. "You did have to be taught a second-time, yes."

"Thank you," Matlock griffled. "It can't have been easy."

"It wasn't," Chatsworth griffled. "But you had a peffa kind, patient and loving teacher."

Matlock gave him a hug. "I most peffa-certainly do, and I'll always be grateful to you for doing that for me." He thought for a moment, watching the festival below as distant sounds of chickling and music lazily drifted towards them on the warm breeze. "But why choose me, when I couldn't even majick a saztaculous vroosh?"

"Doing saztaculous vrooshers is just one oidy part of being Most Majelicus, Matlock. It can be taught quite easily. What you need to understand is that there are many Most Majelicus creatures in these dales that aren't hares at all, and have never even thought to majick a vroosher, and most probably never will. Being Most Majelicus, Matlock, is about being something else, entirely. It takes different qualities, ones hidden deep inside yourself, which helped by your Sisteraculous, Oramus and others, can eventually flourish and become the very living being of you. As your Most Majelicus master, I saw the beginnings of these qualities in you, above all the other majickal-hares I have ever taught. It's why I nominated you to undertake the three tasks, the same ones I completed, many, many moon-turns ago." He turned to Matlock. "But be warned, 'tis a perilous and peffa-twizzly journey, and one that you are only just starting. Your first Most Majelicus task is to find the answer to the riddle of Trefflepugga Path."

Matlock frowned, remembering his time on the path. "But that's glopped-up, it's impossible!" he protested. "No one even knows if the riddle's real, or if it's just a spuddle."

Chatsworth smiled, lightly bliffing Matlock around the ears. "But I managed to solve it," he griffled, "and every Most Majelicus creature before you has, too."

"So you can griffle me the answer, then?" Matlock asked, seizing the opportunity.

Chatsworth chickled. "Matlock, just like the path itself, the riddle changes all the time. The answer for you will be very different from the answer for me. You have your own answer waiting for you, and no-one else's. The path will know when you've found it."

Matlock let out a breath. "But I just don't know where to begin

Chatsworth. I've been on the path. I found nothing. I ended up glopped-up in Alsfisc Dale with just…" He paused, ears twitching as the memory of an oidy furry creature suddenly shot into his mind, "…with just my dripple."

Chatsworth nodded. "And every majickal-hare needs a dripple." He stood, brushing his robes. "So now I suggest we go and find yours."

"My dripple's here?" Matlock asked.

"Well, if Laffrohn's managed to do everything in time," Chatsworth griffled, pointing to the tents, "it'll be somewhere down there – the annual Currick Dale Dripple-Fair." He began slowly pid-padding from the shadow of the woods. "Shall we go? Laffrohn will have her very own guzzwort tent, and after that broomstick ride, I could most peffa-certainly do with one."

The two of them made their way down the gently sloping dale towards the tents and festivities, Matlock noticing red-robed hares pid-padding around with green-robed hares just like himself in the crowds. "I've been here before, too, haven't I?"

"Indeed, Matlock you have," Chatsworth griffled. "Many moon-turns ago, when you first became a majickal-hare. We found your dripple here. Now, as a returning hare on the journey to becoming Most Majelicus, you simply have to find it again from amongst all the others." He turned to Matlock, "And believe me, there are a peffa-lot to choose from."

He led Matlock into the heart of the festival, memories of his previous trip to the dripple-fair returning all the while. "But the first time," Matlock griffled. "my dripple simply chose me. I didn't have to do anything. It just came to me."

Chatsworth nodded, leading Matlock into a ganticus tent filled with creatures drinking guzzworts at long wooden tables; griffling, chickling and some even singing happily. "Last time it was too peffa-easy," he griffled above the noise. "Nothing about being Most Majelicus is easy, Matlock, nothing. You should know that by now. But I have faith you will succeed."

A familiar figure with a freggle of guzzworts in each ganticus paw pushed through the crowd to greet them. "Matlock!" Laffrohn griffled. "So you be here, after all!" She pushed a guzzwort into his

259

paw. "Just the one for you, mind. You'll be having to be choosing your dripple in a snutch of moments, and 'tisn't easy." She pulled him close, whispgriffling in his ear, "But I knows you can be doing it, Matlock. Just be using that head of yours, and only be remembering the most peffa-important things."

Chatsworth took Laffrohn by the arm. "We need to griffle," he griffled, looking around the crowded tent. "Somewhere quiet."

"It be about Proftulous?"

"Who's Proftulous?" Matlock asked.

"Never you be minding about that," Laffrohn quickly griffled, taking his guzzwort and vilishly pid-padding him to the back of the tent, where a thick canvas doorway flapped in the breeze. "You's got a job to be doing now. Concentrate on that and leave Chatsworth and I to be griffling about other, more important matters. Out you be going now, Matlock, and be remembering to use that head of yours."

She turned, disappearing back into the crowded tent, leaving Matlock outside gazing in astonishment at the largest number of dripples he'd ever seen. He tried to think back, recall the first time he had come to the fair as a young leveret, but the only memory he had was of holding Chatsworth's paw until a dripple had approached him, scrittled up his robes and nestled in his hood. Beyond that, there was nothing, and certainly no memory could match the sight that greeted him as he stood in the flapping doorway of the tent. There were dripples everywhere, as far as he could see, all trying their peffa-best to impress, dancing on guzzwort barrels, performing tricks, pretending to read, racing round with fresh brews, all determined to be chosen. Matlock hadn't the oidiest idea where to even start.

"So you must be Matlock, former majickal-hare of Winchett Dale, and now on the beginnings of his journey to becoming Most Majelicus!"

Matlock turned to the griffles, making out an elderly hare in saztaculous blue robes, shindinculously embroidered with golden dripples of all kinds, making his way slowly between the army of excrimbly dripples, a welcoming paw outstretched.

"I'm Baselott," he jovially griffled, adding a wink for good

There were dripples everywhere, as far as he could see, all trying their peffa-best to impress, dancing on guzzwort barrels, performing tricks, pretending to read, racing round with fresh brews, all determined to be chosen.

measure. "Appointed Officer of Dripple Selection." He pulled out a small leather-bound book and quill, vilishly scratching an entry into it. "Just recording you as 'here', Matlock. Some candidates don't even get this far. Good trip?"

"Well, it's all been rather confusing, really," Matlock griffled.

Baselott chickled, accepting a brew bought by an eager dripple. "'Confusing' is a good griffle for it, I'll give you that, Matlock. But it all tends to make some sort of sense in the end. That is," he dug Matlock playfully in the ribs, "if you ever get that far, of course!"

A dripple suddenly leapt from the roof of the tent onto Matlock's shoulder and began brushing his long hare's ears ears with an oidy, bone-toothed comb.

"This one yours?" Baselott asked.

"I'm not sure," Matlock griffled, craning his head to try and see the creature properly. "I mean, I don't think so. But there are so many of them, aren't there?"

"Oh, indeed there are," Baselott griffled, putting the grooming dripple back onto the grass. "Pid-pad this way, Matlock. I have something to griffle you."

Matlock followed the blue-robed hare deeper into the field, having to fend off dripples desperate to please and be noticed with every pid-pad.

"What do you remember about your dripple, Matlock?" Baselott griffled, lowering his voice and putting a paw up next to his cheek. "Strictly between you and I, Laffrohn has told me some rather shindinculous things about it."

Matlock thought for a snutch of moments, as memories of his time outside The Nifferie begging for drutts came flooding back. "Well, it griffled."

Baselott's eyes brightened, as a broad smile broke over his furry hare's face. "So, it *is* true? It actually griffled?" He made a vilish note in his book, then danced a sudden oidy jig, his excrimbly feet thumping the ground in celebration. "Matlock, you have no idea just how long I have waited to hear such news! Tell me, how many griffles would it griffle?"

"Two," Matlock griffled. "It could griffle 'For…you'."

Baselott nodded, writing it all down. "And of course, you've read *Majickal Dalelore (Volume 68 – revised edition)*?"

"I've started it," Matlock griffled, remembering how he had sat somewhere quite dark, as Chatsworth had patiently taught him how to read. "With Chatsworth, my master. But I haven't finished it yet. We were chased away by krates, and had to escape with witches, and…"

Baselott held up his quill, frowning and studying Matlock's face intently. "So you *haven't* read the revisions section?"

"I haven't had time," Matlock confessed, as Baselott made another note in his book. "Should I have done?"

Baselott rubbed his chin thoughtfully. "Probably not yet, Matlock, no." He placed an arm round Matlock's shoulders as they both pid-padded further from the tent, still surrounded by urgent, attentive dripples. "Your master, Matlock, is Most Majelicus."

"Indeed he is," Matlock griffled.

Baselott nodded. "The thing is, I used to be just like him, once. But then I moved on. Or perhaps got moved on, it's so peffa-difficult to know what's in the Elders minds at times. Anyway, somehow, in the way of all these things, I became more than just Most Majelicus. It's why I have to wear these glopped-up blue robes."

"I think they're quite saztaculous," Matlock politely griffled.

Baselott shook his head. "Nonsense, they're far too heavy. But it's all part of the job. Once a year I return to your world and supervise the dripple-fair. It's mostly quite dull, really. But at least it gets me out for a sun-turn."

"You're…?" Matlock's eyes widened.

Baselott chickled. "Stroffed? Indeed I am, Matlock, many moon-turns ago. But only in terms of what you understand by being stroffed in the dales." He gave Matlock another playful poke in the ribs, pointing high into the lid. "Honestly, if you were ever to meet me up there, you'd never recognise me, I swear!"

Matlock's jaw hung open.

"But anyway," Baselott griffled, "once a year I'm let back down here to supervise the dripple selection. I suppose you could griffle that I have this 'thing' about dripples, you see." He beckoned Matlock in close, lowering his voice. "Because, Matlock, my dripple used to griffle, too."

"It did?" Matlock griffled.

Baselott nodded. "I thought mine was the only dripple that could griffle, but then Laffrohn told me about yours, Matlock. So now there's two griffling dripples; mine, and yours." They began pid-padding again, walking back towards the tents and flags. "All I can griffle to you is that your journey to becoming Most Majelicus is to be no ordinary one, Matlock. There are too many signs, too many rules being broken, too much peffa-strangeness going on all around you. Shortly before I stroffed and passed from these dales, I tried to tell everyone about my griffling-dripple. I wrote a long revision to *Majickal Dalore (Volume 68)*, but it was changed to just a few lines, denying that any dripples could ever griffle." He lowered his voice to a whispgriffle. "Someone, for reasons I can't begin to understand, never wanted those pages to be read. I was informed that the original thirteen pages of parchment had been lost. But I suspect they were hidden, and I have an oidy feeling in my Sisteraculous that one sunturn you will be the hare that finds them, reads them, and discovers something in them that might well change the history of the dales forever." He stopped, put both paws on Matlock's shoulders, his jovial face now peffa, peffa serious. "But be sure of this, Matlock, if we meet again, it will be under very different, more glopped-up circumstances. There will be no crumlush sunshine, or chickling, or guzzwort-tents. It will be twizzly and glubbstool. But if you have found and read my lost revisions, all will be fuzzcheck in the end, I promise." He reached out for Matlock's paw, before slowly pressing it to his own head. "But right now, I need you to close your eyes. What do you see?"

Matlock closed his eyes, feeling a peffa-powerful extrapluff running from Baselott's forehead, up through his arm and scrittling into his mind. He saw a lone tree in a field, with rain pouring from a heavy, grey lid above. And sheltering beneath it, a nifferduggling hare, its ripped and tattered clothes scattered around on the long wet grass. "I see...me," he slowly whispgriffled.

Baselott nodded, his griffles utterly serious. "You must griffle no-one of this, Matlock. No-one, do you understand?"

Matlock nodded, eyes firmly closed, still watching himself, seeing a small creature reach up and give him a hug, its mouth clearly moving. "My dripple. It's griffling, it's griffling to me."

"What?" Baselott urged. "What does it griffle?"

The image began to fade, dissolving into just sunlushed orange behind his eyelids. He opened his eyes.

"You must think," Baselott griffled. "Think peffa-hard and try to remember. Did it griffle 'For…you'? Or something else? Think, Matlock, it's peffa-important."

Matlock rubbed his eyebrows, trying to remember.

"Feel the rain as you lay out in The Great Beyond, Matlock," Baselott whispgriffled. "Feel it on your fur. Be in that place, Matlock, be there. Listen to the storm, really try and listen to it. Try to remember everything."

Matlock closed his eyes again in peffa-concentration, brows furrowing from the effort.

"You were asleep," Baselott whispgriffled to him. "But something inside you would have heard what your dripple griffled. Find that place inside yourself, Matlock, find it."

"It's no good," Matlock griffled. "I can't."

"You can. You just need to try again. Find it."

Matlock took a deep hare's breath, trying to clear his glopped-up mind of far too many distracting memories flooding in from all sides. He held the breath for a snutch of moments, before peffa-slowly letting it out and opening his eyes, a broad smile slowly spreading over his face.

"You heard its griffles?" Baselott asked, his face alive with excrimbly anticipation.

Matlock took another breath, nodding. "I did."

"And were they saztaculous and shindinculous?"

Matlock nodded again. "They were."

Baselott took a pid-pad back. "So are you ready to find your dripple, Matlock? Because it did not stroff out in The Great Beyond, Laffrohn made sure of that. She has bought it here, this sun-turn, for you to find again. It is here, somewhere amongst all these."

"I'm ready," Matlock griffled.

"There are rules you have to obey. You only have one chance, just one question to ask them before you make your choice. Find the wrong dripple, and your journey will end, you will wake once more in your field under the tree in The Great Beyond, never to visit the dales again."

"I understand," Matlock calmly griffled, watching as Baselott clapped his paws twice, signalling all the many dripples to smartly line up in front of them both, each one now standing peffa-still, just their black, oidy eyes occasionally blinking, pleading with Matlock to be chosen.

"Last time you were here, your dripple pid-padded to you," Baselott griffled. "Now, you must ask your one question and pid-pad to your dripple. But be sure to choose your question peffa, peffa carefully, Matlock, as all dripples are be desperate to be chosen to be with a majickal-hare on his Most Majelicus journey. 'Tis the highest honour for them, the very height of their dripple lives."

Matlock looked up and down the long line of waiting dripples, his heart racing. He cleared his throat, the noise suddenly loud in the quietly stilled air. He took a breath and began griffling his question. "Which of you," he shouted, pausing to scan their faces, "goes by the name of...Gurrup?"

In a blinksnap all the dripples raised their paws, agreeing to anything to be chosen. Matlock began vilishly pid-padding up and down the dripple-row, Baselott behind, notebook in paw.

"That was it?" Baselott griffled, shocked. "That was your one big question? 'Which of you goes by the name of Gurrup?' Matlock, even if your dripple has a name, even if it griffled you its name, even if it was actually called Gurrup – they're *all* going to put their paws up, because they all want to be chosen."

"All except one," Matlock griffled, stopping by the only dripple in the line with its paws still by its sides. "The dripple that goes by the name of Ayaani." He swooped the excrimbly dripple up into his arms, turning to see Baselott's amazed face. "*My* dripple, Baselott... Ayaani, my peffa-crumlushed and dearest dripple!"

"It...griffled you its name?" Baselott gasped, vilishly flicking through his notebook, as the other dripples broke into raucous pawplause at the completion of the choosing.

"*Her* name," Matlock corrected him, slipping his dripple back into his hood, where she resumed her natural place, smiling and hugging her master's neck for all she was worth. "She griffled me *her* name, Baselott."

Baselott ran a trembling, excrimbly paw down the pages, vilishly flicking through them until he found the right entry, matching Matlock's name to his dripple. "You're right!" he exclaimed. "It *is* Ayaani. But majickal-hares are never supposed to know the names of their dripples until they both pass from the dales." He scratched the side of his head, mumbling and hopping around. "Oh, dear, this is peffa, peffa-twizzly indeed! This is all wrong and gobflopped." He stopped, stared at them both. "I need to hear it griffle, Matlock. Please, will it griffle just for me?"

"Why?" Matlock asked. "Do you not have all the proof you need?"

"Because, all my many lives I have waited for such a sun-turn," Baselott pleaded. "No one believed me that dripples could griffle. Please, just to hear one griffle would make my many lives work complete."

Matlock turned to his dripple. "Would you like to griffle to Baselott, Ayaani?"

"No," she griffled, turning her head away and nuzzling further into Matlock's neck.

"By Oramus himself!" Baselott griffled, breaking into another oidy foot-thumping jig. "I have heard it at last! A griffling-dripple, that can *really* griffle, and not just imitate!" He shook Matlock by the elbow, his face peffa-excrimbly. "It griffles, Matlock, it really griffles!"

"Yes," Matlock griffled, reaching a paw behind his neck and tickling Ayaaani under her chin, "she does."

Baselott tried to compose himself, taking deep breaths, as the next majickal-hare in green robes stepped out through the flapping tent door. "You are finished here, Matlock," he griffled. "Take your dripple and find Laffrohn. She will griffle you what to do next." He lowered his voice to a whispgriffle once more, unable to resist lightly stroking Ayaani's head. "But be peffa-careful, Matlock. I have seen many hares raised to being Most Majelicus, including your master, Chatsworth. But your raising is different. Your griffling-dripple proves it. Rules are being broken with you, and while there may be peffa-good reasons for that, they will come with many twizzly dangers, too. I wish you the briftest good-luck on your journey, and remember, if we meet again, it will not be in such peffa-excrimbly

267

circumstances." He briefly shook Matlock's paw, before turning away to greet the nervously waiting majickal-hare, quill in one paw, his notebook in the other.

With the dripple safely back in his hood, Matlock pid-padded back into the noisy guzzwort tent, trying to find Chatsworth amongst the sea of red and green Most Majelicus hares and apprentices. Some, like him, already had their correctly selected dripples in their hoods, waiting obediently by their master's sides as they loudly swigged guzzworts, griffling and chickling all the while. Occasionally, one might nod at him, a slight acceptance of their situation passing from hare to hare, but most simply stood and waited, uncertain what to do next. Other apprentices queued by the flapping entrance for their turn in the dripple-field, taking deep breaths and trying not to look or feel too twizzly. In the far corner of the tent, Matlock made out a pile of abandoned green robes, shoes and hats, lying in a glopped-up pile.

"They used to belong to all the apprentices what's be choosing the wrong dripple," came Laffrohn's crumlush voice, as she appeared by his side, thrusting a guzzwort into his paw. "Chances are the poor hares will already be back in The Great Beyond, without an oidy inkling of what's just happened to them." She fussed Ayaani, who held out her paws for a sip of guzzwort. "You can tell she's been spending too much time at an inn, can't you?"

Matlock drank the guzzwort in one, wiping his lips. "Chatsworth found her?" he griffled. "When he came to fetch me back from The Great Beyond?"

Laffrohn hesitated slightly. "Let's just griffle it was something like that, yes."

"I touched Baselott's head," he griffled, leaning closer to be heard above the noisy guzzwort tent. "I saw everything; where I was, where Ayaani was. I heard her say her name. Then she went still. She looked stroffed, she…"

Laffrohn quickly put a finger to his lips, whispgriffling in his long hare's ear. "Hush now, Matlock. You can't be griffling about *any* of this. Baselott isn't allowed to be helping any hare finding their dripple. They're not even supposed to ever be let out into The Great Beyond. If anyone finds out, there could be a ganticus amount of trouble for us all. Just be standing here and drinks some guzzworts until I's be ready to leave, then you be coming with me. And whatever you do, don't even begin to look like you're griffling with that dripple of yours. You's be understanding me?"

Matlock nodded, searching the crowded tent. "Where's Chatsworth?"

"He's been called away for a while," Laffrohn griffled, threading her way back through the crowd to fetch more guzzworts. "You'll see him later, don't you be all worrying about that."

Matlock spent the time waiting for Laffrohn to finish by sitting quietly in a corner of the tent, watching the line of green-robed candidates disappearing outside, some returning a short while later, peffa-excrimbly with their dripples to be greeted by their exuberant red-robed and guzzworty masters. Other times, Baselott merely appeared, throwing more green-robes on the pile, before calling the next twizzly apprentice outside. He never once acknowledged Matlock, looking for all the world like a peffa-officious krate about his work, the sight of him pulling Matlock's thoughts back to Winchett Dale, as he tried to piece together what he could of his life from recently discovered memories.

He wondered just what was happening in his beloved dale, remembering his dripple surging though the stone archway at The Cove of Choices to bring him his hawthorn wand, as Goole led the last of the krate wagons down into Winchett Dale. He remembered Alfisc Dale and his glopped-up time there, wondering just how successful Note's system of drutts and cages would be in Winchett Dale, and if he should have done more to protect his fellow creatures from Note's dark intentions.

He thought about the whole Most Majelicus business, watching the red-robed hares, wondering if he would ever wear the same robes one distant sun-turn, and indeed, if he really *wanted* to. It didn't seem to be that different from being just a normal majickal-hare, simply a different set of robes and rules to follow. He thought of Baselott, a hare who apparently had ascended beyond being merely Most Majelicus, but whose briftest sun-turn in the year was returning to run the Currick Dale Dripple Fair – hardly, it seemed, the most peffa-saztaculous of existences for any creature.

269

And yet, for whatever reasons, Chatsworth had nominated him to become Most Majelicus, and there seemed very little he could do to stop the process. He'd been forced onto Trefflepugga Path simply because he'd had no alternative. Once on the path, it had taken him to wherever it wanted him to go, and if it hadn't been for Ursula, then he'd still have been begging for drutts in Alfisc Dale. He thought of the first flight on the white-hare witch's broom, but there the story seemed to end, becoming just an oidy few disjointed memories of his time in the field, all now fading with each passing moment, as if these too were soon also to be denied him for ever.

"Now, you be looking like a hare that's got too much on his mind," Laffrohn suddenly griffled, interrupting his thoughts. "There's no more guzzwort to be had, so's I be thinking it's time for us to go."

Matlock looked up, noticing how the crowd had thinned to a last group of Most Majelicus hares singing in the far corner of the tent, their green-robed apprentices still waiting patiently for them to leave. "I hadn't even realised everyone had gone," he griffled, standing. "I've just been thinking about things, trying to remember things."

Laffrohn smiled. "Lost, deep in your own thoughts, eh? 'Tis a glopped-up place to be, Matlock. I's try not to be thinking about things too much. You should be trying it, too."

"But there's so much I don't understand," Matlock griffled.

Laffrohn chickled. "Matlock, you just wait 'till you be my age. There'll be a peffa-lot more, I promise. But right now, methinks 'tis time we pid-padded back to The Vroffa-Tree Inn for a crumlush bowl of niff-soup. What you be griffling to that?"

"Saztaculous?" Matlock tried, not feeling the oidiest bit hungry at all.

"You do remember The Vroffa-Tree Inn, don't you?"

Matlock nodded. "On Trefflepugga Path? We're going there now?"

"Well, not exactly *on* the path," Laffrohn smiled. "I'd griffle, more *under* it."

"Under it?"

"Just makes sure you be holding onto my paw at all times when we're in the tunnels, Matlock. You not's be being Most Majelicus yet, so you always having to be holding onto me, you understand?" She took hold of Matlock's paw, and the two of them left the tent together, pid-padding out into the sunlushed late-afternoon.

A short distance away, Baselott was still about his final duties, puffing and panting as he put the last of the unchosen dripples back into a ganticus wicker trunk, their noses poking through the gaps, still desperate to be chosen in any way they could. He vilishly motioned them both over, Laffrohn helping him secure the leather buckles that held down the lid on the constantly jiggling trunk.

"Don't you go worrying about all these dripples," Baselott griffled, seeing Matlock's alarmed face. "They'll all be back next year." He pointed towards another three empty ganticus trunks. "Must have shifted close on to three-quarters of them this year, mind." He turned to Laffrohn, his voice suddenly serious. "You using the tunnels, then?"

Laffrohn nodded. "I've griffled Matlock to hold on at all times."

Baselott looked around furtively, checking that apart from the writhing trunk of dripples, they were alone. "And Chatsworth?" he griffled.

Laffrohn nodded. "He left some time ago. We griffled. He's made up his mind. He's going to do it."

Baselott took a deep breath. "Oh, my. So it really begins, then?"

"He be determined, Baselott. And he feels that it's time."

Baselott nervously fiddled with his whiskers. "So everything changes, then? No going back for any of us?"

"Chatsworth felt there were enough signs," Laffrohn griffled, turning to stroke Ayaani's nifferduggling head, snug in Matlock's hood. "Including this one, methinks."

Baselott nodded, put a paw on Matlock's shoulder, looking him straight in the eye. "Now you be looking after that dripple of yours, Matlock. She's peffa, peffa-saztaculous and special. She was prepared to come and find you with your wand. She stayed with you right until her twizzly end out in The Great Beyond. Of all the grillions of dripples I have ever known, your Ayaani is the most crumlush and shindinculous. You must reward her loyalty with yours, and she will make your journey to being Most Majelicus more saztaculous than you ever thought." He briefly nodded to Laffrohn. "So we wait for news from Chatsworth, then?"

"'Tis all we can do," she griffled. "We simply has to be waiting to see what happens."

Baselott stroked Ayaani's head one final time, before ordering Matlock and Laffrohn to stand well back, jumping on top of the dripple-trunk in one effortless bound. "Don't worry," he griffled. "The journey back's always easier. Not so much to carry, you see?"

A ganticus dark blue vroosh suddenly streaked across the sky, swirling around the field and vilishly encircling Baselott and the trunk, before becoming smaller and smaller, then just an oidy dot, finally disappearing, leaving nothing.

"Where's he gone?" Matlock asked, eyes smarting from the stinging brightness of the vroosher.

"Never you be minding about Baselott," Laffrohn griffled, taking Matlock by the paw and vilishly pid-padding away from the festival and up towards the woods. "It's where we be going now that's important. Methinks it'll just about be time for that bowl of niff-soup of yours when we finally get there."

A snutch of moments later, they had entered the wood, Matlock amazed to see a large tree uproot itself in front of him to reveal a long dark tunnel stretching ahead.

"Be holding onto my paw at all times," Laffrohn instructed. "'Tis safe down here, there's nothing to get peffa-twizzly about at all."

In a blinksnap they had disappeared inside, the tree slowly righting itself behind, all traces of them completely gone in the cool quiet of the crumlush woodland.

"Your Officiousness!" the eager krate cried, as Fendeslene Note pid-padded into the stone Great Hall. "We have the dworp! Caged this morn'up, by the lake that leads to Trefflepugga Path."

Note nodded, pid-padding slowly towards the centre of the nearly completed hall, where a group of excited krates guarded a ganticus cage set on a creaking wagon, housing a slumped and glopped-up dworp. "And you have been here with this dworp all sun-turn?" he griffled, suddenly turning on the nearest krate, who looked as if he'd been badly singed rather recently.

The sheepish krate nodded. "We were waitin' for you, Your Officiousness."

"What?" Note barked. "*All* sun-turn?"

The krate winced. "An' we didn't want it to be escaping, you see, so we thought…"

Note stamped his foot hard on the floor, the sudden sound echoing all around the bare stone chamber. "You aren't paid a drutt each sun-turn to think!" He turned to the others, noticing how they all appeared to be in some pain, and smelt curiously like burning fur. "Have you been stood too near to a piff-tosh? What's happened?"

Another krate hesitatingly raised a paw, the others all nodding at him, urging him on. "Begging your pardon, Your Officiousness, but when we was up at the lake caging the dworp for you, we came under peffa-heavy and sustained vrooshing from what must have been grillions and grillions of witches." He took a slight breath, his voice shaking. "So…we's been thinkin' that perhaps there might be some form of recognition for our heroics? A medal, perhaps, or…"

"Just get out!" Note barked, causing them all to start. "Your 'reward' has been your sun-turn spent here, sitting on your burnt softulousses, guarding the dworp, instead of helping with the grillions of tasks to try and civilise this dale! Out! Or I will personally see to it that you are all sent to take your miserable, glopped-up chances on Trefflepugga Path! And from what I gather, there's nothing more a long, long-nosed krellit likes to get his yechus teeth into than a lightly toasted, peffa-lazy krate!"

The krates vilishly headed for the creaker, leaving Note alone in the empty hall with just the caged dworp. He went to the bars, watching as it slowly lifted its head, its juzzpapped eyes meeting his, twizzly fear and distrust written large in them both.

"Well, Proftulous," Note griffled, "We meet again. Not that you'd even remember your name, would you? I doubt you remember anything, do you? All that you were is nearly gone, all your achievements as worthless as drutts. For what have you really achieved with your glopped-up life, Proftulous? What heights did it take you to? How saztaculous were your sun-turns; eating tweazle-pie, everyone chickling at you behind your back, knowing you to be the most peffa-clottabussed creature of all of them?"

273

The dworp let out a low moan, trying to heave itself away from the intensely staring krate.

"And your life with the hare, the so-called 'majickal' hare, was that as peffa-shindinculous as you expected? It didn't seem to last peffa-long, did it? And you gave so much to it, didn't you? All that friendship and trust. But for what, Proftulous, for what? For when the end came, I'll bet every drutt in this glopped-up dale he left you without so much as an oidy glance back, didn't he? Without so much as a single 'thank-you' for your glopped-up gesture of eternal self-sacrifice. Oh, dworp, it can be a peffa-cruel and glubbstooled world, can't it? Look at you now. You crawl on all-fours like a creature from The Great Beyond. You can't griffle a griffle. You have no-one and nothing. You have given everything to the hare, who has taken it all too willingly, then simply left you caged and ready to be stroffed."

Note suddenly flung his arms out wide, a ganticus smile on his face. "But look at me, Dworp! See what I have achieved! This hall will soon be ready, rebuilt in stone, to last a grillion generations, a testament to Frendeslene Note. Whereas you have nothing. I have respect, you have a cage. I have loyalty from my subjects, you have none. You gave everything, dworp, and took nothing in return – hence you have nothing. You, my dowrp friend, *are* nothing."

Note took a long breath, pid-padding slowly around the hall, organising his thoughts. "I'm going to griffle you a story, Proftulous, not that you will ever understand or remember a single griffle of it." He pid-padded to the cage, running a pointed claw along the bars, circling it slowly as he griffled.

"Many, many moon-turns ago, long before you made your glopped-up way into this dale, a majickal-hare was chosen to undertake the three tasks to becoming Most Majelicus. In the course of undergoing the first task, he was returned out into The Great Beyond in order to test his true desire to return to the dales. As custom dictates, his dworp eventually found him, took him back and selflessly and willingly taught the hare how to pid-pad, dress, griffle and read once more, despite knowing what would happen. When his thankless task was completed, the hare simply left, never to see his dworp again, all memories of it quite gone."

274

The dworp moaned again, trying to put a paw over its ganticus ears.

"You think this is about *you*, dworp?" Note griffled. "It's not, believe me." He looked deep into Proftulous' eyes. "But many moon-turns later, after becoming Most Majelicus, the hare managed to discover the true purpose of dworps." Note took a breath. "And it horrified him."

He paused, slowly looking around the empty hall, his thoughts lost, somewhere far, far away. He pulled down on his robes, straightening them, recomposing himself before continuing.

"Now, this Most Majelicus majickal-hare was quite different from all the others. He couldn't live with the knowledge that his own dworp had freely given so much for him, yet was taken from him, too. So he set out to find it, travelling all the dales, but finding nothing. Other majickal-creatures far superior to him warned him not to, demanding that he simply concentrate on the Most Majelicus business of selecting hares from The Great Beyond to train as possible apprentices. But their griffles meant nothing to the hare, nothing. Each sun-turn was peffa-glopped, his mind constantly filled with endless regrets over the dworp he had so cruelly lost."

Note cleared his throat, closing his eyes in deepest concentration for a snutch of moments. "One sun-turn, the hare resolved that this would never happen again. He never wanted another Most Majelicus hare to feel the loss he had suffered, and when his own time came for him to choose his briftest apprentice for the three tasks, it would be a peffa-different story. Dworp and majickal-hare would be bonded for all their sun-turns in the dales together. This time the sacrifice the dworp would make would be rewarded, not forgotten.

"Now, he had no idea how to make this happen, and knew that others far more important than him would be peffa, peffa-russisculoffed if any of their rules were ever broken. But this hare didn't really like rules, he thought they were peffa-clottabussed and glopped up. So he simply waited, thinking and extrapluffing all the while just how to make it happen."

Note reached into his pocket, pulling out an oidy piece of peffa-glopped up pie, wrapped in cloth. "Some time ago, Proftulous,

I made you eat a ganticus tweazle-pie. You remember?" He carefully unwrapped the cloth and offered the pie up to the bars of the cage, wafting it under Proftulous' nose, watching him all the while. "A pie that was cooked from the flames of the majickal-driftolubbs, making it the most peffa-majickal, ganticus tweazle-pie in the history of all the dales."

Proftulous looked at the pie, his dulled dworp instincts making his yechus-nose slowly begin to twitch.

"Then I made you eat the pie, Proftulous, every last mouthful – all except this one final piece, which I have kept for this very occasion, and which you will shortly eat."

A thin sliver of drool ran from Proftulous' mouth as he tried to shift his ganticus body around in the cage.

"And when you've eaten this piece of pie, Proftulous, everything will change. Everything. It will awaken all the other majick that you ate in that pie." Note began unlocking the door to the cage. "You will be restored, and able to lump-thump, read and extrapluff again. You will be Most Majelicus, Proftulous, and know exactly what to do next." He opened the door an oidy amount, vilishly slipping the piece of pie inside, watching the dworp sniffing at it. "I do this," Note griffled, "for a hare who never had the chance to thank his dworp for the love it gave to him. May Oramus give his blessings and forgiveness from on high to us all."

Note backed away as the dworp settled over the pie, watching from a darkened concealed corner as it pushed at it with its nose along the cage floor. "When you leave this hall, I will report you as escaped. There will be krates hunting you everywhere. Use your extrapluffs, Proftulous, and they will guide you to where you have to go. Be strong, and know that you are fully restored and Most Majelicus; the only Most Majelicus dworp in the ganticus history of all the majickal-dales."

The dworp slowly opened its mouth, using the last of its energy to eat the peffa-yechus remains of the majickal-tweazle pie, chewing hungrily on it, griffles from the majickal-driftolubbs coming alive inside its softulous, melding, meeting and reforming, energising it to stand once more on his hind legs, open the cage and lump-thrump down onto the cold stone floor, its mind shindinculous with extrapluffs griffling exactly where to go. Mirrits dropped all around as it headed for the hall creaker and vilishly lump-thumped away into the early even'up.

Note swept away the mirrits, sending them scrittling into oidy gaps in the stone walls, before lying down by the wagon and loudly calling for help, instantly summoning an eager band of krates from outside. "The dworp!" he gasped, pointing to the cage. "It's escaped! Get after it! Bring it back, you hear me? Vilish!"

The krates rushed outside, leaving Note alone. He went to the cage, wiping away the last few crumbs of tweazle-pie onto the floor. "So it begins," he whispgriffled. "Matlock, I simply hope you are ready."

Proftulous had never felt so energised or alive, lump-thumping out of the village more vilishly than he'd ever been able to imagine. A group of krates chased him from behind, but their noisy shouts and griffles began to fade as he headed into Wand Woods. He felt like he had just awoken from the deepest nifferduggles. He smacked his lips with his tongue; the slurpilicious taste of tweazle-pie freshly distinct in his yechus mouth, although he had no memory of eating one, whatsoever. The last thing he remembered was teaching Matlock to extrapluff by Thinking Lake, and after that simply waking up, vilishly lump-thumping away from the village.

He stopped deep in the woods, listening for tell-tale sounds of any chasing krates, extrapluffs telling him he was safe, before becoming mirrits and scrittling ahead, intent on leading him to Zhava.

"Oh, you're not going to be making me do that tunnel-thing again, are you?" she griffled, as she saw him approaching.

"Even'up, Zhava," Proftulous cheerfully griffled. "I's be sorry, but all me extrapluffs is bringing me here, and be griffling to me that I has to be going inside."

"Very well," Zhava sighed, slowly creaking over. "But really, I am The Last Great Elm, you know. Would've thought I would have demanded an oidy bit more respect."

"I be's as quick as I can," Proftulous griffled. "And I always been respecting you, Zhava, you knows that."

"Well, get those yechus mirrits away from me, then," she griffled.

"I thoughts you not be finding them so peffa-glopped-up any more?"

"A lady," Zhava griffled, "can *always* change her mind. Now just go, for Oramus' sake, and leave me be."

Proftulous lump-thumped into the darkened tunnel, Zhava closing the entrance behind as his eyes perfectly adjusted themselves to the pitch black darkness. "Tis like I be's all Most Majelicussy again," he griffled. "Matlock's been making me all better and saztaculous, while that Chatsworth don't be knowing what he's griffling about. Peffa-glopped, he be."

A little way further on, he noticed something hanging from a tree root poking through the tunnel roof. "Well, I'll be a dreffle's uncle," he griffled. "Tis me tweazle-pouch!" He grabbed the leather pouch, putting it round his waist, as more extrapluffs and mirrits guided him further along the many tunnels, Proftulous having a growing feeling in his Sisteraculous that somehow he already knew just exactly where they were taking him...

"Welcome," Laffrohn griffled as she and Matlock finally pid-padded into the ganticus cavern, "to where I be calling home."

Matlock eyes slowly adjusted to the shindinculous sight of The Vroffa-Tree Inn floating above the still, saztaculous waters of the underground lake, torches blazing between each of the waving vroffa trees, sending saztaculous shadows high into the cavern walls, revealing the many tunnel entrances all around. "This is where you live?" he griffled.

"For most of the time, Matlock," she griffled. "Right under Trefflepugga Path. Though sometimes, I has to be going up and floating above it for a while."

"Like when I first saw you?" Matlock griffled. "With the witches?"

Laffrohn chickled. "And other times, too. But you don't be needing to know anything about those, Matlock. Laffrohn's business be her own business, and you'd do as well to be remembering that." They began pid-padding across the small wooden bridge. "Right now though, 'tis time we be preparing that slurpilicious niff-soup, methinks. It's been a peffa-long sun-turn, and I be right juzzpapped with all of it."

"Last time I was here," Matlock griffled, "I was juzzpapped, too."

"Indeed you were, so's I be sending you off to bed for crumlush nifferduggles."

Matlock nodded. "But then I woke up in The Vale of Dreggs," he griffled. "And the bed got all broken and garrumbloomed in the waterfall."

Laffrohn chickled. "Oh, don't you be worrying your hare's head about it, Matlock. That bed always finds its way back. 'Tis made from the wood of fallen trees along Trefflepugga Path, so it will always take you where you need to be. 'Tis like a peffa-crumlush short-cut, that bed. It be thinking you needed to be in The Vale of Dreggs, so that's where it be taking you." She lightly bliffed him around the ears. "Methinks you should be thanking that majickal bed of mine, for it's been saving you a ganticus lot of unnecessary pid-pads along the path, Matlock."

"I will," Matlock griffled. "Just as long as I never have to nifferduggle in it again. The peffa-last thing I want to do is return to Trefflepugga Path."

Laffrohn turned to him, her griffles quiet and serious. "But you *have* to, Matlock. Or how else are you going to be solving the riddle and completing your first Most Majelicus task? There be more at stake in your becoming a Most Majelicus majickal-hare than you will ever realise, Matlock. You must complete these challenges; you must return to the path and solve the riddle. And remember, just like the path, it changes for every creature that ever tries to solve it."

They stopped by the wooden creaker, Matlock taking a deep hare's breath. "But what happens if I can't solve it, Laffrohn? Creatures have been stroffed trying."

"True," Laffrohn griffled, opening the creaker and ushering Matlock inside. "And that's where you be taking your chances, Matlock, just like everyone else." She went to the ganticus piff-tosh, whispgriffled to it, causing it to splutt into crumlush, warming life. "But just like this piff-tosh can stroff you, it also gives you warmth, cooks your food and gives you peffa-crumlushness in the long winter."

"But I don't have any idea where to even begin to start looking,"

Matlock insisted. "How can I solve a riddle, if I can't even find it?"

Laffrohn chickled. "Peffa-nonsense, Matlock. You just got to be opening those clottabussed eyes of yours, for once. The riddle is all around you, you just be needing to look."

Matlock looked around the inn for a clue. "But I see nothing but an inn," he griffled. "Just an inn."

"Then you not really be looking," Laffrohn griffled. "And I don't just be meaning here, Matlock, I be meaning everywhere; in all the dales, even in Winchett Dale. 'Tis everywhere, if only you be stopping long enough to really look. Everywhere."

Matlock slumped into a chair, sighing heavily, his dripple still nifferduggling contentedly in his hood. "Laffrohn," he griffled. "I just don't know how I can do this."

Laffrohn, disappeared behind the bar for a snutch of moments, returning with a wooden bowl, spoon, some niffs and a large cauldron of water that she hung above the piff-tosh. "We'll have no more of that sort of griffling, Matlock," she griffled, putting the niffs, a knife and a chopping board down on the table. "Right now you've got far better things to do, like be making some slurpilicious niff-soup." She clapped her hands, and the oidiest witch Matlock had ever seen suddenly scrittled up the table-leg and sat cross-legged in front of him, then vilishly began chopping the niffs. "This be Bruttel," she griffled. "She sometimes lives here with me, and is a peffa-good oidy witch to have around the place."

The oidy witch raised her pointed black hat at Matlock then resumed chopping.

"Does she know the answer to the riddle?" Matlock griffled, amazed at the speed Bruttel expertly chopped and prepared the crumlush orange vegetables, de-seeding, then cutting them into thin slices in a vilishly growing pile.

Laffrohn chickled. "Why would she ever be wanting to? She's simply a peffa-oidy witch, and she be perfectly peffa-happy with that."

Bruttel nodded, still chopping and slicing, but then suddenly pointed to the window towards the distinct sound of heavy lump-thumps on the wooden bridge outside.

"You be staying here," Laffrohn ordered, pid-padding to the

creaker, opening it and welcoming a ganticus creature into the inn that Matlock immediately recognised from the morn'up by Thinking Lake.

"Tis a dworp!" he griffled, becoming twizzly at the sight of the ganticus yechus creature having to almost bend double to get through the creaker. "The one by the lake this morn'up! It got caught and caged by some saztaculoulsy brave krates, I saw it! Stay away from it, Laffrohn, for it will stroff us all!"

"Methinks stroffing us will be the last thing on this dworp's mind, Matlock," Laffrohn griffled, giving the ganticus creature a welcoming hug, then checking to see if it still had its leather tweazle-pouch. "This dworp be here to help make you your niff-soup, and you will show him courtesy and respect. I be the landlady of The Vroffa-Tree Inn, and I be deciding who I lets in and out." She turned to the dworp. "You be knowing what you have to be doing?"

The dworp nodded, getting a thin book from his pouch, as Bruttel vilishly took the niff pile, scrittled to the cauldron and dropped them in the boiling water.

"That's my book!" Matlock griffled, pointing. "The yechus dworp has my diftolubb! He's stolen it, Laffrohn!"

Laffrohn silenced him with a twizzly glare, Matlock watching in shock as the dworp went to the piff-tosh and threw the driftolubb into the flames, turning its yechus head to almost smile at Matlock. Bruttel stirred the cauldron with a ganticus ladle, the flames splutting green, reds and blues as the ancient griffles were released and began swirling around the cauldron. A snutch of moments later, Laffrohn passed Bruttel the bowl, the oidy witch ladling hot niff-soup into it and passing it back to Laffrohn, who set the steaming majickal-broth right under Matlock's nose. "Now this will be the most peffa-slurpilicious and Most Majelicus niff-soup you've ever be having the pleasure to be eating, Matlock."

Matlock sat, still in shock, as all eyes watched him. Bruttel quickly scrittled back onto the table, sitting cross-legged, passing Matlock his spoon, nodding at him to begin. He dipped it in the bowl and slowly raised it to his lips, completely twizzly and uncertain.

"Matlock," Laffrohn warned, "I suggest you be eating that soup, or else this dworp will be taking offence, and I'm not sure I's like to be seeing him if he got all russisculoffed with you."

Matlock looked at the yechus dworp one final time before closing his eyes, taking a deep-hare's breath and swallowing the soup.

The majickal force of the first mouthful hit Matlock like a ganticus bolt from a cracksploding, garrumblooming lid. His whole softulous trembled, from the tips of his long hare's ears to the very bottom of his shoes. Light and colours garrumbloomed in his mind, and he felt as if was falling from the most ganticus heights, memories swirling all around, reaching for each other, joining themselves together in a never ending chain of unanswered questions, until finally everything turned the most brilliantine white, warm and peffa, peffa-crumlush.

"Matlock?" came a concerned, yechus voice close by. "You needs to be opening your eyes. You be being alright, Matlock? Laffrohn, he not be looking fuzzcheck at all."

Matlock opened his eyes peffa-slowly, making out the blurred, ganticus face in front of him as it gradually came into focus. "Proftulous?" he gasped. "It's you?"

"It be me, Matlock," Proftulous griffled, in his most peffa-excrimbly voice. "It be me! And you be you, too! You be all coming back to us!"

Matlock stood, rushed to his briftest-friend, giving him a hug, and trying not to get too eyesplashy. "I've missed you so much, Proftulous," he griffled. "Every peffa-yechus and ganticulously clottabussed oidy bit of you!"

"Me's been missing you, too, Matlock," Proftulous griffled. "Things have been right glubbstool and strange since you pid-padded up Trefflepugga Path."

Laffrohn gently guided Matlock back to his chair, insisting he finish every mouthful of the majickal-niff-soup, the three of them chickling, griffling and drinking guzzworts, each telling stories of their times apart and together, until finally Matlock was able to make an oidy bit more sense of it all.

"So you stole my driftolubbs," he griffled to Proftulous, "and hid them in your cottage?"

"No," Proftulous griffled, slightly offended. "I not be stealing them. I's be having an extrapluff up at Thinking Lake, and I be

The majickal force of the first mouthful hit Matlock like a ganticus bolt from a cracksploding, garrumblooming lid.

finding them near some glopped-up kraarks who be singing too much. I's be taking them to my cottage to be looking after them for you. But then Mr Coat be finding them, and burning them in my piff-tosh, then be making me eats a ganticus tweazle-pie cooked from them all. And after, I be feeling all saztaculous and be doing shindinculous things, so I can be finding you, Matlock." He chickled. "Methinks that Mr Coat is more clottabussed than me, Matlock, because he be accidentally making me all Most Majelicussy."

"You're…" Matlock was almost stuck for griffles. "You're Most Majelicus?"

Proftulous proudly puffed out his ganticus chest. "I be that, Matlock, I really be that. 'Tis why I can lump-thump down the tunnels on my own, and be seeing in all the peffa-darkness."

Laffrohn topped-up their guzzwort jugs. "But that has to be a peffa, peffa-secret between all of us," she griffled. "If it's ever discovered that you are Most Majelicus, Proftulous, then we'll all be in the most twizzly danger." She turned to Matlock. "Matlock, you are the luckiest majickal-hare ever to undergo the three tasks. You already be having a griffling-dripple; now you also have a Most Majelicus dworp. Together you will have to be looking after each other and use all your majickal-saztaculousness to solve the tasks."

Ayaani woke in Matlock's hood, yawning and stretching, noticing Proftulous. "Even'up, dworp."

Proftulous looked slightly hurt. "Me's not just a dworp, me's Proftulous, named after a star."

"Still a clottabussed dworp to me," she quietly griffled, climbing over Matlock's shoulder to settle lazily in his lap.

Laffrohn stood. "But now, Matlock," she griffled, "be the time when you must be back on Trefflepugga Path. There be a riddle to find and solve."

Proftulous clapped both his ganticus paws. "The riddle of Trefflepugga Path!" he griffled, his face all excrimbly. "I's already be solving that, Matlock, so's I can be Most Mejlicus. Was peffa-easy it was, even for a clottabus like me."

"Of course!" Matlock griffled. "You must already know the answer. What is it?"

Proftulous thought long and hard as the piff-tosh gently crackled,

Matlock waiting patiently and searching his yechus-face intently all the while. Finally, he let out a deep breath. "I honestly not be knowing. But I knows I must have been solving it."

Matlock put Ayaani back in his hood, standing. "What good is that?" he griffled. "How does that even possibly help me an oidy bit?"

Proftulous was still thinking. "The answer could have been tweazles, but I not be peffa-sure, really."

"*Tweazles?*"

"Matlock," Laffrohn griffled, sensing Matlock's growing russisculoftulation, "it doesn't matter what Proftulous' answer is, yours will always be something peffa-different. Remember, the riddle changes for every creature that tries to solve it."

Matlock nodded, apologising to Proftulous, as Laffrohn slowly opened the wooden creaker by the piff-tosh. "Leave Ayaani with me," she griffled. "You must go alone. Up these stairs, lie on the bed and close your eyes. The path will do the rest. And may the Most Majelicus wisdom of Oramus be with you, good Matlock, every pid-pad of the way."

13.

Plusa, the Riddle and Tiftoluft

Matlock opened his eyes peffa-cautiously. It had only seemed like the oidiest blinksnap since he had lain on the bed and closed them, alone in the bedroom at the top of the stairway, trying not to get too twizzly about what things might happen.

But in that single blinksnap, so much had…

He sat up, immediately recognising his surroundings; The Vale of Dreggs, its small brook idly trickling just a few pid-pads away, gently rolling slopes giving way to higher hills and sheer limestone cliffs beyond.

He took a deep hare's breath, composing himself, trying to forget the peffa-twizzly memories of his previous visit; the long line of marching dreggs, their black empty eyes and haunting, yechus moans.

"So," a gentle voice whispgriffled in his ear, "you have returned."

Matlock turned, startled, but grateful to see a familiar spritely face drift in front of him, twirling and dancing crumlush circles in the air. "Plusa!" he griffled.

"Plusa to you," she griffled, "Rihaana to Ursula. You remember?"

Matlock nodded. "You told Ursula that there was another way to fly me away from Alfisc Dale and take me home, didn't you?"

"I did," Plusa griffled. "Although perhaps it wasn't the 'home' you were expecting, Matlock."

286

"It wasn't," Matlock agreed. "She took me out to The Great Beyond."

Plusa darted closer to his face. "Because she had no choice, Matlock. Solitary white-hare witches are peffa-torkly; the peffa-tzorkliest witches of them all. Everything they do is both considered and tzorkly at the same time. You have the powers of Oramus and the Sisteraculous to guide you. Ursula has neither, simply her tzorklyness, which in your griffles means 'to rise above'. She can rise above all things but one peffa-important one – her destiny – which, Matlock, is somehow intertwined and connected with yours."

Matlock reached into his pocket, pulling out the small leather-potion bottle. "She gave me this."

Plusa smiled. "I know. I know many things. It's better that way."

Matlock turned the bottle over in his paw, trying to remember. "She griffled me to open it when I thought the time was right."

"And is it?" Plusa asked.

"I don't know," Matlock griffled, sighing. "There's just so much of everything that I don't know. I can remember most things and how they happened, but nothing seems to make any sense. It's all just oidy bits that I want to reach out and pull together, but it's like they're floating, and every time I try, they move."

"Like me?" Plusa griffled, playfully darting through Matlock's ears and circling him several times.

"Just like you, Plusa," Matlock vilishly agreed, missing her twice with his paws.

Plusa chickled. "You remember what happened to this bed and the singing kraark's leg, the last time you were here?"

He thought about Goole, hearing his glopped-up singing coming from under the very same bed. "He was trapped," he griffled. "I accidentally landed on him."

Plusa shook her head. "This griffle of yours 'accident', is most chickle-making for us sylphas. Nothing in the dales, on Trefflepugga path, or underneath it, happens by 'accident', Matlock, you must have realised that by now. All has a purpose; from the most oidy thing, to all those times you feel you have peffa-gobflopped. Everything happens for a reason, no matter how twizzly or glubbstool it may first appear. Just like your friend, the singing-kraark. His leg got glopped, and is no more. But he has a new one now, carved from the collar-beam of the old wooden Great Hall in Winchett Dale."

"Oh my difflejubbs!" Matlock griffled, shocked at the news. "That is most peffa-glopped. I never meant for him to lose a leg, Plusa. I feel terrible."

Plusa chickled. "Matlock, what have I just griffled to you? Everything happens for a reason. The kraark is fuzzcheck, and able to scrittle peffa-saztaculously." She turned a small circle in the air. "But the most glopped-up thing is that his new wooden leg is also saztaculously important on your journey to becoming Most Majelicus, Matlock. You see, everything has a reason, only you refuse to see it."

Matlock frowned. "A wooden leg is important to me?"

"One sun-turn you will discover why." She hovered in front of his face. "But now I go. You must find the answer to your riddle on this path, and you must do this alone. Good luck."

"Wait," Matlock griffled, "don't go!"

"There are twizzly times ahead for you, Matlock. Everything has changed. You have been out to The Great Beyond, so the path has no memories of your previous two journeys along it. But the blinksnap you leave this bed and take your first pid-pad on the ground, the path will wake and show you many things, some will be helpful to you, others will be peffa-yechus. Extrapluffs will not work on the path, so you must seek another way to find and solve the riddle."

Matlock swallowed, trying not to feel too twizzly, as a light wind blew heavy grey clouds across the lid, sending dark shadows sweeping across the dale. "At least I won't have to see a dregg of myself, as the path can't remember me from before. I should be grateful for that, I suppose."

Plusa chickled. "Trefflepugga Path has many surprises, Matlock, peffa-many indeed. You have returned here, so you must begin."

"Please!" Matlock pleaded, as the drifting sprite rose into the darkening gloom. "Plusa, come back! You must griffle me how you know all this!"

She stopped, hovering in the same spot, before slowly drifting back down. "What do you know of mirrits, Matlock?"

288

"Mirrits?"

Plusa nodded, waiting.

"Well," Matlock griffled. "They're just oidy creatures. Perhaps even the oidiest." He looked to the ominously threatening skies, noticing a slight mist beginning to splutt, churn and bubble from the brook, a twizzly feeling rising in his softulous. "Is this important, Plusa?"

"Why shouldn't mirrits be important, just because they're oidy?"

He tried to think, rubbing his paws on his robes, looking into the distance, his breath becoming shorter as he heard a distant garrumbloom begin to rumble over the vale. "I don't want the dreggs to come again, Plusa."

"Then think about mirrits," she gently griffled. "What are they, Matlock? You already have all the answers inside you. Don't let the path distract you. Close your eyes, clear your twizzly mind and simply think about mirrits."

Matlock shut both eyes, trying to think as the garrumblooming grew closer. An image shot into his mind, a page from a book, one he instantly recognised, its pictures and griffles detailing all he ever needed to know about the oidiest creatures in the dale. "They're born from extrapluffs," he griffled, reading the page as clearly as if it had been in front of his face. "They spend the beginnings of their lives tunnelling!" He opened his eyes. "Plusa, this is shindinculous! I can read every griffle. It's the soup, isn't it? The niff-soup I ate at The Vroffa-Tree Inn. The griffles are there, in my mind, every one of them, as clear as the light of any sun-turn!"

Plusa smiled. "*Majickal Dalelore (Volume 68 – revised edition)*, the least read but most peffa-important majickal-driftolubb of the entire collection. Most of all you will ever need to know for your journey is there, Matlock, right inside you. You simply have to find it."

"It's saztaculous," Matlock griffled, closing his eyes and reading from the page once more.

"What else does it griffle about mirrits?" Plusa pressed. "Turn the page, Matlock. There's more."

"But how?" Matlock griffled, trying not to panic as another garrumbloom cracksploded across the sky. "How in Oramus' name can I turn the page of a book that's not really there?"

"Just reach out and do it," Plusa griffled. "But be vilish, for I must leave before the path gets too twizzly with me. See your paw turning the page, and it will happen. Trust me, reach out."

Matlock reached out a paw then, to his amazement, saw the same paw in his mind, finding the corner of the page and slowly turning it, revealing a large image of a sylpha on the other side. Breathlessly, he vilishly read the griffles, before suddenly opening his eyes. "And mirrits," he griffled to Plusa, "scrittle up trees to nifferduggle on the backs of leaves, before finally changing into sylphas!" He reached out to her, Plusa elegantly landing on his paw. "From an extrapluff, to a mirrit, to a sylpha. You began your life as an extrapluff."

She nodded. "And not just any extrapluff, either. One of *your* extrapluffs, Matlock. The most-peffa important one will you ever have in all your time in these dales. I was born a mirrit from the very first extrapluff you ever had, up by Thinking Lake, as your master instructed you as a young apprentice majickal-hare."

Matlock shook his head, trying peffa-hard to think, take himself back to when Chatsworth had first taught him how to extrapluff. "But I can't remember what it was," he griffled.

"What *I* was," Plusa corrected him. "What I *still am*, Matlock."

"Griffle me," Matlock begged. "Please, I just can't remember."

Plusa vilishly darted to his ear, whispgriffling as the lid crackspoded and garrumbloomed overhead. "Your first extrapluff revealed your destiny, Matlock. All that you will do, and all that you won't, everything that will happen to you in this life of yours. It's always the first extrapluff of any majickal-hare; a life's pathway laid out in front of young eyes that are too blind to see it, ears too deaf to hear it. And yet it still rests somewhere in your mind, waiting to be played out. As the mirrit born from that extrapluff, I have now become its sylpha-guardian to ensure that all happens for you just as it was foretold; that Oramus' will through you in these dales is completed according to his highest and Most Majelicus wisdom and needs." She twirled back up into the air. "But now, 'tis time for you to take the path, Matlock. Answer your riddle. Trefflepugga Path is waiting."

Matlock grabbed at her, but Plusa simply vanished as vilishly as she had appeared. He called out for her many times, each griffle of her name louder than the last, becoming more hopeless and glopped-up as he realised that she wasn't coming back, he was truly alone, sitting on a bed in a twizzly dale, trying to solve an answer to a riddle that he couldn't even begin to find, as the swirling mists and fogs grew thicker with every blinksnap. Nothing made sense, everything seemed unfair, or impossible, or simply just too glubbstooled.

"Oramus!" he called, shouting into the lid. "Why have you left me like this? You're supposed to be the one showing me the way, yet you're nowhere! Sistcraculous! You're supposed to be pid-padding by my side, so where are you? Everything is gobflopped, and why should I believe in either of you? You're just spuddles, made up to make young creatures feel fuzzcheck and crumlush, yet when the time comes for you to help, you're nowhere!" He got off the bed, defiantly setting both feet on the ground and pid-padding to the swirling brook; rage, anger and peffa-russisculoftulation beating in his brave hare's heart. "What use are you, *either* of you? If everything's been already decided according to your will, then what destiny does any creature truly ever have? What destiny do *I have?* What possible glopped-up use are dreams and ambitions, if you know everything that's going to happen, anyway?" He stamped both feet angrily. "This path, this Trefflepugga Path of yours, why did you even make it? You're supposed to have made everything, so why make something so glubbstooled as a path that does nothing but change all the time, taking creatures where they don't want to go, and stroffing those unlucky enough not to solve its ridiculous riddles!" He shook an angry, shaking paw at the last of the fast disappearing sky. "Send your fog, then! Send your mists! Send your dreggs! What can be worse than I stroff here, anyway? It's probably already written down in one of your glopped-up driftolubbs; 'Matlock gets russisculoffed and twizzly, doesn't solve the riddle, and gets stroffed!' Is that what it says? Are those the final griffles of my destiny? Are they? Answer me! Show me, if you're supposed to be watching over me!"

He stopped, panting from the effort, feeling suddenly cold, the wind sending icy peffablasts that swirled around his robes. "Please," he quietly pleaded, juzzpapped, "just answer me."

From the corner of his eye he noticed a red-robed figure vilishly pid-padding across the other side of the misting brook, carrying a hare by its ears. Matlock instantly looked away, his heart beating faster than a winter-flutthropp's wings, shielding his face with his paws, aware that as the figure drew level, it had stopped, the narrow trickling water now the only thing separating them.

"Be gone!" Matlock griffled. "You're not Chatsworth! And that's not me you're holding! You're just dreggs with pitch-black empty eyes, and I'm not looking at you!"

There was a pause, before the figure began to slowly chickle. "That's funny," it griffled, in a voice which chilled every bone in Matlock's peffa-twizzly softulous, "a snutch of blinksnaps ago, you griffled you wouldn't mind being stroffed. And yet now, you fear it. But I do need you to look into my eyes."

"Leave me!" Matlock griffled. "Just keep on pid-padding and leave me."

"You recognise my voice, don't you, Matlock? You know who I am. I won't leave until you have looked into my eyes. For you must, for both our sakes."

Matlock screwed his eyes even more tightly shut, holding his ears with his paws, never wanting to hear the dregg's voice again, for he knew it to be his own. The glopped-up and peffa-twizzly dregg was griffling in Matlock's *own voice*. "Just leave me be," he moaned. "You're a trick of the path!"

"Matlock," the figure griffled. "I am no trick. Open your eyes. Look at me. Listen to me. I am you."

"No!" Matlock griffled, trying to hum and sing, do anything to block out the griffles.

"Listen to me," the figure urgently griffled. "It's peffa, peffa important. I'm not a dregg. Think, Matlock, think. The path has no memory of you now, so there *can't* be any dreggs of you. I'm not Chatsworth, Matlock, I *am* you."

"No!"

"Matlock, you must look into my eyes, however peffa-yechus they look. You *must* do it."

"Leave me, dregg!" Matlock griffled as the lid violently cracksploded above, shaking the ground beneath his feet.

"If you don't look," the figure griffled, "then I promise you that very soon you will be stroffed. Then everything will end, Matlock –

From the corner of his eye he noticed a red-robed figure vilishly pid-padding across the other side of the misting brook, carrying a hare by its ears.

right at the beginning for you, and at the end for me."

"All lies!" Matlock shouted, paws still closed around his ears, but unable to block the griffles. "How can you be me? Your griffles are all lies!"

"In your pocket is a potion bottle," the figure griffled, "given to you by Ursula Brifthaven Stoltz. You can't remember what's in it, but I do, Matlock, because I am you, the you of many moon-turns hence. I am you as you will be, Matlock. I have completed the three tasks, and now I return along Trefflepugga Path with my chosen hare to train as apprentice. Look, Matlock, look at the hare I'm holding. It's not you, and I'm not Chatsworth." The figure took a deep hare's breath. "Look and see, Matlock. It has eyes, it is no dregg, and neither am I."

Matlock peffa-cautiously opened one eye, his whole softulous shaking, staring at the ground by his feet, not daring to even glance across the brook. He needed to find a question, a way of testing the figure's glopped-up claims. "So what's in the bottle?" he griffled. "What did Ursula give me? If you're really me, then you'd already know."

"Her feelings, Matlock.," the red-robed figure replied. "A potion of her feelings that she griffled to you to look after until the time was right."

Matlock took another breath, slowly nodding, seeing Ursula's face and remembering her words as they griffled together The Nifferie.

"I'm right, aren't I?" the figure vilishly urged as another garrumbloom rumbled across the vale. "So I *must* be you, Matlock. Just trust me and look into the eyes of this hare. Please, we don't have long. Do this and save yourself, save me, save Ursula, save everyone! Just do it! Look!"

Matlock nervously rubbed at his whiskers, not knowing what to do. The voice sounded exactly like his, yet still he couldn't find the courage to look. "You have Most Majelicus robes on," he griffled. "If you are me then that means I must complete all the three tasks."

"You will," the figure griffled. "And it is a long and twizzly business, Matlock. But one sun-turn these robes will be yours. Then you will be me, exactly where I am now, griffling to you, just like this, listening to yourself from long, long ago, begging with yourself to look at this hare and see that it is no dregg. And when that sun-turn comes, Matlock, when you are stood on this side of the brook, you, like me, will also be blind."

"Blind?" Matlock gasped

"It is the only way," the figure griffled. "Remember, to me, *you* are a dregg, Trefflepugga Path's first new memory of you. If I were to look at you, I would be stroffed, and everything would end here."

"I'm going to lose my eyes?" Matlock griffled, completely peffa-twizzly, and without realising looking up from the ground and seeing the glopped-up apparition of himself, dressed in the red-robes of a Most Majelicus majickal-hare, but with just black, empty, yechus pits for eyes. He let out a scream, shocked at the twizzly horror of it all.

"Don't be afraid," the figure griffled. "We haven't much time, and there is something you must do; something you won't want to do, but something you must, or many will be in peffa-twizzly danger."

"What happened to my eyes?" Matlock whispgriffled, unable to stop looking at the empty sockets. "How does my face get like that?"

"When you become Most Majelicus, you will be able to do and discover many shindinculous things. But you will discover other things, too; ones that perhaps you didn't want to know. They will put your life in danger, from creatures you haven't even begun to imagine yet. But everything will be fine, Matlock, all will be well if you just give me Ursula's potion."

"No!" Matlock vilishly cried. "I griffled her a promise that I'd keep it safe at all times!"

"And she griffled to you that you'd know when the time was right to use it, Matlock. And that time is now. I have to use it now!"

"You're not having it!" Matlock griffled. "She griffled me that *I'd* know. Me – not you."

"But Matlock, I am you!" the figure cried. "The potion bottle was destroyed in the course of my completing the third task. But it is more valuable than you will ever realise. The only way I could get it back was to find you, as I was, pid-padding along this path many moon-turns ago. Matlock, if you value anything about Ursula, your friends and Winchett Dale, you *have* to give me that potion bottle!"

"Only if you give me the answer to the riddle!" Matlock

suddenly shouted back. "If you really are me when I'm Most Majelicus, then you must already know it. What is it? Tell me!"

"I will do," the figure griffled, "as soon as you give me the bottle!"

"No!" Matlock griffled, as the brook began to sprutt and churn more violently, widening, separating them with every blinksnap. "I don't trust you. You're too yechus! The time *isn't* right, I know it."

"Matlock," the figure pleaded, "we don't have long. The path is making it impossible. The time isn't right for *you*, but it is right *for me*! Throw it to me, vilish! Believe me, Ursula will be stroffed if you don't! Just throw the bottle to me while you still can!"

Matlock looked into the black eyes one final time and took a deep hare's breath, reaching for the potion bottle in his robes. "Forgive me, Ursula," he whispgriffled, taking aim and throwing the bottle across the churning brook with all his might, watching as it sailed across, landing next to the figure, who vilishly bent down, blindly searching the ground for it, before finding and putting it safely into its red robes.

"It won't make sense to you now," the figure cried, "but it will in time. And you will need this!" It reached into its robe and pulled out a wand, holding it high in the air, calling across the swirling waters. "This is your old hawthorn wand. However, it is now Peffa-Majelicus, and has saved me many times. Use its majick wisely, Matlock, and it will help you with all three tasks." It threw the wand across the river, Matlock vilishly scrabbling for it, as the figure cried out once more, "Both wand and potion have crossed the waters of time, let all be right according to Oramus' will for us both!"

Fog was rapidly descending, Matlock barely able to make out the receding figure. "But what about the riddle?" he desperately cried. "Griffle me the answer to the riddle!" He strained his eyes to see through the dense white blanket, the figure disappearing beneath it, rising water crashing around so loudly that it was impossible to hear any more griffles. "Griffle me the answer!"

But no more griffles came, just the deafening roar of the ever-widening river, waves smashing against the banks, sending spray high into the mist and fog. Matlock turned, pid-padding as vilishly as he could, remembering the safety of the crumlush bed that had saved him from being stroffed before. But this time, the fog was too thick, and he could barely make out a paw in front of his face. He didn't have the oidiest chance of finding it, but simply knew he had to keep vilishly pid-padding away from the angry, thrashing river, stumbling over rocks, bumping into trees, trying his briftest to find higher ground, his juzzpapped lungs burning from the effort.

"I'm not going to be stroffed here!" he panted through the griffles. "Tis no place for a majickal-hare to be stroffed! 'Tis all too glopped-up and peffa-glubbstool!"

Gradually the roaring began to recede, the fog thinning as he finally felt the ground begin to rise under his feet, the effort of pid-padding becoming harder as he slowly climbed the slope at the edge of the vale. He could begin to see the ground beneath his feet and was able to pid-pad around rocks and trees, climbing higher all the while, utterly peffa-juzzpapped, looking for a place he could finally rest, get some breaths back.

"I...am...Matlock," he griffled, panting heavily, his paws tearing at the slope. "I...am the majickal-hare of Winchett Dale! I have...a Most Majelicus dworp. I have a...Most Majelicus wand, a dripple than can griffle. I will be...Most Majelicus one sun-turn, for I have already seen myself. I know it happens!" He stopped, turned, looked over the vale, the fog below starting to swirl back into the river, gradually quietening and narrowing into the gently bubbling brook one more.

He took deep breaths, tried to calm his shaking softulous and all the peffa-russisculoftulation he felt building inside, before suddenly throwing both arms out wide, and shouting in his loudest ever voice, the griffles echoing all around the vale. "And you are just Trefflepugga Path! You have none of those things! Yes, you can change, but it's all you can do, isn't it! Well, *everything* changes, doesn't it? Everything! You're no different from the extrapluff that becomes the mirrit, that becomes a sylpha! You're no different from *me*! For I've changed, haven't I? From a normal hare, into a majickal-one! Proftulous has changed and become Most Majelicus! Even your own riddle changes for each and every creature that seeks to solve it! Everything changes, and...that's your riddle, isn't it?"

He took a ganticus breath, reaching into his robe, searching for his two wands, but only finding the one that had been hurled across the raging river. His old wand had simply vanished, as if it had never existed at all. He turned the new wand in his paw, recognising the twisted hawthorn as his, but now blackened with burns, gouges and streaks in the wood, scars from many vrooshers and battles it had fought along the way. Its end fizzed bright-red, and it jumped in his paw. He'd never held anything so powerful in his life.

"Even this wand," he cried out to the vale, "has changed! And it will change me, too! I *will* become Most Majelicus. I will solve your riddle! And you might try your peffa-glopped-up hardest, but that's one thing you *can't* change, isn't it? You can't change a future that I've already seen as my destiny!"

The wand suddenly shot a bright red vroosher into the lid, the force almost knocking Matlock off his feet. He steadied himself, then bliffed his head. "Of course!" he griffled, his voice peffa-shakey and excrimbly. "That's the riddle, isn't it? *What changes, but never changes at all?*" He took a ganticus breath, thoughts finally tumbling and folding into his mind like missing pieces of a puzzle. "Everything's been about change, hasn't it? All of it, every oidy bit of it. Everything's changed. Plusa once griffled to me 'I am, but I am not'. She was, but *wasn't* the riddle. She's changed, but then again, she hasn't. She's still that original extrapluff I had up at Thinking Lake, but is now a crumlush sprite."

The ground beneath his feet began to rumble and garrumbloom, the wand shaking in his paw, pointing down to the brook below, then vilishly leading him back down the slope, Matlock desperately trying to hold on, pid-padding and jumping over and around rocks and trees until he stood at the edge of the calm waters, the wand insistently pointing at the stilled surface as he frowned in concentration, trying his peffa-hardest to understand.

"What changes, but never changes at all?" he whispgriffled, searching the waters for some sort of clue, a creature perhaps, that wouldn't ever change, but do exactly the same things; over and over, sun-turn after sun-turn, moon-turn after moon-turn. "I don't know, I just don't know."

He saw his reflection, an answer vilishly shooting into his mind. "Me!" he griffled, pointing to the water. "The answer's me! I change, yet I don't really change at all!"

The wand turned in his paw and sent out a vroosh that frizzed and bliffed his ears.

"Not the answer, then?" he griffled, stroking the lightly burnt tips of his ears. He sighed. "Still, at least I suppose I've finally found the riddle. That's some progress."

The wand jumped again, urgently pointing back at the water.

"But I've tried water already," Matlock griffled. "I suggested a snowflake to Plusa, because it's a form of water that changes, and then she griffled me that I was right but I was also wrong…" He stopped, recalling the sprite's griffles. "*I am, but I am not. I was, but am no more.*" He griffled the griffles out loud a snutch of times, staring into the water. "She griffled to me that I wouldn't ever find the answer on the path, but that it's everywhere."

He put a paw to his mouth, suddenly breaking into the most ganitcus smile and thumping the ground with his feet, jigging and turning on the spot. "This is about 'time', isn't it?" he griffled. "Time changes everything, yet still pid-pads on every sun-turn, every moon-turn. Time changed Plusa. Time changed me, time changed Proftulous, time even changed this wand!"

He chickled out loud, skipping along the bank, his whole softulous peffa-excrimbly. "And the reason I'll never find the answer on the path, is because it's the one place, the *only* place, where time always changes, isn't it? Time has no meaning on the path. But in all the dales and way out in The Great Beyond, time *can't* change, can it? It changes things, but it doesn't change at all, it just is – blinksmap after blinksnap, sun-turn after sun-turn, moon-turn after moon-turn, from the very first beginnings of the twinkling-lid, right to this moment and beyond into the hereafter." He held the wand aloft triumphantly, calling out to the lid. "Trefflepugga Path! The answer to your riddle is 'time'!"

The wand vrooshed once more, sending a most ganticus red vroosher streaking high into the lid, knocking Matlock to the ground, leaving him gasping at its sheer strength and majickal-power. He held on with both paws, struggling desperately, the wand directing the vroosher back to the ground, then suddenly and unexpectedly rocketing Matlock high into the lid, the path below twisting and writhing like a wounded creature, mountains becoming arms, their paws angrily reaching for him, swiping the air as he vilishly flew by. Rivers and lakes became one gigantic whirlpool, it too soaring high into the lid, its centre a looming, peffa-yechus mouth threatening to swallow him into its dark, watery churning depths.

Matlock held tight to the wand, his robes and ears vilishly flapping in the wind, trying to take breaths, eyes tightly shut as he was thrown in a grillion different directions; Most Majelicus wand and majickal-hare outsmarting, dodging, twisting and turning from all that Trefflepugga Path could throw at them. Clouds reached down as they hurtled by, trees launched themselves like arrows, cliffs broke into crackslpoding showers of rocks and boulders – raining in, missing, then turning to chase them like a ganticus pack of the most yechus, snarling creatures in all the dales.

"I am Matlock the hare!" he managed to griffle in the peffa-twizzly chaos. "I have already solved your riddle, and I command this to end!"

The most peffa-ganticus garrumbloom ripped through the sky, lightning bolts streaking in every direction as Matlock heard the loudest, most peffa-yechus moan he'd ever heard, watching as the rocks, trees, mountains, rivers and lakes all suddenly fell back, crashing to the ground far below, the earth shaking and roaring in endless twizzly protest, until finally all was quiet and calm once more.

The wand levelled as the lid began to clear, clouds drifting away, to leave Matlock gently flying, the sun crumlush on his face, watching in fascination as the wand bought him slowly back down to earth in a place he instantly recognised.

"The Cove of Choices," he griffled as his feet touched the ground, looking around the ganticus cove and seeing the archways begin to slowly rumble open. He put the wand back peffa-carefully into his robe, the tip still red-hot. "Methinks you'll be peffa-useful," he griffled to it. "Just as soon as I can work out how to use you properly. Not sure I care too much for the flying, though. Gets a bit twizzly and glopped-up for a hare."

He turned round, seeing the many open archways leading to all the majickal-dales, including his own beloved and unmistakeable Winchett Dale. He sighed in pure peffa-relief and began vilishly pid-padding towards it, only to be suddenly startled by a series of perfectly clipped and peffa-sophisticated griffles from behind.

"I say, excuse me, dear fellow, just one or two oidy bits of procedure to go through first, I'm afraid."

Matlock turned, gasping to see a creature that was so peffa-yechus, it made Proftulous look like the most crumlush sylpha, pid-padding straight towards him. Its skin was revoltingly scaly, with lumpen hairy boils breaking all over it, and it had quite the longest, pointed and constantly moving nose he'd ever seen. The only crumlush thing you could ever griffle about it was that it wore a golden monocle over one yechus eye, had a rather fetching scarf around its throat and was wearing immaculate white leather gloves.

Matlock had his wand out in a blinksnap, pointing it at the creature. "Get back!" he cried. "I'm warning you, this is a Most Majelicus wand, and one vroosher from me could leave you stroffed!"

"Now, now," the creature griffled. "No need for any of that unpleasantness. Just put it away, there's a good fellow."

"Who are you?" Matlock griffled, frowning and slowly lowering the wand.

"Tiftoluft," it griffled. "Long, long-nosed krellit in charge of overseeing all successful Most Majelicus candidates who have successfully solved the riddle to the Trefflepugga Path." He held out a gloved hand. "Don't take offence, I always wear these, as sometimes I simply haven't the oidest idea where you majickal-hares might have been."

Matlock slowly reached out, lightly tapped the glove, trying to avoid the ganticus pointed nose that seemed to have a life of its own, sniffing and snorting all around his softulous and robes, then slipping into his paw and vilishly taking the wand. "Hey," he griffled, "give that back!"

Tiftoluft chickled politely. "In good time, dear fellow, in good time. Now, if you'd like to follow me, we'll have this annoying business over as peffa-quickly as we can."

Reluctant to leave his wand, Matlock had no choice but to pid-pad after the long, long-nosed krellit as they made their way to the last remaining unopened cliff in the cove. "Will this take long?" he asked, slightly twizzly, then watching in complete amazement as the whole cliff-face slowly slid open; rumbling, clanking and garrumblooming to reveal the most ganticus set of bookshelves he had ever seen, tended by dozens of long-long nosed krellits on golden ladders, sliding back and forth, using their long and yechus noses to reach and open books, constantly checking them and passing relevant ones down to each other in a truly glopped-up chaos of fevered activity.

"Oh, my drifflejubbs," Matlock gasped, amazed at the sheer scale of everything. "That's…"

"Saztaculous?" Tiftoluft griffled, his nose sliding Matlock's wand back into his robe pocket. "It is rather, isn't it? But between you and me, you try cataloguing a library that size. Can all go rather gobflopped at times, I can griffle you that."

"It's ganticus," Matlock griffled in awe, craning his head to see to the top, trying to count all the long, long-nosed krellits scrambling over it, watching the ladders endlessly trundling along shelves heavy with books and majickal-driftolubbs of every colour and size.

"Take a seat," Tiftoluft griffled, gently pushing Matlock back into a chair made entirely from books that had suddenly appeared from behind, as another long, long-nosed krellit vilishly pid-padded over with a guzzwort in the most shindinculous mug Matlock had ever seen, before setting it neatly on the armrest.

"With the compliments of Trefflepugga Path for solving your very own riddle it set for you," Tiftoluft griffled.

Matlock blinked, astonished. "It's…it's given me a guzzwort?"

"All part of the new service. Frankly, we felt that our candidate after-care was somewhat lacking, and thought that with just an oidy snutch of changes we could make the whole experience far more saztaculous. Been doing this for a few majickal-hares now, and they all seemed to have liked it. You approve?"

Matlock took a sip, not quite knowing what to griffle. "Yes, thank you, that's…er…very welcome…at the end of…er…a long, hard riddle-solving sun-turn."

"Excellent!" Tiftoluft beamed. "That's the spirit! Now then, just a few questions, and you'll be on your way, I promise. So, my dear fellow, what's your name?"

"Matlock."

"Good. See, wasn't too peffa-difficult, was it?" He turned and clapped his gloved hands, officiously griffling to the others. "Fetch me *Most Majelicus Candidates – Book M.*"

"There's a book for that?" Matlock griffled, watching the instant activity of noses, ladders and books, until a book was finally selected from high in the ganticus library, making its way slowly down to the ground, where an eager long-long nosed krellit vilishly pid-padded it over to Tiftoluft.

"Matlock, my dear fellow," he griffled, "you'll discover there are all sorts of books and majickal driftolubbs for nearly everything in The Grand Library of the Elders." He waved the krellit away, lowering his voice and trying not to chickle. "Believe me, there's some spuddles to be found on those shelves that you wouldn't even dare to griffle to your mahpa!"

"You read?" Matlock griffled, watching as Tiftoluft expertly flicked through the pages, tracing names with his gloved hand. "I thought you were peffa-yechus things that stroffed creatures and crunched on their bones."

Tiftoluft nodded, adusting his golden monocle. "Well, sometimes some of us do an oidy bit of crunching, my dear fellow. I mean, someone has to clear up the mess if a creature gets stroffed by the path, don't they? But mostly, we're here, tending to the books. The Elders tend to get rather russisculoffed if we're away too long." He found the right entry on the page. "It griffles here 'Matlock, taken by Chatsworth from The Great Beyond, named by him, nominated by him to undertake the three tasks.' All correct?"

Matlock nodded, taking another sip from his guzzwort, and noticing a small doorway at the bottom of the ganticus bookcase, a constant stream of long, long-nosed krellits entering and leaving with books under their arms.

Tiftoluft continued. "And the answer to your riddle was?"

"Time," Matlock griffled.

"Correct!" Tiftoluft replied, closing the book with a satisfied snap. "All seems to be in order. Saztaculous! Now, the thing to remember, my dear fellow, is that every time you pid-pad along the path from now on, you will be led straight here. All doors will open for you as long as you griffle the griffle 'time' to them. 'Tis like your very own majickal key, which is why, of course, no two can ever be the same. From then on, where you choose to go is your own decision. No more of all that changing-path nonsense for you, dear fellow. All understandable?"

Matlock nodded.

"Well, I won't be keeping you. Doubtless you've a grillion things to do."

"Can I just ask what's through that door?" Matlock griffled, intrigued, pointing to the bottom of the ganticus bookcase.

"Indeed, you can," Tiftoluft griffled, taken aback, but smiling broadly. "And may I griffle that 'tis a peffa-splendid pleasure to have one of your kind finally kind take an interest in what we do here. Most simply want to pid-pad off as vilishly as possible to begin their next task." He chickled slightly, his long, yechus nose wrapping itself around Matlock's shoulder like an arm. "Mind, they do tend to be the ones that get stroffed, so I've heard. Too vilish, they are, for their own good. Daresay, I've probably crunched on a few of their bones, myself." He chickled out loud. "Pid-pad this way, dear hare-fellow, and I'll show you what's behind the creaker. Prepare yourself for The Great Cavern of All Revisions."

Matlock had no choice but to follow, Tiftoluft's long nose practically forcing him to pid pad to the creaker, then through it into one of the most peffa-ganticus caverns he had ever seen, many times the size of the one that was home to The Vroffa-Tree Inn. It was hung with hundreds of lanterns illuminating endless rows of desks, a long, long-nosed krellit sitting at each one, all in the peffa-deepest concentration, silently copying and re-writing hundreds and hundreds of books, the only noise the echoing scratch of quills on parchment.

"There," Tiftoluft proudly griffled. "What do you think? Pretty peffa-impressive, eh?"

"It's saztactulous," Matlock whispgriffled, trying to take it all in. He'd never seen so many creatures in one place before.

"Your set of drifftolubbs would have originally come from here," Tiftoluft griffled, as the pair of them began pid-padding along one of the rows. "Each one patiently copied by a long, long-nosed krellit, deep in a cavern on Trefflepugga Path. Each and every picture and griffle. 'Tis a shindinculous skill, and takes many, many arduous moon-turns to learn, but once mastered it will become a life's

"Pid-pad this way, dear hare-fellow, and I'll show you what's behind the creaker.
Prepare yourself for The Great Cavern of All Revisions."

work." A nearby krellit accidentally sneezed, shattering the silence and knocking an ink-bottle all over his work. "Of course," Tiftoluft apologised, shooting the embarrassed krellit a stern look, "Some of them are rather better at it than others."

An excrimbly commotion was beginning at the far end of the cavern, Tiftoluft turning and adjusting his monocle. "Ah, this should be interesting for you, dear fellow," he griffled. "Follow me, I think there's a revision from the Elders on its way."

Matlock followed, pid-padding along the end of the long row to a ganticus roaring piff-tosh, its chimney disappearing up into the inky blackness of the cavern roof way, way above. Tiftoluft gently shooed the other long, long-nosed krellits out of the way, then placed a blank piece of parchment on a grill set just above the flames.

"Happens every few sun-turns," he griffled to Matlock. "Standby, everyone! Another Elder revision on the way!"

Matlock watched as the ganticus chimney began to shake, pitch-black soot falling from its cracks. The orange flames in the piff-tosh began turning blue and green, licking at the parchment, but never once burning it.

"Watch," Tiftoluft griffled, pointing to the parchment as gradually griffles began to appear, moving vilishly as if being written by an invisible hand, filling the entire page. "Looks like a long one, this one. Some are just a few griffles. Terrible pain, those, as it means re-writing an entire driftolubb for just one or two lines."

"My driftolubbs all got burnt," Matlock griffled, still watching the parchment, trying to make out what it said.

"Probably the best thing for them, dear fellow," Tiftoluft quietly chickled. "Chances are, they were out of date, anyway. So many revisions coming in all the time, you see."

"But can I get a new set from you?" Matlock asked. "The latest, most complete set?"

Tiftoluft wagged a gloved, yechus finger and claw at him. "Only one set of Majickal Driftolubbs per majickal-hare, per lifetime, Matlock. It's in the rules." He removed the parchment from the grill, reading it carefully, the flames dying back to orange and yellow. "Well, I never," he griffled, showing the revision to a waiting krellit, its long nose already twitching in anticipation. "Who would ever have thought *that* about short-winged trillers, eh? Well, you learn something new every sun-turn in this job." He passed the parchment to the krellit, who vilishly pid-padded away with it.

"What did it say?" Matlock asked.

"Oh, I'd love to tell you, dear fellow, I really peffa-would, but it's not in the rules, you see?" Tiftoluft opened his yechus mouth and bared his glopped-up teeth. "And then I'd have to stroff you right here and crunch on your bones, and really, that would be peffa, peffa uncivilised, as you seem to be quite a fuzzcheck sort of a fellow." He made an arm of his nose again, looping it around Matlock's shoulder and marching him back towards the doorway. "Besides, you've probably seen too much in here, already. But it was utterly saztaculous to have a fellow take such an interest in our humble labours and honest endeavours for once."

Matlock saw the light from outside beckoning in the distance, realising he didn't have much time to discover what he needed to know. "Do you remember a revision that was made to *Majickal Dalelore (Volume 68)*?"

Tiftoluft chickled. "My dear fellow, there have been grillions of revisions made to all these books and driftolubbs over the years. To think that I would even begin to remember each and every one of them would be peffa-clottabussed, indeed." He stopped, suddenly turned, his eyes narrowing in curious suspicion. "And just *why* would you be interested? For if memory serves me rightly, *Majickal Dalelore (Volume 68 – revised edition)* is the oidiest and least important of all the majickal-driftolubbs. Why, I'm wondering, would you be even the least interested in a revision made to it?"

Matlock cleared his throat. "No reason, I just…"

"You just, what?" Tiftoluft slowly griffled, then end of his long nose beginning to flare as it snaked in the air.

"I just must have confused it with something else," Matlock griffled, trying to stay calm and ignore the thin string of yechus drool running from Tiftoluft's mouth. "It must have been the guzzwort I had after all the excitement."

There was a long and peffa-twizzly pause, Tiftoluft studying Matlock's face intently throughout. "Well," he slowly griffled, "I suppose that can happen."

307

"Oh, it most peffa-definitely did to me," Matlock vilishly griffled. "Made my mind an oidy bit glopped, it did. I don't know why I even griffled the question. What question was it, anyway? You see, I've forgotten it already. It's gone clean out of my mind. Just a juzzpapped hare, I am, all clottabussed from your peffa-generous complimentary guzzwort and saztaculous hospitality."

Tiftoluft narrowed his eyes even further for a snutch of moments, searching for the truth, before suddenly opening them and slapping Matlock on the back with his nose. "My dear fellow! How can I have misjudged you? Just because a fellow goes a bit glubbstooled with a guzzwort, doesn't mean I have to stroff and eat him, does it?"

"I hope not," Matlock griffled, trying to chickle without looking as peffa-relieved as he felt.

Tiftoluft smiled. "Anyway, enough of all this griffling of crunching on your bones, dear fellow. 'Tis time for you to be pid-padding on your way."

Matlock took a thankful deep-breath. "Indeed, and it has been most peffa-kind of you to show me all this, really peffa-kind."

"The crumlush pleasure was all mine," Tiftoluft cheerfully griffled, as they made their way towards the open creaker, and the welcome release of warming sunlight outside. "There is one more thing, though."

"Oh?"

Tiftoluft took him to a large wooden cupboard set into the cavern wall by the doorway. "You'll be pid-padding back to Winchett Dale, I trust?"

"Peffa-much so," Matlock griffled, watching as he opened the cupboard's heavy creaker to reveal shelves full of boxes, crates and trunks of every size, all moving and twitching as light spilled over them.

"Sometimes, we have what we can only describe as 'gobflops' here on the path," he griffled, searching the rows of boxes, Matlock hearing all sorts of strange griffles, cries and noises coming from inside. A paw suddenly reached out from one of the boxes, only to be sharply bliffed by Tiftoluft's nose, before its lid vilishly snapped shut again. He selected a box, opened the lid, peered inside then passed it to Matlock. "I believe these were yours, dear fellow. Or at least, they set off along the path with you at the same time."

Matlock opened the box, seeing four twizzly ploffshrooms

cowering amongst some oidy broken instruments at the bottom.

"We found them wandering around a few moon-turns ago," Tiftoluft explained. "Seems the path took them to Sveag Dale, but it must have gone glubbstool for the poor chaps, as pretty soon they were trying to find their way back and got hopelessly lost. We checked the records and traced them to your journey, so we kept them here for you to return to Winchett Dale, if you ever got this far."

"That's peffa-kind of you," Matlock griffled, gently placing each twizzly ploffshroom in his hood. "I'll be sure to get them back safely."

"There were seven originally," Tiftoluft griffled, lowering his voice. "But frankly, we tend to use this cupboard as a bit of a food store if we get peckish. Sorry about that. And the trinkulah player was completely dreadful, was driving us all quite clottabussed, so he *had* to go."

"I understand," Matlock griffled, relieved that at least some of the ploffshrooms were safe.

Tiftoluft smiled. "From a vibrant seven-piece to a glubbstooled and twizzly four-piece. Life can be so unfair at times, can't it?" He took a book from one of the shelves, blowing on the dusty cover and opening it, then passing Matlock a quill. "Now, I simply need you to sign for the ploffshrooms to say you received them in peffa-crumlush condition, and you can be pid-padding on your way."

"Erm…" Matlock hesitated, caught, reading the griffles. "It says here that I'm signing for all seven of them?"

Tiftoluft nodded. "Is that a problem, dear fellow?"

"Well, an oidy bit, yes. You've eaten three of them."

Tiftoluft sighed. "Now listen, I've had a peffa-hard sun-turn, you've absolutely not the oidiest idea. You've had a complimentary guzzwort and tour of our cavern, dear fellow. I think we can overlook the oidy matter of a missing ploffshroom of two, don't you?"

"Three, actually," Matlock quietly griffled under his breath, reluctantly signing the book and returning the quill.

"Excellent!" Tiftoluft smiled, snapping it shut, his nose lightly bliffing Matlock's ears in yechus appreciation, before closing and locking the cupboard doors. "You're clearly a hare after my own heart, dear fellow. Just because a chap makes an oidy mistake and eats a few ploffshrooms shouldn't mean he should get into a heap of glopped-up bother, should it?"

"No," Matlock griffled, grinding his teeth and anxious to leave, for however fascinating he found The Great Cavern of All Revisions, and however much he wanted to discover the real truth about Baselott's lost revisions to *Majickal Dalelore (Volume 68)*, he knew in his Sisteraculous that now simply wasn't the time. Tiftoluft, for all his smiling bluster, elegant posturing and clipped griffles, was as untrustworthy as any creature Matlock had ever come across, and clearly had no regard for any of the rules he was supposed to be enforcing.

However, Matlock did have one thing over the yechusly-smiling long, long nosed krellit, but he'd need to leave vilishly in order to get away with it. Tiftoluft hadn't yet checked the signature he had left in the book. And it certainly didn't say 'Matlock'.

"I must be going," Matlock griffled, extending a paw and vilishly shaking the white gloved hand. "Many thanks for all your time."

Tiftoluft graciously bowed, ushering Matlock outside into the light. "Farewell, good fellow. I'd like to griffle that it would be a pleasure to see you again, but frankly if that ever happened, I'd be forced to stroff and eat you."

"I'll bear that in mind," Matlock griffled, pid-padding towards the open archway to Winchett Dale.

"It wouldn't be personal!" Tiftoluft called out from behind. "It's just the rules, dear fellow!"

Moments later, Matlock had disappeared under the archway, gratefully emerging into the warm, welcoming, crumlush summer of Winchett Dale. He turned, looking for any sign of The Cove of Choices but there were none; no sliding archways, no long, long-nosed krellits, no cliffs of ganticus bookcases – nothing. Everything looked exactly as it did when he had first pid-padded along Trefflepugga Path so many moon-turns ago. And what a journey it had been, taking him to places he couldn't imagine, meeting creatures he'd never forget, doing things he never even realised he could. But now he was back. He'd solved the riddle of Trefflepugga Pat and had completed the first task to becoming Most Majelicus. Now, he resolved to himself as he made his way slowly back down towards the village, things were going to peffa-definitely change...

He hadn't gone another ten pid-pads before he was vilishly surrounded and roughly caged by a waiting group of officious krates.

14.

Wands, Ploffshrooms and Dungeons

Frendelsene Note watched impassively from the balcony above the wooden stage of the stone Great Hall as Matlock's wagon and cage were slowly hauled inside by an army of excrimbly, puffing and panting krates. He could hear a commotion building outside, looking out of the windows at the hoard of glopped-up and clottabussed creatures that had jubilantly followed the wagon on its journey through the village, only to be finally stopped at the ganticus oaken doors by krates struggling to bar their way. There were excrimbly shouts of joy and cries of 'Matlock's back!' as more Winchett dale residents flocked to the hall, eager to catch a glimpse of the shindinculous return of their majickal-hare.

Curiously, none made even the oidiest attempt to stop the wagon and rescue Matlock, because he was obviously in a cage, and therefore quite the most popular and crumlush of places to be in. Besides, they reasoned, if he was in any real trouble then he wouldn't have been allowed to be in the cage in the first place, as they knew to their cost when krates banned them from being locked up if they glopped-up too badly. And further, this was obviously a prized cage, a cage on wheels, and even though Matlock might have looked a little gobflopped and russisculoffed, the residents of Winchett Dale merely assumed this was because he wasn't being pulled fast enough by the struggling krates, resulting in some of the creatures helping to push the wagon as it trundled by, in what they honestly believed was a saztaculous gesture of goodwill.

"Get them all back to their homes!" Note ordered, slowly descending the ornate stone stairway. "Griffle to them that any creature remaining outside will *not* be locked-up for another three moon-turns!"

Matlock watched from inside the cage, paw resting on the wand deep inside his robe pocket. The krates vilishly left the hall, closing the heavy creaker behind them, their officious barks and griffles filling the square as they ordered everyone back to their homes.

Note waited until the commotion had died down, standing next to the most ganticus pile of drutts Matlock had ever seen, so tall it reached halfway to the saztaculously carved roof of the hall. "Well," he griffled. "I must hand it to you, Matlock, all this time away, and you still know how to make an entrance."

"I think your krates had more to do with it than I did," Matlock calmly griffled.

Note smiled without the oidiest hint of warmth. "Ah yes, the cage. I would apologise for that, but frankly seeing you in it gives me far too much crumlush satisfaction. As it seems to do with most of your clottabussed neighbours, too. Although I'm sensing just the oidiest bit of lingering russisculoftulation from you, Matlock." He clicked his tongue. "And after all the trouble and effort I went to, as well. Seems to me that sometimes there's no pleasing some creatures, there really isn't."

"I'll ask you just once to let me out. If you don't, then it could all get peffa-glopped-up in here."

Note vilishly rushed to the bars, gleefully baring his teeth. "Oh, a threat! I *do* so love those! Especially when they're about as empty and hollow as the mind of every creature in this gobflopped dale!" He took a few pid-pads back, gesturing all around. "Well, what do you think to my 'improvements', eh? Pretty peffa-impressive, even if I have to griffle it myself. A shindinculous testament to the everlasting power of krates, our officiousness and hard work. Built by krates, to last a magnificent grillion lifetimes."

"I preferred the wooden one," Matlock griffled, tightening his grip around the wand. "Now are you going to let me out of here?"

But Note simply shook his head, chickling to himself then slowly sighing. "Do you know there's a disidula that's so glopped-up and clottabussed that it actually *prefers* to live in a cage? Imagine that. It has quite a following. That's just how clottabussed this dale is. Quite unbelievable, and I've seen some things in my officious time, believe me." He paused, looking Matlock in the eye. "As I suspect you saw quite a snutch of things, too, didn't you, during your travels on Trefflepugga Path?"

Matlock produced the wand from his robe, pointing it right at Note. "I won't ask you again," he griffled, his voice even and determined. "Let me out right now, or I will have no choice but to use this."

Note put both paws to his mouth, pretending to be peffa-twizzly at the sight. "Oh my drifflejubs! 'Tis a stick! An oidy majickal stick! Just what will the peffa-brave hare try and do now? Bliff me on the nose with it?"

Matlock aimed the wand straight at Note's head, the end beginning to glow and splutt bright red, humming powerfully in his paw. "Unlock this cage. Let me out."

Note chickled. "What do you actually use that thing for?" he mocked. "Lighting piff-toshes? Is that your big plan, to burn your way out? For Oramus' sake, Matlock, you're just as peffa-glopped as the rest of them around here, which is a ganticus disappointment, believe me. I had hoped you'd return a far brifter opponent than this, really I did."

"This is a Most Majelicus wand and…" But Matlock didn't get the chance to finish his griffles, watching dumbstruck as the wand suddenly jumped from his paw and out through the bars, spinning gracefully in the air before obediently sliding into Note's waiting, outstretched and beckoning paw.

"And first, Matlock, I suggest that you know how to use it," Note griffled, looking at the wand and smiling. He took a deep breath, nodding to himself, examining the charred and scarred hawthorn peffa-carefully. "Perfect," he whispgriffled. "Just peffa-perfect." He turned to Matlock. "I must griffle that I do have to thank you, hare, for finding this wand and bringing it safely back to me. There were times, I confess, when I thought you wouldn't make it. But

313

I shouldn't ever have doubted you, should I? Not the great and saztaculous Matlock the hare."

Matlock angrily hammered at the bars. "Give it back, Note!"

Note shrugged his shoulders indifferently. "Not sure that would be such a saztaculous idea, really. After all, I've gone to such a peffa-lot of trouble to finally have a Most Majelicus wand resting in its rightful place – my paw. All the effort and hard-work; the deceptions, half-truths and endless planning, just for this one peffa-shindinculous moment, this saztaculous crowning and Most Majelicus glory. You're witnessing history in the making, Matlock, 'tis a peffa-special privilege, one to griffle to your grand-leverets about. That is, if you live long enough to have any." He walked to the bars, softly chickling. "All this time and poor, glopped-up Matlock thought this was all about him. All those things he did, all those gobflopped and twizzly times he had, and all the while he was simply being used to bring this wand back to me." Note lightly tapped the bars with the wand. "Comes as something of a surprise, I would think?"

"Just give me back the wand," Matlock griffled, eyes narrowing.

"Or what, Matlock?" Note chickled. "What do you intend to do without it? Try and bliff your way out of the cage? Now that, I wager, would be something even the clottabussed creatures of this dale would pay good drutts to see."

Matlock kept his voice calm and level, his mind churning all the while. "It has powers you will never understand, Note, and in the wrong paws…"

"The *right* paws," Note vilishly interrupted. "My paws!" He turned, suddenly sending a bright red vroosher high into the stone roof, watching as it bounced and twisted all around the hall, sending showers of hot sparks onto the cold stone floor. "The paws of the first krate ever to become Most Majelicus! Me, the Most Majelicus Frendeslene Note!"

"You're completely clottabussed!" Matlock cried, frantically pushing at the bars.

"Am I, indeed?" Note griffled, blowing on the glowing tip of the wand. "Have you even the oidiest idea, Matlock, how it *feels* to be an officious krate? To be openly griffled at, defied and despised? To spend your sun-turns trying to enforce rules for clottabussed

314

creatures for their own good, only to have them turn to the likes of majickal-hares for guidance? To know that long-eared, wand-waving, pathetic, robe-wearing fools from The Great Beyond command their respect, over the likes of us? Think, Matlock, think how that must really feel."

"It's the way of things," Matlock griffled, still pushing at the bars. "How it's always been, how it always will be."

Note waved the wand, tutting. "But not any longer, Matlock. This wand changes everything, can't you see that? All I ever wanted was the chance to hold one, and know that from that one defining moment that the time of majickal-hares would peffa-soon be over." He looked Matlock straight in the eye. "And you, Matlock, you will go down in history as the clottabussed majickal-hare that ended everything! Reams will be written about your betrayal in all the driftolubbs. You will be as despised, mocked and gobflopped as krates are. The end of all majickal-hares' power in these dales will be put entirely down to you." He started to chickle. "Can't you even begin to appreciate the shindinculous beauty of my plan?"

Matlock stared back intently. "But I already know that won't happen, Note."

Note's eyes widened, his face peffa-excrimbly. "Ah, yes, of course!" he griffled, pid-padding to the ganticus pile of drutts. "Because you saw yourself in the Vale of Dreggs, didn't you?" He pulled a face. "Mind you, you didn't look so good without the eyes, did you? But it was one of the peffa-briftest bits for me, watching that wand gently sailing over the widening brook, and you pathetically grovelling to pick it up. I thought for a moment that you would leave it too long, and it would merely land in the river. Peffa-relieved, I was, when I saw you had it safely in your clottabussed paws."

"You…saw that?" Matlock gasped.

Note nodded, his face a peffa-perfect smile. "Oh, and *so* much more besides," he chickled. "You could griffle that I had the peffa-perfect view of everything that happened on your travels, right here in Winchett Dale, watching as you struggled and gobflopped, every pid-pad of the way." He turned to the ganticus pile of drutts, suddenly barking out an order. "Find Matlock!"

A rumbling filled the hall, Matlock watching in peffa-twizzly horror as the pile began to slowly move, drutts from the top falling to the bottom, alive and seeking spaces, vilishly re-arranging themselves to form the beginnings of an outline of a cage set on a wagon, exactly the same size as his. In a snutch of moments, the grey stone statue became complete with a peffa-perfect replica of himself inside the cage, its face staring out from the bars directly at him, jaw hanging open in exactly the same shock as his. Matlock gasped, and the figure gasped too, perfectly mirroring his every move and gesture, the drutts eerily crunching and scrunching in the empty hall.

"Impressive, isn't it?" Note griffled. "Want to see some more?" He clapped both paws together, addressing the moving statue. "Show me Matlock and the witch in The Nifferie!"

The pile vilishly began reforming, the cage disappearing, saztaculoulsy re-forming to make grey stone figures of Matlock and Ursula deep in conversation at a restaurant table. Matlock watched in transfixed shock, seeing Ursula's pebbly statue giving him the potion-bottle, both mouths silently moving as they griffled.

"Of course," Note explained, reaching into his pocket for two small stones, "to actually hear the griffles, you need to use some of these; drutts from garrumbloomed, griffling colley-rocks." He vilishly placed a stone into each statue's mouth. "Quite an art to get the timing right. These statues may only be made of pebbles, but they're exact down to the peffa-last detail. Get it wrong, and you'll still get quite a bite from them." He expertly placed a colley-pebble into each mouth, then turned to Matlock. "Useful things, colley-rocks. I had the entire dale swept for them when you'd gone. Found and garrumbloomed them all with Trikulum. All except the four you kept in your garden. But they'll be mine, too, peffa-soon." He clapped his paws four times. "Griffle!"

Matlock stared, open-mouthed, as gradually griffles of a conversation he'd had many moon-turns previously echoed all around the hall.

"*Because I wanted it to be peffa-perfect when I…*"

"*When…?*"

"*For when I saw you again.*"

"*The tzorkly majick of a white hare-witch is peffa-different to yours,*"

Matlock. It works on feelings, not griffles from a book. This bottle is a potion of my feelings, and only someone who wanted to protect them and keep them safe from all harm would never open it. Keep them safe, Matlock. And keep me safe, too."

"Make them stop!" Matlock cried from the cage, despairing at the sight. "Just make them stop!"

Note vilishly clapped his paws twice, the statues freezing. "Almost makes one an oidy-bit eyesplashy, doesn't it?" he griffled, pretending to wipe away a tear. "All that trust she put in you, and you simply threw it all away like a glopped-up rag." He clapped both paws again, turning to the statues. "Take me to the Vale of Dreggs! Show me when Matlock all too eagerly hurls the witch's feelings into the abyss, in return for the wand that will make me Most Majelicus!"

Note studied Matlock carefully as the stones busily re-arranged themselves into the all too familiar trees and river bank, the oidiest ones clumping together to form swirling clouds of drifting fog. "Trust me, this is saztaculous. I just wish I had some coloured drutts for real authenticity. But on reflection, I sometimes wonder if the black-and-white doesn't give it all a touch more drama. A matter of personal choice, I suspect."

Matlock watched with a heavy and gobflopped heart, seeing his grey statue throwing the small bottle into the stony fog, and just a snutch of moments later, a grey stone wand re-appearing and landing at his feet.

"Oh, I could watch this a grillion times!" Note griffled, clapping his paws again, the drutts freezing at the precise moment Matlock picked the wand from the ground. "Peffa-useful things, drutts, but only if you know how to use them properly. Most creatures haven't the oidest idea what they're really for, what their real power is. 'Just a glopped-up pile of pebbles,' they griffle; including yourself, Matlock." He went to the statues, picked a drutt from the ground, pid-padded to the cage, holding it up close to the bars, turning it slowly in his paw. "The trick is to give them some value. Make clottabussed creatures think they're worth something, then you'd be surprised what they'll do to get more of them, without ever really knowing their true, majickal purpose."

"Like Goole?" Matlock griffled contemptuously.

317

"Exactly like Goole, yes!" Note griffled, smiling. "Offer him some of these, griffle him they're worth something, and suddenly you have a greedy, glopped-up kraark, who'll do anything for more of them."

"Including stealing my furniture and driftolubbs?" Matlock angrily griffled. "And leading you and your army of krates here with wagons full of these glubbstooled pebbles?"

Note nodded. "Greed makes things so much easier, Matlock. 'Tis really quite the most peffa-crumlushed thing. Mix it with a ganticus dose of clottabussedness, and really, you can't go wrong. You want to see some more of your highlights? I quite like the bit when your mahpa and pahpa got all eyesplashy when the dworp came to take you away. Oh, how I chickled at that!"

Matlock narrowed his eyes. "I've seen enough," he slowly griffled.

"Shame," Note cheerfully griffled. "I'd let you have a go with the drutts yourself, but the unfortunate fact is that they only respond to me." He paused. "And now I'm thinking that you're probably wondering why I went to all this trouble to build this hall?"

"Not really. I was wondering just how long you've been as clottabussed as you are."

Note ignored the griffles. "The problem was, your old hall was made from wood. Drutts refuse to work if they are surrounded by wood. Hence, I had it pulled down as vilishly as possible and then had work begin on this stone hall immediately. I knew full well the feeble-minded and peffa-lazy residents of Winchett Dale would be no help whatsoever, and would always do their briftest to stay away from anything involving hard work, so it became all too easy to have my drutt-pile in here, keeping a majickal-pebbled eye on you without anyone ever knowing, or guessing their real purpose."

"Am I supposed to be impressed?" Matlock griffled.

"And if any creature ever came too close, or even through that creaker, then I'd simply do this…" Note clapped both paws once, and the frozen Vale of Dreggs vilishly reformed itself into the original ganticus pile in less than a blinksnap. "Nobody suspected a thing. All anyone thought was simply that I lived here, alone with some worthless drutts. How wrong they all were." He sighed, smiling contentedly at Matlock. "All in all, I think things have gone peffa-well, don't you?"

Matlock didn't griffle a griffle, as the grim and glopped-up reality of his situation began to finally sink in. Everything he'd done, everything he'd worked so peffa-hard to strive for, every juzzpapped sun-turn and pid-pad he'd had on his journey had led to this, caged, humiliated and outsmarted in front of Frendeslene Note, without a single majickal-vroosher or friend to help him.

Note smiled. "The actual truth," he quietly griffled, "can sometimes be something so very different to the one you have been led to believe, can't it?"

"You'll never be Most Majelicus," Matlock griffled through the bars. "All your plans will gobflopp, Note! You have a wand, but you don't have any vrooshers. You don't have any driftolubbs, and you can't read."

Note wagged a pointed claw at his prisoner. "Which is *precisely* why I had your clottabussed dworp friend eat that ganticus tweazle-pie, cooked from flames of your very own set of burning driftolubbs. Who needs to read when you already have a Most Majelicus dworp with all that information safely stored away inside it? T'will simply be a matter of caging him, then training him to accept me as his new master."

"You'll never find Proftulous," Matlock griffled. "He's safe, where no krate can go."

Note threw back his head, chickling loudly. "Oh, I won't have to find him!" he griffled. "He will come to me! The moment he learns of the unfortunate fate of his brave and briftest friend who sacrificed his own life so valiantly fighting and trying to stroff the peffa-twizzly 'something' he will soon show his peffa-yechus head in this village. And when he does, my krates will be waiting for him, just as they were for you."

"It's how you knew I was coming, wasn't it?" Matlock quietly griffled. "Your drutt pile saw me at The Cove of Choices, griffling with Tiftoluft."

Note nodded, grinning and baring his teeth. "Each and every griffle, Matlock. The drutts never lie." He licked his lips. "And it was most amusing to hear that pompous long, long-nosed krellit Tiftoluft griffling that he would be forced to eat and stroff you if he ever met you again. Fortunately, it's nothing you need to worry about, because I will be the one that stroffs you, Matlock." He slowly shook his head, pretending to sound eyesplashy once more. "So peffa-cruel, but so peffa-true."

"Stroffing me won't change anything!" Matlock protested, rattling the bars with all his might.

"Well it'll certainly change things *for you*," Note calmly replied, pid-padding around the hall, lazily twirling the wand in his paws. "Let me explain what's going to happen tomorrow even'up, as you won't necessarily be in a proper state to appreciate the peffa-shindinculousness of my plan. It will be a saztaculous and most memorable night for all, I can assure you of that. With the obvious exception of yourself, of course." He suddenly and viciously aimed a red vroosher at the bars, Matlock jumping back and yelping with pain, holding both burnt paws. "Sorry about that. Just need to know I had your complete attention. Now then, everyone will assemble here for the grand opening of the new Winchett Dale Great Stone Hall. All will be peffa-excrimbly to finally see inside this shindinculous place. Imagine their faces, Matlock, as they feast their eyes on such krate magnificence and peffa-saztaculousness. They'll be lost for griffles. Most will also be wondering just where you are, and then I will have to make my way up onto that balcony, to deliver in my most solemn tones the tale of how their once brave majickal-hare was cruelly stroffed as he battled to cage the peffa-twizzly 'something'. I promise you this, Matlock, I'll do my briftest job for you, I guarantee there'll be plenty of eyesplashers when I've finished. I'll griffle them that you were swallowed whole as you finally caged the 'something', but that you wouldn't have wanted us to be too eyesplashy about it, and that your peffa-last griffles before you were eaten and stroffed were, 'Make sure everyone has a peffa-crumlush even'up tomorrow night!'"

"This is peffa, peffa-clottabussed!" Matlock griffled, blowing on his throbbing paws smarting from the vroosher. "No one will believe you!"

Note nodded, conceding the point. "Not normally, no. But then Winchett Dale is completely peffa-clottabussed in itself, isn't

320

it? They'll believe every griffle that I griffle to them. You must remember, I have been planning this peffa-carefully for many moon-turns, Matlock, right down to the oidiest detail." He pid-padded to the bottom of the stone stairway. "And then after a snutch of silent, respectable moments, I shall announce that the grand opening is to continue as you would have liked, and introduce the glopped-up kraark with his wooden leg to sing us all a song or two." He paused, smiling, imaging the scene, lightly rocking back and forth, lost in the bliss of the moment, before calling across to Matlock. "How do you like the show so far? Think it's going peffa-well?"

Matlock griffled nothing, simply staring with burning hatred in his orange hare's eyes at the gently swaying figure.

"And then," Note griffled, wide eyed, his voice peffa-excrimbly, "there comes the highlight of the even'up! The real showstopper. The floor right where you are now opens, and up comes the caged, peffa-twizzly 'something' that you fought so hard to stroff!" He vilishly twirled the wand in the air. "All are terrified to see such a yechus-monstrosity in their midst! They yell and scream and flee from the hall, as I then proceed to dispatch and stroff it with repeated vrooshers from this Most Majelicus wand! And when at last the 'something' stroffs with a ganticus, agonising cry, I will leave this hall to be greeted with the most peffa-ganticus pawplause that's ever been heard for any krate in the entire history of all the dales. And everyone will know that I, Frendeslene Note, was the only creature to stay and peffa-bravely stroff the 'something'." He paused, smiling and slowly nodding, savouring every blinksnap of the moment. "I become legend, Matlock, in all the dales. A Most Majelicus living legend."

"But there is no peffa-twizzly 'something'!" Matlock shouted. "It's just a spuddle you made up so you could build your stone hall to watch me with your glopped-up drutt pile!"

Note climbed halfway up the stairway, nodding. "True," he griffled, levelling the wand, its red hot tip now pointing directly at the cage. "There is no 'something' *at the moment*. So perhaps it's time we made one up, just you and I. Put our heads together, eh? Officious krate and majickal-hare. I'm sure that between us we could come up with something peffa-twizzly and yechussly glopped-up. How about I go first?" He scratched at his chin for a snutch of moments, mulling over possibilities. "How about it has a great big horn? That would be rather saztaculous, wouldn't it?"

Matlock flinched, yelping as a red-hot vroosher vilishly flew from the wand, streaking across the hall and hitting him in the head. He fell to the floor of the cage, gasping in pain, feeling he would garrumbloom, a peffa-yechus crunching noise filling the inside of his skull as a hooked horn suddenly began to grow, inch by agonising inch from the bridge of his nose.

"Your turn!" Note griffled, chickling in ruthless delight as Matlock thrashed on the cage floor, screaming out in pain. "Oh, I see you're an oidy bit preoccupied with the horn-thing. No problem, I'll take your turn for you." He calmly levelled the wand again. "How about the 'something' has cloven hooves for feet?"

Another red-hot vroosher streaked across, angrily finding and stinging Matlock's feet, his screams echoing off the cold stone walls.

"Oh, my drriffljubs," Note griffled. "Now this is fun! Your feet really are truly yechus! Saztaculous!" He lightly skipped up two more steps. "Now, what else would the 'something' have?" He considered the question for a snutch of moments, ignoring the frantic lump-thumping of Matlock's feet pounding the cage. "Hmm. Methinks the ears will have to go." He sent out another bright red-vroosh. "And let's have just the one eye. And ganticus, scaly legs of a glopped-up pond-blaarper!"

Two more vrooshers followed, Note gleefully watching his creation come to peffa-yechus life in front of his very eyes, before sending more vrooshers vilishly streaking across the hall with each glubbstooled suggestion he could think of…

"Why not have the arms and talons of a twisted-flapper? A yechus blob of dangling skin under your jaw! The tentacled tail of a sea-beast! The hair of a dworp! Ears that are cavern-owls wings!"

The vrooshers kept coming, on and on, rocking and frizzing the cage, the creature inside roaring with each stinging blow, filing it with its grotesque bulk, until finally they stopped, Note breathless from the effort, the creature simply moaning on the cage floor.

"Now *that*," Note cheerfully griffled, putting away the wand, "is the briftest, most peffa-yechus and glopped-up, twizzly 'something'

I've ever seen! I do surprise myself at times, I really do." He cleared his throat, then pid-padded up the remaining steps to take his place in the balcony. "Of course, there is one final reason I had this hall built from stone," he griffled, his paws closing around a small lever by his side. "It allowed me to build this, too!" He pulled the lever, the stone floor under the wagon suddenly falling away, sending wagon, cage and screaming creature plunging into the eerie darkness below. "Useful things, dungeons," he griffled. "An oidy bit of elementary engineering, and they're so much fun."

Note pulled the lever a second time and the floor closed itself in a peffa-loud garrumblooming blinksnap, leaving no trace of anything in the empty hall. "Until we meet again tomorrow even'up, Matlock," he quietly griffled. "Sweet nifferduggles, my friend."

"Just how long is this going to be taking?" Proftulous griffled, tucking into his third tweazle-pie as he sat by the splutting piff-tosh at The Vroffa-Tree Inn. "Matlock's been gone for far too long, Laffrohn, and I'm really beginning to get all worried and peffa-twizzly about him."

"It'll take as long as it takes," Laffrohn griffled. "T'isn't being the peffa-easiest thing, you know, the solving of riddles. And sometimes Matlock can get things more than an oidy bit gobflopped, can't he?"

"That's what I be worrying and getting twizzly about," Proftulous moaned. "I think he might be much in needing of my help."

Laffrohn smiled. "Oh, I peffa doubt that. With the two of you together, methinks that it could all go peffa, peffa, *peffa*-gobflopped! I doubts you two clottabusses would be even able to be find the path in the first place, let alone solve any riddles."

"I just don't be liking all this waiting business," Proftulous complained. "I's already be solving the riddle, and I didn't even know I was even doing it. So, if a clottabussed glop-up like me can be doing it, then it shouldn't be taking Matlock more than a snutch of moments."

"None of us likes to be waiting," Laffrohn griffled. "But sometimes that's all we can be doing. And mostly, there be peffa-good reasons for that."

Proftulous frowned. "But I be Most Majelicussy, Laffrohn. I be able to be helping him, whatever you be thinking about it."

Laffrohn firmly shook her head. "Matlock needs to be doing this by his own good self. He'll find and answer the riddle, you'll see."

"And then everything will be all peffa-crumlush and excrimbly again?"

Laffrohn lightly bliffed his ganticus ears. "I hope so, Proftulous. I do so peffa-hope so."

Another two tweazle-pies later and there was still no news from Matlock. Proftulous had eventually fallen into heavy nifferduggles by the piff-tosh, leaving Laffrohn to simply wait and wonder, with just Ayaani perched on her shoulder for company.

"He'll be alright, your master," she soothingly whispgriffled to it, tickling the dripple under her chin.

"I know," Ayaani griffled over a yawn, still watching through the window for any sign of Matlock's return into the cavern. "I want to thank you for making me all better when I was stroffed out in The Great Beyond."

Laffrohn clicked her tongue. "T'was nothing," she griffled. "The griffles in the majickal-driftolubb that I had you lying on did most of the work, didn't they? Besides, I have an oidy feeling that you're going to be peffa-useful for Matlock in completing the next two Most Majelicus tasks, Ayaani. You and Proftulous, both."

"How?"

"Well, if I knew that then I certainly wouldn't be landlady of The Vroffa-Tree Inn, now would I? I would be being the most saztaculoulsy crumlush Laffrohn, ever. And I don't think that would be ever happening, not in a grillion lifetimes. Not even a Most Majelicus Sacred Majickal Elder can be seeing into the future, Ayaani, and 'tis peffa-probably a good thing they can't."

The piff-tosh spluttered, sending a sudden shower of blue sparks up into the chimney, catching Laffrohn's eye. Ayaani began to get excrimbly, pointing through the window at a figure with long ears, dressed in ornate blue robes, standing on the small wooden bridge outside.

"Baselott?" Laffrohn quietly griffled, wiping the window with her ganticus paw. "That be you?" She pid-padded to the creaker, trying not to feel too twizzly, Ayaani still gripping onto her shoulder.

A visit from Baselott would mean only one thing – things hadn't gone well for Matlock up on the path. She stepped outside, pidpadding towards the bridge, realising from the robes that this wasn't Baselott at all, but another Elder majickal-hare entirely. Instead of Baselott's saztaculoulsy embroidered dripples, this hare had peffashindinculous moons and leaping-hares ornately stitched in gold and silver threads all over its crumlush robes.

"Bow," the hare demanded in tones that Laffrohn immediately recognised, causing her to gasp as she closely studied the familiar face.

"Matlock?" she whispgriffled, awestruck and dutifully bowing. "It be you? It really be *you*?"

The figure nodded, smiling an instantly recognisable curved and crumlush smile. "How are you, Laffrohn?"

"I'm...I'm..."

"Lost for griffles?" the figure replied. "That's not like the Laffrohn I used to know at all, not one oidy bit. And the last thing I ever intend to do again is sleep on that bed of yours."

Laffrohn dropped to one knee, bowing again. "Oh my drifflejubs! By all the might and wisdom of Oramus, it *is* you, Matlock!"

The figure soflty chickled. "Please, Laffrohn, stand. There's no need for all the bowing. I simply wanted to try it out once, that's all. Methinks a hug is more in order, don't you, old friend?"

Laffrohn stood, went to the familiar figure, gave it a ganticus hug, then stood back, her paws still on its shoulders, her smile disappearing, her face clouding and becoming twizzly. "So you got stroffed on the path, then? You never found the answer to the riddle and got stroffed, instead? Oh, but this is the most peffa-glopped-up news, Matlock, completely glubbstooled!"

The figure gently put a hushing paw to her lips. "Laffrohn, calm yourself. I didn't stroff on Trefflepugga Path. Far from it."

Laffrohn blinked, relieved but peffa-confused. "So what be happening, then? I don't understand. You be wearing the robes of an Elder, so you must be already stroffed. 'Tis the only way to finally become an Elder."

"You will discover, in time, Laffrohn." The figure reached into his robes and pulled out an oidy leather potion bottle. "But right now I need you to do something for me."

"So…so you be from times that haven't even happened yet?" Laffrohn whsipgriffled, utterly awestruck.

The figure nodded. "Indeed; from times many, many moon-turns hence, Laffrohn. Long after I have finally stroffed in these dales, and ascended to the Hall of the Majickal Elders."

Laffrohn tried to swallow, her mouth completely dry, as the figure gently placed the potion bottle in her ganticus, shaking paw.

"Many moon-turns ago, I had need of this," it griffled. "T'was as I neared the end of a perilously twizzly journey, when I was simply a Most Majelicus hare. The only way I could bring back my apprentice from The Great Beyond safely was to use the peffa-majickal powers of this bottle, but it had already been destroyed during the journey. Its loss placed us all in peffa-twizzly danger, as you will discover when the time comes. But I discovered a way to find the bottle, and was finally able to make everything fuzzcheck and crumlush again."

Laffrohn stared at the bottle. "I've seen this before," she griffled. "It used to belong to Ursula Brifthaven Stoltz."

The figure nodded. "And she gave it to me for safekeeping, right here, the first time I ever visited this inn. But now that it has done its majickal duty, you must return it to me when you see me next, in order that the cycle is complete. Will you remember to do this for me, Laffrohn? 'Tis most peffa, peffa-important. To forget would change the history of everything, and place us all in the most twizzly danger; even me, where I am now."

"I will be remembering, Matlock," Laffrohn promised. "I be sure to be remembering."

"Then I must leave," the figure griffled, lowering its voice to a familiar whispgriffle. "I've rather bent the rules, anyway, and haven't really got permission to be here at all. So please, not a griffle of this to anyone, Laffrohn."

"Tell me what it's like," Laffrohn suddenly griffled. "Griffle me what happens when you get stroffed."

The figure smiled, pausing slightly. "'Tis the beginnings of your greatest ever journey, Laffrohn. And every pid-pad you take along it is crumlush." He reached out and stroked Ayaani on her shoulder, taking her in his paw and holding her close. "Good Ayaani, keep me safe, won't you?"

The dripple nodded, then let out a sudden oidy gasp as a second saztaculoulsy robed dripple appeared from the figure's long hood and began to excrimbly whispgriffle in her ear.

"That be Ayaani?" Laffrohn gasped.

The figure nodded. "As she is now, yes. She has much to griffle to her younger self, peffa-important things she'll need to know before undertaking the next Most Majclicus task."

"I just not be believing my own eyes, Matlock," Laffrohn griffled, shaking her head and watching the two dripples whispgriffling to each other. "Tis like it all be a some kind of crumlush dream."

"And that is most likely how you will remember it, Laffrohn."

She looked into the figure's familiar bright orange eyes. "So you be knowing everything that will be happening in all our lives?"

"Your future is already my past, Laffrohn. I can no more see my own future than you can see yours. But if you remember to give me this potion bottle the next time you see me, then hopefully all will be well for us all." He placed Ayaani back on Laffrohn's shoulder, before lightly resting a paw on her forehead. "The briftest thing Trefflepugga Path ever taught me, Laffrohn, is that the true nature of everything will only reveal itself in time. Farewell, Laffrohn, landlady of The Vroffa-Tree-Inn, and one distant sun-turn, so much saztaculoulsy more, besides."

Laffrohn's eyes widened, as she was suddenly surrounded by the brightest blue light she had ever seen…

A snutch of moments later she awoke in a chair by the piff-tosh, Proftulous still soundly nifferduggling by her side, Ayaani gently snoring on her shoulder. She shook her head, trying to recall the strangest dream, but remembering nothing, wondering why she had Ursula's potion bottle in her ganticus paw, yet feeling it was somehow peffa-important and had something to do with Matlock.

"Well," Frendeslene Note griffled, as a limping-kraark made its way slowly into The Great Hall, it's wooden leg clacking with every scrittle it took on the cold stone floor, "if it isn't my glopped-up friend and clottabussed accomplice, Goole, the self-proclaimed singing king of the Trefflepugga-kraarks."

"Even'up, Your Officiousness," Goole griffled, bowing and raising his tricorn hat.

"And what do you think of my improvements?" Note griffled. "Not bad for a glopped-up army of krates, eh?"

"I reckon they be most saztaculous," Goole griffled, looking around. "Fair makes me want to be eyesplashy in me one good eye, it does, just thinking about doing me ganticus showstopper, right here, in such an illustrious and crumlush venue. 'Tis a hall peffa-much fit for a singing kraark-king, methinks."

Note frowned distastefully. "Do you even know what 'illustrious' means?"

"Not really," Goole shrugged. "Sounds right peffa-crumlush, though, doesn't it?"

Note sighed, pointing. "And griffle me, how is that wooden leg of yours? Will it stand up to the exertions of your much-anticipated showstopper? I really don't want it flying off and bliffing someone on the head, halfway through."

Goole waved a wing at him, its rings jangling and echoing in the ganticus space. "Don't you be worrying about that, Mr Note," he griffled. "Me and the brother-kraarks have been practising non-stop up at the wood-pile for the last few sun-turns. There'll not be any wooden-leg related gobflopps, I can promise you that. Been driving Serraptomus crazy, we has." He sighed. "But that's what it takes to be a leading artiste, these sun-turns. Proper peffa-dedication. I keep griffling him that, but he just seems to spend his time looking right glubbstool."

Note pid-padded towards the griffling kraark, tapping his wooden leg with his wand. "He made this for you?"

Goole nodded. "Carved and whittled it from the one of the most peffa-important timbers of the old Great Hall, the collar-beam. Some creatures griffle that it was majickal wood. Imagine that? We was 'aving a right good old chickle the other sun-turn, griffling about how this here leg of mine could be having majickal-powers all of its own, on account of what it's made from." He half-closed his one good eye, imagining the scene, then suddenly threw both wings out wide, a ganticus twisting smile appearing on his beak. "Be a proper peffa-saztaculous showstopper that, wouldn't it? 'Goole and his Majickal Leg.' I could get myself to the top of all the briftest places in Svaeg Dale, couldn't I?"

"How about we just concentrate of tomorrow even'up, first?" Note suggested. "One scrittle at a time, eh?"

"Of course, Mr Note," Goole griffled. "I's just be getting all peffa-excrimbly. You know me." He playfully poked Note in the ribs, instantly regretting it.

"You do that again," Note snarled, "and you'll be getting all peffa-stroffed!"

Goole nodded vilishly, spending the next snutch of moments apologising and grovelling as eagerly as he could, until Note silenced him with a paw.

"You have one last task to perform for me, Goole," he griffled. "As you will have heard, the hare returned from Trefflepugga Path earlier this sun-turn."

Goole nodded. "I be seein' him, Mr Note, when he was bought here all caged up. There's lots of excrimbly griffling in the village about why he's come back."

Note lightly stroked the ends of his whiskers. "I want you to griffle to everyone that I have allowed him back into Winchett Dale for one peffa-important reason."

"Very good, Mr Note," Goole griffled, turning and limping towards the creaker. "I'll do that right now."

"Wait, you clottabus! You haven't heard what it is, yet!"

Goole turned. "Haven't I?"

Note counted inside his head, trying not to get too russisculoffed. The way he felt, he wanted nothing more than to vroosh the glopped-up kraark into the peffa-darkest recesses of its next miserable life, wherever or whatever that may be. "No," he calmly griffled. "You haven't."

"Fair enough," Goole shrugged. "Griffle away, I'm all ears."

"The reason that the hare is here is that he suspects the 'something' is already right here in Winchett Dale."

Goole began to get an oidy bit panicked at the thought. "But that be most peffa-glopped up, Mr Note! Last thing I need is for it to be eating and stroffing my audience! Who'll be able to come and watch me sing if they're all stroffed and scoffed? The showstopper must always go on, Mr Note, 'tis peffa-important for me, and you made me a promise that it would!"

"Calm yourself, kraark," Note griffled. "Your majickal-hare has managed to convince me that he is now fully restored and able to vroosh saztaculous vrooshers that will leave the 'something' quite stroffed as soon as he finds it. As a result, I have shown great leniency, and released him to find and deal with it as he sees fit. I'm peffa-sure all will be saztaculous and shindinculous for tomorrow even'up's grand opening."

Goole paused for a snutch of moments. "So you want me to griffle to everyone that Matlock is currently stroffing the 'something'?"

Goole nodded. "And they're all to nifferduggle well and not get too twizzly."

"Right, ho," Goole griffled, a puzzled expression crossing his beak. "Just one thing, though, Mr Note."

"Yes?" Note sighed, wondering just how much easier he could have made the task for the clottabussed kraark.

"What's 'leniency', mean?"

"Out!" Note barked, as Goole scrittled through the creaker as vilishly as his wooden leg would allow.

Matlock gradually came to in pitch-black darkness, his whole softulous aching. He tried to slowly move his head, but it felt all wrong, too heavy and terribly misshapen. He moaned, but the voice wasn't his, belonging to a yechus and twizzly creature that he couldn't even begin to describe or imagine.

A muffled boom somewhere above his head startled him, as if a ganticus creaker had just been slammed shut, vibrating the broken wooden bars of the smashed cage. He tried to call for help, his voice bubbly and glopped, the sound of it in the cramped black space making him feel even more twizzly. Memories of a streaking red vrooshers flashed in front of his mind, seeing Note twirling the wand from the stairway, unable to stop them, crying out in pain as each one struck and changed another part of his writhing softulous. He remembered the cage and wagon falling, and the peffa-twizzly feeling in his stomach as he plunged into the dungeon below… Then nothing…just the black…and the oidiest thoughts beginning to slowly resurface in his mind…

A noise somewhere close made him jump; not from overhead this time, but from the ground, the sound of oidy creatures scurrying and scrittling somewhere just in front of him.

"Matlock," a high-pitch voiced griffled out in the black, "now don't you go worrying. We've played in worse places than this, believe me. What we need is an oidy bit of light on the situation. Now, we haven't got most of our original instruments, so if you'll forgive us, we're just going to have to improvise. And please, if the tune's not to your liking, don't be eating us. We're already down to a four-piece as it is, and we're simply trying our briftest for you. Ready, lads? A-two, three, four…"

A fast-tempo rhythm began to slowly fill the pitch-black dungeon, together with gradually glowing light, flickering and illuminating everything in time to the beat. Matlock looked down, seeing to his peffa-grateful astonishment the soft head of four ploffshrooms now brightly glowing in the dark.

"Oh, my!" one griffled, glancing up at Matlock as he shook a pair of rattling poppy-heads, "Forgive me, but I have to griffle that you don't look too fuzzcheck at all, my yechus friend." The ploffshroom looked around the dungeon at the four stone walls just beyond the smashed bars of the cage. "That thing I griffled about playing in worse places? It's not true, believe me, and we've been in some truly yechus joints in Svaeg Dale, we really have."

Matlock glanced down at his yechus solftulous, holding what had once been a paw up close to his one eye, gasping as he saw just how glopped it looked. Next, he felt the sharp horn protruding from the top of his nose and let out a low moan.

"Keep your chin-thing up, Matlock," another ploffshroom holding two oidy sticks helpfully griffled. "We'll soon find a way out of here. Put me on your head and I'll be like a lamp. We'll both have a good look around. I'll just keep knocking out a rhythm on that horn of yours to give us all the light we need."

Matlock placed the ploffshroom on his head as gently as he could, the oidy sticks tickling him as it energetically kept playing.

331

Matlock placed the ploffshroom on his head as gently as he could, the oidy sticks tickling him as it energetically kept playing.

"Sorry about the inconvenience, friend," it griffled, panting slightly. "But if we were to stop, we'd all be plunged into darkness again, and we'd never get out of here." He looked around, searching for any sort of creaker, but simply finding all four walls, floor and ceiling to be stone. "Well," it griffled, "looks like we're going to need all your peffa-briftest majicky business this time, Matlock. There doesn't appear to be any sort of a way out at all."

Matlock tried to stand, wobbling dangerously, and almost crushing the ploffshroom against a nearby wall in the process. He yechusssly griffled an apology, turning his attention to the smashed bars, using newfound strength to free himself from the broken cage, then cautiously stepping down onto the cold stone floor, just managing to squeeze into the narrow gap between the broken wagon and dungeon wall.

"Try bliffing it," one of the ploffshrooms suggested. "You're ganticus and strong enough. Chances are, you could have us out of here in no time."

Matlock bliffed the wall, pounding it with all his strength, but nothing moved even the oidiest amount. The walls were made from solid stone, and Matlock knew it would be easier to persuade Proftulous to give up eating tweazle-pies than it would be for him to break the them down.

"It's just too hard," Matlock griffled, slumping down exhausted.

"Don't give up," a breathless ploffshroom playing a small horn griffled. "There's got to be a way. You'll think of something. You're a majickal-hare, after all. Just keep trying and perhaps you'll have a saztaculous extrapluff about how we can all get out of here. But do it vilishly, please, as my scrud-joints are really beginning to ache." He glanced up at the drumming ploffshroom on Matlock's head. "How about we change the tempo and dim the lights a bit? I'm juzzpapped, I really am, and it might help the hare think."

As the rhythm slowed, so the light dimmed, Matlock trying to calm himself and think of a way out of the cold, stony gloom. There *had* to be a way, he griffled to himself, it couldn't end here, not like this, alone in a yechus dungeon with just a juzzpapped ploffshroom band for company. He hadn't travelled the length of Trefflepugga Path, found and solved its riddle, simply to be stroffed looking like the most glopped-up creature ever imagined. It couldn't end this way, Matlock resolved – and it *wouldn't*.

"What did you griffle just now?" he suddenly asked the horn-playing ploffshroom.

"I griffled that me scrud-joints are peffa-juzzpapped. 'Tis all this blowing, especially in the mid-sections. I'm having to cover the trinkulah part as well, seeing as he got eaten. 'T'isn't easy, you know."

"No," Matlock griffled, trying not to shake his head too much in the narrow space. "I meant about me thinking?"

"I griffles that if we get the tempo down, then you might be having some extrapluffs how to get us out of here, what with you being majickal, an' all."

Matlock tried to smile, as a most ganticus and saztaculous plan began to form itself in his glopped-up mind. But the sight of his smile turned the ploffshrooms so twizzly that they all stopped playing, and the dungeon was suddenly plunged back into darkness. "Play!" Matlock griffled in the goom. "I won't smile again, I promise! I need to see. Play!"

The band struck up once more, their heads glowing in time to the rhythm, lighting the nearby walls, as Matlock closed his eyes and tried to clear his mind, offering up a short prayer to Oramus that if ever he needed an extrapluff, now was the moment to have it. He sat peffa-still for what seemed like an age, waiting…

"Matlock?" a ploffshroom griffled. "You be alright?"

"Quiet," another griffled. "He be all thinking. Just keep playing and let him be extrapluffing how to be getting us out of here."

Which is exactly what Matlock did, remembering what he had read in *Majickal Dalelore (Volume 68 – revised edition)* about the evolution of tunnelling mirrits. He thought of the majickal-niff-soup Laffrohn had made him in The Vroffa-Tree Inn, suddenly seeing the pages crystal clear in his mind, reaching out with his yechus talons to turn them to the relevant section, trying not to get too peffa-excrimbly as he re-read the ancient majickal-griffles.

The life-cycle of the Mirrit is one of the most peffa-majickal things. Born from the extrapluffs of majickal-hares, oidy mirrits soon take to tunnelling, before one day becoming sylpha-sprites, who like nothing better than to glide on falling autumn leaves. As extrapluffs are griffled to be given to us by Oramus himself, then these tunnelling mirrits can be seen to form a constantly changing and expanding network of goodness that is rumoured to run across the lengths and breadths of all the dales, even under Trefflepugga Path itself, although to use these tunnels, any creature must first be Most Majelicus, or travel with one who already is.

A yamamantally-spious extrapluff suddenly coursed through Matlock's ganticus body, rattling the smashed sides of the wooden cage. A blinksnap later, an eager snutch of mirrits dropped from his softulous onto the dungeon floor, vilishly scrittling towards the walls, searching for narrow gaps and cracks in the stone, forcing and tunnelling their way in.

"Well, I never be seeing anything like that before," a ploffshroom gasped, still shaking its dried poppy-seed heads.

"Just keep playing!" the ploffshroom drumming on Matlock's horn urgently griffled. "Them oidy creatures might just be able to find us a way out of here!"

Matlock watched as the last mirrit disappeared into a tiny gap between two stones, knowing he'd need more mirrits for the job, which meant more extrapluffs. He closed his eyes once more, before suddenly realising with a sinking heart that even if the mirrits *could* find a way of loosening the stone and somehow tunnelling out of the dungeon, he'd never be able to escape along it, as he wasn't Most Majelicus. All he'd have would be a tunnel to freedom that he'd never be able to use.

Undeterred, and knowing there must be a way, he took a breath, trying to think.

"You be making more of them oidy-burrowers?" the stick-playing ploffshroom asked. "Only you'll have to be vilish about it, because even at his tempo, we're all starting to get peffa-juzzpapped, and when we stop, we'll be back in darkness again."

Matlock tried bliffing the stone with his horn to dislodge it even an oidy amount, but even though the mirrits had burrowed somewhere inside, the wall still held firm. "Stop your playing," he quietly griffled. "It's no use. We would need a grillion mirrits to even begin to get us out of here, and even then, we couldn't use the tunnel, as we're not Most Majelicus. It's hopeless, I'm sorry."

But the ploffshrooms wouldn't stop. "Listen up, Matlock, and be listening peffa, peffa-good," the poppy-seed rattler griffled. "We may be just an oidy bunch of glopped-up musical ploffshrooms, but the one thing we've never done is to give up." He turned to the others. "Have we fellas, eh?"

"Never!" the other three all griffled as one.

"And believe you me, Matlock, we've had some peffa-twizzly times, including having to do some things we'd rather not have to griffle about back in Svaeg Dale."

"Peffa-glopped-up things," the nuttar-player quietly agreed.

"And all through the bad times, including some of our members being stroffed and eaten, we've always ploffed on, regardless, no matter how juzzpapped and gobflopped we felt, no matter how glubbstool things were, because music is in our very ploffshroom life-blood, you see. Not that we actually have blood, as such, I was just trying to bend a figure of speech into me griffles."

"Having blood would be an oidy bit yechus, methinks," the stick-player agreed.

The poppy-seed rattler nodded. "We're bonded by the saztaculous beats and tempos of the fuzzcheck rhythms, you see, and nothing gets us down or eyesplashy. We just don't be giving up. Just like the singing kraark we used to play for. He was utterly glubbstool, but at least he didn't give up trying to perform his ganticus showstoppers, did he? Like when you was being vrooshed by that glubbstooled krate with his wand up there, and we was still all hiding in your hood and…"

"What did you just griffle?" Matlock vilishly interrupted.

"I was griffling about when you got yourself all vrooshed into this yechus creature…"

"Of course!" Matlock cried, slapping the side of his ganticus head with his talons. "That's it! You've done it!" He began chickling in a yechus, bubbly voice. "Oh, by Oramus, why didn't I extrapluff this before? I was vrooshed with a Most Majelicus wand!"

"So?" the ploffshroom griffled.

Matlock closed his eye and let the extrapluff ripple through his softulous, causing an eruption of scrittling mirrits to fall from every part of him, vilishly burrowing into the cracks in the dungeon wall, wave after wave of them, an unstoppable army of tunnelling mirrits.

"You care to griffle me what's just happened?" the ploffshroom asked.

Matlock opened his one eye. "There's an oidy chance that Frendeslene Note has made a ganticus mistake," he griffled, smiling his huge yechus smile. "By using that wand, he might just have made me Most Majelicus, in which case all my extrapluffs will be Most Majelicus, too."

"And the mirrits," the ploffshroom eagerly griffled, watching as more fell from Matlock's softulous onto the floor," they'll be all Most Majelicus, too?"

"I peffa-hope so," Matlock griffled, pushing at the stone with his horn and feeling it begin to dislodge in the wall just an oidy amount, forming a larger gap for the mirrits to stream through. "In which case, we might be able to dig ourselves out of here." He gasped as the stone fell away, seeing the beginnings of just the oidiest tunnel being vilishly eaten in the earth behind.

He turned to the ploffshrooms, his yechus face peffa-excrimbly in the gloom. "Methinks we're going to need more light in here to see what we're doing. Up the tempo, good ploff-folk! The more vilishly I can extrapluff, the more vilishly we can get out of here!"

15.

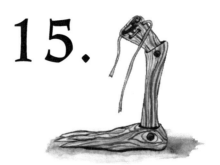

Testaments, Showstoppers and New Beginnings...

It had been a peffa-long sun-turn of excrimbly preparations for the grand opening of the new stone Great Hall in Winchett Dale. Officious krates had been hard at work on the finishing touches, moving ganticus rows of benches inside, cleaning and polishing, draping the outside with shindinculous flags, all supervised with peffa-perfect officiousness by Frendeslene Note, resplendent in saztaculous robes and a satisfied smile.

Residents themselves, meanwhile, occupied the time in their all too peffa-familiar way of watching the krates hard at work, chickling and criticising, drinking guzzworts and griffling about how fuzzcheck they all felt to know that Matlock was busy stroffing the 'something' in order that they could have a yamamantally-spious even'up without the oidiest fear of being eaten or stroffed themselves. Some creatures began to wonder where Matlock's act of stroffing was taking place, asking the krates for any news, but were being told that they'd have to wait for the even'up, when Mr Note would have a 'peffa-important and most officious announcement on the matter.'

Indeed, such was the excrimblyness running through the whole of Winchett Dale that for once, all of the cages were empty, with everyone determined they weren't going to miss the ganticus celebrations by spending it behind bars. With, of course, the exception of Fragus, who stuck rigidly to his preferred option of life in his cage, insisting that when the time came, he should be wheeled from the inn directly into the new Great Hall with saztaculous ceremony. Note had tried to griffle with the determined disidula, explaining that the even'up was more concerned with a celebration of the hall itself rather than any individual creature from Winchett Dale, but Fragus was having none of it, griffling that he wouldn't be attending unless he was wheeled in by at least six krates, all dressed in their peffa-briftest finery for the occasion.

"And after the celebrations," Note had griffled, "would you consider leaving your cage and pid-padding back home?"

"What for?" Fragus had griffled, clearly confused. "This be my home, Mr Boat. And a right peffa-crumlush one it is, too. What thinks you to my new roof? Has got myself my own chimney for my very own piff-tosh, I has. Right cosy in me chair, now, 'tis."

Note had tried not to look too closely at what had once been a perfectly functioning wagon-mounted cage, but now resembled the most crumlushly oidy cottage he'd ever seen, albeit set on wheels. He'd even heard rumours that the stubborn disidula was considering asking for another wagon to be attached so that he could begin work on building a garden, as his pot-plants and window-boxes were nearly full and he wanted to sew niff-seeds in the coming autumn.

Inside the hall itself, Goole and his singing kraarks were trying their briftest to rehearse their ganticus showstopper for their imminent performance; the single-eyed, wooden legged, tricorn wearing kraark becoming increasingly impatient with all the officious krating activity going on around. Some of the more ambitious moves weren't proving at all successful, together with the fact that his wooden leg had the rather unforeseen habit of becoming far too peffa-easily detached, and had at one point sailed through the air, only narrowly missing a scowling Note's head by the width of a burrowing mirrit's leg.

"I thought you griffled there'd be no leg-related glop-ups," Note growled, returning it to the embarrassed and increasingly agitated kraark. "This comes off another time, Goole, and it'll be curtains for your so-called 'showstopper'!"

"I'll work on the bindings, Your Officiousness," Goole vilishly griffled, before promptly turning and taking out his anger on the fallen heap of complaining kraarks behind him. "You lot! Up you get! Positions, from the top! Come on, we've got a show to put on!"

By mid-afternoon'up things were starting to take shape a little better. The hall now had enough seating to accommodate the entire village, all arranged and pointing towards the large balcony above the wooden stage. Note surveyed the work with a satisfied and peffa-officious smile, taking a snutch of moments to congratulate the juzzpapped krates for all their hard work, asking them to be seated as he climbed the stone staircase to address them from the balcony.

"My fellow krates and foot-soldiers of officiousness," he griffled in booming tones. "We find ourselves this sun-turn at the dawn of a new beginning for this glopped-up and frankly, peffa-clottabussed community. It hasn't been easy for us. Indeed, at times, it has sometimes felt like an almost impossible task. But let it be known across all the dales that this shindinculous Great Hall in Winchett Dale stands as a fitting and long-lasting testament to the saztaculous and honourable values of our officiousness."

A slightly twizzly krate in the front row cautiously raised a paw. "Excuse me, Your Officiousness, but what's a 'testament'?"

Note frowned slightly. "Tis like a tribute."

The krate shook his head. "No. Still lost."

"A monument, then," Note tried. "A sort of physical representation of all we have achieved, and are capable of doing."

"You mean, like this hall?"

"Yes," Note sighed, "Tis exactly like this hall."

"So, a 'testament', is a hall, then?"

"No, you clottabus!" Note griffled. "A hall is a hall. But a 'testament' can be a testament to anything."

"Like a paw?"

Note screwed up his eyes. "How in Oramus' sake would you even *begin* to have a testament to a paw?"

The krate stared back, unblinking, peffa-confused. "But you just griffled that I could have a testament to anything. So I giffled about paws to you, and now you're griffling that it couldn't be like that, and…"

"Just shut that griffle-hole of yours!" Note barked, taking a deep breath and looking high into the vaulted ceiling for some

"You lot! Up you get! Positions, from the top! Come on, we've got a show to put on!"

sort of inspiration. "Methinks you've all been too long in this dale. You're all starting to go clottabussed in the head like the gobflopped creatures around here." He dropped his gaze, looking them in the eye and trying his briftest to adopt a calmer, more appreciatve tone. "What I'm trying to griffle is that this saztaculous hall will be a *reminder* to every creature of just how our officiousness and hard work will always be brifter than anything that could ever be done by a grillion majickal-hares, or indeed, Most Majelicus creatures of any kind. For inside each and every one of your softulousses, there beats a shindinculous heart of rules, logic, and officious hard-labour – a testament to krates everywhere."

"Wait," the krate at the front griffled. "So now you're griffling that our hearts can be a testament-thing, but our paws can't? I just not be understanding any of this, I'm really not."

"What about our noses, Your Officiousness?" another krate asked, signalling a frenzy of raised paws, all vilishly suggesting other body-parts that might or might not be considered to be testaments.

"Just listen!" Note barked over the eager griffling, silencing the confused crowd. "Forget about testaments! It's just a griffle, that's all, and one that I now rather regret griffling in the first place, I really do. What I'm simply trying to griffle is…"

A sudden scrunching and rumbling noise silenced his griffles, as the whole hall trembled for a snutch of rather ominous moments.

"What be that?" a krate griffled, looking towards the floor. "I felt the stones move under my feet."

Another krate stood and pointed with an officious paw at a large crack that had appeared on a far wall. "The wall's moving, too!" he griffled. "'Tis like the ground moved, and the hall's falling down!"

Panic ensued, as twizzly krates began to pid-pad towards the creaker, only to be vilishly ordered back to their places by an increasingly anxious Note. "This hall is safe!" he cried out. "It has been built by officious krates, and will last a grillion lifetimes!" He pid-padded towards the crack in the wall, pounding it vigorously with his fist. "This is the briftest stone, it will never fall down. You will repair this before the even'up. 'T'was merely a slight shifting of the ground beneath, that's all. Everyone will work to repair this, and tonight will go ahead exactly as I have officiously planned.

There will be no more twizzly clottabussedness from anyone!"

Gradually the krates recomposed themselves, following Note's orders, reluctantly fetching more stone and mortar to repair the worrying crack, trying to ignore the increasing rumblings and tremors beneath their feet as they did so.

By nightfall, the hall was finally as ready as it ever could be. Flaming beacons had been lit outside, throwing saztaculous dancing shadows all over the building, as a crowd of excrimbly creatures slowly made their way into the shindinculous new hall for the first time, all eagerly anticipating the even'up's events.

Smartly dressed krates politely greeted them at the ganticus wooden creaker before showing them officiously to their seats, Note keenly watching it all from the balcony. Fragus was duly hauled and wheeled inside by six krates in their robed finery to ganticus pawplause and chanting from the audience, the krates then struggling to put the piff-tosh out that threatened to fill the entire building with choking smoke, as the smiling, chickling disidula happily waved to the crowd through the bars all the while.

After a snutch of awkward and embarrassing moments in which two krates had to roll on the ground to put out their burning robes, Frendeslene Note finally called for order, holding out both paws in his most sincere gesture of welcome. "Creatures of Winchett Dale!" he griffled, "At last the even'up has arrived when you get to see inside your new stone Great Hall. Gone is that glopped-up wooden hall, torn down and re-built in saztaculous stone by great and officious krates. Look around you! See its peffa-shindinculousness! Is this not a Great Hall fit for a great dale? A hall fit for Winchett Dale, soon to be the peffa-greatest, and most officiously saztaculous dale of all the dales!"

"Couldn't you have made the windows an oidy bit bigger?" someone suggested. "Only I'm not sure that they be looking the right size, what with this being all stone, an' all."

"Good point," another griffled. "And methinks some of the actual stonework looks glopped, too, almost as if it could have been done by us, and we be just clottabussed glopp-ups, don't we? And the ceiling and roof be far too peffa-fancy, really. We only be Winchett Dale, after all, Mr Coat. Not like all them other shindinculous dales."

Note's jaw hung lose, utterly stuck for griffles in the heavy silence, horribly aware all eyes were now staring straight at him. "You...you don't like it?" he finally managed.

"It'll do," a creature halfway back conceded. "Don't get us all gobflopped and ungrateful. It's sort of fuzzcheck, but we just be thinking that it might have been brifter if you'd thought about where the hall was, and who it was for, before you be starting to pull things down and be building new things in their places."

"It's 'sort of fuzzcheck'?" Note gasped, astonished. "Is that *really* all you can griffle about it, after we've been working and slaving all these moon-turns, right through the winter, every sun-turn, our paws frozen to the bone?" He banged the side of the balcony. "One sun-turn, it was so peffa-cold in here, I had four krates hanging from their tongues from this very balcony because they got frozen onto the side! They suffered for this hall, as we all did!" He searched the audience for a familiar face, finding it in the third row, just about to nod off into nifferduggles. "Serraptomus! Wake up!"

Serraptomus jumped, startled. "Yes...what is it, Your Officiousness?"

"This hall," Note griffled, "is it not the most peffa-saztaculous Great Hall that you could ever imagine?"

Serraptomus thought for a snutch of moments, looking around and scratching his chin. "You want an honest opinion, Your Officiousness?"

"Completely honest. Peffa, peffa-honest."

"Couldn't the windows have been an oidy bit bigger?"

Pawplause and chickles broke out, Serraptomus smiling and enjoying the moment without even the oidiest idea why, Note frowning and blowing out his cheeks in pure russisculoftulation. "So," he griffled, trying his briftest to be calm. "Let me try and get this straight. What you're all griffling is that after all this planning, effort and hard, hard labour – you don't really like this hall at all?"

"We like the cages, Mr Boat," a creature called out, trying its briftest to be encouraging. "They be right proper fuzzcheck, they be."

"Griffle you what," a tweazle from the front-row griffled, "how about you and your krates be pulling this down and be making the most peffa-ganticus Great Cage, instead?"

344

"A ganticus cage?" Note griffled, his voice rising to an oidy squeak. "I've never heard something so peffa-clottabussed in all my officious life!"

"Well that's because you don't be spending enough time at the inn, methinks," the tweazle griffled. "It gets really peffa, peffa-clottabussed of an even'up in there, it really does."

The rest of the hall readily agreed, as Note tried to silence them all once more.

A long-pawed grubble raised its long paw. "Cheer up, Mr Coat. 'Tis supposed to be an even'up of saztaculous celebration, after all. We sort of likes the hall, 'tis simply that we be thinking that if Matlock had been involved from the beginning, then…"

"Ah, yes! Matlock!" Note gleefully griffled, grateful to finally turn matters back to the fate of the majickal-hare. "The good and saztaculous Matlock! Now I'm afraid I have some most glopped-up news about him that might make some of you peffa-eyesplashy."

"Why be that?" Fragus called from his cage, sitting in his favourite chair and supping on a guzzwort. "He's been battling the 'something' all sun-turn to be stroffing it, so we can be safe and fuzzcheck again. We's all been griffling about it, and peffa-excrimbly news it is, too. He always be the saviour of Winchett Dale."

Cries of 'Matlock! Matlock!' vilishly filled the hall, the creatures pounding and drumming the floor with their feet in appreciation, causing oidy particles of dust and stone to fall from the ornate roof above.

Note held out both paws, appealing for silence, insisting that he had it before continuing. "I'm sorry to have to griffle that it is my peffa-sad duty to inform you all that your dear and most beloved Matlock the Hare lost his brave and courageous battle with the 'something' earlier this sun-turn."

"What did he lose?" a triple-winged duxop griffled, pulling a ganticus murp-worm from her ear. "Hope it not be his wand."

"No, you clottabus!" Note griffled, his russisculoftulation rising again. "He lost his life!"

"That be peffa-careless," the duxop griffled. "But if we all be looking for it, one of us will be finding it for him, surely?"

"I meant, he got stroffed!"

"What, before or after he be losing his life?"

"Both!" Note cried, frantically balling his fists, talons digging into his palms.

"Well that not be possible," Fragus called from his cage, as others nodded in agreement. "You can't be losing anything after you be stroffed, so he had to be losing his life before he got stroffed, didn't he?"

"Don't you even *begin* to understand?" Note pleaded, surveying the sea of confused faces with a sinking heart. "Matlock, your Matlock, your saztaculous majickal saviour of the Winchett Dale, is stroffed."

"But he did be losing his life before he be getting stroffed?" Fragus griffled. "Only we's all an oidy bit clottabussed, Mr Coat, and we needs to be getting the order of things all proper and fuzzcheck in our minds."

Note took a breath, counting in his head before continuing. "Please, just *try* to understand. Being stroffed and losing your life are the same thing. Just different griffles for the same thing."

A krate raised his paw. "You mean, like a testament, Your Officiousness? The hare got stroffed as a testament to losing his life?"

It was more than Note could take. "Right, that's it!" he angrily griffled, reaching into his robes and pulling out the Most Majelicus wand. "I've had enough!" He shot a bright red vroosher high into the roof, the sheer startling intensity of it instantly silencing the entire hall. "Now, all of you glopped-up, gobflopped clottabusses are going to listen to me! *No one* is going to griffle out, or question any of my griffles until I have finished. You are all going to simply sit and listen in complete silence! Does everyone understand?"

The dumbstruck hall lazily nodded, still watching the end of the vroosher as it slowly fizzed and faded in the arched roof above.

Note cleared his throat, trying to order his thoughts. "Now I realise that some of you may be wondering why it is that I have Matlock's wand. As I griffled to you before, Matlock got stroffed in caging the 'something' this late this afternoon-up. He battled it right here with me, in this very hall, the three of us locked in a saztaculous battle to finally capture and cage the most peffa-yechus beast ever seen in all the history of the dales. But, as we bravely managed to shut the creaker, Matlock's arm became horribly caught in the creature's ganticus mouth. But like the true hero he was, and knowing he was going to be eaten and stroffed, he threw me this wand, griffling that because I was just as saztaculous and brave as him, he could think of no one more suitable to wield its Most Majelicus power. Indeed, he further griffled, as his second arm was being eaten, that he thought I was so peffa-yamamantally-spious, that if any krate ever deserved to be Most Majelicus, then it must be me."

The hall simply listened, trying their briftest to understand.

"I watched in both twizzly horror and grateful appreciation, good creatures," Note griffled, holding the frizzing wand high in the air. "Thankful to witness such bravery, to be finally recognised for my own saztaculousness, yet also peffa-eyesplashy to see him stroffed. However, this wand stands as proof of Matlock's intention that I be recognised and referred to from now on as Most Officious Majelicus Frendeslene Note.

"But, of course, this even'up isn't all about me, peffa-fascinating and shindinculous as I am. I also want you to know that just before Matlock was dragged through the bars and the last of his long, soft and peffa-furry ears slipped down the throat of the peffa-yechus 'something', he griffled to me that no one is to be eyesplashy tonight, as together, we had captured the ganticus beast, and made everything peffa-fuzzcheck for everyone, and no one is to get twizzly anymore. He also wanted to griffle that it had been the most peffa-perfect honour in his short life for him to have been able to serve under me as we caged it together. He learned a lot from the all too brief experience, but he would remember it for those last agonising snutch of moments before he was finally crunched and stroffed. I believe it gave him the strength to be eaten, and at the end I was simply glad to have been able to do that for him."

Note hung his head respectfully in the silence, before peffa-slowly raising it, hoping to see a hall full of peffa-shocked and eyesplashy creatures. Instead, everyone simply looked straight back at him, as if waiting for more griffles. "That's all there is," he griffled, not really knowing what else he could possibly have added. "Matlock got stroffed."

347

Again no-one griffled a griffle, not even the oidiest eyesplash appeared. It felt to Note as if the entire silent hall had been frozen into one of his ganticus drutt statues, completely still and unmoved by all they had heard. He began to panic, searching for the young bespectacled disidula who had once gone to Matlock on the High Plateau to confess his faith in the gobflopped hare.

"You!" he griffled, pointing to it as it sat between its mahpa and pahpa. "Disidula thing! Did you hear any of my griffles? I griffled that Matlock is stroffed. You remember, him, don't you? The crumlush, majickal-hare who once pulled a thorn from your paw, and you griffled that you'd always believe he was majickal, even though he couldn't vroosh a single oidy saztaculous vroosher?"

The young disidula nodded. "Matlock be stroffed," he quietly griffled, looking at his paw, feeling for the place where the thorn had been.

Relieved that he might finally make at least one of the creatures eyesplashy, Note vilishly descended the stone stairway as another ominous rumble shook the ground below. "Come to me," he beckoned from the front, taking the youngster and lifting him into his arms for all to see, then gently griffling into its ear. "Now, I want you to know that it's not a yechus thing to get eyesplashy. And I think Matlock would have wanted you to do that, don't you? After all, you've just heard the most glopped-up news a young creature could ever hear. Your saztaculous majickal-hare has been stroffed by the peffa-yechus 'something', and you will never see him again. Your oidy heart must be torn in two; you must be peffa-desperate to get all eyesplashy…aren't you?"

The disidula simply looked out at the sea of watching faces.

"Please," Note pleaded, whispgriffling. "Please, peffa-please. Just one or two splashers will do."

"Why?" the youngster griffled, blinking from behind his spectacles.

"Well…" Note quietly griffled, shifting uncomfortably, beginning to wish he hadn't picked the creature up in the first place, as it was far heavier than he'd realised, "…because then everyone else will be all peffa-sad and eyesplashy, too. Then, afterwards, I can make them feel all fuzzcheck again, and they will like me even more. It…it's like

348

a game, you see; me and you are on this side, and everyone else is on the other side, and the winner is the one who can make the most creatures peffa-sad and eyesplashy."

"That's doesn't sound like a nice game."

"I know," Note whispgriffled, aware other creatures were starting to get restless, and fearing things might turn peffa-gobflopped any moment. "But please. Just one eyesplashy will start it."

The young disidula shook its head, beginning to struggle in Note's arms. Realising the cause was lost, he set the youngster back on the ground, watching it happily pid-padding back to its parents. He cleared his throat, looking at Fragus' cottage-cage and wondering if stubbornness and opportune resilience were common traits in all disidulas, and if he'd been foolish not to have spotted their true talents earlier on. Disidulas, he supposed, might well have made a better job of building the hall to the rest of the creatures' expectations than his own officious krates, who frankly had proved something of a disappointment since arriving in Winchett Dale.

"So," he slowly griffled, attempting to regain an oidy bit of dignity after what had proved a rather unsuccessful even'up so far, "bearing in mind Matlock's last griffles were for us to make sure we still had a shindinculous celebration tonight, I have the most ganticus pleasure in announcing the peffa-briftest singing act in all the dales to entertain and lift our spirits. But before I introduce them to you, could I just ask why not one of you seems the oidiest bit upset about the stroffing of Matlock the hare?"

All eyes in the hall turned to Fragus, who gradually stood from his chair, opened his cage and slowly pid-padded to the front, putting one short disidula's paw around Note's shoulders and pointing to the silent creatures with the other. "What you see here, Mr Boat," he slowly griffled, "is everything that Winchett Dale is, all that it has been, and how it most certainly will be for grillions of sun-turns after we have all stroffed, too. We may be glopped-up and clottabussed, and not do things in the peffa-perfectly 'right' and officious way, but that's simply how it is here, how we all are. But the one thing we do know is that when our own time eventually comes to be taken to Oramus, then much of ourselves, and the way we have lived our lives, remains right here in Winchett Dale. Just like our old Great Hall that you so vilishly pulled down. It had memories, lifetimes and majick in every beam, every roof-tile. How many of our forebears looked from its windows? How many softulousses had sat in the glopped seats, nifferduggling through endless public-grifflings then rushed for the inn the moment they were done? And those kind of things, Mr Coat, those saztaculous memories, are still just as much as part of us as we all are.

"Life for us is like a saztaculous white summer cloud in a shindinculous blue sky. It passes above, changing all the time, then slowly drifts away as another comes to take its place. Matlock is with us now, just as he's always been. We enjoyed, loved and sheltered under his cloud. We watched it float on high, right across our dale and into our hearts, and even though we know him to be stroffed, we know he be here, still. We welcomed him to Winchett Dale as we've always welcomed all majickal-hares down through the ages of this crumlush place we call home. And while he pid-padded amongst us, he was one of us, as he will *always* be one of us. So although he be gone, we have lost nothing, because he gave everything to us, and for us. We all be richer for knowing him, richer than the most peffa-ganticus pile of your glopped-up pebbles will ever make any creature. So no eyesplashers from us, Mr Note, only the most shindinculous and peffa-perfect memories of Matlock's majickal cloud. And I hope that be answering your question."

Note watched as Fragus made his way slowly back to his cage in complete silence, shutting the door behind him and settling back in his chair once more. He cleared his throat, rubbed his face with both paws, trying to think of something to griffle. "Well," he griffled. "How about we have a little entertainment to lighten the mood, eh?"

"It's not the singing kraark, is it?" the young disidula griffled. "He's glopped-up, and he's got a wooden leg."

"Er…yes it is, the peffa-same!" Note griffled, trying his briftest to sound excrimbly. "But let's not judge him just because he's only got one leg…"

"And only one eye," someone else griffled.

"True," Note conceded. "Only one leg and one eye…"

"And he can't sing."

"Well," Note griffled, "now that's not *entirely* true…"

"Yes it is," a rupplesnarler griffled, "He's peffa-gobflopped at it!

Everybody knows that. Is this the briftest you've got for us? What's he going to do, take his wing off, so it matches his leg?"

Note appealed for calm, deciding now would be the briftest moment to vilishly introduce the entertainment before things went any more gubbstooled than they already were. Though frankly, he had no idea how that could ever happen. "Creatures of Winchett Dale, please give a saztaculous Great Hall welcome to 'Goole and the Trefflepugga Kraarks'!"

A snutch of restless moans rippled across the hall as Goole and his backing kraarks nervously scrittled to their places, finally ready for their saztaculous showstopper.

"Good even'up Winchett Dale!" Goole enthusiastically called out, his beak beaming with pride. "We're here to make your saztaculous opening night one to truly remember!"

"Does that mean we can all be going home, then?" someone immediately asked, as another distant rumble shook the ground beneath the hall.

"What be that garrumblooming?" the rupplesnarler griffled. "I don't be thinking that this stony hall of yours be as peffa-safe as you griffle, Mr Boat."

Note vilishly pid-padded back up to the balcony. "There's absolutely nothing to get twizzly about," he griffled. "Everyone stay in your seats, we're all peffa-safe. This hall will stand as it is for a grillion lifetimes. The only thing that's going to bring this house down in Goole's showstopper. Now please, put your paws together and show some good old Winchett Dale appreciation for a very talented, if an oidy bit glopped kraark; Goole!"

A weak ripple of unenthusiastic pawplause broke out, the distracted creatures pointing at thin trails of dust falling freely from the roof, watching as oidy cracks appeared in the ornate stonework, high above their heads.

"Thank you! Thank you, and a peffa, peffa-kind thank you, Mr Note!" Goole griffled, his one good eye still saztaculoulsy shining with excrimbly anticipation. "Now normally, folks, I has me own crumlush little seven-piece ploffshroom band what performs with me, but somewhere along the way they seemed to have all ploffed off."

"Them ploffshrooms are smarter than you think," a driftingborticus mumbled under his breath.

"But with the aid of me brothers, we have fashioned a few musical devices to help us, whittled and carved by Serraptomus, all from the old timbers of your former Great Hall."

"Can we go now?" someone griffled from the back.

Goole ignored the griffles, clapping his wings together as three more kraarks scrittled on with a trinkulah, a musical neffle-hammer and a high-skinned strimple drum, vilishly arranging themselves at the back of the stage, before breaking into a light, brisk rhythm that gradually built over Goole's excrimbly griffles.

"Now folks, I've made up so many saztaculous songs in me long career as a singing-kraark, that it was difficult to select one that suited the occasion this even'up. But, seein' as this be the beginning of a new age for us all, I've come up with a brand new showstopper especially to mark these shindinculous celebrations in a truly saztaculous and memorable way. It's called *'I'm Not Glopped-up 'Cause I've Got a Wooden Leg.'*"

Note immediately silenced him from the balcony. "Are you sure, Goole? A song about a wooden-leg? I mean, is that really fitting?"

Goole nodded eagerly. "Oh yes, Your Officiousness. Very fitting. The bindings have never been tighter."

Note ignored the raucous chickling from the crowd, ordering the kraarks to play on, Goole tipping his tricorn hat to everyone as he jauntily launched into his song:

Now you may think that your life has stopped,
If you lose a leg and it's gone a bit glopped.
But thanks to Serraptomus and his whittling,
Look at me now, just how I'm scrittling!

Goole skipped, danced, scrittled and rushed frantically around the stage as his backing-kraarks tried to form a high-kicking line behind, trying to avoid a volley of niffs from the excrimbly, chickling crowd.

It's life with a wooden leg! Life With a wooden-leg!
With all this talent, I'll never need to beg,
Because it's life with a wooden-leg!

One or two boos began to ring out around the hall, as Goole, undeterred, went into the second verse.

I used to think that you needed two,
Turns out I was wrong about that, too.
'Cause the only real way to have the briftest fun,
Is not on two legs, but one one!
It's life with a wooden leg! Life with a wooden leg!
With all this talent…

"Just stop, for Oramus sake!" an elderly shuttler cried out, pid-padding towards the front, as the kraark band came to an embarrassing halt. "Just how much more of this glopped-up song is there?"

Goole looked around the hall, his breathing heavy in the awkward silence. "Er…about fifty-three verses."

"*Fifty-three?*" the shuttler gasped.

"I had seventy-four originally," Goole griffled, defensively. "Was peffa-hard enough cuttin' it down to what it is."

"But it's pefa-glubbstool," the shuttler gently griffled to him. "We've never heard anything worse. Hasn't anyone ever griffled to you just how gobflopped you sound? None of us wants to be hurting your fellings, Mr Goole, but sometimes you be needing to be facing the truth, and that be that you can't sing. I'm sorry to be the one telling you, but someone has to be doing it."

Goole nervously scratched the end of his beak with a wingtip. "But I've cleaned me hat specially for tonight."

The shuttler shook her head, trying her briftest to be as diplomatic as possible. "Mr Goole, it wouldn't matter if you be wearing the most shindinculous crown. Don't you see, you're making a clottabus out of yourself, and we're all chickling at you." She turned to the rest of the creatures who all nodded in agreement. "We don't mean you no harm, Mr Goole. We just don't want you to be making a gobflopped spectacle of yourself. Why don't you be quietly scrittling away, and be forgetting about all this singing nonsense, eh? It's not right for a kraark, Mr Goole. Krarks be made for flapping and scrittling, not singing, and perhaps that's what you'd best be doing."

Goole's one black beady eye narrowed as he watched the shuttler pid-pad back to her seat. He took a ganticus breath, slowly nodding, his beak fixed, mumbling to himself in the heavy, awkward silence, taking his time to find the right griffles as everyone watched and waited.

"Because that's what I *should do*, isn't it?" he suddenly shouted, startling them all, his one good eye blazing in indignation. "Just scrittle away! Oh, you'd *love* that, wouldn't you, eh?" A pointed wing shot out, the rings trembling and jangling. "Look at you lot, eh? Oh, so *I'm* the clottabus, am I? When was the last time you looked at yourselves, eh? I can tell you, I've played to some glubbstooled crowds in my time, but never to such an ungrateful bunch of clottabusses like you!"

"Goole!" Note sternly called from the balcony. "I think that's enough!"

"No!" Goole shouted back, throwing his hat to the floor. "That's *not* enough, Your Officiousness! That's not enough at all! It's not even the oidiest bit enough!" He stopped, took several deep breaths, the last button from his tattered waistcoat plinging onto the floor, the only sound in the completely silent hall. He looked at it for a long time, composing his thoughts before taking another breath, slowly reaching down and putting it in his waistcoat pocket.

"What you don't seem to be able to understand," he griffled, his voice shaking a little, "is that I already *know* I'm not a shindinculous singer. It's not news to me, any of it. Deep down inside my Sisteraculous, I already know that I gobflop at it. And you might griffle why would a glopped-up kraark like me even *have* a Sisteraculous? But I do, peffa-deep down I do; just as every other creature in these dales does, no matter how Most Majelicus or peffa-yechus and gobflopped they are. We all do." He took breath. "And my Sisteraculous told me to sing. Yup, that's what she did, one sun-turn she told clottabussed old Goole to sing. And do you know – he did, he tried it, he tried to sing. And he was just as gobflopped at it that sun-turn as he still is this even'up. Never improved, ever, not even the oidiest bit." He held up a wing. "But, in singing those first precious griffles, he felt something he'd never felt before; a crumlush glow inside, for all the world as if the most shindinculous star from the twinkling-lid had filled him up with its Most Majelicus glory."

"Please, Goole," Note griffled. "Is this going to take long?"

"Let him griffle!" the elderly shuttler called out. "Go on, Mr Goole, we all be listening to you."

Goole swallowed. "So, I suppose what I'm really trying to griffle is that even though I won't be bringing the brother kraarks back here to waste your time with any more of my showstoppers, it won't stop me from doing them. I'll just do them on my own, and perhaps try to imagine what it would have been like to once have had heard a shindinculous round of pawplause, or seen a crowd of peffa-happy faces enjoying our show. Because we have tried really hard for you, what with all the brothers learning the dance and playing the music, we really have. It's not been easy for us, but at least we tried. And even though we've made ganticus clottabusses out of ourselves, we can all leave this hall with our beaks held high, knowing that we came here in good faith and chanced to do something that so many others would have shied away from. We simply tried to put crumlush smiles on all your faces, and bring just an oidy bit of that shindinculous shining star into each and every one of your hearts." He bowed his head. "I'm peffa, peffa-sorry. I'm just a kraark, who likes to sing."

The hall sat in absolute silence; the only noise a lone figure rising from his seat and slowly pid-padding to the front to join Goole on the stage.

"Oh my drifflejubs!" Serraptomus griffled, as he peered out over the audience. "All looks so peffa-different up here, doesn't it?"

"What you be doin'?" Goole whispgriffled.

Serraptomus noisily cleared his throat and stood proudly by his friend's side. "Something I've never really done before," he griffled. "But something I've always wondered what it would be like to do." He winked at Goole. "Let's see if there's any of shindinculous shining star in this old whittling krate, eh?" He took a deep breath and began to sing...

He's just a kraark, who likes to sing!

"Gosh," he griffled, face beaming. "It really is quite fun, isn't it?" He sang the line again, this time encouraging others to join in, as the musical kraarks began slowly playing along in the background. The elderly shuttler pid-padded to the stage to join them, as she, Goole and Serraptomus all began singing together, soon to be joined by others, vilishly filling the small wooden stage with a mass of singing and dancing creatures.

He's just a kraark, who likes to sing!
He used to think he was a king!
He's just a krarrk, who likes to sing!
With a wooden leg, but no wooden wing!

Gradually, the whole hall began to take up the song, all singing as loudly and enthusiastically as they could, some dancing in the aisles, others standing and clapping along with paws, talons and wings. Goole, with a smile wider than the moon itself, began high-kicking with such peffa-excrimblyness that his leg came loose from its bindings, flying high into the roof and lodging itself between two shaking beams.

Note, standing quietly in the balcony, anxiously watched the growing cracks in the walls, one paw on the dungeon lever, trying to judge the peffa-perfect moment to raise the caged 'something' from its prison below the shaking stone floor.

He's just a kraark, who likes to sing!
It's what he does, it's just his thing!
And to your face, a smile he'll bring!
Our crumlush Goole, our singing king!

Note glanced across at the far wall, noticing mortar falling from the previously repaired crack, stones either side beginning to shake and tremble in time to the musical cacophony, knowing that the time was near – peffa, peffa-near…

Deep beneath the hall, alone except for a peffa-juzzpapped ploffshroom band, their oidy soft heads glowing in the darkness of the slowly growing mirrit-tunnel, Matlock struggled to breathe. The mirrits eagerly ate into the soft ground as he tried his briftest to tunnel further, using his horn and talons, tearing at the earth then shifting it behind, flattening it with his cloven feet, bent double in the choking gloom.

Above his ganticus head, the ground shook with the sounds of muffled singing and stamping from the hall, clods of wet earth occasionally falling into his one glopped-up and yechus eye. He urged the ploffshrooms to keep playing all the while, struggling for griffles in the oidy space, as he tried his briftest to extrapluff more mirrits to help with the tunnelling.

At last the tunnel began to gradually rise, Matlock hoping with all his hare's heart that it had managed to clear the hall, frantically stabbing the earth with his horn, digging as vilishly as he could, desperate to find the surface and fill his lungs with great gasps of clean, fresh air.

More earth fell on his head, as suddenly – peffa-thankfully – the roof gave way and shafts of crumlush evening sunlight streamed through, stinging his one eye. He pushed with all his might, managing to stand, his yechus softulous heaving itself out of the tunnel, until he could finally lie on the welcoming ground of the village-square, taking ganticus breaths and thanking Oramus and all his peffa-luckiest stars in the twinkling-lid that he had finally escaped.

A snutch of moments passed before he slowly stood and looked down, seeing himself fully in the golden light for the first time. He gasped at the yechus sight, gently setting the juzzpapped ploffshrooms on the ground.

"We've done it," he whispgriffled, thanking them, watching crowds of mirrits vilishly scrittling away across the square. "We're out."

The ploffshrooms collapsed in an exhausted heap. "All it took was an oidy bit of the old rhythm," one managed to griffle. "Don't get me wrong, though, but I never want to see another tunnel in my life. All me tunnelling sun-turns are peffa-definitely over."

Matlock tried to smile, turning for his first proper sight of the newly decorated Great Hall. It certainly did look shindinculous, draped in flags of every colour and hung with flaming lanterns. From the sounds of singing and chickling from inside, it certainly seemed that everyone was having a most saztaculous time. Though the more he looked, the more he noticed the hall was almost beginning to move, the roof cracking, sending oidy bits of stone dropping below.

"Oh, by Oramus!" he griffled, vilishly pid-padding to a small side-door. "'Tis the tunnel! It'll cause the whole hall to fall down!"

He was just about to burst through the creaker, when suddenly the singing stopped, and he heard the familiar tones of Frendeslene Note, addressing everyone inside.

"And now," Note griffled from the balcony, as the last chickling creature had returned to its seat, "we come to the highlight of the even'up!"

"The bit where we all go to the inn?" someone hopefully griffled.

"No," Note calmly answered, his paw closing around the dungeon lever. "The bit where you finally get to see the peffa-yechus 'something' that your courageous Matlock and I captured this afternoon'up."

"Then can we go to the inn?" the voice called back.

"No-one is going to the inn until they have seen me stroff the 'something'!" Note barked, brandishing the Most Majelicus wand above his head and vilishy pulling the lever. "Behold, good creatures of Winchett Dale! The peffa-yechus and glopped-up 'something' that I, the great and Most Officious Majelicus Frendeslene Note, will now save you all from with my Most Majelicus vrooshers!"

The stone floor at the front of the hall fell away, the creatures gasping in surprise, Note sending a ganticus red-vroosher down into the dungeon, his eyes closed, face twisted in concentration, slowly raising the smashed cage and wagon out from the depths and high into the air.

"There be nothing there!" a creature cried. "Its cage be all glopped-up!"

"It's escaped!" another shouted, causing a ganticus twizzly panic, as creatures vilishly began to rush for the creaker, overturning benches and crying out, taking youngsters by the paw, pushing and shoving as the hall shook and garrumbloomed all around them.

Note opened his eyes and immediately stopped the vroosher,

sending the wagon crashing back down into the dungeon and causing a large roof-support to suddenly give way, stone dangerously plummeting down onto the stage, shattering and smashing into the crumbling walls.

The creatures pushed open the ganticus creaker, pouring outside and vilishly pid-padding into the square, cries of twizzly-panic filling the air as they searched for loved-ones, calling to each other to make sure they were safe, before turning to watch in horror as the entire hall suddenly lurch to one side.

"It be all falling down!" one cried. "And Fragus still be inside!"

A group dashed back towards the creaker as a complete side wall fell away, crashing to the ground, rock and stone tumbling all over the square.

"Look!" Goole cried, pointing with a wing as Fragus' wagon and cage were hauled through the gap by a peffa-ganticus and yechus creature. "'Tis the 'something'! And it's saving your Fragus!"

Matlock hauled the wagon with all his might, straining every muscle and sinew, just managing to get it far enough into the square before the rest of the hall spectacularly collapsed, falling in on itself with a peffa-ganticus garrumblooming crash, covering everyone in a billowing dust-cloud, until finally a heavy silence settled over the shocked square.

For a long time, no one griffled a griffle; krates and creatures stood shoulder to shoulder, stunned, simply looking at the mountain of stone that been their new Great Hall.

"Well," Fragus eventually griffled, his voice clear in the summer even'up. "You certainly bought the house down, Mr Goole, I've got to griffle you that."

The creatures turned to the cage and the yechus creature breathlessly panting beside it, cautiously approaching, youngsters hiding behind their mahpas and pahpas, looking and pointing, whispgriffling to each other. A circle formed around it, watching as it slowly sank to its yechus knees and slumped against the side of Fragus' wagon.

Slivert Jutt, landlord of the Winchett Dale Inn, peffa-cautiously pid-padded into the circle, his long whiskers twitching. "You be the peffa-yechus and ganticussly twizzly 'something', be you?"

Matlock, utterly juzzpapped from tunnelling and hauling the cage, weakly shook his head.

"So what you be, then?" Jutt griffled. "For you surely look most peffa-yechus to us."

"Matlock," he managed to quietly griffle. "I…be…Matlock."

"Matlock?" Jutt griffled as the crowd began to murmur. "It really be you in all that glopped-upness?"

Matlock nodded, looking at the sea of confused faces with his one yechus eye.

Jutt took a moment, frowning slightly. "You griffle that you be Matlock, but how do we really *know* you be him?"

"I know a way!" Fragus suddenly griffled from inside the cage. "You need a test, Slivert. Be asking him a question, and if he gets it right, then we all be knowing he be Matlock."

The other creatures all nodded and murmured their approval of such a saztaculoulsy clever idea.

Jutt pulled at his whiskers, deep in thought and concentration, searching for a question as everyone waited. "Alright," he eventually griffled. "What colour be the grass?"

"No, you ganticus clottabus!" Fragus griffled. "Be asking him a question that only Matlock would be knowing the answer to!"

"Oh, I see!" Jutt griffled. "I be getting your meaning now, Fragus. I'll be twisting me whiskers again and be thinking of one. Just be giving me a snutch of blinksnaps."

The creatures all waited patiently for a second time until Jutt suddenly snapped his paws in triumph. "Got it! Got meself a question that only Matlock would be knowing!" He bent down and addressed the creature in his most peffa-serious tone. "Be… you…Matlock?"

Matlock weakly nodded, Jutt eagerly turning to the others. "That be sorted, then!" he griffled. "He *must* be Matlock to know if he *is* Matlock! Honestly, some creatures think I'm a clottabus, but I really surprises myself sometimes, I really do."

With the matter of the peffa-yechus 'something's true identity calmly established according to the clottabussed traditions of Winchett Dale, the excrimbly creatures set about gently pulling him to his cloven feet and offering him some of the remaining niffs they had saved to hurl at Goole, as the one-eyed kraark scrittled away on his one remaining leg to find more from the rubble for his ravenously hungry friend.

"'Ere we go," he griffled dropping a pile at Matlock's feet. "And see what else I've found when I've been rooting around. Mr Note's Most Majelicus wand. Normally, I'd be keeping that for meself, but seeing as I've been a bit harsh on you in the past, Mr Hare, I guess this be rightfully yours. 'Tis the peffa-least I can do, really."

Matlock took the wand. "My wand," he griffled. "The wand he stole from me when he turned me into this yechus glop-up."

"Oh, I don't know," Goole griffled, scrittle-circling Matlock and looking him up and down. "It's not *that* yechus. The squishy tail-thing's quite fetching in its own way. You turn up in Svaeg dale with a tail like that, and trust me, they'll all be wanting one."

"Thanks," Matlock griffled. "I know you're just trying to make me feel fuzzcheck."

"Got to, haven't I?" Goole griffled. "I mean the rest of you is so peffa, peffa glopped-up."

"Where's Note?" Matlock asked, looking at the huge pile of rubble and stone.

"I don't think he be making it out in time," Slivert Jutt replied. "He be gone to do some peffa-apologising to Oramus, I be reckoning, for all the trouble and gobflops he be causing. In the end, he wasn't being the most crumlush of officious krates, so perhaps t'was Oramus' will he ended up stroffed under all that glop-up of his own making."

An instinctive extrapluff suddenly coursed through Matlock. He narrowed his one eye, straining to listen. "Hush!" he suddenly called, slowly pid-padding to the pile. "No more griffles from anyone. I can hear something from inside!" He pressed one of his cavern-owl's ears to the stone, just making out distant scratching and the faintest tapping noises from below. "It's Note!" he cried to the others. "He's still alive! Everyone start moving these stones, vilish!"

But not a creature moved in the square.

"Hurry, we can save him!"

Slivert Jutt pid-padded forward. "But we not be doing that, Matlock," he slowly griffled, "for two peffa-important reasons. Firstly, for all the glubbstooled mess he be making in our crumlush dale."

The others all nodded and griffled in agreement.

"He be coming here," Jutt griffled, "and be going about all sorts of gobflopped ways to be changing things, when we don't be needing him to be changing anything at all. We's not be being inviting him here, and we's not be wanting his ways of drutty-pebbles, either. Our old Great Hall was crumlush as it was, and now we be realising that all his griffles of the 'something' were just a spuddle to be making us twizzly so he could be building this new one, which then nearly got us all stroffed."

"And the second reason?" Matlock asked, puffing and straining as he tried to move a ganticus piece of stone.

"Them rocks be far too peffa-heavy."

Matlock took a breath, trying not to get too russisculoffed. Instead, he glanced towards the top of the pile, noticing Goole's upturned wooden-leg poking from between the stones, pointing straight to the lid above, the sight of it suddenly causing him to have a another ganticus extrapluff, sending mirrits dropping and scrittling over the pile. Knowing what he should now do, he carefully climbed back down and took out the Most Majelicus wand, brandishing it high in the air.

"This wand," he griffled out loud, "was given to me, by me. Not the me from now, but a me from many moon-turns hence, a me when I finally become Most Majelicus."

"Begging your pardon," Jutt asked, "but how's can you be giving yourself something?"

"It doesn't matter!" Matlock cried out, turning sharply. "It just happened! Accept it, accept that sometimes the peffa-strangest of things happen for the most unexpected and sometimes saztaculous reasons that we have no hope of ever even beginning to guess at! It's just how it simply is at times, Slivert!"

"Right you are, Matlock," Jutt quietly griffled, awkwardly pid-padding back to the others. "I only be griffling the question, is all."

Matlock looked into all their confused faces. "Look," he apologised, taking a breath, "I don't want to get russisculoffed with anyone, least of you, all my friends. But whatever we all think of him, whatever he has done, this krate is still alive and needs help.

And while I understand he has done many things to hurt us all…"

"He sometimes wouldn't let us go into the cages for a whole moon-turn!" someone griffled.

Matlock nodded. "I know, I know. And many other glopped-up and glubstooled things, besides. But how many of us can honestly stand by and do nothing, knowing that he's still in there, alive, and most probably peffa-close to stroffing this very moment?"

"Well, we all are, aren't we?" another creature griffled. "That's exactly what we be doing, Matlock. Just standing around and watching. 'Tis quite boring though, because really all we're doing is just looking at a ganticus pile of rocks. You'd think it would be far more interesting and exciting, wouldn't you?"

Matlock sighed, looked to the lid above, streaked red and gold with the setting sun, and offered a short hare's prayer to Oramus. His extrapluff had told him exactly what he should do to save Frendeslene Note, and from that moment it should have been so simple. Yet the longer he waited in the expectant silence of the square, the more doubts he began to have. Why save a creature who had been so cruel, had used him every pid-pad of the way, subjected him to a peffa-twizzly journey simply to get his greedy paws on a Most Majelicus wand? And what would happen if he *did* save Note? Would the deranged krate ever stop in his ruthless ambitions? By saving Frendeslene Note, would it simply make matters worse for other creatures in other dales?

"Mr Matlock?" came an oidy voice beside him. "What you be waiting for?"

Matlock looked at the young disidula looking up at him, a light film of dust covering the lenses of his spectacles. "Sometimes," he quietly griffled to it, "it's really, really peffa-difficult to know the right thing to do."

The disidula nodded. "But you took the thorn from my paw, didn't you?"

"I did, yes."

"And it wasn't majick, was it?"

"No," Matlock quietly griffled, "it wasn't."

The disidula beckoned Matlock down, whispgriffling in his cavern-owl ears. "That's because it didn't *have to* be majick, did it?

But now, I be thinking, this *has* to be."

Matlock watched the youngster pid-pad back to the crowd, his mind made up. "Creatures of Winchett Dale!" he griffled to them all, brandishing the wand once more, its red tip starting to splutt and fizz ferociously. "Here's a saztaculous vroosher I should have vrooshed for you all many moon-turns ago, up on the High Plateau! Move back, all of you!"

A bright red vroosher shot from the wand and high into the lid, as creatures scurried, pid-padded and scrittled in all directions towards the edges of the square, watching in awe as Matlock fought with its immense power, grimacing as he slowly managed to direct it down onto the ganticus pile of rock and stone and focus it to settle exactly on the protruding wooden leg at the very top, the whole pile beginning to groan and garrumbloom, glowing bright red as the vroosher vilishly descended.

"By all the Most Majelicus majickal-powers of Oramus!" Matlock cried out. "I charge this wand to give rise to the new age of Winchett Dale!"

More rocks were flung to the sides, the noise rumbling over the whole village, as to everyone's astonishment the wooden leg firstly began to sprout branches, then a ganticus growing trunk, burying itself down into the pile, scattering and throwing chunks of stone until at last it rooted itself into the ground becoming the most saztaculous and crumlush tree, its shindinculous leaves shimmering gold in the evening light.

Matlock gasped as the last of the vroosher vilishly fizzed back into the wand, his whole softulous shaking from the effort, taking deep breaths and looking at the saztaculous tree, standing magnificently where the rock pile had been only a snutch of moments earlier. He turned as pawplause broke out from all sides of the square, Winchett Dale's excrimbly creatures waving, chickling and pointing with sheer majickal delight at what they saw.

Goole scrittled over to him. "Well, I be supposing Serraptomus can always whittle me a new leg," he chickled. "Quite some vroosher, that, Matlock, I've got to give you that."

Matlock nodded. "It was quite some piece of wood," he griffled.

"Majickal-wood, methinks," Goole griffled, winking with his one eye. "Carved from the old Great Hall. Me and Serraptomus always used to griffle that it could be majickal one sun-turn. And I'm guessing that perhaps this was just that sun-turn."

"Yes, perhaps it was," Matlock griffled, distracted, his one yechus eye now settling on a familiar figure in red robes beckoning him over to the base of the tree. "Chatsworth?"

The figure held out his paws as Matlock pid-padded over. "Well, it took you a while, but you got there in the end."

"Where's Note?" Matlock griffled, looking all around.

Chatsworth simply smiled. "Standing right in front of you, Matlock."

"You're...?" Matlock griffled, his yechus jaw hanging open in shock. "You're Note?"

"Well, not permanently," Chatsworth griffled, chickling a little. "Just when it suited over the last few moon-turns." He produced his own wand from his robes. "But underneath, I'm no more Frendeslene Note than you are the glopped-up creature that stands before me now. Time to vroosh you back to yourself, methinks. Be still, Matlock. I've seen enough of the peffa-yechus 'something' to last me many lifetimes."

Chatsworth expertly span the wand three times in the air, vrooshing a crumlush red cloud that quickly covered them both completely, Matlock closing his one eye, then opening two, noticing to his great relief that his horn had gone, his squishy tail vanished, his feet were back as he remembered them. He held a talon to his face, watching as it majickally changed into his own familiar paw before his orange hare's eyes. He felt his hat slide over his long brown ears, green robes wrapping themselves back around him, before finally his long purple shoes scrittled into the cloudy vroosh and slipped themselves onto his peffa-grateful feet.

"There!" Chatsworth griffled, surveying his wandwork. "A grillion times better, methinks."

Matlock didn't know what to griffle, where to even begin. All this time Frendeslene Note had been Chatsworth?

The elderly Most Majelicus hare read his thoughts. "Your task wasn't simply to solve the riddle of Trefflepugga Path, Matlock," he griffled. "I needed to be sure that one sun-turn, you would also be able to save the very thing that you despised the most. The creature that had taken everything from you, used you, changed you, threatened to stroff you and imperilled the lives of all your friends. Because one sun-turn, Matlock, you *will* have to do that, only it will be far worse than this even'up, far worse."

"I...just don't understand," Matlock griffled, peffa-confused. "I don't understand at all."

Chatsworth smiled. "That's because you're not meant to, Matlock. But you will, one sun-turn, I promise. All will make peffa-perfect sense, and that's all you have to know." He put an arm around his weary former apprentice. "Besides, this should be an even'up of saztaculous celebration. You solved your riddle on Trefflepugga Path, and in doing so have completed the first of the three Most Majelicus tasks, and I think we both deserve a freggle of guzzworts. All this being Frendeslene Note has given me a ganticus thirst, I can griffle you that. Not sure I'll get this dust out of my throat for many moon-turns."

Matlock frowned, still trying to make sense of it all. "But what would have happened," he suddenly griffled, "if I hadn't escaped from the dungeon?"

Chatsworth's smile faded. "Then you wouldn't have been right for the peffa-important tasks and choices you will have to make in the future, Matlock. Remember, whenever I was having to be Note I could follow your progress with the drutt-pile every pid-pad of the way, until you finally ended up in that dungeon. It was the only time I couldn't see what you were doing. But I'd given you all that I could to help you; ganticus strength, the horn, talons, the hooves and even cavern-owl ears. I'd vrooshed you with a Most Majelicus wand, ensuring that for all the time you were the 'something' you were Most Majelicus, too. I simply prayed to Oramus that you would find a way out. When the hall was collapsing, I knew you were on your way. The rest was simply a matter of timing. The last thing I did was throw the wand towards the creaker as the building fell around me, hoping you'd find and use it."

Matlock tried to smile, but couldn't. "I should be so peffa-relieved, but part of my Sisteraculous is griffling to me that this has only really just begun."

Matlock tried to smile, but couldn't. "I should be so peffa-relieved, but part of my Sisteraculous is griffling to me that this has only really just begun."

"Peffa-true, Matlock," Chatsworth griffled. "Oh, so peffa-true. But no more griffling for now, we have friends waiting at The Vroffa-Tree Inn, who will all be eager for news."

The two robed majickal-hares, one in red, one in green, slowly pid-padded from the base of the tree, as excrimbly cries of 'Matlock! Matlock!" rang all around the square in the saztaculously glorious and peffa-crumlushed even'up.

The journey back through the mirrit-tunnels seemed to last an age, Matlock clinging to a corner of Chatsworth's robes as he lead the way in the pitch black, trying to ask his old master all manner of questions, but being greeted with silence. His mind swam with possibilities and unresolved conclusions as he tried to make even the oidiest sense of everything that had happened.

When at last they reached the welcoming sight of The Vroffa-Tree Inn, its crumlush flaming beacons throwing golden light all around the ganticus lake-filled cavern, Matlock felt too juzzpapped to take another pid-pad, his mind unable to think any more.

Laffrohn, Proftulous and Ayaani were already waiting for them on the bridge, the excrimbly dworp carrying Matlock inside, his griffling dripple vilishly snuggling back to her place inside his hood. A snutch of moments later, they all sat on a long table in front of the roaring piff-tosh, eating niff-soup and tweazle-pies, drinking guzzwort and trupplejuice, Laffrohn griffling and chickling loudly as she fetched more food and drink.

Throughout the meal, however, Matlock mostly ate in silence, grateful to see his old and briftest friends, but unable to stop the constant stream of glopped-up thoughts and memories spinning and tumbling into his mind. Everything still felt like the peffa-strangest dream he'd ever nifferduggled. He tried his briftest to answer their griffled questions; what it had been like to be even more yechus than Proftulous when he was the 'something'; how it had felt to finally vroosh a saztaculous vroosher; what had been the briftest part of his journey on Trefflepugga Path. He answered each as honestly as he could, yet felt Chatsworth's eyes on him all the time, knowing in his Sisteraculous that their relationship would never be the same. In doing what he'd done; by being Frendeslene Note, Matlock knew something between them had been stroffed along the way. The trust, established and nurtured so many moon-turns ago as Most Majelicus master and apprentice majickal-hare, had gone.

After the meal, Proftulous took a nifferduggling Ayaani from Matlock's hood. "I be peffa-juzzpapped from all the excrimbly waiting," he griffled over a ganticus yawn and particularly yechus belch. "So now I's be lump-thumping upstairs for me nifferduggles." He lightly bliffed Matlock's ears. "It be so good to be seeing you all back with us and crumlush again, Matlock. Everything be working out peffa-perfectly in the end, didn't it?"

Matlock tried to smile, as Laffrohn hurried Proftulous away.

"I expect you two needs to be griffling," she griffled to Chatsworth and Matlock, throwing more wood on the fire. "So's I be leaving you for a while. It be peffa-good to have you back, Matlock. Most peffa-shindinculous, indeed."

The two hares watched in silence as she gathered plates and bowls in her ganticus paws before leaving them alone, the only sound the occasional splutting of the warming piff-tosh.

"Well, Matlock," Chatsworth eventually griffled. "You've had some time to think, and I know you'll have plenty of questions to ask, but before you do, I just need you to listen to what I have to griffle."

Matlock nodded, turning his wooden mug in his paw, watching the last of his guzzwort rippling at the bottom.

Chatsworth quietly cleared his throat. "When, one sun-turn, you complete all three tasks and become a Most Majelicus majickal-hare, your life will be given over to the dales in your duties of finding and training majickal-hares in the way and wisdom of ancient dalelore. And when the time is right, you will be called before The Most Majelicus Council for Majickal Hares and asked which of the hares you have trained should be considered to undertake the three tasks, and be raised to being Most Majelicus."

"And you chose me," Matlock quietly griffled.

"Because you were the briftest apprentice I ever had, Matlock," Chatsworth insisted. "Far and away the briftest. I knew in my Sisteraculous that out of all the majickal-hares in all the dales I had taught, you were always going to be the one, right from the moment I first saw you out in The Great Beyond."

"And yet you never griffled me a griffle of this?" Matlock griffled, still looking into his guzzwort mug. "You knew I'd be having to do these three tasks, and you never once thought to even griffle me even the oidiest snutch of griffles about it?"

Chatsworth shook his head. "It can't be done that way, Matlock," he quietly griffled. "There are rules, as you will discover when you become Most Majelicus."

"Then they're peffa-glopped-up rules, methinks," Matlock griffled, finishing the last of his guzzwort and slowly setting his mug back down. "Peffa, peffa-glopped-up and glubbstooled."

Chatsworth nodded.

"So what happened next?" Matlock griffled, looking his former master in the eye. "You nominate me, then suddenly decide to become some other creature entirely, nearly stroffing me?" His voice rose as anger began to overwhelm him. "Is that one of your 'rules', too, or is that something you simply did for fun? Because I can griffle you this, Chatsworth, you hurt me peffa-badly, and not just when you vrooshed me into the 'something', either. And to discover that you were calmly watching it all from your drutt-pile is peffa-gobflopped!"

"Matlock," Chatsworth calmly griffled. "Please let me finish, please let me explain."

"What *point* are your explanations?" Matlock griffled, suddenly bliffing the table with his paw. "How can I believe a single griffle of them, when you can so easily hurt me? How can I believe in *you*, anymore? How?"

Chatsworth waited a snutch of moments, letting Matlock's anger subside. "The first task is to solve the riddle of Trefflepugga Path. During it, the chosen majickal hare will have to join the path of his own freewill, without his wand or dripple to help him. Their Most Majelicus masters are allowed to influence how this happens, but on no condition must they reveal themselves to the chosen-hare. Perhaps you're expecting me to griffle that I'm peffa-sorry how it happened to you, but gobflopping on the High Plateau when you had no driftolubbs was peffa-easy for me to arrange and worked crumlushly, I think you'll find. By the end of that sun-turn, you had taken your first pid-pads on Trefflepugga Path of your own freewill. You might have thought of it as a glopped-up sun-turn, but for me, it was quite saztaculous, the true beginnings of your journey."

"Why?" Matlock griffled, trying his briftest to control his russisculoftulation.

Chatsworth leant forward, his face now eager and excrimbly. "Because it was the very same even'up The League of Lid Carving Witchery visited this inn, of course! The one sun-turn in the whole year that it happens, and I had to get you there on time. The inn rose, you met Laffrohn, pid-padded inside, met Ursula, then nifferduggled on the bed that took you straight to The Vale of Dreggs the next morn'up." Chatsworth beamed a ganticus smile at the memory. "I watched it all from Goole's drutt pile in his wagon, saw your every pid-pad and move, Matlock. Everything was working so well, much brifter than I could ever have expected."

"So that's why you had Goole believe the pebbles were worth something?"

"Indeed. Once I knew your selection for the three tasks had been approved by The Most Majelicus Council for Majickal-Hares, I made my plans then set about crossing the dales, looking for a greedy, clottabussed creature just like Goole. When I found him, I knew he was the one, with his glopped-up dreams of showstoppers and singing. All he needed was a dream to believe in."

"Which you all too keenly gave him," Matlock sourly griffled.

"Because I *had* to, Matlock," Chatsworth griffled. "Don't you see, don't you even *begin* to understand just the oidiest bit? He was peffa-perfect for my plan, and that was always to make sure you had the briftest chance of completing the task. I needed the drutts to be able to watch you. With Goole gone from his wagon, it was the peffa-perfect place to do exactly that until the rest of the drutts could be bought into the dale and building of the new Great Hall could begin."

Matlock simply sat, tight lipped, his hare's smile as narrow and unforgiving. "I'm not sure who was the greediest," he slowly griffled. "You, or Goole. You both wanted drutts, so there's no real difference in either of you. He mistakenly thought they were worth

371

something, yet you always *knew* they were, and kept their real value secret and hidden. You used his greed in order to feed your own greed, just so you could enjoy watching me glopp-up, every pid-pad of the way."

Chatsworth angrily pointed a paw, the smile gone, replaced by an increasingly russisculoffed frown. "Don't you *ever* griffle to me about the value of things!" he griffled accusingly. "What in Oramus' name do you know about the true 'value' of *anything*? You had to find the real value of mirrits from a driftolubb that you couldn't be bothered to even read before! A driftolubb that had to be turned into majickal-niff soup before you would ever begin to understand all its contents!" He paused for a snutch of moments, shaking his head, calming his breathing, lowering his voice. "You value nothing, Matlock. You know nothing of worth, nothing. Have you even thought about why I had to make you into the 'something'? Has it even begun to cross your mind why I had to do that?"

"Because you enjoyed it?" Matlock coldly suggested.

"There, you see! A peffa-perfect example!" Chatsworth griffled. "Only thinking about yourself! Think, Matlock, think! I needed you to hate me more than any other creature you've ever met. I also needed you to be Most Majelicus for a short time, in order that you could escape in a mirrit-tunnel. Vrooshing you into the 'something' with the Most Majelicus wand was the only way I could make that happen, Matlock, the only way. Don't you understand? Don't you see that? I did all of that to help you."

"I think if you'd really wanted to help me you could have griffled all this to me far earlier," Matlock griffled.

"Listen Matlock," Chatsworth tried, "I know you are peffa-russisculoffed with me right now, but that's only because you don't see the bigger, peffa-ganticus picture. Majickal-hares sometimes get stroffed while undertaking the three tasks. Many have to be returned to The Great Beyond. Remember the dripple-fair? The pile of robes from hares who failed to find their dripple? It happens, Matlock, believe me. Completing the three tasks is full of peffa-twizzly dangers for any majickal-hare. But for all the fates of all the dales, it is more peffa-important that you alone succeed, rather than any other majickal-hare that has ever attempted them before…"

"But why?" Matlock vilishly interrupted. "Everyone keeps griffling about how my being made Most Majelicus is going to be 'different', or 'more peffa-important' than any other hares. That rules are being broken. Well, I don't see that, Chatsworth! I don't see the oidiest bit of it."

"So what do you 'see', Matlock?" Chatsworth griffled.

"What do I see? I see someone I was once glopped-up and young enough to love, trust and admire. I see the red-robed hare that took me from my family, that I learned from, that taught me many majickal-things. And I also see that that hare has gone." He looked across the table, unable to stop the griffles. "You might as well be Frendeslene Note all the time! And I'm thinking that being him was also probably peffa-easy for you, wasn't it? Because, really, all I 'see' is him, the officious krate who didn't give a mirrit's leg of any concern for anything – except himself!" He took a deep hare's breath. "You griffled me the question. The truth is I don't see *you* anymore, Master. I don't see you. I just see your rules, your deception and your excuses. I see your cruelty. There, I've griffled it; I see someone who cares more for following the 'rules' than about anything else. That's all I truly 'see'."

Chatsworth slowly stood. "One sun-turn, you will see properly."

"How can I?" Matlock angrily griffled, his patience worn far too peffa-thin. "I already saw myself as Most Majelicus in the Vale of Dreggs, you remember? You saw it too, in your moving drutt-pile. I had no eyes, did I, Chatsworth? How will I ever be able to see anything with no eyes? Griffle me that, oh peffa-wise and Most Majelicus one!"

Chatsworth looked at Matlock for a peffa-long time, the silence glopped and heavy between them. "One sun-turn, you will understand," he quietly griffled, slowly pid-padding towards the creaker. "I wish you well, Matlock." He opened the creaker, Matlock watching through the window as he left the inn, then pid-padded over the wooden bridge into a mirrit-tunnel without ever looking back.

"Well," Laffrohn griffled at Matlock's side, placing a ganticus paw on his shoulder. "I be thinking that perhaps that didn't go quite so peffa-saztaculously."

"He's just gone," Matlock whispgriffled, still watching through the window. "I got peffa-russisculoffed with him, and he just pid-padded away."

Laffrohn sat down. "Oh, now don't you be worrying about Chatsworth," she griffled, her voice as soothing and peffa-crumlush as always. "He's been hearing a lot worse from all sorts of creatures over the years, believe you me. 'Tis what be making him so peffa-special, methinks."

"Is he coming back?" Matlock asked.

"When the time be right, Matlock."

"When will that be?"

"Why, when it be right, of course," Laffrohn chickled. "He couldn't be coming back when it be wrong, could he now? That would most peffa-glopped. Besides, Chatsworth has a much on his Most Majelicus mind right now, and a lot more important things to be sorting out." She poured a guzzwort from her jug, refilling Matlock's mug. "And you might find this peffa-glubbstooled to believe, Matlock, but he's doing nearly all of it for you."

Matlock slipped at his guzzwort. "He only cares about his rules, Laffrohn. That's all it is, just his 'rules'."

Laffrohn chickled. "Well now, let me griffle you something about Chatsworth when he was your age, undertaking the three tasks. Part of the first task is that Treffflepugga Path returns you to The Great Beyond. 'Tis a test, you see, to find out if you'll return to the dales. Some hares simply stay with their families, all memories of their majickal-time completely forgotten. Others return, but only if they are found and bought back by a Most Majelicus creature, for they are the only creatures from the dales who can pid-pad into The Great Beyond without stroffing, just as your good Ayaani did."

Matlock listened, memories of his short time with his family flooding back.

"Now, once the hare is returned to begin its majickal learning all over again, it be the job of its dworp to do that. The dworp must undertake the task knowing full well that when the time comes for it to teach the hare to extrapluff, it will be forgotten by the hare and

374

left simply to roam the dales with a glopped-heart until eventually it stroffs. It can no longer griffle, or lump-thump; 'tis the most glopped thing to see, Matlock. The hare it freely gave everything to never remembers the sacrifice the dworp made.

"When Chatsworth became Most-Majelicus, he managed to discover the lonely truth about dworps, and vowed that when the time came for his own chosen majickal-hare to undertake the three tasks, he would never let this glopped-up thing happen again." Laffrohn lowered her voice to whispgriffle. "So he became the only Most Majelicus hare to *break* the rules, Matlock. The only one. He found a way to make it happen. Disguised as Note, he had your Proftulous eat a ganticus tweazle-pie made from your majickal-driftolubbs, making him the only Most Majelicus dworp in the history of all the dales. He never wanted you or Proftulous to suffer the sadness that he had, and feel the loss of a dworp who had given everything only to be forgotten. 'Tis why you still have Proftulous here with you, now. 'Tis all down to Chatsworth making it happen.

"He also found a way of giving you a Most Majelicus wand, too. And to do that, he had to break more rules, Matlock, just as you will, in order to complete the cycle that has been set in motion. No other majickal-hare has ever seen a future version of themselves, it is utterly forbidden by the Grand High Council of the Elders. But you have, Matlock, and once again, it all be down to Chatsworth breaking the rules, not following them."

"But why?" Matlock griffled. "Why is he doing this?"

"There are things that are happening," Laffrohn whispgriffled, "peffa-dangerous and twizzly things, Matlock, that one sun-turn could change these dales forever. We made you eat majickal-niff soup cooked from the burning pages of *Majickal Dalelore (Volume 68 – revised edition)* so it always be with you in your mind. And with a Most Majelicus wand and dworp, not to mention a griffling dripple, we have tried our briftest to make sure you have everything you could be needing in order to complete the next two tasks and finally become Most Majelicus. But they won't be easy, Matlock, far from it. The Elders always do all in their ganticus powers to ensure the rules are never broken. But they *must* be, Matlock, if the dales are to be safe. Chatsworth knows this, and so does his master, Baselott."

An image of the blue-robed Elder hare with his notebook at the dripple fair flew into Matlock's mind. "Baselott…is Chatsworth's old master?"

Laffrohn nodded. "He taught Chatsworth, just as Chatsworth taught you. He also be the first majickal-hare to ever notice that dripples could griffle. He wrote a thirteen-page revision to *Majickal Dalelore (Volume 68)* on sacred parchment, but it was never included in the driftolubb. Someone amongst the Elders themselves must have disapproved of Baselott's revisions, and the parchment disappeared without the oidiest trace. T'will be your job, Matlock, to be finding those thirteen pages, and find out what be written in them that made the Elders so peffa-twizzly. This be your real and peffa-secret task, Matlock. Baselott knows this, Chatsworth knows this, and I be knowing this. 'Tis what makes you so special, Matlock, and 'tis why we all be looking out for you as briftest as we possibly can."

"But how has Baselott been looking after me?" Matlock griffled, puzzled and more than a little overwhelmed by everything he was hearing. "I only met him for that one short time."

Laffrohn took a snutch of moments. "Because, Matlock," she slowly griffled, "as an Elder, he broke one of the most sacred and peffa-important rules for you."

"Which was?"

"Secretly passing a spell from the Elders to Chatsworth," she griffled. "The *Mutato Corpore*, the changing spell. 'Tis a spell that's meant only to be used by the Elders, and it be utterly forbidden for any Most Majelicus creature to even attempt. But t'was the only way Chatsworth could change himself to become Frendeslene Note when he needed to."

"So he broke another rule, too?"

"Indeed, Matlock," Laffron griffled, her face peffa-serious. "Baselott and Chatsworth both broke one of the most peffa-ganticus rules. And in doing so, by Chatsworth using the majick of the Elders in this way, he and Baselott have done a dangerous and twizzly thing. If anyone discovers Baselott has taught Chatsworth the *Mutato Corpore* there will be all manner of glopped-up and glubbstooled consequences."

"And they did all this for me?"

Laffrohn nodded. "In order to be helping you as much as they could in the completion of your first task." She refilled his guzzwort. "So if I were you, I wouldn't be judging Chatsworth too harshly, Matlock. He be doing a peffa-lot more for you than you could ever realise."

Matlock slowly rubbed his juzzpapped eyes, trying to understand. "And what if I fail?" he griffled. "What if I fail the other two tasks, and don't become Most Majelicus? What if I let everyone down, and gobflop, or get stroffed, or…"

Laffrohn chickled. "Fail, Matlock? With Baselott, Chatsworth, Proftulous, Ayaani, a Most Majelicus wand and the landlady of The Vroffa-Tree Inn all on your side? How could you *possibly* be failing? Besides, you already majicked a saztaculous vroosher by making that tree and saving the life of a creature you had been deliberately made to hate. Chatsworth needed to know you could do that, don't you see? 'Tis why he had to be so peffa-glopped up towards you, and be Frendeslene Note. He had to know that you would find it in yourself to do exactly what you did."

"But I still don't understand why he didn't just griffle me all this in the first place? In fact, why didn't *any* of you griffle me anything about it?

Laffrohn lightly bliffed his ears. "Oh Matlock, it all had to be coming from *you*, not him, you clottabus. Mind, I'd have given a freggle of guzzworts to see what you looked like as the peffa-yechus 'something'." She chickled quietly. "By my eyes, I bet that be something to see!"

Matlock allowed himself just the oidiest hint of a smile. "I did look peffa-glopped."

"But you be all back to yourself, now," Laffrohn griffled. "Everyone be fuzzcheck for now, and that be the most peffa-important thing. But now, I be thinking that it's time for you to be getting some nifferduggles."

Matlock's eyes widened, his paw pointing to the ceiling above his head. "Not in *that* bed?"

"Calm yourself," Laffrohn griffled. "It will not be taking you anywhere glopped-up this time, I be promising you that." She reached into a small cupboard by the wall, rooting around the shelves.

"So who bought Ayaani back from being stroffed?" he griffled.

"T'was Chatsworth," she griffled, "helped by the majickal-driftolubb she be lying on, the same one in Proftulous' tweazle-pouch when he bought her back from the dale. Ayaani be peffa-important, Matlock. Chatsworth needed to know just how much she be loving you, and she had to be stroffed for him to be finding that out. But her loyalty to you was peffa-shindinculous. 'Tis why Chatsworth makes sure she brought your wand to you in The Cove of Choices. He was waiting outside to meet the drutt wagons coming through, and let her vilishly pid-pad through the gap, breaking, I must griffle, yet another rule. Remember, Matlock, majickal-hares undertaking the first task are forbidden their dripples to help them. 'Tis why they're all normally removed and taken to the dripple-fair. Chatsworth thought this was wrong, and sensing just how important Ayaani could be for all of us, he made sure she was with you as much as possible."

Matlock thought for a long time, slowly putting the pieces of the puzzle together, trying to understand the ganticus picture. "It's just like he griffled to me when he was being Note. He had this all planned, right from the very first blinksnap he arrived in Winchett Dale. He knew everything that was going to happen to me, didn't he? Every oidy thing."

Laffrohn softly chickled. "As much as he could, Matlock. But remember, it was still up to you to do the most peffa-important things. They would always be down to you, not him, or anyone else. He could only be helping as much as he could, and we all be simply crossing our paws that you be succeeding, every one of us, all of the time." She turned to him, closing the cupboard. "You see, all those times you were thinking you were all alone and peffa-glopped-up, but really, we all be with you, one majickal way or another, every pid-pad of the way."

"What are the other two tasks?" Matlock griffled.

Laffrohn waved a ganticus paw at him. "Oh now, 'tis not for me to be griffling you that, Matlock, not at all. T'would be a rule that's far too peffa-dangerous to break, even for me. But you'll find out in time." She held up an oidy leather potion bottle. "There be just one more thing, though – this."

"Ursula's potion bottle?" Matlock gasped, taking it as she offered it to him. "But how did you…?"

"Not for you to griffle, or for me to answer," Laffrohn firmly replied, before lowering her voice to a crumlush whispgriffle. "Let's just griffle that I had's meself the strangest dream and then I wakes up with it right beside me."

"A dream?"

"Methinks there could well be someone else looking over you, Matlock, and if my suspicions be right, then it turns out he might not be that peffa-good at keeping the rules, either." She looked at the potion bottle. "All he'd griffle is that when the time is right, it really does work."

"But…"

"Off for nifferduffles," Laffrohn firmly ordered. "And no more griffles of this to anyone, not even a whispgriffle. Good night, Matlock, and be nifferduggling saztaculoulsy. And may all your dreams be peffa-crumlush. I'll see you in the morn'up."

"And will I see Ursula again?"

"Oh, so you be wanting to, do you?" Laffrohn griffled, smiling. "Matlock hare, I do believe you be blushing under all that fur of yours!" She clapped her paws, and Bruttel, the oidiest witch, vilishly scrittled onto the table and looked up at Matlock's face expectantly. "Seems Matlock might be having something of a soft-spot for Ursula, Bruttel. As a witch yourself, you think this be a peffa-good or a glubbstooled thing?"

"Both," Bruttel griffled. "But because it be both, it could also be peffa-shindiculous. 'Tis always the way with majickal-hares and solitary witches, especially white witch-hares from across The Icy Seas."

"No, no," Matlock anxiously griffled. "I didn't mean…"

Lafrrohn chickled. "Bruttel has spoken, Matlock. And in The Vroffa-Tree Inn, the griffles of Bruttel may not be the loudest, but often they be the wisest. Now, no more griffles from you, Matlock. 'Tis time you be off for your nifferduggles, and not be thinking about any of this anymore."

Matlock still held the potion bottle in his paw as he opened the creaker by the piff-tosh, Bruttel watching his every pid-pad as he slowly climbed the stairs.

He awoke in the first light of the morn'up, his hare's eyes gradually focussing on a ganticus, excrimbly head grinning back down at him.

"Up we be getting, Matlock," Proftulous griffled. "Come and see what we've all been doing for you while you be all crumlush and nifferduggling."

Matlock slowly sat, looking around the room, recognising his own bedroom, all its furniture placed exactly back as it had been many moon-turns previously.

"I'm home?" he griffled, breaking into a broad smile.

"We be getting everything back from Goole and majicking it all back together for you," Proftulous griffled. "We be doing the whole cottage for you, then the bed be bringing you right here." The excrimbly dworp passed Matlock his robe, hat and slippers. "You be getting all dressed, and be coming down for breakfast when you be all ready."

Matlock stretched, yawning as he dressed, crossing to the window and looking outside at his crumlush cottage garden, seeing Goole, Serraptomus and the other trefflepugga kraarks hard at work trimming puttle-nettles, niff-plants and chasing curious tricky-rickets back over its surrounding wall. The colley-rocks were back in their rightful places, their faces upturned to the morn'up sun in each of the four corners, as Fragus pushed a gretteling-spurritt up and down, its long beak expertly cutting the grass.

He opened the window, calling down to them. "Morn'up all! I see you're out of your cage at last, Fragus!"

"Only while I be cutting your lawn, Matlock," he griffled. "Can't wait to get meself back in there. Got's meself some crumlush new purple curtains, I has, from the hall what all be falling down."

"I'll have to pid-pad over for a guzzwort or two one sun-turn," Matlock griffled. "Have a look inside."

"You'd be most welcome, Matlock," Fragus griffled. "I's be in a competition to find the briftest cage in all the dales, soon and I be reckon I could be having crumlush chance of winning, methinks."

Matlock smiled, closed the window, taking his time to contentedly look around his bedroom, then watching in surprise as the bed began to suddenly pid-pad towards the creaker.

"I'll best be getting back," it griffled. "Nice place you've got here, but I prefers it at The Vroffa-Tree Inn, if I'm honest."

"I had no idea you even griffled," Matlock griffled, amazed.

"What, just because I'm a majickal-bed?" it griffled. "Anyway, got to go. It'll take me a while, and these four legs aren't what they used to be in me youth. Done too many trips up the path, I have. Age, it comes to us all."

Matlock watched in awed silence as it kicked open the creaker, flipped to one side and squeezed itself through the narrow gap, before righting itself and carefully pid-padding down the stairs.

"Bye, Matlock," it griffled as it left. "Had a few excrimbly chickles with you, I did. Especially going all garrumbloomed and glubstooled over that ganticus waterfall. That'll be one to griffle to the rest of the pillows and sheets about for years to come, I reckon. Shindinculous, it was, peffa-shindinculous."

"Bye," Matlock griffled, running his paws through his long hare's ears and shaking his head a snutch of times, wondering just what else he would discover about his long journey along Trefflepugga Path. It seemed the whole business was one constant surprise after another.

"Slippers by the piff-tosh!" came a stern voice from the bottom of the stairs. "I make a new rule in this cottage. Slippers and shoes always by the piff-tosh, and the dworp must wash its yechus feet in the ganticus bucket I put outside."

"Ursula?" Matlock griffled, unable to contain an instant smile. "You're here?"

The white hare-witch frowned. "Of course I am here, you splurk. Someone had to be in charge of all these fools putting everything back together again. How can I be somewhere else, when clearly I am here, tidying your cottage, which let me griffle you was peffa-glubbstool, even for a majickal-hare."

"Well, in truth, I haven't lived here for almost a year," Matlock tried.

"Excuses!" Ursula snapped, clicking her tongue. "Some of this dust and yechus mess was many, many moon-turns old! Much more than just one year. It looked like a snutch of the most peffa-splurked dworps had been living here."

"Sorry about that," Matlock mumbled. "It's just that I'm not really used to having so many visitors."

Ursula nodded. "Rihaana griffled me as much. 'Tis why she thought it best I came to organise things properly."

"Plusa told you to come here?"

"And I do it more as a favour to her, not you, Matlock. I am not wanting any of your mixed-messages or splurked interpretations with this. I am simply here to help, that's all."

"Of course," Matlock vilishly griffled. "I wasn't thinking anything else, I was just…"

She held up a paw. "Enough griffles!"

Matlock cleared his throat, looking around his pristine and saztaculoulsy clean living room; the piff-tosh swept, the grate gleaming and a neat stack of logs waiting at the side. "You've done the most saztaculous job," he griffled, reaching into his robe pocket and showing her the oidy leather potion-bottle. "I still have this."

"Of course," Ursula griffled. "Why would you not have it? I gave it to you to keep."

"And I remembered what's inside," he griffled. "A potion of your feelings."

She stared at the bottle for a while, unable to look Matlock in the eye. "Then…I…"

A ganticus crash from the potionary interrupted her griffles, loud cursing filling the cottage. Matlock pid-padded through the creaker, seeing Proftulous standing beside a heap of broken glass jars and majickal equipment. "I be peffa-sorry, Matlock," he griffled. "I just be bringing this lot in, when I be bumping into that bed, pid-padding its way out." He looked at the floor. "I be spilling all the Pronosticulus powder and be making the most glopped mess of everything."

"Don't worry about it," Matlock sighed. "We can always go to the mine in the morn'up and get some more."

Proftulous, true to form at the mere mention of anything involving hard-work that might be even the oidiest bit twizzly, began

It was evening and the three of them slowly pid-padded into the crumlush garden and sat on three chairs Serraptomus had carved from beams of the old village-hall, Ayaani bringing them each a steaming mug of brottle-leafed tea.

rubbing his knee. "I be thinking I've glopped my flarrkers, too, I really do. I not sure I'd be any good down a mine, Matlock, I really don't."

"Now why doesn't that surprise me?" Matlock griffled.

Together the three of them cleaned up the mess, spending the rest of the sun-turn finishing the cottage, cleaning every oidy nook and corner, before finally griffling goodbye to Goole, Fragus, Serraptomus and the trefflepugga-krarrks. It was evening and the three of them slowly pid-padded into the crumlush garden and sat on three chairs Serraptomus had carved from beams of the old village-hall, Ayaani bringing them each a steaming mug of brottle-leafed tea.

"Well," Proftulous griffled, "I must be griffling that there be times when I not's be thinking that this could ever be happening again."

"This does not surprise me one tzorkly-bit," Ursula griffled. "You spend most of your life not thinking about anything at all."

"Except tweazle-pies," Proftulous griffled, "I be loving my tweazle-pies."

Ursula sighed, turning to Matlock. "Do you sometimes wish Chatsworth *hadn't* made him Most Majelicus?" she griffled. "And you'd simply forgotten about him like all other majickal-hares eventually do?"

Matlock closed his eyes, smiling in the moonlight. "I don't think I could *ever* have forgotten about Proftulous."

"Indeed. He is like the peffa-bad case of schtorple-bumps I had as a leveret. Some yechus things just seem to stay with you for a lifetime."

Matlock chickled. "Ayaani? What do you think? Would you have forgotten Proftulous?"

"She not be answering your glopped-up questions," Proftulous griffled, a little hurt. "As she most probably be nifferduggling in your hood."

Matlock lazily reached round, feeling for his dripple's ears as an oidy dark cloud slowly drifted across the shindinculous moon, bringing a sudden chill to the even'up. "She's not there," he griffled, calling her name outloud and trying to ignore a sudden ominous feeling in his Sisteraculous.

"She will be inside, washing pots," Ursula griffled. "She will come soon."

"Perhaps," Matlock griffled, as the cloud cleared the moon and the three friends returned to griffling and chickling in the crumlush cottage garden, all thoughts of Ayaani gone from their minds.

And as for the oidy griffling dripple herself, she was at that peffa-same moment vilishly pid-padding through Wand Wood, drawn by a strange and strong desire she had never known before, driving her deeper into the woods, away from the cottage and towards the beginnings of something that made her Sisteraculous peffa-twizzly at just the oidiest thought of it.

Ayaani couldn't stop, or turn back. Whatever it was that lured her on was too powerful, and she knew in that blinksnap that she was being taken straight to the second of the three Most Majelicus tasks.

She simply prayed to Oramus that Matlock would be ready…

Griffle Glossary

Welcome to the 'griffle-glossary'; a peffa-handy 'start-griffling' guide to the language of the dales. Whilst far from comprehensive, it intends to give the interested observer a beginner's guide to 'griffling', and perhaps a further oidy glimpse into the world of Winchett Dale…

Good luck, and good 'griffling'!

Abbrolatt – (n) Slow moving, yet largely harmless giant *moffashlobb* – eats tops of trees, so *shortwings* have to be careful. Won't mean to squash you with its feet, and will *eye-splash* for many *sun-turns* if it does. Useful for scaring long, long nosed *krellits* away. Not as effective at scaring short, long nosed *krellits*, though…

Bliff – (v) To lightly strike something, as opposed to using a *peffa-bliff* (n) to cause some really glopped-up damage.

Blinksnap – (n) The *oidiest* moment; from the time it takes the average creature to blink an eye. *(all except grated-joolps, who for peffa-long and complicated reasons that can sometimes cause embarrassement, are the only creatures in Winchett Dale to take more than a minute with each blink.)*

Briftest – (adj) What you know as 'the best'.

Chickle – (v) to laugh. From the guttural noise created by much mirth-making.

Cloff(s) – (n) Chores. From the *cloffing* noise made at the back of the throat by creatures doing chores, who'd much rather be doing *fuzzcheck* things instead!

Clottabus – (n, colloquial) A bit of a fool. Distinct to Winchett Dale, after Clottabus the owl once tried to actually prove he could turn his head a full circle, and found himself back to front for nearly a whole *moon-turn*.

Creaker – (n) Door; from the noise most often associated with opening one.

Crimple – (n) Stomach. Traditional repository for *tweazle-pies* and *niff-soup*. Can tend to grumble if too full.

Crumlush – (adj) The feeling you get inside when all's *saztaculoulsy* well. Cosy, warm, lovely.

Ebberback – (n) A type of beetle, tastes *herreuck*, so don't bother. From the same family of *Coleodaletera*, frequently seen skrittling all around the dale and sometimes from some of the more *glopped-up* creatures themselves. Examples include – *murp-worms, slidgers, dilva-beetles, cloff-beetles* and water-dwelling *slipdgers, jellops* and *blurfs*. Not to be confused with *mirrits*, which are quite another *saztaculous* thing, entirely.

Eye-splashy(ers) – (v/n) To cry; tears.

Excrimbly – (n) Exciting, or excited; as in '*becoming all peffa-excrimbly*' at the thought of something *saztaculous* about to happen.

Foffle – (n) Small cheese-eating creature, much like an *oidy* kitten, with a hard belly and long pointed nose, who will guard your *piff-tosh* all night from *frizzing* embers, softly *greeping* as he does so.

Freggle – (coll n/slang) much the same as a *snutch* (meaning 'few') *freggle* is most often used in association with *guzzworts*.

Fritch – (n) Most popular board game in Winchett Dale. Involves putting up tiny fences to wall your opponent in. *Peffa* opportunities for cheating, and Matlock is most definitely not allowed to use any *vrooshers* during the game!

Fuzzcheck – (sl) When everything's completely graggly and so fine! Used by Winchett Dale to approve of a really good *vliff*.

Ganticus – (adj) Somewhere between 'large' and 'huge'. Although *peffa-ganticus* is most definitely vast.

Garrumblooms – (n) Deep rumblings, of the kind sometimes made by *Foffle Mountain*; or more likely from Proftulous if he's eaten too much *tweazle-pie* for his supper. At this point, most creatures tend to make their excuses and go outside...

Gobflop – (n) to fail at something.

Glopped-up – (n phrase) When something has gone wrong.

Glubbstool – (n) When something has gone *peffa*-wrong! Not the sort of *sun-turn* you'd ever want to remember – could well be time for a *crumlush brottle-leaf* brew in front of the *piff-tosh*...

Greep – (v) Contented noise made by *foffles*, as they slide their hard undershells on any cinders that might pop from your *piff-tosh* during the night. Helps to keep them warm during the winter months.

Griffle(s) – (n) Word(s). (Also used in verb-form – '*to griffle*')

Guzzwort – (n) The favourite even'up drink of Winchett Dale. Brewed on the premises of the saztaculous Winchett Dale Inn, landlord Slivert Jutt's crumlushly famous ale is a rich, nutty bown slurpilicious treat. However, it can sometimes lead to a slightly glopped and glubbstooled head in the morn'up... *(Visitors to Winchett Dale Inn: please be warned NOT to drink from Jericho Krettle's tankard, as even though he is a peffa-infrequent visitor, he's peffa-particular, and will bliff you quite severely if he finds out.)*

Juzzpapped – (n) To feel really tired, especially at the end of a *peffa*-long and *glopped-up sun-turn.*

Lid – (n) the *crumlush* and *saztaculous* sky above all our heads.

Long, long-nosed Krellits – (n) Avoid these at ALL COSTS!

Majelicus – (adj) *Peffa*-majickal, the most majickal majick, that can't be *vrooshe*d from books, tinctures or potions, the very heartbeat of our majickal world.

Moondaisy – (n) Small, singing yellow and blue flower found in Wand Wood. We even have our own *Moondaisy* choir – auditions are *peffa*-hard, though, and most *moondaisies* will merely hum a bit, and never really have the chance to showcase their true floral singing talents to a wider audience beyond just a few *skrittling druff-beetles.*

Moon-turn – (n) The time taken for the moon to turn full-cycle – 28 *sun-turns*, or 'month'.

Niff – (n) *(niffcapiscum dalus)* Orange vegetable, similar in appearance to peppers, grown all over the dale, mostly in creatures' back-gardens, picked anytime from June onwards, and used in a variety of *slurpilicious* dishes, the favourite being sliced, roasted *niffs* lightly tossed in a *cloff-beetle* salad.

Oidy – (adj) Tiny, really *peffa*-small...

Nifferduggle(s) – (n) Sleeping. To go to *nifferduggles* is sometimes the most *crumlush* part of our *sun-turn*...

Parlawitch – (n) Official language of all witches, both in the dales, and also solitary white hare-witches living across *The Icy Seas*. Developed over countless generations, *Parlawitch* is a combination of traditional witch-*griffles* blended with distant Scandinavian dialect. However, you don't have to be fluent in *Parlawitch* to griffle with a witch, as by and large, they have learnt to *griffle* many languages in their *vroffa*-broomed travels, but having a few *Parlawitch griffles* to hand is always polite, and perhaps the *briftest* way to ensure they don't get *russisculoffed* and try and turn you into some *yechus* creature for the rest of your *sun-turns*...

Peffa – (adj) Very.

Pid-pad – (v) To walk. You humans go '*bud-thud*'; whereas we, more delicate creatures of Winchett Dale simply *pid-pad*. Except Proftulous, who for obvious *dworped* reasons, lump-thumps along, instead.

Piff-tosh – (n) Fire, of the kind that you have in your home, to settle in front of when the *sun-turn* has left you *peffa-juzzpapped*. Needs a gently *greeping Foffle* to guard it while you're *nifferduggling*, though! From the noise made by the fire as it burns in your grate.

Pronosticulus – (n) Type of rare metal, also found as an element running through parts of the *Trikulum* mines. Can be ground to powdered form for use in some healing spells and occasional *vroosher*. *(Griffle gratefully discovered and supplied by the peffa-good Mr James Edgerton of Meole Brace School, Shrewsbury...)*

Russisculoffed – (n) Irritated. From the gutteral noises made by *Russicers* if you go too near to them while thay are hoarding *shlomps*. Be warned, they much prefer their *schlomps* to you!

Scrittle – (v) How *oidy* creatures and *flappers* get around on the ground. From the slight scatching noise they make.

Saztaculous – (adj) Something that is quite *peffa*-wonderful.

Shindinculous – (adj) Something that it so *peffa-saztaculous* that it shines out from anything that might be at all *glopped*.

Sisteraculous – (n) The absolute being of you! The complimentary part of your *softulous* that if you really listen hard to, has some truly *saztaculous* answers to questions you never thought to ask. Something so many have forgotten how to trust, but we at Winchett Dale rely on every sun-turn!

Softulous – (n) Body; be it furry, scaly or otherwise…

Sluffsday – (prop n) Monday. From the generally disappointed 'sluffing' heard across Winchett Dale as we realise it's another five *sun-turns* before we can say 'Thank Oramus it's Yaayday!'

Snutch – (n) A few.

Sploink – (n) *Ganticus* raindrop, tending to fall from a *peffa*-dark *lid* and landing with an audible 'sploink'.

Splurk – (n) *(Parlawitch slang)* A fool, a *clottabus*.

Spuddle – (n) A tale, story, or legend, sometimes told by parents to their cubs, kittens and leverets. The *spuddle* of the *Berriftomus* is one, which tells of a *peffa-yechus* creature that will come to you at night while you *nifferduggle* if you've been naughty.

Sun-turn – (n) A day. The period of *time* it takes for the sun to rise and fall, before leaving just the *saztaculous twinkling-lid*. What you would call a 'day'.

Sweeniffs – (abrv) Sweet-Nifferduggles. Said to cubs, kittens and all manner of young creatures in the Dale by exhausted parents as they finally put their offspring to bed at the end of each *sun-turn*.

Trikulum – (n) Highly explosive purple powder, used to make *ganicus cracksplosions*. Must be handled with *peffa*-care at all times! Can sometimes be found in the abandoned *Trikulum* mines running under *Foffle Mountain*.

Tricky-Ricketts – (n) *Peffa*-intelligent garden weeds that only grow in completely inaccessible places. Can be heard *chickling* at you when you try and remove them.

Trinkulah – (n) *Crumlush* willow-harp that Matlock will sometimes play to the wind.

Twinkleabra – (n) Ornate candelabra, often lit with *saztaculous* candles in different colours, depending on what festival is currently being celebrated.

Twinkling Lid – (n phr) The *shindinculous* sky at night, alive with *saztaculous* stars.

Tweazle – (n) Rodent-like creature, a *peffa*-distant cousin of *dripples*, that won't stop *griffling* in a way that makes them sound peffa-important. Nearly always at the front at *public-grifflings* of any kind, keen to air their views, but also to be safe from any hungry *dworps* in the nearby vicinity.

Twizzly – (n) To feel scared, or an oidy bit ill – when your *softulous* and *sisteraculous* aren't properly aligned, and you sense danger lurking somewhere close…

Tzorkly – (adj – *Parlawitch*) Literal meaning – 'to rise above', but used amongst witches to mostly mean '*Peffa-fuzzcheck* and witchy'.

Uggralybe – (n) A *Peffa*-lazy plant, that will only decide to grow if you sing softly to it at the end of each *sun-turn* – what we first called an *uggralullyby* – and the origin of your human word *lullaby*.

Vilishly – (adv) Quickly. From the noise made by a woodland creature rushing through the undergrowth, searching for berries, or trying to escape a hungry predator.

Vroosher – (n) A wand-assisted majick spell. From the *saztaculous vrooshing* noise they make!

Whupplit – (n) an *oidy* rain-drop. From the sound it makes when falling on leaves, or even *whuppling* into the Thinking Lake.

Yamantally-spious! – (excl, slang) Used by the creatures of the dale, when something's gone *peffa-fuzzcheck*.

Yechus – *(adj)* Something that is truly glopped-up and horrendous.

The Dale Bugle.

➡ **Where it is always peffa-good news** | **Every sun-turn!**

HOME AND DRY!

DISIDULA FRAGUS WINS CAGE OF THE YEAR!

 elebrations rang across Winchett Dale last even'up with the news that Fragus the disidula had beaten off stiff and peffa-glopped-up competition to win the coveted *'Best Cage of All the Dales'* competition in a truly paw-biting finale that saw him claim victory for what judges griffled to be *'the briftest and most crumlushed cage based on a traditional cottage theme.'*

EMOTIONAL AND CLOTTABUSSED

Beating three-times winner and perpetually caged Melwine Freckle from Clivert Dale in the final round of judging, our Fragus was peffa-proud to finally lift the saztaculous trophy and bring it back to Winchett Dale.

'It's been peffa-emotional' Fragus griffled as he celebrated in the Winchett Dale Inn last even'up, excrimbly residents passing him guzzworts through

(CONT. OVERLEAF)

STILL DON'T HAVE A
Dudge-Whammet?

WHY NOT?

THEY'RE SAZTACULOUS!!!

the bars of his prize-winning luxury home. *'I know most folks be thinking we's all peffa-clottabussed in Winchett Dale, but this proves that sometimes we do be capable of doing things that don't go totally glubbstooled all the time.'* Asked whether he intended to stay in the cage from now on, Fragus declined to comment as he was too busy drinking guzzworts.

SECRETS

Landlord Slivert Jutt intends to place the cup behind the bar for all visitors to see. *'It'll be here as proof of our great victory. Each and every one of this glopped community helped with Fragus' cage, bringing him all sorts of things to be getting it looking shindinculous. All except Mrs O'Button, who griffled she couldn't even be bothered giving him a single dudge-whammet, which we all be thinking was harsh, but fair, as Fragus swallowed the last one he had.'*

Asked who it was that had supplied Fragus with the original chair in his cage, Jutt wouldn't be drawn, instead winking at this reporter and griffling with a smile, *'There be some secrets in Winchett Dale that will always be remaining that way...'tis better, we thinks.'*

FRIANOZZ TO STAY

ree-dwelling, flute-playing glop-up the frianozz griffled yesterday that he had no plans to leave Winchett Dale, despite the fact that some residents have complained that he only knows one tune and continues to play it all sun-turn, and that he's not very good at it, either.

'My fledglings could do better than him,' an irate pruckle-flapper nesting nearby griffled last even'up. *'I've heard more musical noises coming from Proftulous' grimmett than the racket that thing makes!'*

However, the Frianozz is adamant he'll stick to the tree. *'Just like this tree,'* he griffled to our reporter, *'music is in my roots. And besides, I was majicked here by the hare. It wasn't as if I ever asked to end up in Winchett Dale.'*

Some residents, however, are more than happy with the cross-legged flute-playing clottabus, sending their youngsters to stand and listen for hours if they've been naughty and gloppedup. *'I'll be good for all the rest of my sun-turns,'* an eye-splashy hurrupyuppitt griffled this afternoon'up. *'Please, can I just go home, now?'*

Classifieds

THE NUMBER ONE DIRECTORY FOR ALL THAT'S SHLONKED AND PEFFA-GOBFLOPPED IN THE DALE...

LOST

DELVING-WETTLER
Last seen climbing a binding-affimilator, griffling it was 'off for a brew'. If found, please return brew-mug immediately.

KRICKLE
Hardly ever used, an oidy bit smelly, answers to the name of `Gillup'. Friendly, if approached, but will sometimes accidentally bite legs off.

LAST SCRUFFSDAY
I can't for the life of me remember where I put it, or even if we had it in the first place. Any ideas?

SCUTTLING-TORP
And it's not the first time it's scuttled off, either. Honeslty, I'm getting peffa-sick of this! I send my husband for a stoic-torp, but, oh no, he has to come back with a scuttling one... that's right ladies, because he *always* knows best...

FOUND

BLOFFREY'S FRONT-TOOTH. No, wait a moment, I'm Bloffrey, it's mine, and it's still in my mouth! Phew, peffa-close one...

LONG-BACKED SHICKLE-CHAIR. And just by looking at it, you can tell why someone would have wanted to get rid of it. Even more uncomfortable than sitting on a raging-skreeder. Why do creatures even make such things?

THE MEANING OF LIFE. No, wait a minute, it's gone again! Frickles. It was all just one of those peffa-annoying dreams...

GANTICUS PILE OF DRUTTS but seein' as they're pretty useless to everyone, I'll just be keeping `em in me wagon for now... Goole.

SHORT-WINGED FRETTLE. I just woke up, and there it was, staring down at me. Yechus thing, someone please come and collect, vilish!

WANTED

LARGE NEFFLE HAMMER
Will swap for a grugeon-saw and dammill-sander. Come on, there must be someone out there who has one...

A GROWING SENSE OF PURPOSE
Would collect, but frankly only if it was really worth all the effort and bother.

BEARDED-SKRETTLE
Peffa-urgent as I just lost our last one (it was my pahpa's, and if he finds out, I'll have to listen to the frianozz playing glopped-up flute for hours)

SERVICES

TILT-CLEANING
– by experienced tilt-cleaner. End your tilting problems and begin leaning with peffa-confidence this sun-turn! See Verticus Scrutt in Grifflop Marshes (next to the grutta-bog)

PLOFFSHROOM BAND FOR HIRE
– saztaculous 4-piece, peffa-oidy rhythm-combo, will play all your briftest favourites. As seen and heard all over the dales, and sometimes even underneath them...

(Trefflepugga Path and Svaeg Dale approved for a shroomtaculous time!)

MATLOCK THE HARE

will return in

THE PUZZLE OF THE TILLIAN WAND

To discover more about Matlock the Hare and Winchett Dale,
visit www.matlockthehare.com this very sun-turn…

228952UK00001B/1/P